This is dedicated to my son Dyonne.

Thanks for always giving me
the time and the space to write.

Right now, you've got yourself at the start
of a really exciting road: enjoy the journey.

We're all really proud of you.

A Glenmill Publication

© Mark Frankland, 2004

The moral right of the author has been asserted.

First published in 2004

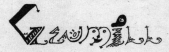

Glenmill Publishing

Dumfries

Scotland

DG2 8PX

tel: 07770 443 483

http://www.thecull.com

British Library Cataloguing in Publication Data.
A catalogue record of this book
is available from the British Library.

ISBN 0 9535944 9 1

*Cover painting: 'The Ailsa Course at Turnberry' by Kenneth Reed
available from www.golfingprints.com*
Glenmill logo: *Andrew Carroll AKA 'Gizmo'*

Printed and bound in Great Britain

TARGET ONE
MARK FRANKLAND

Contents

Prologue

Chapter 1
Kirkonnel, Scotland 1925

Roland McMillan glanced at the clock for the fifth time in four minutes. Eleven fifty-two. Or was it nearer eleven fifty-three. Yes. Definitely nearer eleven fifty-three. He felt sure that he had seen the minute hand move along the dusty face like some kind of exhausted animal crawling towards its death. He had read in books about time passing slowly. Sometimes he had heard the other clerks bemoaning the passage of the day during their ten-minute tea break at nine-thirty in the morning. It had never troubled him before. For Roland, his Saturday morning job in the accounts room had always been a time to be treasured. He relished the hours of silence broken only by the slow ticking of the old clock and the remorseless scratching of pens. When he had first won himself a Saturday morning job at the Co-op on the High Street he had been thirteen. Initially he had been allocated the task of stacking shelves in the storeroom. He had been moved into the accounts room at the behest of his headmaster, Mr Rotherham, who had pointed out to the manager one afternoon on the bowls green that young McMillan was a boy of quite exceptional talent. He had taken to the discipline of the ledger books with unusual relish. For him they held the same pleasure as a crossword and he always felt a slight disappointment when noon arrived and it was time to go home. Home to the cold little terraced house on Mons Street. Home with his father.

Another glance. Still eleven fifty-three? How could it still be eleven fifty-three? How typical it would be if the clock had indeed chosen this day of all days to slow down. He felt the frustration rising in his chest.

"McMillan. Settle down now. There's still work to be done boy. Work a plenty."

The chief clerk had noticed. His harsh words cut through Roland and he thrust his head down over his ledger. He was mortified to feel the blood filling his cheeks, and out of the corner of his eye he could sense the smirks of the other clerks. He vowed not to look up again. He would concentrate on his ledger until he heard the sound of the horn. If the small accounts room of the Co-op was regulated by the ticking of the old wall clock, the town of Kirkonnel ran to the sound of the horn at the Fauldhead coalmine. Kirkonnel was one of those places that had no other reason for their existence other than a coalmine. For hundreds of years it had been a small village by the River Nith surrounded by hills. The land was not particularly fertile and only able to support a handful of modest farms. The nearest towns of any note were Dumfries and Kilmarnock which were both a good half-day's coach ride away. There was nothing natural in its location that would ever have made Kirkonnel much more than a hamlet.

Then the Industrial Revolution started to rage and Britain became addicted to coal in greater and greater quantities. The first mines in the valley were sunk in the mid-nineteenth century and the work sucked in new people. In 1850 Kirkonnel was a village of one street and home to 400 souls. When Fauldhead Pit opened in 1897 everything changed. The population swelled tenfold and Kirkonnel became a town. All life revolved around the pit which employed 1,200 men. Their 1,200 women kept the small terraced homes and their 600 children packed into the tiny school that was built for a fraction of that number. The blast of the pit horn marked time for the whole town as it rang out across the dark valley. Start of shift. Break times. End of shift. End of war on 11th November 1918. 4,000 souls ran their hard lives around the booming sound of the pit horn, a sound that Roland now waited for as he cursed the blush that had taken control of his face.

It was indeed a special day, definitely one of the biggest days in his fifteen years. From his very first days at school it had become apparent to his teachers that Roland McMillan was different. He learnt to read and write with the same ease that his classmates had learnt to walk. Mathematics and Latin caused him no less trouble. He had never shown much interest in the chaotic mayhem of the playground. Instead he would spend his break time at his desk reading. His studious nature earned him a fair amount of ribbing but it was never too severe. Even the toughest of classmates were drawn back from outright bullying by the legend of Hamilton McMillan, Roland's father.

In the small isolated world of Kirkonnel the legend of Hamilton McMillan was a large one. He had settled in the valley in 1904 with his young wife Irene. Rumour had it that they had come down from Ochiltree in Ayrshire. He was a very big man who soon became one of the foremen at the pit. Working on his team was considered to be a very mixed blessing. The upside meant top bonuses as every year the McMillan team won every one of the production prizes. The downside was the methods that the foreman would employ to maintain his record. Deep in the belly of earth Hamilton McMillan was the king of his world. He worked with a ferocious strength that never seemed to flag. Shirkers had to deal with his gnarled fists. The attraction of the money made being on the McMillan team a goal for many of the young men of Kirkonnel. Not many could stick it more than a week or two. They would be seen about the town on a Saturday afternoon with bandaged faces and an air of humiliation and defeat. To be accepted by the hardened regulars of the McMillan team would automatically earn any young man a new place in the town as well as a fat pay packet at the end of the week. Only the hardest would ever make it.

The influence of these "McMillan Men" was felt beyond the deep shafts of Fauldhead Pit. For years they always made up the defence of the local football club Kello Rovers where they viewed the rules of the game with a similar disregard to the code of conduct at the mine. Strikers often developed injuries in the week leading up to a clash with Kello Rovers. They certainly got injured enough on the day of the match. Looking to the referee for any kind of protection was a rather hopeless pastime. In 1911 a particularly zealous referee down from Cumnock astonished the watching crowd of 1,100 when he sent Hamilton McMillan from the field for delivering a nose-splitting head butt to an opposition defender whilst waiting for a corner. After the match the man in black was hustled down an alleyway on his way to the station and beaten so badly that he was hospitalised for a week. Following this incident, other referees got the message loud and strong. It was another landmark in the McMillan legend.

TARGET ONE

When Britain declared war on the Kaiser in 1914 the whole McMillan team took the train down the valley and volunteered their services for king and country. The town turned out to cheer them on their way and referees all over the south west of Scotland breathed a sigh of relief. When Hamilton returned in 1919, he returned alone. Those who had marched away with him never made it back to watch the grey clouds swallow up the hills of the valley. Not many had much of a time of it in the trenches of the Great War, but the miners had it worse than most. Their skills were in constant demand. Initially it meant long hours digging and buttressing the deep trenches that ran from the Channel coast to the Swiss border. They got less leave than the other frontline troops. They had more time under the pounding German artillery. Then, the battle of the Somme brought on a new kind of war. Both sides took the fight underground. Miners from coalfields in Scotland and the valleys of Wales vied with those from the Saarland and Saxony as they sunk shafts and tunnelled under each other's lines. The goal was simple, to make it all the way under the opposition lines and set an enormous explosion to open up a breach for attacking infantry. The dangers were appalling. As one side dug, the other side listened. When work was detected, the enemy would sink a tunnel close by and set a charge to bury their opponents alive. Other times they would breach the tunnel walls and a savage hand-to-hand fight would be waged. That was how it had been for the McMillan Men in March 1917 in a shaft under Beaumont Hamel on the Somme. A team of men from Gelsenkirchen breached their walls a hundred yards back from the face where they were working. Once the opening had been achieved a unit of storm troopers launched into the Kirkonnel men at the face. They fought with their backs to the wall of cold French clay. They fought with picks and shovels and their bare hands. They fought with the grim murderous intent of hard men who knew they had not long left in this world. One by one they were knocked to the ground and finished off with bayonets through their necks and chests and stomachs. The men from the Ruhr were under orders to bring back a prisoner for interrogation. It wasn't hard for them to pick out Hamilton McMillan as the leader. He was the largest, the loudest, the most vicious in his rage. They beat him into oblivion and dragged him out to the German side on the lines.

PROLOGUE

When he came round he was tied to a wooden chair in a deep bunker. They beat him for three days until they realised it was a pointless exercise. He said nothing. He just sat it out and took it, staring all the time with eyes bright in his filthy face. They sent him back down the line to a prisoner of war camp near Cologne.

He came back to the valley a changed man. He never told a soul of the fight to the death deep under the ground. All anyone knew was that he came back with a Military Cross and that he and his men had fought it out to the last. The legend grew so large that the narrow valley could barely contain it.

It soon became apparent that it was a very different Hamilton McMillan that slowly stepped off the train in 1919. Before Beaumont Hamel he had always been known as a hard man, sometimes violent, certainly not a man to be crossed either above or below ground. This reputation wasn't at all unusual in the new mining communities all over Europe. Mining wasn't a job for the faint-hearted. Conditions were dire, the management was brutal and proper safety procedures were more or less non-existent. Nobody in Kirkonnel ever blamed Hamilton much for thumping first and talking about it later. Even the mothers of the boys who returned home all battered and broken, having failed to make it through their initiation onto the McMillan team, bore little or no grudge. Even the unfortunate referee from Cumnock secretly felt that his crooked, badly set nose was something of a badge of pride. Everybody was happy to forgive Hamilton his occasional excesses because at heart he was always seen as a proper fine sort of a man. He was never shy of recycling his fat bonuses on drinks all round at the pub on a Saturday afternoon. He was always the first to throw a generous donation in the hat when it was passed around to help out the family of a miner who had been injured and left destitute and unable to work. Everyone always knew when Hamilton was in the pub at his regular spot at the bar. He was loud and funny. Everyone agreed, he was good sort.

His wife Irene was no less popular. Plenty of Irish blood ran through her veins and a smile was never far from her pretty face. She was always at the very heart of the life of the street where they lived, always providing a sympathetic ear, a bag of sugar or an extra pair of hands. There was a great celebration in the pub on the night when their first born, Roland, arrived in 1910 and all the women turned out in the rain to watch Irene bring her baby home. There was a great air of sadness on the two occasions when she failed to carry her next two children. By the time that Hamilton marched off to war it was clear that Roland would be alone.

His memories of his dad before the war were thin. He had only just turned five when his mother took him to the station with the whole of the town to cheer the small train away down the valley to France. His memories were of his father's size and his huge beaming face. From the moment he arrived he had been the apple of Hamilton's eye. As they hung out their washing the women chuckled at the way the big, hard man worshipped his infant son. By the time he was fifteen, Roland's memories of the time before the war had become akin to those of the whole of the world. He was convinced that it had been an era when the sun always shone. Wonderful Saturday afternoons watching his dad and the others scythe down the strikers from the other towns and villages of the valley. Sunday afternoons fishing for trout in the clear bubbling waters of the Nith. Evenings at the table filled with laughter. A dream time. The perfect time.

He had just turned seven on the day that the telegram had arrived. By this stage every household had come to dread the postman. The town was in a permanent state of shock at the level of slaughter that was going on over the Channel. Never a week passed when the postman didn't seem to deliver the worst of all news to one or another of the families of the valley. It was snowing hard on the April morning when it was the turn of Irene McMillan to get her telegram from the ashen-faced postman whose job had become a nightmare. It didn't say he was dead. It said he was missing in action. The letter from his commanding officer left no room for doubt. The legendary McMillan team had been ambushed underground. They were heroes one and all. The Empire was both grateful and proud. Her husband had been awarded the Military Cross. A seven-year-old Roland watched his mother's face collapse and age ten years in ten seconds. All down the street the curtains twitched and then fell still. They had learned to leave it an hour or so before calling round to try and support what was unbearable. Roland was mature far beyond his years and had no difficulty in understanding that his father was gone. That evening he went out to the river in the driving snow and threw his scrapbook of the war deep into the swirling black waters. He had watched the distant glory of his dad's war with the enthusiasm of any seven-year-old. Now he saw it for what it was. He never again stuck his drawing pins in the map of France.

It was many months later that Uncle Frank arrived on the scene. Uncle Frank of course wasn't an uncle at all, it was what his mother asked him to call him. Uncle Frank was a train driver from Kilmarnock who had met his mother when she was working behind the bar at the pub trying to make ends meet. Irene McMillan wasn't made to be the grieving widow for very long. She was too young, too full of life, and in the train driver who had been invalided out of the army having been injured at Loos she found a match. The neighbours didn't think much of it. There was too much laughter about the new couple as they took their long walks along the banks of the river when he got a Sunday off. Times were deemed too hard for laughter. Nobody begrudged Irene a little bit of happiness after what had happened, but it was plain for all to see that she had found rather more than a little bit. The new couple were so ridiculously obviously head over heels in love that it caused offence. A fling was one thing, but there was too much tragedy in the small community for it to be able to stand such overwhelming joy.

It all came to a halt when Irene received her second telegram in the summer of 1918. The words turned her legs to liquid. Hamilton McMillan was very much alive and well in a POW camp in Germany. The Americans were now in France and the German War Machine had thrown its last dice in the spring. The Great War only had a matter of weeks left. Then Hamilton McMillan would return to the valley. Roland could not understand why the greatest news of his young life caused his mother to turn as pale as death.

Uncle Frank stopped coming to the valley on his Sundays off and a smile was now a million miles from Irene's face. She became distant and withdrawn. The neighbours steered clear and looked elsewhere for a bag of sugar and a sympathetic ear. The gossip of the street grew and grew as the day approached when Hamilton would return. Would anyone tell him? What would he do if they did? It was generally agreed that the fate of the referee from Cumnock would be as nothing compared to what would happen to the unfortunate train driver if he ever dared show his face in Kirkonnel.

Irene tried her very best for her husband when he came back. She had used the time to prepare herself. None of it had been his fault after all. Neither had it been hers. It had been the war, the filthy war that had destroyed so much and so many. She tried with all her heart but nothing could get her close to him again. Her man was changed: changed beyond all belief. He had more or less starved in the camp and watched many of those around him perish from cold and disease. All the weight had fallen from him leaving the big sharp bones protruding from his face. Like many millions of other men, he refused to speak about any of it. Night after night Irene would be jumped awake as he screamed out in his sleep. When they opened, his eyes would be unnaturally bright and he would push away all of her efforts to give him comfort.

It was on Hogmanay 1920 that he heard about Uncle Frank. Just a chance comment by a colleague who was drunk almost to the point of oblivion. Hamilton had dragged the man outside and beaten the whole story out of him whilst those inside crowded to the window of the pub to watch. A terrible silence had fallen across the room as he came in without a word and roughly lifted his wife to her feet. He marched her through the streets as the revellers stopped in their tracks and felt terrified at the look of total hatred wrapped across his fearsome face. Roland curled himself into a ball and clamped his hands over his ears to try and blank out the sound of the beating his father gave to his mother. She never screamed. She never uttered a sound as he released all the savagery of the horrors that ate away at him. He smashed four of her ribs. He ruptured her kidney. He pulped her face and when he had finished he left her on the floor almost for dead. The next morning he awoke early, gathered up his fishing rod and reel, and left for the river even though it was icy cold and there was no chance of catching a fish.

Roland managed to get his mother into bed and fetched the doctor. It was many weeks before she was able to leave the house, and when she did the state of her face made people gasp. The legend of Hamilton McMillan grew once more, but now the legend was becoming a dark one. In the months that followed, Roland seldom heard his parents speak. They were like machines. His father had stepped back into his former life down the mine and his mum got on with the chores of the house in silence. Roland felt as if he were forgotten. On a few occasions his mother would grasp him to her and not let go as she finally gave in to the tears. It seemed that he had ceased to exist for his father. He never attended the parents' evening at the school and so he never learned that his son was considered to be prodigy.

Roland retreated into his books. He read endlessly, hiding away from the relentless nightmare of his life in the magical world of Huckleberry Finn and Moby Dick and Robinson Crusoe. By the time he was eleven his days were filled with dreams of the day when he could leave the valley and the cold hatred of his home for the fantastic world that waited beyond the endless rain and the dark hills. In the midst of all the fantastic places that filled his hours one stood out ahead of all others.

America.

Endless, thrilling America. A land of mountains and deserts and sparking blue oceans. A land of cowboys and Indians where dreams would always come true. The dream suddenly came closer to reality in the summer of 1922. He awoke on morning to the sounds of smashing plates and cups. By the time he dared to creep down the stairs the rage had washed out of his father. He was sitting at the table with his head in his hands wearing a mask of utter despair. He looked at his son blankly for a long minute before getting up and stumbling out of the back door. There was a letter on the table. Just a short letter whose words burned into the young Roland and destroyed him somewhere deep inside. His mother had gone away. Away with Frank. She urged her husband not to try and follow her. She begged him to look after her son. She said that she was sorry for everything.

Over the months that followed the rumours gathered strength and credibility. Irene McMillan had indeed gone far away with the love of her life. She had gone all the way across the ocean to America.

Irene's departure led Hamilton into a darker world yet. The demons that had crowded his mind since the savage fight deep in the bowels of the earth under the Somme chewed and clawed at him. Night after night he would wake up with a scream of primeval terror. Once awake, sleep would never return and he would sit out the cold hours before the dawn at the table in the kitchen smoking cigarettes until the ashtray overflowed. Then he would shuffle out of the front door like a zombie, timing his walk to arrive at Fauldhead Pit minutes before the sound of the horn would shake the heavy damp air of the dawn. In the months after the departure of his wife Hamilton went over the edge on three occasions.

The first was an argument in the pub. He had long ceased to be the life and soul of the place on his favoured stool at the bar. Instead he had taken to drinking alone at a table in the corner. He was given a wide berth by one and all. No longer did he keep himself to beer, more and more he spent his hefty bonuses on whisky which seemed the only thing that could keep the demons at bay. One Saturday night a member of a visiting football team drank more than he had intended to and allowed his mouth to run away with him. In the years before the war Hamilton had barged his big brother to the ground during a particularly ill-tempered Cup-Tie. The brother had dislocated his shoulder and missed five weeks of wages whilst it healed. Not surprisingly, he had harboured a grudge ever since and probably held on to it right up to the moment when a German shell blew him into a hundred pieces during an advance at the third battle of Ypres. His younger brother had filled out into six-foot-two of farming brawn and on the back of several fast-guzzled pints of beer he took it on himself to honour his brother's memory.

He was in the middle of a somewhat slurred tirade at the quiet man at the corner table when Hamilton's arm shot out and broke a glass in his face. The boy was completely stunned by the unexpected speed and ferocity of the strike and could do nothing as the older man dragged him from the bar by his hair as the blood cascaded down his face. After a few moments the faces at the window were forced to turn away such was the ugliness of the beating that Hamilton handed out. Even those who had seen the worst of the horrors of the trenches found it hard to stomach. When he was done Hamilton quietly re-entered the pub and resumed his seat without so much as a word.

Three months later there was an ugly incident at the mine. Yet another hopeful youngster was trying to gain acceptance on the newly rebuilt McMillan team. Hamilton caught him sneaking a crafty fag and broke his arm with a lump hammer. There were mutterings about how McMillan was getting out of control but nobody had the courage to say anything. The boy stuck to the story that his arm had been trapped when one of the coal wagons had become uncoupled.

PROLOGUE

In the autumn of 1924 a young midfielder mistimed a sliding challenge and caught Hamilton hard underneath his knee. Once again the red mist descended and it took every one of his team-mates to drag him off. Later when he waited outside for his revenge he was disappointed. Everyone knew what was about to happen and so the boy had been smuggled away from the ground. It was with some relief that the rest of the team learned that the tackle had caused lasting damage to Hamilton's leg and forced his retirement from the game at the age of 40.

By now things were changing at Fauldhead Pit. The old order had marched out to war in 1914 to protect and secure the way that things had always been. As a mission it had been a catastrophe. The young of Europe's aristocratic classes had been slaughtered in the mincing machine of the trenches. The millions who were frog-marched out to fight for their kings and Empires now demanded their share of the cake as some kind of compensation for the millions of gallons of blood that had been spilled. Unions started to prosper as working men began to fight for better lives. The union gave a new focus for the rage that burned away inside Hamilton McMillan. The firebrand speakers who laid the blame for the carnage of the trenches at the gates of the aristocracy and the owning classes found him a willing convert. For years he had struggled to make any sense of the horrors that he had endured. He had tried to maintain a patriotic loathing for the Germans who had butchered his friends with their bayonets. It was something he had never quite settled with. He could never get his mind away from the fact that those in grey uniforms who dug the tunnels for the German High Command were no more than mining men just like himself and his friends. Had the roles been reversed the McMillan team would have butchered with the same lack of pity that they had been shown themselves.

Now at last he was hearing voices that made sense of the nightmare. He should not blame his fellow working men simply because they spoke a different language. It was the bosses who should carry the weight of the blame, the one who make fat fortunes on the back of the blood spilt by so many millions. It was the bosses and the landowners who had sent so many to their graves in order to protect their fine houses and huge fortunes. When the first strike came to the mines of Nithsdale there was nobody more feared among any potential scabs than Hamilton McMillan. When the men of Fauldhead downed tools and walked out, they all downed tools and walked out. Not one miner ever dared to break ranks and face the retribution of the born-again union man who could use his raw-boned fists like hammers.

From the moment that he had read the note that his departing mother had left on the kitchen table, life had become more or less relentlessly miserable for Roland McMillan. His hours in school were generally his best. Even though his teachers had to struggle with upwards of 50 children in classrooms designed for half that number, they still managed to find time to dedicate to their most gifted pupil. The headmaster, Mr Rotherham, gave Roland particular attention. James Rotherham was a man of the church and he had taken on the role of running Kirkonnel school with a religious zeal more akin to Victorian times than the Roaring Twenties. His creed demanded that with proper dedication from teacher and pupil alike there was no reason why the very highest academic achievement should elude even those from areas of grinding poverty. After fifteen years in charge of the tiny red brick school his greatest ambition had still to be fulfilled. There had been many very bright young pupils, but he had never managed to lift their sights further than following their fathers and uncles and brothers down the family road to Fauldhead Pit. He reached his 60th birthday early in 1925 and he was acutely aware that time was running out.

For five years he had known that Roland McMillan was probably his last hope of achieving his dream.

He managed to find time for the boy at least for an hour a day after school. The main drawback was that Roland was adamant that his father must not know of his extra studies. Once Irene McMillan had departed for America, little Roland had been forced to take on the role of the woman of the house. Even though he could easily have afforded to hire in help, his father made the boy do all the cleaning, washing and cooking. Every day it was expected that the hot water would be poured in the tin bath in the kitchen ready for his father's return.

Luckily his father was seldom in. Every evening he would come in and wash, change and eat with barely a word to his son. Most of the time Roland felt as if he didn't even exist. He doggedly got on with his chores and filled in the empty hours with his books. For months he had worried that his father might get wind of the fact that he was going to sit the exam to win a scholarship to the Academy in Dumfries. In the end there had been no need. Trouble was brewing at the pit and Hamilton McMillan was consumed by the business of the union. Roland sat the papers in the empty classroom whilst his headmaster quietly marked books at the table at the head of the class. He couldn't make any judgement as to how well he had done. The papers if anything seemed almost ridiculously easy. Too easy? It didn't seem possible that they could be so straightforward. He was convinced that he must have made some terrible mistake. Maybe he hadn't read the questions properly. Maybe the questions demanded something completely different from him and which he wasn't nearly clever enough to see. He tried to put these feelings into words to Mr Rotherham but the old headmaster had merely smiled and patted him gently on the shoulder and told him not to worry himself too much.

That had been in July and now was the day when the results had arrived at the school. Mr Rotherham had sent word to the Co-op that morning and had said that he would be waiting for Roland to call round once he had finished work. All morning he had watched the agonising progress of the minute hand of the clock and all morning it had seemed as if it had become stuck. At last the sound of the pit horn wandered across the town and the clerks began to pack away their ledgers and pens. The young man who worked at the desk next to his leaned across and gave him a dramatic wink.

"All I can say Roly is that I hope she's worth it."

Roland had no clue what the clerk was talking about.

"Sorry. I don't understand."

The clerk grinned. "Of course you do. The girl you are meeting. You've been looking at that clock all morning. Has to be a girl. Only one thing can make a chap so jumpy. I just hope that she is worth the wait."

Roland was about to reply but it suddenly all seemed very complicated. The clerk gave him a friendly tap on the shoulder and made his way to the door shrugging on his jacket as he went.

The senior clerk looked disapproving as he handed over Roland's meagre wages.

"Not very good this morning, McMillan. Not very good at all. I expect better than this. Much better. There are plenty out there who would give a lot for your job. Better buck your ideas up before next week. I'll be watching by Jove. Oh yes, I'll be watching. No room for slackers here boy. None at all. Now off you go."

Roland stood and took the lecture with a suitably blank expression. He may have been watching the clock, but as usual he had managed at least twice as much work as anyone else in the room. All the others were being paid at least five times more than him to boot. But he kept his counsel. He had learnt that arguing with anyone in authority in Kirkonnel was pointless.

Outside, the High Street was Saturday afternoon busy. Mothers, sisters and wives were getting Friday's wages turned into groceries and other vital provisions before their men had the chance to put the whole lot into a landlord's till and leave the family without for a week. It had been a dry spell for the time of year which meant that the whole town seemed more than ever consumed by the black coal dust from the pit. There was never an escape from it. In dry weather it blew around on the wind that funnelled up and down the valley and found its way into every nook and cranny. When the skies opened up the streets were inches deep in black filth.

As he jogged towards the school he barely registered the looks on the faces of the women with their headscarves and bags and prams. Normally he did. Normally the pity on their faces made him blush. His situation was well enough known in the town. Most of the women on Mons Street had knocked the door to offer his father help with the chores of the house. They had all been sent packing and told that their charity was not needed. It was generally agreed that Roly was a good lad. A bit odd of course, always with his nose stuck in some book or another, but a good lad all the same. They all knew that it would be hard on him when the day came to leave school and go down the pit. God help him if that father of his forced him to work on his team.

When he arrived at the school Mr Rotherham was waiting at his table at the head of the class. It was quiet in the room compared with the noise and bustle of the High Street. He had dreaded the moment of reading the letter. Would he be able to control himself if it contained failure? More than anything he didn't want to cry in front of his headmaster. In fact it wasn't at all as he had expected. He knew that he had passed the exam the minute that he walked into the room. The reason being that for the first time in all his years at the school his headmaster's face was one big smile, it transformed him completely.

James Rotherham handed him the letter and it confirmed what he had already guessed. ". . . happy to offer a full scholarship . . ." It was true. Right there in black and white. A ticket out of the swirling coal dust and the boom of the pit horn and the father who had left his humanity deep in the earth beneath the Somme. It took a moment to realise that Mr Rotherham was speaking to him.

"Now then McMillan. I know your father's reaction to this is causing you some concern."

Roland felt the elation driven from him at the very mention of the subject.

"Yes sir."

The old man nodded. "I am aware that your father is an unusual man. I am also aware that your family's situation has become difficult. However, he is also a man of some influence and importance, particularly with his work with the union. I find it impossible to believe that his reaction to such exceptional news as this will be anything but proper pride."

How Roland wished that he could believe him. He didn't know what to say. Rotherham continued.

"I think that it is best that I accompany you to give the news. I know that it will come as a shock and possibly it will be better if he hears it from me. After all, as headmaster, I also enjoy a certain position in the town. Difficulties are put in front of us by the Lord, McMillan. We are the Lord's most magnificent creation and by overcoming our difficulties we prove his greatness. Come McMillan, let us go."

Part of Roland was horrified. What would happen if his father lost his temper and hit Mr Rotherham? That would be too much, even his father would not be forgiven. A much bigger part of him was desperately grateful and relieved. He had been unable to find any way of broaching the subject. Now the terrible responsibility had been taken away from him. Once again there were looks on all faces as they made their way through the town to Mons Street. Roland opened the front door and stood back to allow Mr Rotherham in. His father was not due back for another few minutes, Saturday afternoon being the one day when he would drop off at the pub in his work clothes. Rotherham took a seat at the table whilst Roland filled the tin bath with the water that he had left heating through the morning. He occupied himself making tea as the minutes dragged by.

The tea was just on the table when the front door opened and his father came in. The big man stopped in his tracks at the sight of the schoolmaster sitting at his table.

"What's this?" His tone was cold.

Rotherham met his fierce gaze with a stern look of his own, a look that he had perfected through a 40-year teaching career, a look that had terrified hundreds of school children since 1885.

"The school has received some magnificent news this morning Mr McMillan. Your son has become the first pupil from Kirkonnel to win a full scholarship to the Academy in Dumfries. I am sure that it must make you a very proud man indeed. Such news nourishes our faith in the greatness of our Lord."

Hamilton felt the rage rising in him and closed his eyes tight to try and contain it. Nourishes our faith! How he hated these religious swine. They had been there in the trenches, telling them all that they were doing God's work, telling them that Jesus was right there with them. Had he been with them when they killed each other like animals? Had it been his hands who guided the pick axes and bayonets to their bloody work? His body was knotted with tension. It was a real effort not to ball his fists, not to strike the man down to the floor and beat him. He held on and slowly opened his eyes.

"Get out of this house."

Rotherham's face was a picture of surprise. This was outrageous, unthinkable. Never had he been treated in such a manner.

"Really Mr McMillan, I know that this must come as something of a surprise, but there is no need . . . "

"I said out. Out now. Out before I throw you out."

Hamilton was very still. Rotherham was about to speak again, to put his outrage into words. It was the eyes of the man that stopped him short. They blazed out of the bony blackness of his face. He saw madness there, a gleam of insanity. Had it been the war? The years in the mine? His wife leaving for America? It was impossible to say, but he knew there was no reason to be found in Hamilton McMillan. He was suddenly frightened. Very frightened. He got to his feet with all the dignity he could muster and made it to the door. Before walking out, he half turned to find that McMillan was inches behind him.

PROLOGUE

"Really Mr McMillan, I must once again say that there is no need for . . ."

"Out." Hamilton pushed him hard in his back and it was all he could do to keep his feet as he was propelled into the dusty street. He sensed the twitching of the curtains and took care to restore his dignity as he made his way back towards the school. Outwardly his face was grave and composed. Inside he was filled with terror for the boy.

Inside the kitchen, Roland waited with his head bowed. How foolish he had been to think it would ever be any different. His father would never allow him to leave. His destiny was mapped out. Like all the others, he would go down into the depths of Fauldhead Pit. His father stood for a moment when he came back into the small kitchen. Then he spoke.

"There will be no Scholarship boy. Not now, not ever. I've had enough of your ways. No sports. Always with your face in a book. It makes me ashamed. You don't need fancy books to dig coal. No dried-up prune of a headmaster is going to come into my house with his pompous religious . . ."

It was as if the effort of the sentence tired him. It was the effort of dragging himself through each and every cold and brutal day. No wife, no life, just the nightmares that came every night and deprived him of even the comfort of sleep. And now another betrayal. His son this time. His only son. Plotting behind his back with that damned headmaster . . .

Snap.

In a way Roland was lucky. It would have been the worst beating of his life, but the first blow felled him like a rotten tree and left him out stone-cold unconscious on floor. The rage drained out of Hamilton at the sight of the stillness of his son's body. For an awful moment he feared that the blow had killed him, but a check on his pulse proved otherwise. He shook his head to clear his brain. He carried his son up the stairs and left him on his bed. Then he washed himself in the bath, changed, and left for the pub.

Roland awoke three hours later and his head was throbbing with agony. Little by little the pictures of what had happened pieced themselves together in his mind. Each piece of the desperate jigsaw sent him down into depths of misery that he had never known before.

Then at his moment of greatest despair a thought jumped into his head that made him sit up. It was a thought that was so unimaginably appalling that he knew it would never leave him. To his own amazement he never fought the thought. He knew that he would only ever have this one moment to alter the course of his life, and he was determined to take it. He jumped up from the bed and did his best to ignore the pain that rolled around his head. He threw his few clothes into a bag that his father had once used for his football kit. He filled every remaining space with as many books as he could squeeze in. He ran downstairs and pulled on his cap and coat and turned to the wall by the fireplace. Could he really do something so bad, so utterly unforgivable?

He pulled out two loose bricks to reveal a cavity in the wall that held a small biscuit tin. Inside the tin was the money his father had collected for the union's Christmas outing. A piece of paper was covered with his father's careful record of who had given what, when and how much. How much was there? Thirty-two pounds, ten shillings and fourpence. Enough. Enough to take him far away from the gloomy valley and the sound of the horn. He remembered a lesson at school. The poetry of John Donne. "Ask not for whom the bell tolls, for it tolls for thee." Ask not for who the pit horn sounds, for it sounds for thee. For a lifetime. A life wasted and lungs choked up until they gave up the fight for breath. A life of nothing or a life of something. A future for thirty-two pounds, ten shillings and fourpence.

It was enough. Enough to take him to America and far away from the valley for ever. He glanced at the clock. It had been a day of clocks. Twenty to seven. Twenty minutes before the last train up to Kilmarnock. Then Glasgow. Then a boat and a new future. Enough time but only just enough. Time to choose.

He chose.

He thrust the money into the pocket of his jacket, grabbed the bag, and ran out of the back door without bothering to close it. It had started to rain heavily whilst he was unconscious and the black mud squelched under his running feet. He made his way through the darkening streets, and climbed aboard the near-empty train. He was unnoticed as the train gave a whistle and chugged sedately up the valley to New Cumnock and Cumnock and Kilmarnock and the New World.

It would be 79 years before Roland McMillan returned to the valley.

Chapter 2
September

The view in front of him made it impossible for Jonathan McMillan not to smile. The rain of the morning had cleared away and now the sky was a wall-to-wall blue. Ahead of him on top of a low hill the long, magnificent white buildings of the Turnberry Hotel gazed out across the Irish Sea. It was their last stop on a week-long golfing tour that had taken in Royal Dornock, St Andrews, Carnoustie, Troon and now, finally, Turnberry. The four friends made up the core of a college golf team that had pretty well swept the board in the southwest corner of the United States over the last two years. The local media was full of speculation as to how far some or all of them could go if they decided on a professional career.

It was an idea that Jonathan had been toying with. Ever since the age of seven when he had first picked up a club, golf had been at the centre of his life. He was old enough now to realise that he was far from being a natural, but hours of dedicated practice had made him very nearly good enough to turn pro. His game was somewhat mechanical, but his great strength was an ability to get the ball into the hole when it counted most. Mental strength was something that ran strongly through the McMillan family, starting with his great grandfather who had started the dynasty, and running with continuing strength through his grandad and his dad. He was pretty sure that he was cut from the same old McMillan tartan, although the only real tests of his mettle in his short and extremely privileged life had been on the golf course. He still felt a glow of pride when he remembered the three-iron approach and a hole-out from fifteen feet that had secured the birdie he needed to square his match and win the inter-collegiate championship for his team earlier that year. The emotion that he had experienced as he settled over the all-important putt had surprised him. Not fear. Not nerves. Not even much tension. Only a controlled exhilaration at the pressure and the challenge. The ball had never wavered from the centre of the hole.

As he had walked off that green with his arms held aloft to acknowledge the cheers of the crowd, he had been almost certain that a career as a pro-golfer was what he wanted. The last few days had forced him to reconsider. He had always been told how the truest and purest golf you could ever play was to be found on the great Scottish links courses. To come up with the money for the trip he had worked near-suicidal hours in a bar. It was typical. His three friends had been funded by proud parents and relatives to make the trip as a celebration of their successful college careers. His own family probably had a net worth of about 500 times the three others put together. But paying your own way was a McMillan tradition that was far too deeply rooted to ever be changed. He hadn't even bothered asking. He hadn't wanted to. He could have had his pick of jobs in the variety of businesses that made up the sprawling McMillan empire, but he hadn't much fancied a summer of snide glances at the boss's son. Instead, he had preferred the anonymity of the bar, and he had enjoyed the rough and ready company of the oil workers who made up the core of its clientele.

The great Scottish golf courses had been everything he had hoped for. They were magical, ancient, almost mystical. They seemed almost as firmly embedded into the landscape as the hills and the sea. The company had been first-rate too. The only downside to his trip had been his more or less complete inability to adjust his game to play in the way that Scottish golf demanded. All his life he had learned to play on America's manicured parkland courses. Hit a straight drive, and the ball would nestle on a flat, carpet-like fairway. Hit an approach shot into the green, and it would bite and grip in the same way almost every time. It was a scientific game, a game where endless hours of practice helped achieve a predictable perfection.

A week in Scotland made him feel like a bumbling amateur. An arrow-straight drive could shoot off into the rough as if it had landed on a grenade. A picture-perfect approach shot could hit the green and bounce as if hitting concrete. There were bare sandy lies, weird humps and hillocks, greens that could look like a sheet tossed over lumpy furniture. And the crazy changing weather threw another fifteen spanners into the works. He had watched as a couple of his friends had managed to alter their games to accommodate the alien conditions. They had mastered bump and run shots, half-swing punches from awkward lies, and soft-handed floated lob shots that landed gently on the baked greens. He had tried, but he had been found wanting. It was as he had always suspected. His game was too mechanical. Too practised. He lacked the magic in his hands to come up with the variety of shots that the great courses demanded. It had forced him to reconsider whether he really would have a future at the highest level of the game.

He focused his wandering attention and concentrated on the hole ahead of him. The task was so different to the one presented in the morning that it was almost laughable. When his alarm had chased him out of bed at 7.00 a.m., the rain had been lashing at the window as a near gale blew in from the sea. He had barely been able to see beyond the lawn in front of the hotel, let alone out across to the spectacular island lump of Ailsa Craig far out in the bay. The morning round had been a battle against the elements. By the time they had made it to the eighteenth, he had felt as if he had done twelve rounds with a heavyweight champion. He had crunched the best drive that he had hit all week up the right-hand side of the fairway and even then he had had to throw every ounce of his six-foot-two, fourteen-and-a-half stone frame into a three wood that just managed to limp onto the front edge of the green. A fifty-foot putt to four feet and a careful hole out gave him just about the best par he had ever made. His four won the hole and the match.

Now it was all change. The weather had started to clear as they had eaten lunch and the early evening showed of Scotland's rugged west coast at its absolute best. He and his partner were one down and already their two opponents had launched their drives miles down the centre of the fairway. Both balls had finished a good 170 yards further than he had made it into the teeth of the morning gale. His partner Dale over-reached himself, looking to smash the ball within yards of the green. He quit out of his expansive swing at the last second, and the ball ballooned high and right into the very centre of a sprawl of gorse. Jonathan decided that the situation demanded revised tactics and duly selected a three wood. He took an easy, gentle swing and more or less caressed the ball down the centre of the fairway a good 50 yards behind his opponents. It gave him the chance to play first and try to get the ball as close as possible to wind up the pressure a notch or two on his opponents.

As he stood over his approach shot he could not begin to decide what club to use. A quick calculation told him that there was 160 yards to go to the front of the green. The wind at his back was freshening all the time. That morning it had taken the three wood of his life to make it. Now he decided on a hard, high nine iron to land on the gentle upslope at the front of the green. His connection was as sweet as it could have been and he settled at the top of his follow through to watch the sunlight white of the ball arc out towards the pin. It was nice. Really nice. It just needed to drop on the slope, bite a little, and then follow the gentle slope round to the hole. His eyes widened in amazement as the ball landed ten yards further than he had planned on the downslope and took an exaggerated high bounce clear over the back of the green, under a small white chainlink fence and then over the car park to disappear under a blue Izuzu Trooper.

Dale chuckled. "Guess you're not comfortable with those bump and runs yet, hey Johnny."

He couldn't help but chuckle too. He had just played two shots that had been as good as he could make and the old golf course had laughed at him. Maybe it was time to consider where his career lay in the great corporate monolith of McMillan Holdings.

An hour later, showered and changed, he was waiting for his friends in the bar. There was an old framed map of the west of Scotland on the wall which attracted his attention. He was giving it little more than an idle glance when the word Kirkonnel jumped off the page at him. Could it be? Maybe. How far was it? Christ. No distance at all. 30 miles, if that. A mere spit for a man accustomed to the endless straight roads of Texas. He sat down and flicked open his mobile and hit the speed dial.

The call was answered on the second ring by the honeyed tones of the Deep South.

"Hi. You're through to Joanna at McMillan Holdings. How can I help you today?"

"I can think of many things JoJo, but none of them can be said on an open line. Maybe you could put me through to Grandad, if he's free."

"Why Johnny boy, you sure know how to make a girl blush all the way down her neck. My, a'm all of a fluster now you bad, bad boy. Just a minute sugar."

He grinned at the thought of JoJo's ebony black skin blushing. Some things just were not scientifically possible. A few seconds elapsed and JoJo's honeyed southern voice was replaced by the similar tones of his grandfather's secretary.

"Johnny! How are you doing over there honey?"

"Fine Jill. Really fine. Is he free?"

"You got real lucky. Just out of a meeting. I'll put you through."

A few more seconds and then a big, deep booming Deep South voice. Austin McMillan was one of those big men with big smiles and big, big voices.

"Johnny boy. How the hell are you? Tearing it up over there you lucky sonofabitch?"

His grandad loved to play the part of the great Texan cartoon with his cowboy hats and fancy boots and leather jackets with tassels on the sleeves. Jonathan knew it to be no more than a big flamboyant act that played well with the punters and the stockholders. His great-grandfather had been a hard, hard act to follow, but Austin had filled his father's boots and more. Even after a week, it was good to hear the brash home voices of Texas.

"I'm pretty good, sir. Really good in fact."

"And the golf? How is it? Good as they always say it is?"

"The golf is as good as it gets. The trouble is that I think that it has proved that my game is a little short of what these places need. I figure I'll be filling out a CV on the plane home and coming round to see you for a job interview."

The words were said lightly, but he could feel their effect even at a digital distance of thousands of miles. The voice on the end of the phone lost all the big brashness and suddenly sounded more like a disappointed old man approaching his 70th year.

"Hell Johnny, are you serious?"

Austin had been a passionate amateur golfer for most of his life although he had never had the talent to go with it. The sunny uplands of his golf career had been a handicap of twelve which he managed to hang on to for three months in 1972. He had never made any secret of his dreams of seeing his grandson making it all the way to the top of the professional pole.

"I'm afraid that I am sir. Actually, I feel pretty positive about it. It has made the trip really worthwhile. Much better to find out early rather than smacking my head against a wall for years and years."

"Well, I can see some sense it that sure enough. Anyway, is that why you called? If you've run out of cash you can go do some washing up. You know the rules of the McMillan clan."

Jonathan chuckled. "No. It's OK. I've watched my pennies like a proper Scotsman. I want to check something out with you. I remember that your father came from a place called Kirkonnel. Is that in the south of Scotland?"

"Sure. Just outside of Ayrshire. Why do you ask?"

"I've just seen it on a map. It's only a few miles from here, just over the hills. I figure that I might just hire a car and go take a look. Have you ever been sir?"

"Nope. Can't say I ever have. My Daddy never wanted to talk to us about that time. I asked him often enough, but you know how he is. Stubborn as a goddamn mule. Always was. I read up on it some when I was younger. It was a mining town. Never much of a place until they found coal in the nineteenth century, and then it took off. Same as lots of the places we got over here up in the north. I don't suppose it will be much of a place now. I hear most of the coalmines are gone now over there. Hell though, you should take a look. Take some pictures too. I'll look forward to seeing them. In the meantime I best give some thought as to where you're going to make your start in the firm."

"Yes, I would appreciate that, sir. I'll be round to see you when I get back."

"You do that. I gotta go. Another meet. Take care."

Jonathan looked thoughtful as he ended the call. He had not planned to tell his grandfather of the decision he had made. In fact it was only when he said it that he even realised himself that he had made the decision at all. It had suddenly become final. He had planned on a career as a pro-golfer for as long as he could remember. Throughout all the endless hours of practice when he was ten and eleven, in his mind's eye his shots were always soaring into the eighteenth at Augusta or St Andrews to secure yet another major title. All gone now. Gone the very minute that his high nine iron had leapt across the green and under the Izuzu. He felt the beginnings of depression and made a big effort to shake it off.

Half an hour later a hire car had been delivered to the car park and he had made his excuses to his friends. It was the first time that he had driven a right hand drive and the first few minutes were pretty fearful as he headed south on the A77. The map showed a direct route east which he followed. After half an hour he was convinced that he must have gone horribly wrong as he came onto a tiny little road that snaked over barren hills. There was no issue about driving on the wrong side of the road. There was no right or wrong side, only a middle. When he occasionally met oncoming traffic, one of them had to reverse to the tiny lay-bys used for passing. The Texan in him had never seen a road like it. Just as he was becoming seriously worried that he was utterly lost and had entered the land of *American Werewolf in London*, he crossed the top of a hill and got his bearings.

Once through Dalmellington, the going was more straightforward. The first hints of the old coalmining legacy could be seen as he came into New Cumnock. His grandad had been right. It reminded him of the failing little towns in the rustbelts of Ohio and Michigan. Places that had seen their best days before their customers turned east to Japan and Korea for their heavy engineering requirements. McMillan Holdings had shed all its interests in the sector in the early '70s and it had been a brilliant strategic move. There was a quiet desperation about New Cumnock which sank his spirits. Boarded-up shops. Grim pebbledash houses. Nobody about, even though the early evening was bright and warm.

A sign told him that it was just a few miles to Kirkonnel. The road headed back up into the hills now and there was more traffic. The countryside was not displeasing, but he felt that it had a kind of brooding quality about it. It looked pretty good on a sunlit September evening. It would look pretty grim in the rain and wind of the winter. The road started to drop back down to the valley floor and all of a sudden he was in Kirkonnel. A couple of minutes later he was out again. That was it. More or less a one-street town. He pulled over and allowed a couple of trucks to rumble by before doing a U-turn and heading back to park on the High Street.

He parked up with no difficulty and took a walk. In some ways the town differed comparatively little from the days of his great grandfather. It had hardly grown at all and most of the original buildings were still there. The coalmining legacy was all but gone. What was left was a place that felt out of place and out of time. There was a forgotten feel to it that slowly got to him as he walked. He could only imagine the noise and the bustle that there must have been about the place in its heyday. Then the coal from the pits of the valley had been used to power the steamships and the trains that criss-crossed the globe. The sweat and toil of the miners of Kirkonnel and a hundred places like it provided the fuel for the engine rooms of the greatest Empire of them all. It must have given the place a purpose. Now it was a town that had lost its place in the world. A town with no role to play.

He wondered what he had been hoping for. Like so many Americans he had been drawn to the place of his roots like iron filings to a magnet. To find what? Some clue as to who he was? Where he came from? It was only as he walked the streets that he realised that any such thoughts were pretty dumb. The Kirkonnel of the twenty-first century bore no resemblance to the town that Roland McMillan had left all those years ago. He was about to unlock the door to his hire car when he noticed that he had parked outside a small pub. Why not?

Inside, it wasn't much of a place. A brief glance about the room told him that he was the only customer. The landlady was sitting on a high stool behind the bar watching a game show on the wall-mounted TV. She was smoking and a mug of tea was in front of her. She registered his entry with a look of surprise. Clearly it was not a common event for a stranger to come in at seven o'clock on a Thursday night.

He smiled as he reached the bar. "Good evening Ma'am."

The smile, manners, and the Texan accent all had the collective effect of more or less knocking her into next week. She met his smile with one of her own and subconsciously registered that he was the first American customer to visit her pub in the twenty years that she and her husband had been in charge.

"Hello love. What can I get you?"

"Gotta Bud?"

This made her laugh and repeat it. "Gotta Bud? Aye. I gotta Bud."

She shook her head in amusement as she lifted her large frame off the stool and dug a bottle from the cooler and plonked it on the counter.

"On holiday are you?"

He took a swig, having decided that it would spoil things if he asked for a glass. The proprietor obviously had firm views on the way that Americans drank their beer.

"Yes Ma'am. Taking in the golf for a week. Mighty fine it is too."

"Taking in the golf are you then?" She couldn't help but smile. He was like something off Dallas. Nice-looking boy though. All wavy blond hair and teeth that looked like they cost a living fortune. But at least he showed his teeth. It seemed as if most local boys of his age who came into her bar were worried that they would be issued a fixed penalty notice if they were caught out smiling. Certainly that jumped-up pratt that her daughter was dating looked as if he hadn't risked a smile since he was six years old. She collected her cigarette and took a pull.

"Not a lot of golf here in Kirkonnel love. Bit lost are you?"

Again the beaming Marlboro Country grin.

"No Ma'am. Not lost at all, though I was getting kind of worried up in those hills coming over from the coast. The golf is at Turnberry. I'm just here to be the typical American. You know how it is. A man in search of his roots."

This quickened her interest. "What, here in Kirkonnel?"

"Yes Ma'am. This is where my great grandaddy was born. Long time ago. 1910. He left in 1925 and went Stateside. I saw the name on the map and I just had to come. I don't really know what I expected to find. That's Americans all over, guys wondering who the hell we are." He frowned at his use of the oath. "I'm sorry for my language Ma'am."

She laughed heartily at this. "Call that language! Try coming in on a Friday night and most of my customers are quite incapable of stringing together a sentence without using the F-word a half a dozen times."

"Oh. That's too bad."

"It's Kirkonnel love. That's the sort of place it is now. No work. No prospects. No nothing. Lots of men on the dole, young lasses pushing prams and kids on heroin. Welcome to Kirkonnel. Not much like the place your great grandad must have known. This place died the day they closed the pit."

His face was a picture of surprise. "Heroin? Here?"

"Oh yes. Not just here, everywhere. It's the same in all these wee towns. Nothing for kids to do but drugs. Heroin has taken over from coal as the main pillar of the local economy."

He found it extraordinary. He of course had lived an immensely privileged and sheltered life. Drugs had been fairly big at the Campus, but never junk. Junk was New York and Detroit and L.A. He couldn't believe that it could be a problem in such a tiny out-of-the-way place. But the landlady was obviously in earnest. It sank his mood a notch or two. He regretted coming. It would have been better to have taken a swim and a few drinks in the bar at the hotel. There had always seemed a certain glamour about his Scottish roots. The fact that Roland had doggedly refused to talk about his early life for nearly 80 years had made for great family speculation. There had been all kinds of theories about his mysterious early days, all of them worthy of Hollywood. None of them painted the picture of the sad, lost little place in the valley and the pub where no-one could afford a drink until a quick pint before last orders.

His reverie was broken. "So what's your name love? Maybe I know of some of your family."

"Sorry. I was miles away then. McMillan. Jonathan McMillan. My great grandad is Roland McMillan."

She frowned and searched her memory. There was something familiar but it was from long ago, from the early days when they had moved down from Motherwell to take on the pub. It was something that she must have heard from some of the old boys when they talked about their good old days when times had been better. McMillan. There was nobody of that name in Kirkonnel now. Not that she knew of anyway. But there was something. She screwed her forehead into a frown and then it came.

"Of course. I remember now. I knew there was something in the name. God, it was years ago. I remember the old lads talking about him. It must have been . . ." Again she concentrated hard. ". . . 1974. Of course. The Miner's Strike of '74. The one they won. The one that got the Tories out. Of course, there was no strike here. The pit had closed a few years before, but it was still the talk of the town. There were couple of old boys living out their past over a few pints. That's it. Coming back now. They were talking about the strike in 1926. The big one. The General Strike. There had been a massive scandal. Some desperate character had tried to break the strike. He must have been crazy. Scabs never had a chance in these parts. The bosses had tried to drive him into the pit in a van if I remember right. Well, the pickets stopped it and ripped open the back doors and dragged him out. He was beaten to death. The guy who did it was called McMillan. Funny first name. Like a town. That's it. Hamilton. Hamilton McMillan. Apparently he never tried to run away or hide of anything. He just beat the scab to death with a stave and waited for the police to take him away. It was a huge story at the time. They didn't hang him. I suppose they didn't dare. There were those who thought that Britain was about to go the way of Russia and the strike could have turned into a full-on revolution. The last thing they wanted was to make him a martyr. So they gave him life. I seem to remember that they said that he died in prison. Here. Come here."

She jumped off her stool with an alacrity that belied her years and bulk, and marched him across the room to an alcove. The wall was decorated with old pictures from Kirkonnel. The years had taken their tolls and the glass was all stained by decades of nicotine. She pointed to a fairly small old photo that was up in the corner of the wall alongside a cobweb that looked that it had been there for as long as the frame.

"Look. In the middle."

It was team photo. Kello Rovers. Champions. 1921. The team all wore beaming smiles, long shorts and striped woollen shirts. Only one face was serious. The man with the hard bony face must have been the captain. He was squatting down in the middle of the front row. Even squatting it wasn't hard to see that he was the biggest man in the team. His eyes bore into the camera. Through the camera. The eyes frightened him. They were staring out into nothingness. They seemed to be filled with a burning anger. A rage. There was no pleasure there. He was certain that the man's eyes would have sucked him in even if he hadn't heard the story of the murder. He glanced down to the careful, flowing handwriting under the photo and there it was. Confirmation.

Hamilton McMillan. Captain.

The landlady was aware of the effect that her story had had and she felt rather guilty about it. These were not the roots that the nice young man had come for. She had allowed herself to blurt it all out and now she was struggling to think of something to say. In the end she spoke in a gentle voice.

"You've got his hair, but he certainly doesn't have your smile love. I'm sorry. I should have kept my big trap shut."

He pulled himself clear of the eyes. "It's OK. Really." He attempted a smile. "We Americans are a motley bunch. It's what we expect. But that face. I wonder what can have happened to make that face?"

She sighed. "I can't remember much else love. Except . . . yes that's right. They said it had been the war. That's right. They said that he had a bad war. A terrible war. Once he had been a grand bloke. Hard. But always there to give a hand to anyone as needed it. But then he went to the war. The First World War that was. It was a bad war for miners. They fought a little war all of their own underground. There were lots who stayed there. Buried alive or killed in hand-to-hand fighting. A couple of old boys that came in here used to talk about it. They were the ones that remembered Hamilton McMillan. They said how he came back when the army had given him up for dead. He came back with a medal but he was never the same again. Wild. Dangerous. They said it was only a matter of time before he killed someone. The trenches did that to some men. They kept it all bottled up inside until something just snapped."

He spoke more or less to himself. "1926. He killed the man in 1926. That was a year after my great grandad left. He must have run away. Good Lord."

He stood and stared at the picture in silence for a while.

"Can I get you another drink love?"

"No. Thank you, but I'm driving." He forced himself to snap back into the present. "In fact I best be getting along. My friends will be wondering what has happened to me. I hope that you won't think me rude Ma'am, but I would like to make you an offer to buy this picture. I know it is unforgivable, but . . . well, I would really like to buy it."

She smiled. "I wouldn't dream of it, love." She reached up, unhooked the frame and handed it to him. The wall behind left a mark that had been many, many years in the making. "Here. A souvenir from Kirkonnel. Your roots."

His eyes prickled with tears as he took the gift. "Ma'am, what can I say. I'm overwhelmed. I really am."

"Well don't be. It's just a worthless old photo to me. I give it gladly. It's time I put something a bit more cheery on the wall anyway."

He nodded and suddenly found it hard to make his exit. He wanted to say something appropriate but found the words elusive. She helped him out.

"Go on. Stop hanging about. Off you go before it gets too dark. Maybe you'll be back one day?"

And at that moment for some reason he knew for certain that he would be. "Oh yes Ma'am. I'll be coming back to Kirkonnel. You can be assured of that."

Meg Cunningham took a moment to have an expansive stretch as she got out of her car. A glance at her watch confirmed what she already knew. 5.30 a.m. Five bloody sodding thirty in the bloody morning on her day off. It wasn't a state of affairs that she was remotely happy about. She took in the view and tried to get her brain to find a few positives. There was no getting around the fact that it was a downright gorgeous morning. The sun was just a few minutes away from making a swaggering entrance into the world. When it emerged, it would be as big and bold and as full of itself as Sinatra taking the stage in Las Vegas. The birds were already cheeping in delight at the prospect of a September day of warm morning sunshine. There was a soft mist settled down on the valley floor. A glowing dew lined the green grass of the pastures and the cattle were straight out of a milk advert. The whole thing could have been laid on by the Scottish Tourist Board and no doubt there would be plenty out there who would take them up on an offer of a weekend break in the rural idyll of Bruce and Burns.

It didn't work. Meg lived in Dumfries and had done so for her whole life apart from three years at college in Aberdeen. The countryside was there 24 hours a day every week of the year. If she wanted countryside, she could have countryside. She could have countryside at a sensible hour on a Sunday. She didn't need countryside at half-past five in the morning on her day off. The fact that it looked like a postcard was neither here nor there.

The caravan was a good 60 yards from where her car was parked and the grass urgently needed a cut. There was no way that she was going to get her shoes wet unless she had to. Maybe they would be ready and they would come out to her.

TARGET ONE

The caravan lived in a small copse of trees at the end of a track that ran half a mile from the road. The quiet of the morning was mildly interrupted by the soft hum of the generator that provided the caravan with its power. Water came in five-gallon plastic bottles. The caravan itself was not a pretty sight. It belonged to Roger Swann and he had bought it years ago for £100 plus delivery. At the time, it had been a place for him and his shooting pals to take a break from slaughtering the local wildfowl. A basic bit of shelter where they could eat a sandwich or two and pass around their hip flasks. Spartan surroundings where they could exchange jokes and reminisce about the privations they had all endured as boys in their beastly public schools.

It was inconceivable in this day and age that anyone would choose to live in such an aluminium wreck. Then again, it was inconceivable in this day and age that anyone but Archie bloody Banks would choose to live such a crazy and chaotic life.

Meg Cunningham was 32 years old and in every way a successful, sensible professional young woman. She was always smart. She spent generously on her hair and nails. She went to the gym three times a week. She owned her own flat in the right part of town and it was always spic-and-span. She was well liked without being flamboyant. Only a year before, she had become the youngest female to be made a branch manager in the southwest of Scotland for the bank where she worked. Though not an automatic head-turner, she had always enjoyed more-or-less her pick of men and she generally chose well. She chose lawyers and doctors and businessmen. Her men would take her out on her terms, and her terms had always been a light commitment. Her career came first and would continue to come first for the foreseeable future. Her men were taken on board on strict "take it or leave it" terms and they generally chose to take it.

All her life she had been organised, on top of things. At school she had never wavered from the top of the class. She easily made the grades to get to college and at college she easily made the grades to make the graduate entry scheme into the bank. Her career had been smooth and she had found no great difficulties in steering clear of office politics. All was well and all was in its place, just like it always had been. Except for one small blemish. It had always been the same small blemish, and no matter how many times she made promises to herself to change things, the small blemish always stayed with her.

SEPTEMBER

Archie Banks.

Archie Banks had entered her life at twelve years old. It had been her first day at High School. She was decked out from head to toe in new uniform purchased by her solicitor father and shop manager mother. She had been dropped off at ten to nine from the family Ford, having driven into town from their nice semi-detached house in the nice suburban street where they lived. Archie Banks came from a different planet. He had walked in to town with two friends from the flat where he lived on Sunnybank estate. His dad was unemployed and his mum had disappeared from the scene when he was only three. What meagre benefits that were to be had from Thatcher's disapproving purse were never going to paid out to any school uniform shop, the pub and bookies being much higher up the list of his father's priorities. The result was that the only concession to the recommended uniform sported by Archie Banks was a rather tatty tie passed down from a cousin.

Meg had settled into her first day quietly and had concentrated hard on listening to everything that her teachers told her. Archie wasted no time in establishing himself as the class clown, a role he had rehearsed vigorously throughout his years at primary school. Fate decreed that the teacher moved Archie forward from the desk that he had chosen at the back of the class to the desk next to the one that she had chosen at the front of the class. She had glanced across at him disapprovingly. She knew his type from primary schools. Loud boys who were coarse and full of themselves and altogether horrible. Some of her friends were attracted to them, but not Meg. No way. She was far too sensible for that. She always made a point of having nothing whatsoever to do with them, and she had absolutely no intention of having anything to do with this cocky scruff off Sunnybank.

Within three days it was clear that it wasn't going to work out that way. The trouble with Archie was that he was different. He actually was funny, and there was no way she could avoid the fact. She found it impossible not to laugh at his pranks and at one point she had actually got caught with a smirk on her face and was told off. It had left her speechless. Never in all her time at school had she been told off. She had been livid when the teacher turned back to the blackboard and she had turned to give Archie Banks a fierce stare. To her surprise he had shrugged and mimed the word "Sorry". To her amazement, her anger had drained away and the stern look on her face had been replaced by a small smile.

Within the week she had taken to spending her time in the playground with Archie and his two acolytes. Soon she was admitted to their inner sanctum which meant that Archie was Archie no more. He was "Deek". The evolution of his nickname had been typically convoluted. At and early age, "Archie" had been reduced to "Arch". Then one day some classmate had come into possession of a football card depicting a moderate journeyman midfielder called Owen Archdeacon. "Arch" immediately became known to one and all as the "Deacon". Then the "Deacon" became "Deek", and "Deek" it was to remain for ever more. Deek had two staunch friends from the same block of flats and as a threesome they had been involved in every bit of mischief that the Sunnybank estate had to offer since the age of three.

Paul Simpson was small. He had always been small from the moment he had emerged into the world weighing in at just under four pounds. There are many children who spend their early years rather small, and then astound all around them with a vigorous and spectacular spurt of teenage growth. It was never going to be the case with Paul. His dad was a small round man who could make five-foot-five on a good day. His mum was a small round woman who had never once threatened to break through the five-foot barrier at all. Paul was not only small and round, he was also crumpled. His face looked as if it had been stuck in the doors of a lift and had never straightened out. He had been five years old when a playground wag had christened him as "Troll" and the name had been with him ever since.

Dennis McLean was as different from his friend Troll as different could be. He had always been taller than the norm, and by the time he entered High School he was already well on his way to his eventual six-foot-four. However, he was a boy whose body always grew up rather than out, and no matter what prodigious amounts of chips and bread passed his lips, he would never be anything but completely skinny. He passed the six-foot barrier a little after his thirteenth birthday. He sported the chalk-white freckly skin of a pure bred Scotsman coupled with an unruly mop of flame red hair that refused doggedly to respond to any efforts at styling. Somewhere in the dim and distant reaches of their collective past he had collected the nickname of "Banjo". Over the years this became the topic of considerable debate. There was no particular reason why he should have been known as Banjo, it just seemed to have always been the case.

So it was that in the autumn of 1984 Meg was admitted into the world of the Sunnybank Three. She brought the woman's influence to what had always been a wholly male preserve and, to her own amazement, she found out that she was a tomboy at heart. Her mother was appalled when she first arrived at the back door with her new friends. There was a furious family debate that evening where the main gist of her mother's position was that there was no way that any daughter of hers was going to be spending her days getting up to no good on the Sunnybank estate. Her dad was more pragmatic. He wasn't born-and-bred Dumfries and had worked himself up from the harder turf of Glasgow's East End. He knew the difference between mischief and real badness well enough, and he was rather taken with the odd threesome who had attracted his daughter. He started a process that would eventually turn into a rather messy and ugly divorce by refusing to back up his wife's prejudices. If his daughter wanted to spend her time up on Sunnybank with Deek, Troll and Banjo, then that would have to be her decision. She had always been an independent girl and it would do her nothing but good to find out about how life was on the other side of the tracks.

The biggest event of their collective lives happened during their first High School summer holidays. Meg's dad had taken a week off from his practice, and on the Tuesday morning he had taken his daughter to the golf course. Meg had for a few years tried to maintain a very modest enthusiasm for the game of golf. It had always been a great passion of her father's and it filled the hours of his leisure time. He was a good player, and their living-room cabinet was always adorned with silverware. Meg had inherited none of his ability and her only pleasure was the hours that it gave her alone with her father.

That morning he had taken her onto the practice ground to try and coax some kind of effectiveness into her jerky swing. They had the place to themselves apart from Roger Swann, the self-styled "best player in the club", who was thrashing two irons like tracer bullets to the far edge of the fairway.

She had been stopped mid-swing by a cry from the edge of the fairway.

"Go on Meg. Give it a whack."

When she looked round she spotted the familiar faces of her three friends beaming out from the hawthorn bushes. Her dad chuckled.

"Looks like were been sussed." He assumed a dramatic movie "voice-over" tone. "There ain't nowhere a gal can hide from the Sunnybank Three." He waved them out of the bushes. "What are you lot up to then?"

Deek, as ever, was the spokesman. "Not a lot Mr Cunningham. Just knocking aboot you ken. Can I have a go?"

Meg passed over the eight iron she was holding with delight. Her last five efforts had scratched and scuttered along the floor like miserable wounded rabbits. She was in no mood to become the butt of their jokes.

Deek took the club and weighed it thoughtfully.

"Ah have nae got a clue what to do here, Mr Cunningham. Show us a shot."

Frank Cunningham duly obliged and flicked the eight iron gracefully through a shot which flew gently through the warm morning air. Deek watched the slow easy swing with interest.

"So you dunnae whack it then."

"No. Not at all. The harder you try to whack it, the worse it is. Rhythm and timing Deek. Rhythm and timing. That's what it's about."

Deek's first three efforts showed little of either. He had been impressed by the fat divot that Frank Cunningham's shot had taken and he was keen to do the same. He did indeed manage three pretty impressive divots, but the ball on each occasion did not progress much more than five yards. This induced great hilarity from Troll, Banjo and Meg and even Deek had to smile ruefully.

"Hey. It's no as easy as it looks, ken."

Frank tapped the grass just behind the ball. The boy had mimicked his swing as if her were a tape recorder. He was intrigued. "Try and hit the ground here Deek. Right behind the ball. Do you play pool?"

"Aye."

"Think of a backspin shot."

The next effort was better. Deek took slightly too much turf, but the ball still went nearly 100 yards. The next two were crisp and clean and brought a smile of satisfaction to the impish face. He was just about to hit again when he was brought up short by a new voice. It was Roger Swann who had made his way across the practice ground.

"Are these lads members Frank?"

Frank Cunningham's face clouded.

"No they're not Roger. No harm done though. They're only having a go."

Swann's face showed little sympathy for the idea of the three non-member ragamuffins being allowed to have a go.

"Not really on you know Frank. Look at the mess he's making." He waved his club accusingly at the trench like divot holes left in the wake of Deek's first three efforts. "I mean the lad can't play at all . . ."

"Aye I can." Deek had always had a problem with keeping his mouth shut when such a course of action was preferable.

Swann was not remotely amused. "Don't you give me cheek lad or I'll chuck you into those bushes by the seat of your pants. I suggest you all leave now."

Frank sighed quietly to himself. The game of golf had always been something that he had loved, it was just sad that it always seemed to attract jumped-up little Hitlers like Swann. But there was never any point in trying to fight them with their insufferable codes and rules. "I think it might be best if we knocked off now lads. Tell you what, come round later and I'll take you to the driving range . . .."

The expression on Deek's face brought him up short. Gone was the impish good humour. The boy was angry.

"Want a bet mister?"

Swann's face was a picture. "A what?"

"You heard me. Want a bet?"

Little did Deek know that Roger Swann had more or less no ability to say "no" when it came to any kind of wager. It was the main reason that his wife had stormed out of his life a few months earlier amid a torrent of foul language and accusations. Despite himself, he couldn't help but succumb to a twitch of interest.

"What kind of bet?"

Deek pointed out across to the clump of trees at the corner of the practice ground.

"You say I can't play. I bet I can knock one into those trees. Three chances. Three balls. What about it?"

Swann couldn't help but smile. Cheeky little sod. "How much?"

Deek dug into the pocket of his jeans and started hauling out coins. Troll and Banjo looked on miserably. They had all pooled the meagre

resources they had cadged from grumbling parents. £2.12. Enough
for chips at dinner and tea. Enough for a few cans of pop and maybe
a couple of shots in the arcade if they could get away with it. Enough
for a pretty decent sort of day, and now Deek was about to punt the
whole lot on one of his crazy bets. Swann was duly impressed.

"All you've got, hey boy?"

"Aye. Every penny."

Swann glanced over to the trees. It must have been just over 200
yards. "You've no chance. You know that?"

"So you say. Put your money where your mouth is if you're so sure."

This was an unexpected entertainment. "OK then. Tell you what. You
might think I'm a miserable old sod, but I'll be fair. I'll give you odds.
Four-to-one. I win, and its £2.12. You win and its £8.50. Fair enough?"

Deek nodded gravely. "Aye. That'll do me. Could you show me
Mr Cunningham? Hit a couple so I can watch, ken?"

Frank Cunningham decided on a three wood. No way the lad
would handle a driver. No way he would handle a three wood, but
there had been something in the way that he had swung at the eight
iron that made him wonder. He hit three careful shots each one of
which flew well over the required distance. He kept up a quiet
commentary as he hit each shot, pointing out the main requirements.
Swann lit up a cigarette and leaned on his two iron.

"Can ah have a fag mister?" asked Troll hopefully.

"Bugger off," was the predictable response.

After the third shot Frank shrugged and asked. "OK? Get the
picture?"

Deek smiled, and as he smiled Frank Cunningham thought for the
umpteenth time that the boy was born to play the part of the Artful
Dodger. He knew full well that the £2.12 represented dinner money
for the day and he resolved to take all three of them out to the coast
for the afternoon along with fish and chips. He was annoyed at
Swann for taking on the bet. Had the bloody man no idea at all?

"Nae bother Mr Cunningham. How high should I tee it up then?"

Cunningham placed a ball carefully on a tee and Deek addressed
the ball with furrowed concentration. The swing when it came was
altogether too fast and he lost it halfway down. The club head did no
more than glance the top of the ball that bounced along for a
miserable 30 yards.

"One down, two to go" smirked Swann.

"Too fast, hey Mr Cunningham. Ah forgot the rhythm and timing bit."

This time he teed up the ball himself and his swing was half the speed. The ball took off smoothly and bounced along to within ten yards of the tree line. Deek nodded with satisfaction. "Aye. That's more like. Just a wee bit too slow. Two down and one to go hey boss. Best get the wallet out."

A slow smile played on Swann's lips as he took another drag. "Aye, maybe I should. Come on. One last chance lad. Give it your best."

Deek's best was astounding. He quickened his swing slightly and sent the ball off with a sound crack. It was only just dropping as it clattered into the high branches of one of the trees in the middle of the copse. The two adults looked on as if they had both been hit by the same bolt of lightning. Deek turned from an exaggerated follow-through with a wide grin of satisfaction.

"There you go. Money out time I think. That will be £8.48 if ah've done my sums right."

Swann reached into his pocket and pulled out a £10 note. Of all the lost bets in his life this was the one he had enjoyed most. "Here you go lad. Keep the change. So you like golf then do you?"

"Aye it's OK. No chance of playing though is there? Not for the likes of me. I'll stick to ma pool and fitba."

Swann looked over to Frank Cunningham. "Tell you what Frank, if I propose this lad for membership will you second me?"

Cunningham couldn't quite believe what he was hearing. But he could understand it well enough. What they had both just witnessed was something special. Really special. He nodded happily.

Deek seemed confused. "What you's on about. Ah cannae afford no golf club membership."

Swann grinned. "No need. I'll pay. I'll pay and I'll show you how to play."

It was a great turning point in both their lives. Swann had been left a small fortune by his father and was able to live well on his share dividends in the sprawling house a few miles out of town. On the surface of things, he seemed happy enough with his lot. His was a life of golf and the races and shooting. Since his wife had left, there had been a collection of divorcees who had made their pitch at the big house and the expensive lifestyle. All they had done was to make his life seem increasingly empty. He was well past 40 and he was aware that he had missed the boat. The cheeky lad from Sunnybank became the son he had always wanted. By the time Deek turned fifteen, he was playing off scratch and finished fourth in the Scottish Boys Championship. When he left school, Swann swung him a job as an assistant pro at the club. Deek's first home of his own was the old caravan on the Swann estate.

Despite her tetchy early morning mood, Meg couldn't help but smile at the memory of that morning nearly twenty years earlier. Her dad was retired now, but he still never missed following Deek round in any tournament that he played in. She knew that he would be there later on that day. A smart figure with silver hair and the same old warm smile. Despite everything, he had never given up on the boy who had risked everything he had on that three wood into the trees. Roger Swann had been the making of Deek. Sadly he had also been his nemesis. He had done more than find the son that he had always craved. He had also found a fellow craven gambler. A kindred spirit. When Deek turned pro he never gave the game the dedication that it demanded. His real passion was always reserved for the big money challenge games that his mentor loved to arrange. They built a reputation for themselves and there was no doubt that they won more than they lost, but anything they ever won disappeared in the twinkling of an eye in the bookies and casinos.

The balance of her relationship with the Sunnybank Three had changed for ever when she turned sixteen. After four years, the inevitable had happened, and she and Deek had become an item. The lads had all left school whilst she had stayed on to get the grades that everyone had always predicted. Deek had become an assistant pro whilst Troll's dad had got him a job on the bins and Banjo had surprised one and all by becoming a trainee in the Job Centre. For a while it had been fine. Deek often had a pocketful of cash from a successful challenge match and the four of them lived high. Things went awry when she left Dumfries for college. Their relationship became strained and none of her college friends took to the Sunnybank Three when they regularly paid her visits. Rows started. She wanted Deek to come and visit her alone, but he stubbornly refused to come without the other two. She saw the chance to spend some time alone as a chance for romance. He saw it as betrayal of his oldest friends. Worse still, he had started to drink too much, and the drink started to bring out a chip on either shoulder that she had never noticed before. It became impossible for her to go out with her college friends when Deek and the others were visiting. It always ended badly. Deek would hit the drink with a crazed determination and by nine o'clock a fight was always inches away. Everything came to a head one Saturday in March when the fight finally erupted. Michael Harper was a fellow accountancy student and he had become a good friend. Meg knew full well that given half the chance Michael had more than friendship in mind. He came from a large house in Stirling and represented everything that Deek had set himself to hate. All evening the young man from Sunnybank had riled Michael as he relentlessly tipped back drink after drink. All Michael had suggested was that Deek should steady on a bit and maybe go back to Meg's room to sober up. Deek's response had been to launch himself across the table at his middle-class adversary like a madman. It was a pretty major mistake. In his drunken fervour, it had slipped Deek's notice that Michael played in the second row of the college's rugby team and stood six inches taller than the crazed class-warrior. Two short punches finished the job that the drink had already more or less completed and left Deek out cold on the floor. From there it was the A&E for a patch up on the nose and a long, miserable drive home to Dumfries. It was also the last straw as far as Meg was concerned, and she let Deek know that they were an item no longer.

It would be two years before they saw each other again. Meg had thrived at college and emerged with an impressive First in her degree. It easily opened the doors for the graduate entry at one of the country's largest banks that provided her with a preferential mortgage rate to buy a nice flat in the centre of the town. She knew it would only be a matter of time before she bumped into Deek, and she had rather dreaded it. When it happened one evening on the High Street, it was worse than she had anticipated. Deek had always tended towards being skinny, but now it was as if all the weight had been stripped from him. The impish mischief that had always made him so attractive to her was long gone. His face bore deep lines that had no right to be there. He was dressed smartly enough, but the clothes seemed to hang off him all wrong and his hair was a bird's-nest mess.

"Hello Meg. You're back then."

"Yes. Back again. How are you Deek?"

A rueful grin. "Aye well. So so. On the wagon at the moment. Three months now. Well, eleven weeks, four days, six hours . . . " He glanced up at a clock. ". . . and 45 minutes."

"That's great. Do you feel better for it?"

A shaken head. "No. I feel lousy, but maybe it will get better."

"And the golf? How is the golf?"

"Middling. I've been playing more tournaments the last year. Had a couple of top tens, but it's tough going. Lots of keen kids who hit the ball into next week. I don't play so many games with Mr Swann now. He's not been so good himself. Too many bets gone wrong, too many bookies chasing him for cash. He tends to lock himself away in the house most of the time. He comes out every now and then and we have a game, but not often. It's sad really."

"And where are you living?"

"Where do you think? The caravan. Where else?"

"Troll and Banjo?"

"Aye. The caravan. We're all still there. Not good really, but there you are. Old habits and all that."

"But are they well?"

"Oh aye. They're fine. Just like always. You know how it is with those two."

Oh yes. She knew just how it was with those two. With all three of them. The Sunnybank Three were now in their early twenties and they still hung on to a life they had made for themselves when they were twelve. The caravan was their den. They had parted that evening without making any arrangements to meet again.

They hadn't met again properly for a further four years. Her father kept her up to date with the progress of Deek's career such as it was. Every now and then he managed to qualify for one or two of the more modest PGA tournaments, but never troubled the higher reaches of the leader board. One day she received a frantically excited call from her father whilst she was at work. He was following Deek around in a tournament down in the Midlands and he was five under and the tele was there. He told her to get herself home and watch it. She had told him not to be so silly, but when it was the time for her lunch break she had duly returned to the flat and tracked down the golf on the obscure reaches of *Sky Sports 3*.

"Welcome back to Hawksmoor Park for day one of the Rolex Invitational. We still have a surprise first-day leader. When we were last with him, Scotsman Archie Banks had just moved onto six under. Let's see how things are progressing."

The picture seemed to have switched to a view more akin to a nature programme than a golf tournament. The view from inside the trees was the epitome of Britain in springtime. There were vivid hues of green and butterflies. It was certainly a long way from the fairway. Deek stood looking down with a look of disapproval at the clump of thick brambles where his ball nestled. At his side, Troll's squashed face mirrored his concern as he stood with the huge bag on his shoulders. She couldn't help but smile. The bag was nearly bigger than the caddie. To the side of the frame stood the gangling figure of Banjo ridiculously visible in a bright yellow shell-suit that was two inches too short in the legs. Next to Banjo was the dapper figure of her father whose expression mirrored Deek's.

"Well John. Looks like Banks has found himself quite a spot of bother there on fourteen . . ."
    "Absolutely. You may remember that the fourteenth is a dogleg. Nobody so far has taken on the tiger line over the trees and tried to make the green. Banks went with his driver and it really looked as if he had made it. The ball hit one of the highest branches and here we are. This is a disaster. There really is no shot whatsoever. All he will be able to do is go all the way back and take a drop. To be honest he will do well to come off with anything better than six . . ."

Deek was now reaching for a club. Troll was shaking his head unhappily. And Deek smiled, and for an instant there was the boy she had known all those years ago. She couldn't quite believe what she was seeing. He rooted his feet down into the tangled brambles and with a cigarette hanging from his lips addressed the ball. The fact that he was taking on such an outrageous shot seemed nothing compared to the fact that he was taking it on with a fag in his mouth in front of the TV cameras.

" . . . I really think that this is a mistake. If he gets this wrong he could be looking at eight or nine . . ."

Deek's swing was little more than a whirlwind thrash sending a clump of bramble and dry grass into the air. The picture switched to the green ahead. Unbelievably a ball emerged from the thickness of the trees, took a determined bounce forward, and made its way to an unlikely position a few feet from the pin. There was only a handful of people watching but they applauded enthusiastically.

"Unbelievable. I tell you, we won't see a better shot all week. That was reminiscent of Seve Ballesteros in his prime. Fantastic . . ."

Sadly it was to be his high point of the week. Nothing terrible happened, things just drifted away. He finished on Sunday at a respectable two under par and 43rd. A modest payday and back to golfing obscurity.

She was 28 and an assistant manager when he walked into her office. It was no surprise. The appointment had been staring at her for three days. He had told her that he was back on the wagon again. The golf was going well. It was time he took a step forward. He wanted to have a go at the European Qualifying School. It was time. He needed an overdraft and she gave him one against all her better judgement. He actually made it to the second phase, but failed by two shots to get to the final round.

Two years later he tried again, but fell again at the second phase. The next year he was well and truly off the wagon and fell at the first hurdle. By this stage he had become a problem. His overdraft had tipped over £20,000 and it was unsecured. The rest of her ledger was as perfect as perfect could be. Only one account stood out like a festering sore thumb. Archibald Banks. Sole trader. Golf professional. £20,432.25. Unsecured. She had been short-listed for the manager's job at one of the flagship Edinburgh branches and the interview was a mere six months away. Six months to tidy up her ledger. Six months to do something about the account of Archibald Banks. She had telephoned him and told him that he was having another go at qualifying whether he liked it on not. She told him that this time he was going to stay sober and come good. She told him that the overdraft was frozen and she would fund the bloody thing out of her own pocket. She told him that she had entered him for the first stage at St Annes Old Links on 14th September. She told him that she would pick him up herself at five-thirty in the morning and that he had better be ready and sober.

There was still not a flicker of movement from the caravan. She yanked the boot of her car open and pulled out her walking shoes and put them on. By the time she reached the rusty door she was firing on all cylinders. Her knock shook the tired metal and brought no response. It was only after the third time that the door creaked open to reveal the blinking, confused face of Troll in a T-shirt and underpants. At the sight of Meg his eyes became wide open and his odd crumpled face looked as if it had seen the horrors of the world.

"Oh shite."

"Yes Troll. Oh shite. Where is he?"

"He's like . . . well . . . you ken Meg . . . he's . . ."

"Excuse me please Troll."

She eased him backwards and climbed into a chaos of empty beer cans, fast food wrappings and overflowing ashtrays. Troll was appalled at the effect the scene was having. "You see Meg, we hav'nae had time to tidy up, ken, it was . . ."

"Please Troll. Spare me."

On the right bunk a pair of chalk-white feet hung over the edge and a splash of red hair was slowly emerging from under a duvet as Banjo miserably came to life. On the right-hand bunk there was a completely still lump totally buried under the duvet. Meg took hold of the end of the duvet and pulled it off to reveal the bony sleeping frame of Deek curled up into a foetal ball. To watch him climb out of sleep was a painful exercise. He peeled open his eyes and tried to make some sense as to what could possibly have happened to his duvet at such an ungodly hour. Then he saw Meg and his expression moved from astonishment to panic to outright mortified terror.

"Oh bloody hell. Christ. Buggery. It was a challenge match Meg. Down at Southerness. A Jap. Gave him ten-hole start and won on the seventeenth. Won a grand so I did. Got a bit carried away celebrating. Oh Christ."

Her voice was crisp and hard. "£1,000. Very good. Strange I didn't see it going into the account Deek."

"Aye well. It was too late on. The bank was closed and . . ."

"How much is left?"

"Well, you see . . ."

"How much?"

His face fell. Why was it always the same? Drinks for one and all, a big curry and a card game at some flat in Sunnybank. The cab home had eaten up the last remnants of the winnings. What could he say?

"Nothing Meg. Same as usual. Pissed away on cards. I'm sorry. Really."

"Just get dressed Deek. We need to be away in ten minutes. I'll wait in the car."

It took them quarter of an hour to emerge. Troll hefted the large bag into the boot and took his place on the back seat next to Banjo. Deek sat up front nervously smoking. By the time they were half way to Annan, the sound of snoring floated forward from the back seat. Deek's head was pounding and he yearned to do the same as his friends and switch off the lights for a while. He looked over to Meg who whose face was a mask of anger. Why did he have to love the bloody woman so much? It had never gone away, not even for a second. From the very second he had been hauled from the back of the class in S1 and placed next to her he had been lost. There had been one or two flings in the years after they had split, but none of them had meant anything. There was only ever Meg. There would only ever be Meg. It was how it was and he was stuck with it. Every time he sweated it out on the wagon, it was with the hope that he could turn everything around and she would accept him back. Every time he crashed off the wagon it was because he just couldn't handle the sheer depression of waking up to the fact that she was gone. Meg was better than him. She always had been. She was a successful professional woman who would soon leave Dumfries for a big city and a rich husband and a clutch of kids in private school. He had been something to her once, but not any more. How could he be? He was 32 and looked 50. He gambled away every penny he made. He could barely function without half a bottle of scotch and 40 fags a day. He was a born loser on the road to nowhere. He felt he had to say something.

"Meg, look. I really am sorry. You know that, yeah?"

"You're always sorry Deek. I'm sick of sorry. Sorry stopped working years ago. I don't want sorry. I just want some payback. You always told me you would come through when it counted. Just watch the boy from Sunnybank, remember that? Watch him when the chips are down? Yeah? Well the chips are down Deek. I took a flyer on you because of stupid misguided loyalty. Well it's payback time. My future is in your hands whether you like it or not. It's called responsibility. Now I suggest you try and sleep off the booze like the others. I really don't want to talk about it much."

He desperately wanted to say something but the words were nowhere in sight. He rolled the seat back and slept.

His tee-off time was ten-past four. The time on the practice ground had been highly discouraging to say the least. All around him were lads in their early twenties who looked as if they had stepped off the cover of *Maxim* magazine. Designer gear and tanned faces and smooth confident swings. His clothes all needed a good iron and he was painfully aware of the curry stain on his trousers. He couldn't seem to time a shot and he knew that he was being sniggered at. He took a good couple of hearty pulls on the whisky that was hidden in a Nike water bottle and made his way to the first tee. Waiting for him was six-foot-two inches of model young professional. White teeth. Two grand's worth of clubs. A disapproving caddie. Firm handshake. Dry hands. No nerves.

"William Hendricks."

"Archie Banks. Call me Deek if you like."

The handsome face registered the whisky on his breath.

"Yes. Deek. Fine." An accent out of expensive Surrey. Deek bridled.

"Are we having a wee punt on it then?"

"Excuse me?"

"You ken. A wee side bet. 100 quid a shot on the card. Up for it?"

Now the handsome face was rattled. "Well I suppose so. Why not?"

The weather started cloudy and nondescript. By the fifth, the wind was up and the rain was lashing down. The elegant Surrey swing was blown away and the Adonis tramped home miserably with 85 against his name. Deek kept taking a hit of whisky and kept his shots low. He put together one of the finest rounds of his life and finished the day at the head of the field with 69. He handed over the £1,600 cash to Meg before she left the car park.

"Better bank this for me."

She took the cash with a frown.

"What's this?"

"Side-bet with that jumped-up cocky prick from London. I don't suppose he'll be on for another tomorrow."

She smiled despite herself and passed back a £50 note. "Go on. Have a drink. All of you. You can do it Deek. Three more days. You are almost there after today. Just play steady. For me Deek. Please."

And he did. He took safe lines and avoided trouble. The rain lashed the Lancashire coast for three days and he emerged as the winner of a sodden field. A further £2,500 came off the overdraft and he was duly listed to play in the second phase of the qualification process at Girona in Spain in November. As he waited for the train back to Dumfries he had no concept of what the next few months were about to bring.

When it came, the moment that marked the culmination of two years work in the life of Steve Kenton was something of an anti-climax. Hollywood would have demanded a great deal more of the moment. There would have been hatchet-faced bad guys coked up to their eyeballs and firing off their Uzi's in all directions. There would have been black helicopters swooping down through the hail of fire to allow fearless members of the SWAT team to swing down from ropes, firing from the hip. There would have been a ruggedly handsome good-guy looking battered and bruised in his vest, bloodied, but still able to fight out a deadly but successful Kung Fu battle with the bad guy to get the girl. It was how things always were when the great and the good at the top echelon of the drugs world received their come-uppance.

The Hollywood money men would have spat out their tall decaff lattés in disgust had a scriptwriter brought them a screenplay describing Steve Kenton's moment of victory. For a start, he was a rather nondescript-looking middle-aged man of 45 who was thinning on top and had the slightly greyish look of a lifelong smoker. Had he been stripped down to his vest, the viewer would have seen a body which was more designed to win a cross-country race than a Mr Universe competition. But he wasn't in his vest. He was wearing slacks and a plain white shirt with the sleeves rolled halfway up his forearms. The bad guy of the scene, Tom Rushton, was similarly unimpressive. He looked like a bank manager ready for early retirement to Morecambe Bay. Admittedly, the men from the California studios would have been much happier with the two guests who sat across the mahogany table on the patio of Rushton's two million pounds worth of house. They were both extremely fit-looking young black men decked out in pristine designer-gear and sunglasses. They lolled in their chairs like real gangsters and would have offered the producer of the movie a genuine chance of giving walk-on parts to a couple of famous rappers and thereby boosting up the box office of the film whilst not asking for much in the way of acting. The two guests up from Moss Side actually both fancied themselves as rappers, but in truth they were much more suited to being gangsters, a pursuit in which they had both excelled at since the age of ten.

The patio afforded one of the more spectacular views in the northwest of England. The house sat on top of one of the first high hills that separate Manchester from the Peak District. From the city centre it was reached in 40 minutes, through the grinding poverty of east Manchester until the city faded into affluent suburbs and then winding country lanes through fields filled with sheep. The back of the house stared down onto the sprawl of Greater Manchester and on a clear day it was a sight to behold. When they had first arrived, the two guests from Moss Side had been entranced by the view. For a few moments they had allowed their tough-guy image to slip as they had picked out familiar landmarks through the powerful telescope which Rushton kept at the edge of the patio.

Now it was all business. The two men had been customers of Tom Rushton for five years, but it was the first time they had met the big man personally. Secretly they were somewhat disappointed for similar reasons to those of hypothetical Hollywood money men. He seemed more like a schoolmaster than the main man, but they knew better than to let on. They had started out as keen teenagers on the make, spending a couple of thousand a month with the Rushton empire. Over the years their spending had steadily risen to over fifty thousand. They were discreet, they didn't go round shooting people, and they paid up good as gold. Since being released from his one and only stay in Strangeways Prison, Tom Rushton had distanced himself from the drug side of his business. His stretch had lasted nine months but it would be a great deal longer the next time. He was very, very careful. The meeting was not about drugs, he left that to lieutenants who were never to be found within ten miles of his mansion in the hills. The meeting was about his hotel development on the Turkish coast. He had bought a completely undeveloped stretch of land adjacent to the sparkling, clean waters of the eastern Mediterranean and had bought off all the local officials. A 600-room hotel was already halfway built and the complicated network of offshore *Shell* companies offered a wonderful investment opportunity to anyone with large amounts of dodgy cash that needed laundering.

Offering his best customers a piece of his lucrative Turkish scheme made huge sense to Tom Rushton. More and more it was the money that was the downfall of many of the more successful dealers in the commodities that he sold. By persuading them to invest with him he achieved two key aims. Firstly, he made as much profit from handling their money as he did from selling them smack and coke. Secondly, he was able to have some control on what they did with their cash and could keep them trading for longer.

His pitch was going well. Both of his guests were clearly intelligent and had they been born with a different postcode they would have probably been lawyers or legitimate businessmen. The sensible economics of his offer were easy for them to understand and held great appeal. Stashing their cash had become a greater and greater problem the more their enterprise had grown. The deal would be completed, that much was clear to all concerned.

Steve was barely listening. He was already more than familiar with the detail of the Turkish venture. He was idly smoking and watching a kestrel hovering over the next-door field when the moment arrived. Rushton hadn't noticed that his attention had wandered.

"Do me a favour will you Steve. Nip to the office and grab the last bunch of photos we took will you." He tossed across a set of keys and carried on with his pitch. "You'll see from the photos lads. The place is more than half built. These Turks don't hang about I tell you. We reckon we'll be open for trade by next June at the latest . . ."

Steve rose to his feet and suddenly his heart was shaking his ribcage. Two years and suddenly the big moment had arrived. He concentrated on walking as nonchalantly as possible. Not the time to blow it now. Keep the cool. Take it slowly. He felt as if all eyes must have been burning into his back as he crossed the patio to the back door and went inside.

Deep breaths, Stevie boy. Deep breaths. Auto pilot. Don't think about it. Just do it. Up the stairs. Unlock the office door. Close it. Deep breaths. Computer on. Hit the keys. He carried out each action carefully. He hit the keys in the order that he had been trained in and froze the screen before it had started its start-up routine. A winking white line told him that he had got it right. He reached down his trousers and yanked off the piece of tape which he had stuck to the inside of his thigh every day for the last four months as he waited for his chance. The tape took away a clump of hairs and made him wince. Under the tape was a mini-sized CD which he quickly rubbed on his shirt and inserted into the D Drive. Whilst the technology did its bit, he opened the top drawer of the desk and took out the packet of photos that they had taken on their most recent trip to the Turkish coast. The seconds passed by like years until the screen told him that his work was done. He ejected the CD and taped it back to the inside of his thigh before returning to the patio and lighting up another cigarette. There was no sign of the kestrel. Maybe it had got its field mouse. Maybe it had just got fed up and gone looking in another field. He felt a closeness with the bird. He was a hunter too. He always had been. He knew what it was to show patience. He shared the hawk's ability to wait for his moment. Wait and kill. Wait and kill.

This had probably been his hardest ever job. At first he hadn't fancied it at all. It had all seemed too much of a wing and a prayer. Too many 'ifs and buts'. A chess game worked out by the Oxbridge types in London who had never spent a minute of their lives on the wrong side of the tracks. Steve Kenton had been there all his life. He had been born and raised on an estate in Salford. His natural intelligence had taken him to Manchester Grammar and his A-levels took him to Durham University. He financed himself through an Army Bursary and, when he completed his degree, he went straight on to Sandhurst. He duly took up his position as a second lieutenant in the Parachute Regiment just in time to be shipped south to the Falklands. After that it was Ireland and the lethal rainy fields of South Armagh. In 1987 he had successfully made it through a murderous induction to be accepted into the elite undercover 14th Intelligence Unit. For the next seven years he had lived on the streets and in the ditches of North Derry and Belfast. He had become quite a star in his secret little world and had been involved in taking down three major players who were granted a total of 78 years in the Maze Prison.

Peace had left him at a loose end. He had options. He could have returned to the Regiment as a Captain or taken up the offer on the table to work on secondment to the Security Services. He had chosen the latter. The Irish peace gave the Government the chance to move a lot of men like Steve Kenton into the front line on the war on drugs. A few had been shipped out to Latin America to hide in the rain forests and track consignments of cocaine all the way to the vessels which would cross the Atlantic to Europe where they would be stopped by the ships of the Royal Navy. Others like Steve were sent out into the mean streets and estates of Britain to quietly get themselves under the skin of the drugs industry. It was the kind of mind-bogglingly dangerous work that not many would fancy. For the men and women of 14th Intelligence it was merely more of the same. Getting caught merely meant a fate worse than death in some lock-up garage at the hands of different maniacs. Instead of the IRA's much vaunted "Nutting Squad" it would be the semi-psychotic hard men of some dealer or another.

He had done a couple of years as a tramp in Handsworth in Birmingham before being pulled out and offered the Rushton job. At the time Tom Rushton had been sent to Strangeways Prison for a year on conspiracy charges. This had led to the hair-brained scheme dreamed up by the Oxbridge types. At least it had the virtue of being relatively simple. The cover had been that Steve had left the Army under a cloud and gone home to Salford and become bitter and twisted at the lack of reward for his service to Queen and Country. He picked a fight in a pub with a known local face and beat him within an inch of his life. It was plain bad luck that a passing patrol car chose that very moment to stop and take a look. It was generally accepted that the victim had deserved all he got and proper consideration was taken of Kenton's excellent record with the Army, a point that was made vigorously in court by his commanding officer. All of this was taken on board and the judge made great show of having listened. However, GBH was still GBH, no matter how many excuses there were for it. Steve Kenton was duly sent to Strangeways for three years.

That had been the easy bit. The next bit was the gamble. A crazy gamble, but they had taken it anyway. On the wing that was now occupied by both Steve Kenton and Tom Rushton was a lifer called Malkie Jenks. The fact that Malkie was a complete and absolute nutter was common knowledge. He had been in and out of a variety of institutions from the age of fourteen for all manner of violent acts. He had made a career as an enforcer on the bleak edges of the crime world. He had never made it far up the ladder due to the fact that his fuse was far too short for him to be much use to anyone. At the very centre of Malkie's life was his wife Doreen and their only son Ian. One fateful day, a gang of youths in Fallowfield had stopped Ian on his way home from school and roughed him up and trodden his glasses into the ground. Malkie had flipped and killed two of them with a knife. It was generally agreed that life would mean life for Malkie Jenks.

However incarceration did nothing to lesson his adoration of his wife and son and it was fairly clear that they shared his sentiments. The Oxbridge types found a way of passing the word into Strangeways. The word was passed through the right channels and the word was simple. If Malkie topped Tom Rushton, then the missus would get 100 grand and the boy would get private school. The offer was as irresistible as the Oxbridge types had predicted, and Malkie accepted the contract. The news was in turn passed along to Steve.

It had then been a matter of vigilance. Rushton was safe in the midst of a cocoon of security. Malkie's task was never going to be easy. Steve tried to work out when the hit was most likely and decided that the library was the obvious place. Rushton had pulled the required strings to get a cushy job in the library, and Steve arranged for the same. There were always three wardens on duty when the prisoners visited the library, which made it most unlikely that anything untoward would happen. Getting caught was a stone-cold certainty which meant that nobody would try any rough stuff. What Steve rightly worked out was that Malkie didn't care a damn about getting caught, which meant that it was an opportunity he would be bound to take.

He had been proved absolutely right. So it was that when Malkie had made his strike at Rushton's neck with his blade, Steve had been on hand to catch his wrist. He had snapped it cleanly, but that had done little more than send the foiled assassin clean round the twist. Malkie was a good four inches smaller than Steve and gave away 40 pounds but he made up for these physical disadvantages by sheer psychotic craziness. Before Steve had managed to put his lights out with a hard chop to the throat, Malkie managed to slash him three times. He lost three pints of blood and spent a month in the infirmary. He had been back on the block for three days when he received the expected summons for an audience with Rushton.

The older man had waved him to a chair in his cell and offered tea. Two of his cohorts had stood sentry outside with their arms folded. Once Rushton had done the honours with the tea, he had perched himself on the edge of his bed and looked Steve hard in the eye.

"So Mr Kenton. I am grateful. Of course I am. But I would like to know why?"

Steve shrugged. "Instinct I suppose. That and training."

"Training? What training?"

Steve rolled up his sleeve to reveal a maroon tattoo of the wings of the Parachute Regiment. "Three Para."

"How long?"

"82 to last year. Twenty years."

"Rank?"

"Captain."

Rushton nodded thoughtfully. A captain. Very unexpected. He carried on. "I suppose that meant Falklands and Ireland and the Gulf?"

Steve nodded. "That's about right."

Rushton offered a cigarette, which was accepted. "Not just instinct surely. There must have been something else."

Steve allowed silence for a few seconds. "Yeah OK. Maybe there was. I've not found work easy to find. Nobody much wants ex-Paras. People think we're all head-cases. Poxy security jobs and that's about it. Maybe saving your neck might offer me better career prospects."

Rushton smiled. "Maybe it will. Nothing like cutting to the chase. Fair enough. I owe you. That's accepted. I'll need to get a few checks done. I'll be out in another four or five months. Yourself?"

Steve shrugged. "Another ten. Maybe a year. I suppose it depends if they count doing Malkie as good behaviour or not."

"Fair enough. If you check out, there will be job waiting. A good one. I can use your type. You know how it is with the young lads these days. All sunbeds in the gym and too many Jackie Chan movies. They don't tend to be worth a light when things get a bit warm and their mental ability pretty much ends at how to use their fingers and thumbs on a Playstation. No, I feel pretty sure there will be a place for you Steve."

"Excellent. It is all I could have hoped for Mr Rushton. You won't be disappointed. That I can assure you."

Ten months later Steve had emerged into the sunlight of a spring day and a Mercedes was waiting to pick him up. Over the following weeks Rushton was indeed more than happy with his new employee. He had conducted lengthy enquiries and had been perfectly happy with what he had found. Kenton had been somewhat economical with some of the truth. That hadn't been a particular concern. It was to be expected. His investigators had tracked down several Para squaddies who had served under his command. They filled in a few interesting gaps. Kenton had gone undercover with the spooks in 1987 and not re-emerged for many years. No wonder he was bitter and twisted at his lack of job prospects.

Rushton had tackled the issue head-on as the Mercedes had made its way out of the city. "You have told me some lies."

Steve felt a knot in his stomach. How much did the man know? He tensed himself for action. All he said was. "Maybe."

"Ireland. It was more complicated I gather. Undercover stuff. Must have been pretty hairy."

Steve twisted himself round and made the older man jump slightly. "Now please understand this Mr Rushton. I am grateful for the opportunity of this job. Very grateful. Just like I am seriously pissed-off at what had happened since I quit the Army. But what went on in Ireland is a secret. A serious secret. I take secrets seriously Mr Rushton. It is part of the package and one that I hope you will come to appreciate. If this job hinges on me telling secrets then the answer is 'No'. Is that clear?"

Rushton examined the hard face intently for a few moments. Then he relaxed and smiled. "Yes Steve. Very clear. Very clear and very commendable. You may find it hard to believe, but I am actually something of a patriot. You are welcome to your secrets Steve."

And that had been that. Each week took Steve nearer to the core. Rushton had been much more frightened than he had let on by Mad Malkie's near miss. He wanted the tough ex-Captain close by him and he wanted him there all the time. It wasn't long before he started using Steve as a sounding board for ideas. Rushton was at heart a lonely man who had spent too much of his life trusting nobody. So it was that Steve learned of the fantastic array of offshore accounts and *Shell* companies that made up the glorified launderette that washed the huge amounts of cash that flowed Rushton's way. He learned that his boss would flash the money around the globe from the computer at his desk in the house on the hill. The software was state of the art and had cost a fortune. Without the passwords that existed only in Rushton's head, nobody could ever get close.

Now, after two long years, all that was about to change. The CD that had spent a mere few seconds in the computer was about to be Rushton's downfall. A little after two the next morning, Steve slipped out of the house and jumped easily over the dry stone wall that separated the magnificent grounds from the fields of the neighbouring farm. He hummed softly to himself as he walked two miles through the moonlit night to a waiting car. Inside was the familiar face of one of his colleagues from 14th Intelligence.

"All OK?"

Steve nodded. "Yeah. Wrapped and packed. Up to the boffins now."

The driver slipped into gear and they set off. "There's a few cans in the back. In the Tesco bag."

"Nice one Tom." He reached over and popped open a lager. "Nothing like celebrating in style. These on expenses?"

"You joking? They would have a duck fit. On me."

"Cheers."

They were silent after that. Both men had long lost the need for small talk. Steve drank three cans as they slid through the moonlight of an empty motorway system. He nodded off as they passed Stoke and didn't awake until they were making their way through the empty streets of north London. By the time they reached the office everything was done. A team of computer experts had been waiting for the moment that the broadband line between their termini and Rushton's machine was opened a little after two-thirty. They had worked furiously for three hours until every penny had been lifted from every account. It had been a huge sum, far greater than anything they had expected. A third of the fortune was money that Rushton had been investing on behalf of other main players. The empty accounts were a death sentence. The Home Secretary had been made well aware of this before he had confirmed his permission for the money to be taken. Everyone knew there was no point trying to get Rushton in a courtroom. They could never use any of the information from the computer because it had been obtained illegally. The best solution was simply to take it. The money would fill up the coffers of the security services and the bad guys would tear each other to pieces in their rage.

Steve's boss was in buoyant mood. He was still in his dinner suit from a function the evening before. The tie had been discarded and the collar was open. "Ah Kenton. The man of the hour. In you come. Sit."

Steve obliged and took a proffered glass of champagne. The old man bubbled on. "Marvellous job. Outstanding. Big, big result, I'll tell you. The biggest ever. People are very pleased. Very, very pleased. A great day for the Service."

Steve tried not to make it obvious that he wasn't much interested in the bluster. He had done his job and he felt rather sullied. Sure, Rushton was a bad guy, but he had known plenty worse. There wasn't much between Rushton and the red-nosed old boy the other side of the antique desk. As usual, the only real difference was a postcode. Rushton had grown up hard in Fallowfield and had become a villain. His boss had done Harrow and Oxford and had ended up a knight of the realm. Both were ruthless bastards. Now Rushton would be executed and it would be another stain on his conscience that he would have to learn to live with. He pulled cigarettes from his pocket and raised an eyebrow.

"Of course old boy. Smoke away. Smoke the whole bloody lot. Stuff the red tape Walla's. Here. Use the bin."

Steve lit up and wondered how long it would all last. "Now Kenton. We best sort out what to do with you. Obviously you'll need to keep the head down for a month or two. Got this lot for you."

He reached into his desk and tossed an envelope across. Steve looked inside. Passport. Driver's licence. Another Steve. A new Steve. There was a credit card. "The boffins have siphoned of a few quid from Rushton's millions and dumped them in an account for you. I suggest that you bugger off somewhere warm and live it up for a few months. There's heaps of cash to go at. Get a girl and unwind. You've earned it. I would like to see you back in this office on 1st February. Now bugger off and bloody well done."

TARGET ONE

His boss was back gloating on the phone even before he had closed the door. He supposed that it could have been worse. It had been too long since he had known the feeling of a rucksack on his back and the wind in what was left of his hair.

George Albright the Third flexed his considerable shoulders and took a long look down the fairway that stretched 582 yards through the New England countryside. He and the Dane, Jan Sorenson, were the last pair out on the course. It was familiar ground for George Albright. He knew all about being in the last pair out on the last day of a tournament. In his many interviews to TV and the press, he liked to call it his zone. It was the reason why his passion for the game still burned so bright. Money had ceased to matter years before. In fact money had never been an issue for George. His family had about thirty tonnes of it and had done so for many generations. He had more money than he would ever know what to do with.

The majority of the 26,000 spectators were now massed along the narrow fairway, stretching their necks for a view of the players. The rest were crammed into the grandstands that swallowed up the tiny green far in the distance. All week the 18th had been the statistically hardest hole on the course. It was rare for a par five to occupy this particular berth. Normally the top pros would birdie the par fives at least 50 percent of the time. Not this week. The hole was too long, too narrow and a sharp wind had blown into the faces of the players most of the week. Nobody had hit it in two shots. Instead the perceived wisdom was to lay up with two careful shots and try and get close with a seven or eight iron third shot. This was how George Albright had played the hole in the first three rounds.

Now it was different. Now he was in the zone and the adrenalin was coursing through his mighty six-foot-three frame. Two holes earlier he had been two behind with three to play. The Dane had kept his nerve for fifteen holes and his determined features had shown no signs of weakness. Both the sixteenth and seventeenth were tight, long par fours which had yielded little all week. Sorenson had made par on both having taken a careful one iron off each tee. George had used his driver and reduced each hole to a mere pitch and putt. Birdie, birdie. All square and one to play. It was why he was the world's number one and had been so for four years without interruption. The biggest hitter on the planet. The strongest nerves of them all. When the question was asked of George Albright the Third, the answer was almost invariably a resounding "yes".

He had made his mind up to take his driver as he walked off the seventeenth green. However, he played out a charade to keep the crowd and the cameras and his opponent guessing. In front, the penultimate pair hit their second shots and started to make their way up the green. They were out of it. They were merely making up the numbers. As they walked and George stood stock still with his arms folded, the commentators started to get themselves excited. Maybe he was about to go with the driver. Maybe he was trying to make the green in two. How typical of Albright to choose this moment to go for broke.

At last he moved. He strolled to the back of the tee and offered his hand to a surprised-looking Sorenson.

"Good luck Jan. May the best man and all that."

The moment of sportsmanship sent the commentators into predictable raptures. One or two ex-pro experts suspected clever gamesmanship, but wisely decided to keep it to themselves. The big-headed driver was taken from the bag. It was a very famous club, manufactured by Nike, and advertised by a beaming George Albright in all corners of the earth. It retailed at over $800 and sold by the thousand. It was little wonder that the Nike Corporation were so happy with George Albright the Third. His lean frame made him an ideal clothes-horse and their caps looked great atop his handsome craggy face with the year-round tan. They paid him millions and never begrudged a penny of it.

He took a couple of lazy practice swings and stared hard down the fairway. He took a moment to smile. His sponsors like him to smile. His teeth had always been impressive, but several thousands of dollars made them sensational. Slowly, a church-like hush settled over the softness of the autumn afternoon. All eyes were fixed on the big man as he carefully lined himself up. And then the tension of the silence exploded into huge cheering as he threw every ounce he had into the drive. Those at the side of the fairway simply cheered for the hell of it and would have done so had he miss-hit the ball by 100 yards. Those behind the tee gasped in awe at the sheer ferocity of the shot. Then the cheers redoubled as the ball thumped down into the centre of the fairway 342 yards from its starting point. Commentators jubilantly hammered out the statistics measured by their computers. The word 'unbelievable' was used many times.

Sorenson felt like crying. He had played perfect golf and still it was all slipping away. The big American had put himself in range and was playing golf from another planet. For a moment he wondered whether he too should take the driver but he immediately knew that it would be stupid. He steeled himself and found the fairway with his three wood 80 yards behind Albright.

The rest was something of an anti-climax. The Dane laid up his third shot short of the crossbunkers. Albright reached the green with ease with his three wood. Sorenson hit a solid third to 25 feet and missed the putt. The American duly two-putted and took the cheers with a huge grin. Three birdies to finish and another championship under his belt.

He cruised through the post-event interviews with all his usual aplomb and dazzling teeth. He talked of his great love for God and America and doing it for the boys over there in the Middle East. His sponsors were always anxious that he should play the role of the fervent patriot, and he was more than happy to do so. Why shouldn't he? It was a stone-cold fact that America had been more than good to the Albright family more or less from the moment that they had stepped off the boat from England 200 years earlier. He had little idea about what the whole thing in the Middle East was all about, but several of his buddies from school and college were involved, so he was happy enough to give messages of support. Church quite frankly bored him and always had, but it was a family tradition from which there was no escape regardless of the fact that he was the world's number one pro-golfer.

When it was all done and dusted, he retired to the locker room and took a shower. As was always the case, a wave of depression washed through him. Outside, the builders were already dismantling the grandstands. The small roads that led away from the course were clogged with traffic, but in an hour or two they would be empty. By the time he emerged, the old course was all quiet. He lived his life for the brief moments of sheer heart-pounding excitement like pulling out the driver on the eighteenth. There was nothing to touch it, and for a few minutes he would feel as if he was soaring as high as an eagle. The trouble was that it never lasted. The trouble was that there was nothing else that came close. He wondered whether to have a drink in the bar, but decided against it. He felt too gloomy to put on the big show. Instead he wandered over to where his helicopter waited and flew home.

A few hundred miles away the President of the United States had switched off the TV in the Oval Office with reluctance. He had managed to free up an hour in his schedule to watch George Albright the Third do his stuff. The President loved his golf and had done so for as long as he could remember. Not that he could play the game to save his life. He loved his golf and he loved George Albright. The man represented everything that was right about America. Sportsmanship, diplomacy, looks, monumental talent, and when the chips were down, he always came through. Best of all was that he always took the time to tell the whole world about it. As things went from miserable bad to terrible worse in the Middle East, there were few enough who would stick their necks out and say a word or two for the Marines. George Albright always did, and in the eyes of the President, that made him one hell of a damned fine guy. With a sigh he returned to his papers and started to prepare for the next meeting. As usual it was all about the Middle goddamn East.

Anatoly Rykov drained his third cup of coffee and waved for a bill. 21 euros. Outrageous. A month's wages for some at home in Russia. A month's wages assuming they were lucky enough to get paid at all. For him 21 Euros was nothing, but all the old lessons about the decadence of the West had left their mark. He had taken a seat by the window in a quiet street in Monte Carlo. On the other side of the street was the kind of discreet hotel that was affordable only to the super-rich. It barely looked like a hotel at all, more a lavish town house. His investigations had informed him that its suites were available for the bargain price of $5,000 a night. Crazy. Crazy town. Crazy world.

He hadn't expected to see anything untoward, but he had spent an hour looking anyway. It was a habit to Anatoly Rykov. Staying careful meant staying alive. He paid the bill and neglected to tip. No way would he tip the supercilious swine of a waiter for three coffees at seven euros each. He crossed the quiet street and entered the hushed opulence of the reception area. He was dressed well enough in an Italian suit and shoes and an open-necked silk shirt. His thinning hair was cropped close to his head and he wore dark sunglasses. The man at the desk saw nothing that suggested impostor and so he smiled.

"Oui?"

Rykov spoke in lightly accented English. The desk man wasn't interested in the accent, but if he had been pushed he would have guessed at Austrian or Swiss. Certainly not Russian. "Suite 5 please. Tell them it is Mr Eisner."

The call was made. Another smile. "You can go up. Third floor. The lift is just over there."

As usual Abdullah had taken the whole floor. Rykov stepped out of the lift to be met by two security men. They gave small nods of recognition but frisked him from head to toe anyway before gesturing him to an open door. Inside the man he knew simply as Abdullah was waiting in yet another lavish hotel suite. It was more or less the same as several others they had used over the years in cities all over the world. Abdullah was his usual debonair self and he greeted his visitor with an upper-class English accent that he had perfected years earlier during his time at Harrow and Oxford.

"Anatoly, my dear chap. How are you? Come. You must sit down. A drink? Of course. Always a drink. Always the Russian. I have vodka. They tell me it is the very best vodka. You must let me know what you think?"

The Arab took a bottle adorned with Russian writing from the fridge and poured a generous glass. He felt a slight pang of regret as he replenished his own glass from a jug of freshly squeezed orange. He had drunk lots during his younger days in England, but he had stopped when he had discovered his real Islamic roots with the Muhajadeen in the mountains of Afghanistan.

It was where the two of them had first met. 1982. Three years on from the calamitous Soviet decision to invade the land that history had proven many times over to be uninvadable. Before Afghanistan, there had been little remarkable about the life of Anatoly Rykov. He had spent his first eleven years in the kind of miserable industrial town that Soviet planning specialised in. His father worked in a sprawling steel mill whilst his mother assembled machine tools. The teachers at his school spotted an unusual talent in the quiet boy and duly made contact with the local party bosses. He was transferred to an academy in Moscow to be groomed for greater things than milling steel. He proved himself academically capable as well as shining at sports. The academy deemed him to be ideal military material and duly enrolled him for officer training. So it was that he arrived in Afghanistan in charge of a platoon of miserable conscripts in 1980. Once again he was spotted and marked down as a young man of promise and transferred to be trained for the Spetznatz, the elite of the Soviet Special Forces. It was at this point that his defining talent came to light. What set Anatoly Rykov apart from the rest of the recruits was his natural genius at blowing things up. It was a talent that he had been born with.

Over the next year he developed a new tactic in the savage war that was all his own. Working alone, he would infiltrate Muhajadeen camps and plant explosive devices that he would detonate from a hide in the hills. He targeted senior commanders and had a chilling success rate. By this time it was becoming more and more apparent that the Soviets had dropped a horrible clanger and had entered into their own rocky version of Vietnam. Their largely conscript army was up against some of history's most accomplished guerrilla fighters and the news was bad from wall to wall. This all made the successes in Anatoly's sector all the more surprising and his strikes became more than a mere annoyance both to the Muhajadeen leadership and their CIA advisers.

The stakes were raised considerably early in 1982 when one of Anatoly's bombs blew a Langley man into 100 small pieces. By this time more was known of him. Spies employed at his regiment's base as cleaners and general lackeys fed back a picture of a quiet, reserved young man who showed little interest in the adulation shown when he returned from one of his missions. Feverish discussions ensued both in the mountains of the Khyber Pass and in CIA Headquarters in Virginia. Eventually a decision was made that the problem should be dealt with in the time-honoured American way. They bought him.

After a tortuous period of to-ing and fro-ing, a clandestine meeting was arranged and a deal was done. Anatoly Rykov defected to a contract which required him to carry out a total of five of his trademark hits before being furnished with a new identity and a fat lump of dollars in a Geneva bank. His bombs saw off two Colonels and three Majors and made him one of the most hated men in the Soviet Union. The CIA agent who had brokered the deal received slaps on the back from one and all and advanced many places up the Agency ladder.

Rykov and Abdullah had met before he had departed Afghanistan for his new life. Anatoly had always cut an isolated figure with the Muhajadeen. His kills earned him grudging respect, but there was still a well of bitterness that was a result for those he had killed whilst fighting on the other side. It was therefore something of a surprise when the young Arab approached him as he sat by his small fire and spoke in excellent English.

"May I join you please?"

Rykov thought for a moment then nodded. He had studied this one. The boy was interesting. Abdullah, he seemed to recall as his name. Not an Afghani. Foreign. Saudi probably. One of the driven holy warriors doing their bit for Allah. He didn't have the crazy gleam in his eyes like so many. There was a calmness about him that had rather impressed Rykov. The boy was brave enough, he had witnessed that on several occasions. There was something else. Something he couldn't quite figure out. He was interested.

Abdullah spoke quietly. "You are leaving tomorrow?"

"Yes. Tomorrow."

"You have done great things."

Rykov made no reply. Where was this going? He sipped at his coffee. The coffee was much better on this side of the war. American. The young Arab continued.

"I too am leaving soon. This week probably. I will tell you a little about myself. I come from a very rich family. A royal family. They do not know that I am here. They would hate me for it. Our leaders say that there will be more important work for me to do in the years to come. They say that I waste myself as a fighter in this war. Instead I am to go back to the West and wait for my time. There will be more important fights soon, fights where I will be more effective in a suit than these robes. I respect these wishes. One day I may have need for a man like you to help me fight. I ask little. My family use a firm of lawyers in London. Hendricks, Dean and Reynolds. Jeremy Reynolds is the son of one the partners. He was with me at school and university. Should you ever wish to find well-paid work you can call at their offices. Ask to see Jeremy Reynolds and announce yourself as Mr Fiedler. Leave contact details with him and he will make contact with me. That is all. Maybe I will never hear from you again. Then again, maybe I will. Only Allah can know such a thing. You have memorised these things?"

"I have."

"Good. Then I will leave you in peace my friend. May Allah be with you."

Anatoly had fixed the details in his mind, but was quite certain that he would never visit the London office. There had been enough killing. Now was a time for an easier life. The next day he had left the camp and made his way over the mountains and into his new life in the West. Abdullah had left three days later and followed the same route. He stopped in one of the larger camps, close to the border with Pakistan. He spent the evening with a man who he had known from his childhood. His friend was two years older and came from a family that was even richer than his own. His friend had grown up into a six-foot-four giant of a man and was known as a great warrior. It had been he who had persuaded that Allah needed Abdullah to fight the war on different battlefields. It had been he who had patiently cooled the younger man's passion and taught him to think more carefully, more clinically. It had been he who had sent word for Abdullah to approach the Russian assassin on the evening before his departure. The protégé briefed his master on the outcome of the meeting. The tall man had sat listening quietly with his usual stillness. When Abdullah had finished he had nodded.

"You have done well my friend. Now Allah will decide the rest. We will be guided." And Osama Bin Laden had smiled warmly.

For ten years it had seemed that Allah had decided that he had no need of the services of Anatoly Rykov. He had invested his money wisely and settled down in the Austrian city of Innsbruck. He became fluent in German and nearly so in English. The dividends on his stock portfolio allowed for a life that was comfortable, if not particularly lavish. He spent his time reading, climbing and skiing, and life was better than he could ever have expected. However, everything changed when the stock markets crashed in the early '90s. No longer would his share dividends finance a life of ease. He had applied for several jobs, but times were hard all over Europe.

So it was that he pulled the carefully stored information from his memory which had remained with him for the ten years since he had sat by his small fire on the side of the Afghan mountainside. He felt little regret as he travelled across Europe to the discreet firm of solicitors in a London mews. Life had been good and life had been comfortable, but life had also become rather boring. He was intrigued to see if the method of contact would actually work. Mr Jeremy Reynolds was indeed available and showed no sign of surprise to meet Mr Fiedler. He gave the name of a hotel in Salisbury and promised to alert his client that Mr Fiedler would be staying there for a week. As it turned out, Abdullah arrived to see him on his second night.

The young man in the dirty robes of the hill fighter had changed. He wore an expensive suit and looked every inch the part of the powerful businessman. He was confident and assured. Anatoly was impressed. Yes, there was a demand for his work. Enquiries and arrangements would be made. They agreed to meet in a hotel in Cologne in a month. That was to be the first of many meetings. They developed a simple system. Abdullah would send word when he had a job to offer. Rykov would only consider a target if there were a substantial amount of intelligence regarding the man's habits and movements. If he accepted the contract, 20 percent of his fee was transferred into his bank. The balance was paid on completion of the job.

Over the next ten years he killed eight men in the service of Allah. The first two were particularly unpleasant Serbian warlords who had been doing unspeakable things to Bosnian Muslims. Then there was a German Neo-Nazi in Hamburg who was inciting race hate against Germany's large Turkish community. He returned to the Balkans to assassinate another Serb, this time in Kosovo. Then he was sent east to deal with an Indonesian secret policeman and a Hindu firebrand politician in Ahmedabad. The last two contracts before the Monte Carlo meeting were both Russian officers whose conduct in Chechnya had gone well beyond anything that was acceptable.

Eight kills at a million dollars each. Anatoly had no need to worry about the stock market any more. He could retire any time he liked. The problem was that he had become almost addicted to the dark game that he and Abdullah played. Nothing in life would ever compare to the planning, the stalking, the watching, and of course the killing. Others paid great fortunes for a licence to kill big game in Africa. He hunted men for money. Nothing he had ever found in his life could even begin to compare, not women, not sport, not the comradeship of soldiers. He was a hunter and he had come to terms with the fact that nothing could ever replace the thrill of the stalk, of the kill.

Anatoly took a sip of the peppered vodka and relished the warmth as it gently burnt its way down. Over the years they had become comfortable together. They knew exactly where each other stood. On the surface they were well-heeled professional men in their prime. Underneath they were different. A fierce religious fire provided the fuel that drove the Arab. Anatoly Rykov was powered by ice.

Abdullah opened a briefcase and took out a manila folder.

"Maybe you know this one Anatoly. He was in Afghanistan at the same time as us. Major Yuri Krishkin. Did you know him?"

Anatoly shook his head and took the proffered photo. It showed a man of medium height wearing the sandy camouflage of the Soviet occupation forces. He shook his head and took another sip from his glass.

"No. I never met him. I knew of him of course. Everybody knew of him." Of course they had. The man was a monster. He headed up the interrogation team in one of the most notorious internment camps. Even the hardened soldiers of the Spetznatz had shuddered at the tales of torture which leaked out. Krishkin could get anyone to talk. It was what he did.

Abdullah continued in his light, chatty tone, all cucumber sandwiches and the rowing at Henley. "Of course you did. Everyone knew about Krishkin. A very bad man indeed. Well, sadly he has gone from strength to strength. Today he is General Yuri Krishkin. Did you know?"

"I had heard."

"The rank has changed, but not the man. He is still up to all his old tricks. Grozny this time. If anything he is even more unspeakable than ever. Our sources have discovered that he has recently been granted a three-month leave from a grateful Russian people for a heroic two years of work in Chechnya. He has returned home to Moscow. I have pictures. General Krishkin has become a man of routine in his old age. Every day he leaves his apartment at eleven and makes his way to a favourite cafe. See, here. He walks. The big men are all from his regiment. There are always four of them. His minders. He always takes the same table and plays chess with his cronies. No doubt they exchange torture stories over their vodka. He stays until three and makes his way home. Like clockwork Anatoly. Like clockwork. Do you foresee any problems?"

Rykov shook his head. "No."

"You know, I often think that you are a very lucky man Anatoly."

"Really. Why is that?"

Abdullah smiled. "Krishkin will be the ninth. The ninth evil man who you have killed in the name of Allah and all that is holy. For many the task is not so clear. The ones who flew the planes in America were not monsters. They knew that they would kill thousands who were innocent. They had to harden their hearts and their souls to win their place in Paradise. For you there is no need. It is only the monsters we give to you. You are lucky to have the honour of undertaking such a noble task."

Anatoly smiled. "And well paid."

Abdullah reflected his smile as if he were a mirror. "Oh yes. Very well paid. I trust that we still enjoy the normal terms?"

"Of course."

"Then you must proceed my friend. You must proceed. Allah will be with you at all times. Do you know this?"

"I will take your word for it."

Sally Hunter tried to find the required concentration to make the shot. Her mind was everywhere but on the fourteenth hole of her home golf course on the outskirts of Dundee. It was a Sunday and she was playing a quarter-final tie in the club knockout match play competition. Normally her opponent wouldn't have given her any competition whatsoever. Sally was good at golf. She had been good at golf since her dad had taken her out for the first time at seven years old. She had been the captain of the ladies golf team at her university. She had been within an inch or two of being selected to represent Scotland as an amateur. Yet today she couldn't get her mind on the game at all.

In front of her was a stretch of 150 yards of short-cropped fairway that ran up between sand dunes either side. The wind was freshening all the time and was now more or less blowing straight into her face. Normally no more than a five iron, but the North Sea wind was worth at least two clubs. Maybe the best answer would be a gentle three wood . . .

The trill of her mobile phone completely disrupted her thoughts. She nearly tipped over her bag as she dug into the compartment to find it. She wrenched it free on the fourth ring and her heart skipped a beat when the screen announced Private Number. Her opponent pulled a disapproving expression as she watched the performance. Politician or not, it was still not the done thing. Not the done thing at all.

Sally turned her back on the grumpy face and hit the green button. "Hello, Sally Hunter."

"Sally." Her heart skipped another beat as she immediately recognised the familiar tones of the First Minister. Her boss. "Can you talk?

"Yes, of course I can."

"I would like to see you if possible. Can you make it this afternoon?"

"Of course. No problem. I'll be there in just over an hour."

"Splendid. See you then." Click.

The disapproving look had been slightly dislodged by interest. Sally beat her playing partner to the punch. "I'm ever so sorry but I have to go. I concede the match of course." She smiled with amusement at the hungry look of unrequited nosiness in her opponent's eyes and took her leave.

Sally Hunter had been a Member of the Scottish Parliament for just over five years. She had been elected among the pioneer members who made up the first devolved government that Scotland had known for hundreds of years. It had taken her a little while to find her feet. It had all been very different from her life as a headmistress at a chaotic High School on the wrong side of Dundee. Politics had in no way been a lifelong ambition. It was something that she had drifted into by accident. When she was 35 she had discovered that her husband was having a frantic affair with a secretary from his work. She had dealt with him in much the same way that she dealt with the boys from the schemes who came into the school with flick knives or wraps of speed: she kicked him out. The marriage had been childless and she was left with time to fill. The National Union of Teachers had started off as a time-filler, but it soon become a passion. She discovered a knack for the wheeling and dealing of politics that she had never suspected and was soon elected onto the National Committee.

By this time she was in her early 40s. She dressed in classy suits and wore her hair short. She had photogenic features and a firm, clear east coast voice that carried an attractive hint of the school ma'am.

She could face down even the most dogged tabloid reporter and could hold her end of an argument without simpering or evading. Without it ever being her intention, she had unwittingly ticked all the boxes required for a potential Scottish Blair babe. An approach was duly made by the Scottish Labour Party which had come as just about the biggest surprise of her life. She hadn't needed long consider and a matter of months later she took up her place in the new Parliament.

For five years she had been loyal and worked every hour available. For the last few months she had been hearing all the right noises. She had been noticed. She had impressed all the right people. She did well on television. Best of all, she had a cupboard devoid of skeletons. When the Justice Minister had resigned over a prison scandal, a re-shuffle was inevitable. She had waited on a call all Saturday evening and Sunday morning to no avail. She had agonised for an hour about the scheduled golf game and in the end she just couldn't stand pacing the house any more. By the time they walked off the ninth green she had given up and was finding it hard not to become dispirited. By the twelfth she was at the gates of despair and depression. Then on the fourteenth came hope. More than hope. There was no way that she would be summoned on a Sunday afternoon to be informed that there was no ministerial job. Or was there? Was she about to receive pep talk about staying patient and keeping up the good work? Maybe.

She drove through the Edinburgh suburbs far too fast. She kept trying to slow down and take her time, but frustration continually got the better of her. She spent a moment or two composing herself before getting out of the car. A brief visit to the mirror in the Ladies confirmed that she looked presentable. Would it be Education? It had to be Education. Everything in her life made her an obvious choice for Education. Surely. It had to be.

A few minutes later she almost toppled off her chair with surprise. "Excuse me?"

The First Minister had been expecting her shocked reaction. He gave an avuncular smile. "We believe that you are perfect for Sport, Sally. Absolutely perfect."

Composure was coming very hard. She had to take a firm breath. "Really. May I ask why?"

He had been dreading this part. "Well. You play golf of course.

And you know all about school sports. And you are good with the TV. We feel you will bring some real energy to the position. Sport is very important to Scotland. You know that it always has been. It's a key role. A big role."

She managed to unzip a dogged smile. "Well I must say it is rather a surprise, but of course I am very grateful. I can assure you that I will give the role all my energy. Thank you sir."

He rose to his feet to signal the end of the interview. She hadn't bothered to ask who had been given Education. A crony no doubt. She had been handed a basket case. Sport. Of all bloody things it had to be bloody Sport. Was there a country in the western world where the Minister of Sport stood less of a chance? Twelve months a year of rain. Playing fields all sold off to help fund the Thatcher tax cuts. Fried Mars bars. World records for heart disease. Sectarianism in football. Utter oblivion in everything else. Good at pub sports like darts and snooker. Sports to be played with a pint and a fag. A nation whose sporting highlight in twenty years was a Commonwealth Medal in Curling of all things.

As Sally made her way over to where her car was parked, she couldn't begin to understand what she had done to deserve her fate.

The time difference meant that as Sally made her way back to Dundee, it was mid-morning in Washington D.C. The White House was as quiet as it ever got. Larry Weinberg knew that his doctor would have had a duck fit if he had known that his patient was working on a Sunday morning. Rest Larry. I'm being serious Larry. Don't go shaking your dumb head. Seriously. Rest for Christ's sake. You wanna kill yourself Larry? You're 67 years old. You're 60 pounds too heavy. You've got a stomach ulcer and blood pressure off the charts. You're not so young any more Larry. Slow down or you're just going to come to a stop. The big full stop. Yeah, yeah. OK for the goddamn quack to say. Rest Larry. Why not? You're only the White House Chief of Staff Larry. Why not? Take an hour. Take a month down in Acapulco. Sure. Twenty points behind in the polls and an election just over twelve months away, so rest. Sure. Ten Marines a week getting blown apart by the goddamn cloth-heads so rest. Yeah, yeah, yeah.

In front of him the Sunday papers were sprawled across the desk.

TARGET ONE

A Marlboro was burning down in the ashtray and a half-cup of coffee sent out steam to blend in with the smoke. You got to stop smoking Larry. The caffeine is sending the blood pressure over the edge Larry. Goddamn quack. Prick.

A timid knock at the door brought his head up. His cracked voice barked "In".

They trooped in. Four of them. Sulky faces one and all. Body language that screamed "It's not fair". Sunday morning and Larry Weinberg made them come in to work. He smirked at their doleful expressions. He knew all about what they said about him. Of course he did. He had their offices bugged. They were supposed to be the best of the best. Young and hungry and the top of their Ivy League classes and look at them. Sulking like goddamned schoolgirls because they had to come in to work on a Sunday morning. Pricks.

He waited for them to sit and then started throwing the newspapers at them. They held up their arms and looked appalled. He didn't stop until his desk was clear.

"There. Read it. All of it. Page after page. Negative. Negative. We started the week twenty points down. So where will we finish when the American people read this lot? 25 down? 30? 50? I pay you to work the Press. I pay you to emphasise the goddamned positive for Christ's sake. And what do I get? This! So don't look all hangdog. Get the hell out there and pick up your phones and do something! NOW! GO!"

When the door clicked shut he allowed himself a chuckle. He felt a little better. They would pick up their phones and beg and wheedle and none of it would do any good. The Administration was on the skids and nothing seemed to be going right. He had been in the game long enough to know that what they really needed was a bit of luck. Something that could make the President look good again. Something. Anything.

Something to turn the tide back their way.

Chapter 3
November

Deek awoke with the impression that a Leprechaun was trying to drill through the side of his head with a jackhammer. As he came to his senses he realised that it was his mobile phone which he had set to vibrating alert mode. He hit "Send" and "End" in quick succession and was tempted to throw the offending piece of plastic across the caravan. It rang again immediately and he answered with a look of distaste.

"Aye." His mouth felt like someone had left a burst vacuum bag in it.

"That you Deek?"

"Aye."

"It's Gerry. Down at Southerness."

"Aye."

"I've got a young Jap staying. He fancies a match. Five hundred. You up for it?"

Deek clamped his eyes closed to block out the light. His head was hammering. His head always seemed to be hammering these days. He swung his arm to the floor until he located a full can of lager. Gerry Lions ran a hotel on the coast adjacent to the magnificent Southerness course which attracted a healthy Asian clientèle. Many of the visitors found it hard to resist a bet, and Gerry would broker money games for Deek. Two mighty swigs of lager started to normalise him.

"Wha' time is it Gerry?"

"Back of eight."

"Christ."

Silence took over the line. He had an appointment with Meg at two. Couldn't miss that. No way. Then again, it would do no harm to turn up with some cash. He pulled the curtain to one side which revealed a grey November world of lashing rain. The few leaves that remained on the trees were being wrenched from their branches by a sharp wind. The prospect of the weather tearing in off the bay was anything but tempting. But a match was a match, and the cupboards were bare.

"How about half-past nine? I need to be in Dumfries for two. Got to meet Meg."

This brought a chuckle. "Better not be late for Meg."

"Piss off, Gerry."

"All right. I'll fix it. Don't be late."

Gerry's cut was twenty percent of any winnings, which had always made him a more than willing promoter. Deek dragged himself upright and lit the first cigarette of the day, which tasted like undistilled hell. Two more swallows drained the can and washed some of the bitter nicotine from his mouth.

He gingerly leaned across and shook the lump of duvet that covered the sleeping shape of Troll. It took two minutes of increasingly vigorous shaking to get any response. At last Troll's squashed face emerged, his eyes blinking frantically at the light.

"Shape up, Troll. We've got a match."

"Aye?"

"Aye. Some Jap Gerry's lined up at Southerness."

Troll eased back the curtain and took in the wet and wild of the world outside. His small face split into a grin. "How much?"

"Five hundred."

"Nice."

The weather was exactly what they both wanted. Most of the enthusiastic Asians were accustomed to warm sunny weather on imitation American parkland courses and endless hours on floodlit rooftop driving ranges. They had no concept of how to play a Scottish links in the wind and rain.

It took another can, a black coffee laced with scotch, and three more cigarettes to bring Deek to something approaching normality. Troll made a call to a mate who arrived in his taxi just before nine and loaded up their gear into the boot. They pulled up on the empty car park just before half-past nine. Gerry was waiting with four Japanese under the porch.

Deek almost toppled over as he dragged on his rather torn waterproof trousers which had seen many better days. His jacket was from a different set and was two sizes too big, and a bright yellow waterproof fishing hat completed his attire. He shook hands with the young Japanese who also bowed. The tourist was attired in hundreds of pounds worth of the best waterproof gear that the shop on Princes Street could offer. His bag looked as if it could house a family of four for a weekend break and the neatly arranged clubs were all graphite and worthy of a five-year mortgage.

Gerry took control of negotiations.

"OK lads. It's straight match play. Five hundred to the winner. Sudden death if it's all square at the end. Nakata gets a six-shot start."

Deek kept his expression neutral and took a cupped drag from his cigarette. Typical Gerry. No mention of six bloody shots on the phone. He gave a small nod of acceptance and pondered on the old adage of beggars and choosers.

As they made their way to the first tee the real strength of the wind became apparent and the expressions of the spectators became resigned. The first umbrella was blown inside out twenty yards from the clubhouse. Deek gestured for Nakata to hit first and offered him a swig from a half-bottle of Grouse which was rejected. The young man's practice swing was certainly impressive. He carefully placed his ball on the tee and took himself through an elaborate and rehearsed routine as he approached the ball. His swing stood up well to the conditions and he stuck the ball sweetly into the gale. For a while it looked as if it was going to be a good shot. He started the ball down the right of the fairway and it drew gently back towards the middle. After 150 yards the wind took control and exaggerated the draw into a hook and bent the ball away to the left into the middle of a large clump of gorse.

"Hard lines mate." Deek gave his surprised-looking opponent a tap on his Gortex-clad back and tossed his ball down onto the short grass. He didn't bother with a practice swing. He used a cut-down swing with his one iron and fired off a shot that never made it more than ten feet from the ground. The topspin on the ball allowed it to kick and run until it finished 220 yards down the left of the fairway.

Deek kept the club in his hand as he strolled down to his second shot. This was more or less a carbon copy of his drive and sent the ball scuttling onto the front edge of the green, ten feet from the flag which was bent near sideways by the wind. Five minutes of poking around in the gorse bore no fruit and Nakata conceded the hole.

It was all over by the fifteenth and the bedraggled party returned to the clubhouse where cash was paid over. Deek accepted the young man's offer of a drink before heading back for town. One hundred went to Gerry. 50 went on the three-fifteen at Haydock and a tenner went on pie and chips and a thin cup of coffee in a Dumfries café. It left £40 in one pocket for later and £300 in the other for Meg. He wrestled with his hair for a couple of minutes in front of the grimy mirror in the café's toilets, before admitting that it was a lost cause. He took a moment in front of the glass and didn't much like what he saw. His skin had the grey tinge of the big drinker and it seemed to be drawn tighter than ever over his cheekbones. There were far too many lines and his eyes were sunk deep into their sockets. He looked like hell and it was getting worse. He tried all the time to convince himself that he was under control, but it was getting harder. There was no escaping the fact that it now took half a bottle of spirits, several cans and two packs of B&H to get him through the day. He was going to have to do something about it. He had been about to do something about it for ten years and now he was the wrong side of 30 and looking the wrong side of 50. He shook his head and left.

Meg looked everything he didn't. She was smart and looked sickeningly well. She looked better than well. She looked beyond belief. She looked like what she was, the girl he had fallen head-over heels for twenty years earlier. Nothing every changed. Every time he saw her he felt as if he'd been punched in the stomach by George Foreman. He needed a drink. He needed a fag. He needed a life. She gave him a smile that seemed genuine enough and George landed another big left.

"Have a seat, Deek."

He pulled out the wad of notes and passed them over. Best to get the good news in as soon as possible. "Here you go Meg. Few quid. I was up and at it early."

She counted the cash with trained fingers. "Found a sucker then. Was it Gerry?"

NOVEMBER

"Aye."

"A tourist?"

"Aye. Japanese."

She glanced out at the weather that was showing no sign of improvement and laughed. "Poor sod."

"He was'nae so poor."

She laid down the money in a neat stack and assumed a businesslike air. "So. The overdraft. We seem to be going in the right direction at last. £16, 234 before today. Under £16,000 now. How are your plans for Spain."

The second phase of the PGA Tour Qualification process was due to start in three days time in Northern Spain."

"Aye. Nae bad."

"Truth please, Deek."

He looked down at his hands which were gripped together on his lap. "Well I'm getting sorted today Meg. I'll need to spend a few quid. You know. Expenses and all that. Couple of grand should do the trip."

"How are you travelling?"

"I'll get a car from Ian."

"Where are you staying?"

"We'll sleep in the car."

She drummed her fingers and considered. "One thousand. Ian will get you something cheap and alcohol and cigarettes are for nothing in Spain."

He considered trying to argue but not for long. There was never ever point in trying to argue with Meg. "Aye. OK."

He put his head down and stared at the plastic tee he was fiddling with. There was so much he wanted to say. For years he had wanted to apologise about how he had behaved when she was at college. He wanted to explain that it was only because he missed her so much and was so consumed by jealousy. He wanted her to understand that the only reason that he had started to drink so much was that he was so guilty and ashamed at the way that he had behaved. These were things that had eaten away at him for a decade and still he was no nearer being able to talk about them. The Scottish macho culture that he had lived out his life in had never encouraged the baring of the soul. Instead, the common wisdom was to get into the pub and drown the lot out. It was absurd, that he actually looked forward to these meetings. It was the only chance that he ever had to spend a bit of time with Meg any more. How ironic that things had now come to this. She was lecturing him on getting his unauthorised overdraft sorted, so that she could clear her own decks and move on to Edinburgh. She was pushing him to help her do the very thing he dreaded. Somehow as long as Meg was in Dumfries there seemed to be a flicker of hope. Once she was gone, everything would be gone. His mind formed unwanted pictures of Meg with some tanned-looking fellow-banker in their Morningside flat with two kids in designer clothes and big smiles.

"Deek!"

He looked up sharply from the tee between his fingers. "Sorry Meg. I was miles away."

"Remember what you always told me, Deek. Remember how you always said that you would always come through when it counted. Remember that?"

"Aye. I remember that."

"I really need you to come through here, Deek. It's time for me to move on. I know you can do this if you really want to. Can you try and do it for me?"

"I'd do anything for you Meg. You ken that."

His head was back down, his eyes averted from the blush that spread across her pale skin. She felt a small prickle of tears as she looked at his bowed figure. It was impossible not to think of all the other young golfers converging on the course in northern Spain for the second phase of the qualifying process. They would already be there now, comfortably ensconced in nice hotels and getting through two practice rounds a day. None of them would be embarking on a two-day drive in a second-hand jalopy to arrive the day before. Only Deek would spend the night before the competition sleeping in a car. Against all her better judgements she relented.

"I'll tell you what. Make it £2,000. You need a hotel to stay in. Try and get a cheap flight. We need to give you the best chance at this."

He smiled and shook his head. "No, leave it be. We'll be fine. Remember, we're lads off Sunnybank. We dunnae need anything fancy."

She shrugged and couldn't think of anything more to say. He sensed it was time to leave and got to his feet. "I'll come through Meg. Dunnae worry. I'll no let you down. Not this time."

His face looked so sad that she was worried that the tears welling up in her eyes would become uncontrollable. "Thanks Deek."

"See you when we get back."

"Yes. Ring me won't you. Let me know how things are going."

"Aye."

Before making her usual neat notes she stared at the door for several minutes. It was ridiculous that she felt this way every time she saw him. He was irresponsible. He was a compulsive gambler. He was almost certainly an alcoholic. He lived in a caravan and he looked like a wreck. And yet no matter how many years passed she couldn't get him out of her system.

Troll was reading the local paper in the waiting room outside. He looked up enquiringly and Deek forced a grin and nodded. They stepped out and lit up in the sheltered area housing in the cash point machines.

"We off then?" asked Troll.

"Aye. It's sunny Spain here we come."

"How much?"

"A grand."

Troll's face screwed up. "How do we get to Spain and stay there for a while on a grand?"

"Easy. We'll go and get a motor from Ian and we'll sleep in it."

Troll shook his head. "That's it Deek, I'm on the phone to George Albright. Time I started caddying for someone who can keep me in the style I would like to get accustomed to."

"Style maybe, but would he show you a good time? Fancy hotel suites aren't much good if you're expected to go to church instead of the pub. Think before you make that call, boy. Are you ready to meet your Lord my child?"

Troll tossed the butt of his cigarette into the small river that was gurgling along the gutter. "Well, when you look at it that way . . ."

The garage of Ian Garton Motors offered a welcome refuge from the downpour. A radio was playing but all seemed deserted.

"Ian!!"

The shout brought an oil-covered mechanic out from under a Cavalier that would have looked a whole lot different as it rolled off the line the year the Berlin Wall crashed to the floor.

"Deek. How are you?"

"Nae bad. You?"

"You know. Lots of work and nobody wants to pay their bills. How's the golf?"

"Aye. It's all right. Won a quid or two off a Jap this morning. I need a motor Ian. Something that will get me to Spain and back."

"How much?"

Deek grinned. "What do you think?"

The grin was reflected. "Aye. Ten bob and change. Actually you're in luck. Come here."

Outside was a venerable old grey Volvo Estate. Like the Cavalier, it had seen the last years of Maggie Thatcher. Going by the number of dents along the side, some previous owner had never mastered parking the old car in confined spaces. Inside, the leather seats were cracked and worn and the boot wouldn't close properly. Both wing mirrors were cracked. Ian fell intoSalesman mode.

"183 thousand on the clock. Three months MOT. Two months tax. All yours for 100 quid."

"Will it make it?"

"It's a Volvo. It'll get you to Hong Kong and back if you want."

"Straight up."

"Straight up."

Deek looked at Troll who had been indulging himself in his favourite worthless pastime of kicking the tyres. He merely shrugged. Once again Deek contemplated the theory of beggars and choosers before sticking out a hand. "Deal."

Three days later after 1,500 miles of driving, the old Volvo took its place among the Mercs and BMWs of the car park of the golf course in northern Spain. The officials wrinkled their faces in distaste at the two scrumpled Scotsmen as they registered and informed them that their tee-off time was scheduled for eight-thirty the next morning. There was just enough daylight for ten holes of practice. The course was long, magnificent and manicured like a Japanese garden. They found a bar in a small village a few miles away to while away a pleasant evening over four bottles of the local red which cost less than two pints at home. By midnight, the interior of the old car was filled with the sound of snoring.

They had brought four old-fashioned alarm clocks which all belted out at six the next morning and succeeded in bringing the two men slowly to life. Deek reached into the back and popped a bottle of San

Miguel which had got nicely cool through the chilly night, and stepped out into the layby. The dawn was half an hour old and the day was still and perfect. He stretched the stiffness out of his body and lit up. Things weren't looking good. Still, sunny weather and a long park of a golf course were anything but what the doctor ordered. Not his scene at all.

By the time the two of them sat over beers and Spanish omelettes a few hours later his fears had been realised. He had played OK, but he didn't have the length of so many of the younger players. He had carded a respectable one over par 73, but others were tearing it up. When he had left the course, the leader board was already adorned with red "under par" scores, and when play finished he was in the bottom quarter of the field. Depression was beginning to ease into him and he dealt with it in his normal way – in the bars of the small town. They were both asleep in the car more or less stupefied by several hours of cheap red wine when fate made its spectacular intervention a little after midnight. They were completely unaware of the great change in the weather outside. By three o' clock, the old car was shaking gently as a gale-force wind threw itself across Northern Spain. The rain came just before dawn and they awoke to rivers of wet pouring down the windows.

This time as Deek opened his beer he was smiling. This was a lot more like it. Over the next three days the weather was unrelenting in its ferocity. The TV stations reported that it was the wildest weather that they had seen in over 50 years. Deek kept his shots low and knocked in his putts. He added a 72 and two 74s to his opening 73 and finished at five over par and thirteenth. He was through to the final stage of qualifying in Cadiz a few days later with a cheque for 5,000 euros.

Later that night, after steaks and champagne, he got through to Meg.

"Cracked it Meg. Through to the next stage. Nice cheque too. We're on a roll out here."

She could tell that from the sounds of the busy bar in the background. "So I can hear. Try not to be too idiotic Deek. Don't blow it now you are so close."

He smiled. "Dunnae worry Meg. When did I ever blow anything?"

"Precisely. The final stage is next week?"

"Aye. In Cadiz."

"Dad's coming over. I might be able to come too. I'm trying to wangle it."

His heart skipped over. "That would be magic Meg. We'll expect you if we see you then. Got to go. No more change . . ."

The line went dead and he decided that more champagne was in order.

For day after day the weather showed no signs of improvement. They made their way to Cadiz via a succession of bars and arrived in time for a full practice round. This time, an onerous six rounds lay ahead of the competitors fighting it out for the chance of the huge riches on offer for any who qualified for the full European PGA tour. Deek hung on to level par through the gusting winds of the first five rounds. By the time he noticed Meg and her dad waiting by the first tee for the final round he was more or less home and hosed. The weather had at last cleared for the final round and he played out a careful 73 to finish eleventh. After a night of celebration the trusty Volvo was gifted to a surprised-looking mechanic in a small garage and they all took a plane home together. Deek's overdraft dipped under the £10,000 mark for the first time in many years and the first event of the tour in Bangkok awaited him in February.

George Albright the Third was feeling confused. Something was happening. Something strange. Something that had never happened before. He just couldn't be bothered. It was round four of a tournament at a new course in the Arizona desert. For three days he had played OK. Nothing remotely spectacular, but adequate. He had started off the final round at six under par, five shots back of the leader. It had been just his kind of situation. Unlike other competitors, he could afford to go for every shot regardless of the prize money. If he blew it and fell away down the field it hardly mattered. The money was irrelevant to him. All that counted was winning. He loved these situations when he could throw all caution to the wind and take the driver every time. Sometimes it came off. Sometimes it didn't. Whichever way, there were few spectacles in golf that spectators loved to watch more than George going for everything.

Only today it just wasn't happening. His limbs felt tired. He couldn't seen to get his mind on things. For some reason he felt irrationally depressed. There was no explaining it. On every tee he duly lifted his cap and smiled at the crowds who were urging him on. His drives were straight enough but 80 yards light of their usual distance. His approach shots were lamely finding the safe areas of the green. His long putts were barely reaching the hole, let alone threatening it. After fifteen holes he hadn't made a single birdie and had fallen back to three over par. The huge gallery that had assembled at the first was draining away. It wasn't George's day. He wasn't firing and they wandered back to watch the players behind who were in contention.

There had been off-days before of course. Many of them. But this was different. Usually he had to fight a growing anger inside him when things went badly. He had to contain the urge to snap a club over his knee. It would be all that he could do to maintain his famed calm and dignity until the end of the round and when it was finished he would punish himself with hours on the practice ground.

Today it just didn't seem to matter. He didn't need the money. He had already been crowned the world number one for the year. What difference could winning another tournament make to his life? None. Suddenly his whole life seemed pretty empty. He had barely spoken with his trophy wife for three years. She frittered away their cash in beauty salons and took lunch and gossiped with her pathetic friends. They would pick at their salads and take it in turns to stick their fingers down their throats in the toilets. There were no children and there never would be. He felt that she was itching to find some cause to hire in a divorce lawyer to carve out a share of his millions. He barely saw his father who was an industrialist-turned-Congressman whose life revolved around the Defence Committee which was trying to unpick the nightmare of the Middle East. His mother lived out her days in a fog of Valium and gin in the rambling family mansion in Virginia. It seemed as if millions of people wanted to know him and yet he barely seemed to know a soul. He was surrounded by lawyers, financial advisers, image gurus, agents, personal fitness managers and caddies, yet he couldn't call a single one of them a friend.

He completed the round with three more dreary pars and after half-an-hour of forced smiles and anodyne comment to eager TV people, he managed to escape to his suite in the majestic hotel that was attached to the course. Once inside his room he leant wearily with his back against the door and surveyed his surroundings. There was a huge sitting area that could have parked five family cars, and a patio door onto a balcony that looked out across the majesty of the tamed Arizona wilderness. Nothing was missing. Sumptuous leather furniture, a cinema screen of a TV hooked into about a million channels. Drinks cabinet. Teak dining furniture. Doors which led off to an equally magnificent bedroom and bathroom. How much would they charge for a room like this? $1,000 a night? More? Completely out of sight for the regular working man. How many millions were out there who would give their eye teeth for a few days in a room like this? Yet for him it meant nothing. Just another room. Just another stop on the weary merry-go-round of his jet-set life.

He sighed and pulled a Budweiser from the fridge. There had to be more than this. There just had to be. If only there was someone to talk to about it. There was no point in talking to any of his advisors. All they were interested in was to get him into more and more show-pony work for the corporations who queued up to buy a piece of him. Their only interest in him was their ten and fifteen percent, no matter how much they simpered and crawled. He was sick of them. Sick of their false smiles and flashy suits and greedy eyes. In the end he was just a golfer who was getting weary of the game. He wondered how he had ever allowed himself to become such a commodity.

He switched on the TV with little enthusiasm and sank deep into a leather armchair. An anchorwoman with a head of hair which could provide a good home for a colony of seagulls, reluctantly put away her expensive smile and assumed a suitably grave air as she connected her viewers over to Iraq. The usual pictures. Weary-looking Marines, hot and bothered and scared in their flak jackets and body armour. Officers with tight expressions, and eyes filled with resentment. The rubble and debris of yet another bomb. Chanting crowds with faces filled with hate. A Stars and Stripes in flames.

What right had he to feel sorry for himself, sitting in the lap of five-star luxury with his ice-cold beer? The faces passed across the screen one by one. Young. Tired. Dejected. Doing other people's dirty work because it was their job. And all of a sudden an idea jumped into his head which made him sit up bolt upright.

Could he? Well of course he could. He grabbed the phone and started making calls. Eventually he tracked down the Pentagon number for Brigadier Richard Carver. The secretary was all briskness.

"Brigadier Carver's office."

"Is Richard available?"

"Who's calling?"

"George Albright."

A pause. "Of course sir, and I'm Minnie Mouse."

He rolled his eyes in frustration. It took five minutes for the well-trained guard dog to have enough doubt to agree to connect him. Her hesitancy must have come through to the Brigadier whose voice was filled with suspicion when it came on the line.

"That you George?"

The younger man chucked. "Remember when I beat you in a putting competition when I was nine?"

"Sure do." The big officer's voice was its normal self now. George had known him all his life. Richard Carver had been at college with George's father in the 1960s. Albright the Second had gone into the family firm and Richard Carver had followed his own family's military tradition and gone to Vietnam. He had completed three tours and gone on to become one of the Marine Corps, most charismatic leaders. He also played off a five handicap and never let anything get in the way of a round with the young boy who had grown into the greatest golfer on the planet.

"How the hell are you George? I caught that triple birdie finish of yours. Man, was it ever hot. Your game still good? Not on fire today I hear."

"No sir. About as on fire as a wet dish towel."

"That bad huh?"

"That bad."

George sensed the sounds of one of the Brigadier's trademark fat cigars being lit.

"So George. What can I do for you? Got some kind of a problem?"

"I'm afraid so, sir."

"Well shoot."

George took a deep breath. "Sir, I figure I'm having some kind of a mid-life crisis."

"Don't be goddamn stupid. You're only 32."

"33."

"33 then. Go on. Sounds crazy to me. Nice wife. Rich as all hell and the best damned golfer in the world. Nobody has the right to any kind of crisis who can hit a driver like you."

"Sir, my wife hates me, everyone around me is only there for their ten percent and I'm stale as month-old bagel with golf."

"So what do you want me to say? Goddamn it, I'm a Marine, not some women's magazine agony aunt."

George smiled at the horror in the voice that suspected that sympathy was being asked for. "No sir. You don't have to say a thing. I just want a favour."

"Good. I'm not all that good at the shoulder-to-cry-on thing. What do you want?"

"When I was at college I worked up a kind of trick shot routine. You know the kind of thing. A few jokes. Shots with rubber clubs, one-handed shots, shots between the legs, all that kind of stuff."

"Yeah. I remember. You did it at some party once. Not bad actually. But what the hell has some old golfing song and dance act got to do with anything?"

"Sir. I'll lay it on straight. I need a change. I need to do something different. Worthwhile . . ."

"For Christ's sake get to the point man."

"Sir. You've got over 100,000 men in Iraq. They're scared, bored and seriously pissed. I want you to fix it for me to go out there and tour around with my golfing song and dance act. Bob Hope meets Jack Nicklaus. Get it?"

"You serious?"

"Sure I'm serious. Real serious."

The line was silent for a while. "You know it's pretty hot out there. The whole place is Indian country. We couldn't give you any hundred percent security guarantees. In fact we'd need you sign some kind of insurance waiver."

"Fine."

"Your dad will be pissed with me."

"I thought you just said you were a Marine? Think Iwo Jima and get over it."

Another chuckle.

"OK. It's done. When do you want to go?"

"I booked through till mid-January with promotional stuff. How about February, for a month?"

"I'll make it happen. Leave it all to me."

"Thank you sir. I'm obliged."

"Hey. No need for thanks. I'm proud of you, son. Real proud. You'll do a lot for the boys out there. They're all beginning to feel pretty forgotten."

"Let me know how the arrangements go. We'll talk soon."

"Sure thing. I want a game before Christmas."

"Bring your wallet."

"Don't I always?"

It was a different George Albright the Third who took the next bottle of Bud from the fridge. This one looked as if he had taken a heavy load off. He was smiling.

Jonathan McMillan's return home to the States had proved to be a sad one. As his father had driven him away from the airport in Dallas he had informed him that his great-grandfather had been rushed into hospital with a re-occurrence of the angina which had been getting steadily worse for five years. For a few days it had seemed touch and go, but slowly the old man had rallied. When Jonathan had visited him, Roland McMillan seemed to have shrunk to half his old size. His skin was deathly pale and almost translucent. All the drive and passion of the man seemed to have drained into his eyes which still shone out bright and strong. The old man took the news about Jonathan's decision to give up his golf aspirations surprisingly well. The news had been something Jonathan had been worrying about. If anything, Roland had been his greatest supporter in the whole family. He had joked that it must have been his Scottish roots coming to the surface.

When Roland had at last retired as the company Chairman at the age of 82, his first project had been to build a golf course at his vast ranch in Texas. Predictably enough, no expense was spared and three separate course designers were hired to take on the task of creating a small piece of seaside Scotland hundreds of miles from the Gulf of Mexico. Great convoys of trucks carted in sand for false dunes. Biologists were engaged to cross-breed varieties of gorse which could survive the rigours of the Texan summers. A team of carefully selected young Mexican horticulturalists was seconded to various Scottish links courses to learn the art of green-keeping. After seven years the course was at last finished and there were many who said it was one of the finest in America. Though not open to the public, Roland ensured that his creation was always busy. He always made it available for amateur competitions and charity events. He also laid on week-long stays for children from the more deprived areas of Dallas and Houston. Their itinerary included golf tuition from a small resident team of coaches as well as horse riding and camping. The only way for others to sample the course was to pay an extortionate fee to compete in a charity event.

Jonathan had spent many hours honing his skills on his great-grandfather's course, often with the old man following him round in his buggy. Over the years Jonathan had become closer to his great-grandfather than even his own parents. When he broke the news to the shrivelled figure propped up by hospital pillows, he sensed a kind of relief in Roland McMillan. A bony hand wrapped in veins reached up and he took it.

"Actually, I am glad Johnny. I have worried about this for some time. You are a wonderful golfer, anyone can see that. And maybe you could have even made it all the way. But I have always seen more in you."

Jonathan was surprised by this. "More? I'm not sure that I understand."

This brought a small, tight smile. "Not now. I am too weak. Soon. Come and see me when I get home. Not long now. These good people think they have me here for a few weeks but they are in for a surprise. Come and see me then, but don't go making any commitments."

"I was going to see Austin about making a start in the company."

"Don't. I'll tell him. Take a bit of time out. I want to talk to you."

"Of course. Just call when you are ready."

The call came in the second week of November and Jonathan duly made the four-hour drive to the ranch. When he arrived, the sight of Roland came as a pleasant surprise. The old man had made a recovery that was almost miraculous. He was still in a wheelchair with a blanket over his knees, but there was some colour in his face and death was no longer hovering impatiently. They made their way into the large wood-walled lounge area where a fire blazed away. Abe, the manservant who had attended Roland for 40 years, smiled at the sight of Jonathan. "Good morning Jonathan. I trust that you are in good health?"

"The very best Abe. And you?"

"Not bad for an old man. You had a pleasant visit to Scotland?"

"Yes. Splendid thanks. Nothing like going back to the old roots. I would recommend it anyone."

Jonathan was too young to see the shadow that passed for a moment across the servant's eyes. Roots were something that Abe had never talked about and never would. His roots were a small dusty village in the hills above Jerusalem. His roots were all blown up one night in 1948 when he was twelve years old when the Jewish fighters had made him an orphan and set him on his long journey to America. In the village of his roots, Abe had been Ibrahim. Ibrahim for the Moslems was Abraham for the Jews and the Christians. He had changed to Abraham in New York, and by 1955 he had become Abe. His second name, Hassim, became Haston, and by the time he made it out west to Texas nobody suspected that a small village in the hills of Judea had once been home. He had first entered into the world of the McMillans when he had got himself a job as a cleaner at the head office of the Corporation in 1962. His shift started at eleven in the evening and finished at seven in the morning. He would generally arrive at Roland McMillan's office a little after midnight and sometimes the man himself was still in there working away. The two men often fell into conversation over coffee and they would sometimes talk away the night. It had been in 1964 that Abe had been offered the role as Roland McMillan's personal servant and he had been there ever since.

He cleared his mind of the young man's throwaway comment. Nothing had been meant by it. He had watched Jonathan grow into a fine young man who seemed to genuinely care. Of all the McMillans he had been with over the years, this was the one who most closely resembled Roland and he was fond of the boy. He carefully poured out coffees and fussed over the blanket before asking, "Is there anything else sir?"

Roland shook his head. "Abe, I have been trying for more years than I can remember to get you to call me Roland and you have refused every time. You might just have noticed that I am showing signs of age and I dare say I won't be around much longer. I would view it as a truly great favour if you can find it in yourself to call me Roland before I die."

Abe smiled. "I am sure you will outlive me by some years sir. However, I will give the matter some consideration if you wish. I make no promises though."

"I did tell you that I come from a tiny house in a Scottish coalmining village didn't I, Abe? Not a castle. Not a country house. I told you that?"

"Yes sir. Many times."

"Well you consider Abe. Consider well. I'm not too old to fire you."

Abe smiled at the mischief. "I must advise that redundancy after 40 years would not come cheap."

"Might be worth it though."

"Of course sir."

Roland laughed and this sent a small burst of pain through his chest. "Go on. Bugger off. I'll buzz if I need anything else."

The mention of the Scottish coalmining was a surprising break for Jonathan and he was determined not to waste it. He had been trying to think of a way to tell Roland about his visit to Kirkonnel for weeks, and now the opportunity had been tossed to him. Roland's early days had always been the great mystery of the family. It was a period that the old man seldom, if ever, discussed. He was willing to talk about his life from the day that he met his wife to be when she served him coffee in a diner outside of Austin, Texas in 1931. The time before that was never up for discussion. Jonathan had worried that his great grandfather would be mad with him for prying.

"There is something I better tell you sir."

"My, my. Not even noon and it's time for confessions. I am intrigued."

Time for the plunge. "The last course we played over there was Turnberry. When I was waiting for the guys in the bar I got to looking at a map. I noticed that Kirkonnel was just a few miles away over the hills. I gave Austin a call and asked if it was the same Kirkonnel where you were raised and he said that it was. So I hired a car an paid a visit."

Roland sat forward in his wheelchair, a look of keen interest on his face. "Good lord. Kirkonnel. You really went there?"

"Yes sir, I did. I brought you this."

He reached into his small rucksack and pulled out the photo from the wall of the pub; it had been carefully re-framed. He passed it over. For a long time old man stared down and into the past. When he at last looked up there were tears on his tired cheeks.

"Did you hear much about him?"

"Just a little. He sounded like he was quite a guy. You know what happened in the end sir?"

"Oh yes. Yes I know that he died in prison."

He stared out at the flag that fluttered gently on the eighteenth green of the course that he had built. His own small piece of Scotland.

"He wasn't a bad man you know. I remember times when he was as good a father as a boy could wish for. It was the war. He must have had a terrible time in the war. I think it is impossible for any of us to even begin to imagine how it must have been for the miners who fought underground. When he came home he was changed. Terribly changed. Terribly, terribly changed.."

Again the words drifted into a steady, melancholy silence. At last the old man seemed to come to a decision. "As you know Jonathan, I have never spoken of this period of my life. I have my reasons. I dare say that there has always been a certain amount of speculation about it in the family."

"I should say that is an understatement, sir."

"Yes. No doubt it is. As you can see, I am not a well man. At my age I have no right to be. It is time that I start to tidy up my loose ends Johnny. Maybe the best place to start is by telling you my story. The one that I have always kept to myself. You can now become the owner of the story. I have faith that you will act appropriately."

It took the whole of the afternoon. On two occasions Abe came in quietly with more coffee. Roland told of his time as a boy in the valley for the first time since he had caught the train on the fateful night in 1925. He told of the hard few weeks in the chaos of Glasgow. The miserable journey across a stormy Atlantic in the third-class bowels of a steamship. Then there were the months amidst the illness and despair of Ellis Island as he waited alongside thousands of others for a chance at the American dream. Then there were odd jobs in bars and on building sites as he moved from city to city eking out a desperate, lonely living.

Everything changed one night in Chicago in 1929. "I had been working in this bar. Nineteen I was. It was an Irish bar and the guys liked me because I still had my Scottish accent. There were these three in particular who would always demand that I served them and they would tip me a dollar. A dollar was a week's eating in those days. Wall Street had crashed and the place was a hell on earth. You've never seen unemployment like it Johnny. All over America. Families on the move. Disease. Starvation. I was lucky. Those dollar tips kept me eating. The guys were crooks of course. Always with their heads together, making sure they couldn't be heard. They had a corner booth at the back of the bar that was only for them. Sometimes they would have meetings with other crooks. It was their office. That was how it was when everything went crazy. I had just served drinks and they had a suitcase on the table. They quickly closed it when I got there, but not until I saw that it was full of money. And I mean full. I mean thousands. I was just digesting what I had seen when all hell let loose. Some other guys had come in and started shooting. I just dived to the floor and kept my hands over my ears until it was all over. When I looked up everyone was either dead or disappeared. The four guys at the table were all shot to pieces. So were three guys at the door. Everyone else had run. I was alone. Nineteen years old and already I could hear the sirens coming closer."

Jonathan's face was a picture. They had all pondered on all kinds of colourful stories about Roland's early life, but none quite this colourful. "What did you do?"

"What do you think I did?"

"No. You didn't!"

"I did. I took the case and hightailed it out of the back door. I ran to the railway station and took the first long-distance train, which happened to bring me here, to Texas. Three weeks later I paid cash for a small oil field from a company that had gone bankrupt. You know the rest."

Of course he knew the rest. The rest was well-established family legend. One oil field had become twenty. Then steel and shipping and property. Seventy years of corporate wheeling and dealing that had made the McMillan family one of America's richest. For years the family had speculated on how on earth Roland had come up with the cash to buy the first field. And here it was. The strangest of truths. A suitcase full of cash left on a table after a bar room shootout. Unbelievable.

"Are you disappointed?"

What a question. "No. I can't say that I am sir."

"What do you think you would have done?"

Jonathan pondered this. "I just can't say. How could I? Look at the life I have led. No hunger. No trauma. How can I even begin to imagine how it must have been in those times. I can't answer you sir."

"And there is no need. No need at all. I am glad that you know the truth. You have plenty of time to think about it. The whole of your life, which is many years longer than I have. Now. I told you that I wanted us to have a talk. I feel better to have that particular burden off me. After all, it is one that I have carried for many, many years. That is one detail cleared up. There are others. Many others."

"How can I help sir?"

"Oh you can help greatly. Very greatly. If you are willing."

"Try me."

"I fully intend to. The first thing is money. Isn't it always? I am worth a great deal of money, Jonathan. A ridiculous figure. Almost obscene. The company makes a huge profit every year and it will always do so. Our sphere of operations is well spread and if one area goes bad, another will come good. I am going to leave the family the firm. They don't need the cash. All the cash is going into the McMillan Foundation. I have already set it all up. Very discreet. I want you to run it, Johnny. Will you do that?"

Jonathan felt like Tom the cat having had a flat iron dropped on his head from a great height.

"Good God sir. What can I say? What will it involve?"

"About a billion dollars. An income of something like 50 million a year. If you agree, we will both target a board of trustees. We'll get good guys. Guys who have been around the block a time or two. As to what areas you want to work in, that will be your choice. You're a good kid Johnny. You always have been. You care. That's enough for me. No need for me to tell you what to do and what not to do. You will have one of the biggest charities in the world at your disposal. It can be Africa, it can be single moms, AIDS, drug users. Whatever. You call. I know you will use the money right and do some good. No need to say anything now. I'm not at death's door just yet. Take a bit of time out. Think it through."

"I've thought it through sir."

Roland smiled. It was as he had expected.

"And?"

"Yes of course. I am honoured, and I won't disappoint you."

"You'd better not because I'll be watching. Good. Item one done with. Time for item two."

"There's more?"

"Oh yes. There's more. Come. Let's go take a look at the pictures."

The pictures were one of the great joys of Roland McMillan's life. In 1951 he had taken a family holiday in Italy and had spent an afternoon in the Uffitsi Gallery in Florence. Those few hours were to open the doors to one of the great passions of his life. He had returned to the States with two pictures and he had been collecting ever since. In half a century he had spent over 400 million dollars in auctions all over the world. Rumour had it that the collection of Renaissance masters was now worth well over a billion. His insurers certainly took that view, and their premiums would have paid for month-long party in a pretty large town. He had built an extension in 1974 to house his collection. It was hermetically sealed and temperature controlled and a place where he had always spent hours of his time gazing into a world of sunshine and bursting colour. There was something of the church or mosque about the long, silent room. Jonathan had always felt as if he were entering a place that was in its very own time-warp. He could understand how it was that Roland could cut himself off for so many hours under the gaze of the peaceful faces in the pictures.

They made their way around the room slowly. Neither of them spoke. There was no need. Of course the fate of his treasured pictures would be playing large in Roland's thoughts. Jonathan wondered what plans the old man had made. He waited patiently until they returned to the blaze of the fire. Dusk had descended over Texas while they had been in the gallery. Outside the night was inky black as a thick covering of cloud hid away the stars and the moon. Eventually Roland spoke.

"You know Johnny, I have often felt bad about the pictures. I have been selfish. I realise that now. I suppose I have realised it for many years. How very selfish for one old man to hog so much beauty to himself. These pictures should have been there for everyone to see, not just me. It is a thing that I have become ashamed about. I promise there have been many times when I have vowed to myself that I would do something about it, open a public gallery, anything . . ."

His voice trailed away and he looked into the jumping flames of the fire sadly. "I just couldn't do it. Couldn't part with them. Couldn't stand to share them. I'm not proud of it Johnny. Not proud at all." he made a visible effort to find some more energy. The long afternoon had taken a toll on his weak frame. "Anyway. No good moping about it. What is done, is done. Nobody has ever learned how to turn back a clock. Certainly not me. I need to put this right before I die Johnny, and I need you to take control. I am like Gollum with his precious ring. I will put it off and put it off and only when I am on my death bed will I realise that I have left it too late. It mustn't happen Johnny. We need to sort this out now. Over the next few months."

Jonathan nodded slowly. There had been times that he had thought it to be rather out of character for his great grandfather to hide and hoard his art collection like a modern-day Shylock. "So. What have you in mind? Anything?"

A slow nod. "I have a few thoughts. Of course it is all about where, Johnny. I was born in Scotland and despite everything that you now know, I will die feeling like a Scotsman. But America has been good to me and all of my family. It was America that gave me the chance to have . . ." he looked around the magnificent room. ". . . well, to have all this. Not just me. All of us. So where should I choose Johnny? Should I choose Scotland? Or should I choose America? Where, Johnny?"

The young man shook his head and took troubled. "I can't tell you that sir. Nobody can. Only you can choose."

"I know. Of course I know. The problem is, Johnny, I just can't seem to decide. I promise you I have tried. In the long hours of the night in the hospital it was all that I thought about. I just can't."

"Both make good cases, huh?"

"Yes. A dead heat. Nothing to choose between them."

Roland now looked thoroughly miserable. All his life he had been decisive. From the very minute that he had packed his bag and left the valley for the great New World of America. From the split-second decision to take the case full of money and leave Chicago. He had built up one of America's greatest corporations by being decisive. And yet now, when confronted by one of the most important decisions of his long life, he was dithering. Jonathan sensed it.

"OK sir. I can understand that. We need to find a way to find the winner. They're all square after four rounds so we need to come up with some kind of play-off. We need to decide if it is sudden death like the Masters, or best over four holes like at the British Open or even a full eighteen holes like at the US Open "

In an instant Roland McMillan's face was transformed completely. Where before there was a slightly defeated look, now there was a new gleam in his eyes. "My God Johnny, you have it!"

"I do?"

"You have it. The answer. The solution." He couldn't help but laugh.

"Sir?"

"They can play for the pictures. Can't you see?"

Jonathan was trailing far behind. "Frankly sir, no, I can't."

"Golf, Johnny. Golf. In the old days the kings and emperors would send out their champions to fight it out for their realms. We will do the same. Only this time it with be golf clubs instead of swords and axes."

For a moment Johnny was dumbfounded, and slowly but surely the beauty of the idea started to form in his head. It was outrageous, but . . .

"Who will be the champions?"

Roland was firing on all cylinders now. "The number ones. The American number one against the Scottish number one. When do the money lists start for the year?"

"Just the beginning. January first."

"OK. I thought as much. Let's say we can get the match on for June. We will need a cut-off. How about the first of April? Whoever the two leading golfers are for the two countries on the first of April."

"Well . . . " Jonathan slowed down his racing brain. "One or two changes sir. The Masters is at the beginning of April. I think we should make the cut-off at the end of the Masters."

"Good. Agreed."

"Maybe June is not ideal. The US Open is in June. I figure May might be better. Maybe the last fortnight?"

"Agreed again. So Johnny. More questions. What kind of contest?"

Jonathan scratched his head. "Gee sir. Well . . . are you planning on paying the guys?"

"No. If they are not willing to fight it out for their country we will just go down the list until we find someone who will. I will make a heavy sum available to both of them to donate to a charity of their choice."

"OK. I go with that. They'll play. No real question about that. Their sponsors will insist on it. But four rounds would probably be asking a bit too much. 36 holes is probably too little. Why not three rounds? 18 holes on day one and 36 holes on day two. That would make the thing different. Unique."

"And match play?"

"Oh yeah. Got to be match play sir."

"Good. Better and better. OK. What's next? Well, I suppose there is the big question. Where the hell do we play it? Here would be too vain."

A slow smile spread across Jonathan McMillan's handsome young features. "Oh that's easy sir. No choice really. Turnberry. Just a few miles over those dark Scottish hills from that valley of yours. No matter how things pan out on the money list, the Scottish guy is bound to be way down from the American. Turnberry will give him a chance. Plus the facilities are ideal for this kind of event. It will cost a few dollars but you should be able to book out the whole place."

"Yes. Yes, why not. I like that. Just a few miles from Kirkonnel. Maybe it's time that I went home for a visit."

The door opened quietly and Abe ghosted into the room. It took a moment for Roland to notice him. "Oh. Abe. Sorry about that. I was miles away."

"It is after eight sir. May I bring you both something to eat? Possibly sandwiches?"

"No. Not yet. Sit down Abe. Sit down and listen to this idea of ours. You've always been my best sounding board. Tell him, Johnny."

Jonathan outlined the need for a long-term home to be found for the pictures and the scheme they had hatched to choose between Scotland and America. Long before he had finished, the manservant was beaming.

"So?" asked Jonathan.

"I like it. Love it. But who do you think it will be? Got to be George Albright for the States, but what about Scotland?"

Jonathan thought for a while. "You know Abe, I haven't got a clue. Montgomery isn't firing at all these days. Most of their guys who have shown a bit of promise seem to have gone off the boil. Paul Laurie maybe? He's quite consistent. But really, it could be anyone."

"Doesn't matter who it is. Ain't nobody going to handle big George. No way."

Like millions of his fellow Americans, Abe was a big fan of George Albright the Third. His certainty amused Roland.

"Now you be careful Abe. Don't forget that I am the Scotsman here in the room. You underestimate us at your peril. Remember Bannockburn, as my old headmaster used to say."

"Remember what? I ain't never heard of no Bannockburn, but it will take more than any Bannockburn, whoever he may have been, to get in the way of big George."

The old man chuckled. "My, my. Such confidence. It seems that a wager may be in order. I suggest ten dollars."

"But you don't even know who will be playing for Scotland."

"And you don't even know who will be playing for America."

This amused Abe no end. "Ah come on sir. Who else is going to be number one after the Masters?"

"So we have a bet?" A thin white hand snaked out from under the blanket and Abe took it gently and shook.

"So. Is it sandwiches?"

"Yes. Certainly. Roast beef and horseradish sauce please Abe. And I would also like to extend the bet."

Abe looked suspicious. "Should I smell a rat here?"

"Absolutely. America wins and you get to carry on with this ridiculous 'Sir' nonsense. Scotland win and you have to call me Roland. Deal?"

Abe was boxed in and he knew it. All he could do was to maintain dignity. "Yes sir. I am agreeable. Don't build your hopes up though."

Both men were in something of a state of shock. Within minutes their plan had evolved to the point of being agreed. "So where do we start?" asked Jonathan, suddenly feeling a long, long way out of his depth.

"You get on a plane tomorrow and sort things out at Turnberry. Book the whole hotel. Every room and shed on the place. Friday, Saturday and Sunday. We'll play the match over the weekend. Throw as much cash as you need. Tell them I am having a major party for my 95th birthday. Tell them about Kirkonnel. Tell them what you like, just don't tell them the truth. Not yet. As long as we have the hotel and course to ourselves we can sit on the truth for a while. We will need some political help on this. I'll call Senator Morton tomorrow and get him on board."

NOVEMBER

They ate their beef and horseradish sandwiches. They drank coffee and started to fit the flesh on to the bones of the plan. Two days later Jonathan called from Turnberry to confirm that the weight of the McMillan millions had secured the whole hotel and golf complex for the last weekend in May.

Major Yuri Krishkin allowed one of his three security men to open the front door of his apartment complex. Outside, the rain was cascading down. He wrinkled his face in distaste. Ten of his precious days of leave had been filled with a relentless grey rain that made his home city look its absolute worst. Like all Russians, he had a great love for the snow, and he had hoped that his leave would present him with the chance to spend some time out in the midst of the first falls of the winter. Instead, winter had chosen to arrive late and there had only been rain.

He briefly considered taking the car but brushed the thought aside. The walk to the café was part of his routine. It got the blood running through his tired old veins. Too much of his life was spent in cramped interrogation rooms. Time amidst the smell of fear and shit and blood. Time filled with three packs of strong cigarettes every day. Sometimes four. Cigarettes and ferocious coffee. He was determined to take as much air as he could during his leave. His doctor had been adamant. All the signs were there and it was up to him to take heed of them. Drink less. Smoke less. Exercise more. He had no intention of taking heed of anything that decreed less on the drinking and smoking. The exercise he was willing to try.

The walk to the café took him half an hour. He did his best to keep off the rain with his umbrella. His security guards could afford no such luxury. They needed to keep their hands free. Times were dangerous for a man like Yuri Krishkin who worked in the very front line of the endless war against the Chechans. Their faces were blank as their cold, hard eyes flitted over the wet streets. They would have preferred the car of course. When they arrived at the café he waited for a few moments outside while two of his men checked that all was as it should be. Then he went in while the second pair took up a station under the eaves of the front door and lit their cigarettes.

Apart from the wretched figures in rags that filled nearly every sheltered doorway, the place was deserted. On a sunny day the pavements would have been filled with hawkers from all over the crumbled remnants of the Soviet Empire selling their pathetic wares. Not so today. Today the rain would keep customers off the street. There were no more than a sprinkling of pedestrians, all of them with their heads bowed into the cold rain. The guards settled themselves for another damp afternoon of boredom.

A hundred yards up the street, Anatoly Rykov watched the familiar scene develop. He had made the doorway his own. He was invisible in the stinking rags that he had bought for ten dollars from an astounded tramp a week earlier. Moscow was home to thousands of such lost souls, drawn to the centre of the rotten empire, hoping for something better than the grinding poverty of the countryside. The city bore no resemblance to the one he had known all those years before. No longer did the great portraits of Lenin stare down on the masses below. Now his image had been replaced by the gaudy neon of the corporate world. Coke. Nike. Sony. The grey streets had once been empty of traffic and always kept clean by an army of those at the bottom of the Soviet feeding chain. Now there were traffic jams and those at the bottom of the feeding chain lived in doorways and dug around in the bins.

Four days had confirmed the fact that the General was a fool. The text book said, never follow a routine. Never. And yet every day he took the same walk to the same café to sit at the same table and play chess with his cronies over glass after glass of vodka. A fool. An arrogant fool, smugly secure in the midst of his tough guys. Smugly secure in his sprawling capital city and his memories of the days when his country had held the world in a grip of fear.

Anatoly Rykov had broken into the cafe in the wet hours before the dawn. The table where Krishkin spent his afternoon was a relic of the communist days: a rusty silver leg held up a chipped and stained circular table top. The screws that joined the two were tired and weak. It had been a job of two minutes to remove the tabletop. Another five minutes had been enough to place the charge in the hollow steel tube and put the table back together. It had been less than half an hour from leaving his spot in the doorway to returning.

He knew that the General would be doing his rounds of the café now, shaking hands, exchanging greetings. His routine. A few minutes. One of his men would have taken his coat and hung it up over the old radiator to dry. Now he would be taking his familiar seat and sipping at the first vodka of the afternoon. Others would be joining him. The pieces would be laid onto the board. Cigarettes would be lit. The first pawn would be moved forward. Anatoly waited patiently. Fifteen minutes drifted by. The security men smoked and chatted quietly. Twenty-five minutes.

Time.

He reached into the stinking coat and pulled out a small mobile phone. The keypad was locked. He undid it and called up the number onto the screen. A glance showed that the street was bare of pedestrians. He touched the green button and after a delay of barely a second the front window of the café erupted outwards in a rush of orange. The noise took a further second or so to fill the air. The bodies of the two guards broke apart as they were tossed out into the middle of the road. All along the street, the bundles of the dispossessed came to life and ran. Nobody wanted a part of it. Soon the place would be crawling with police and security men. They would need to find themselves new doorways to sleep in. New bins to sift through. The exodus of ragged figures took seconds. Nobody noticed Anatoly Rykov in its midst. By the time the wailing sirens entered the scene of mayhem he was many streets away. Ten hours later he passed through customs at Helsinki airport.

Like Moscow, the rain was lashing the late-night streets of Dumfries. Sally Hunter pulled her coat tighter about her and tried not to think about the state her hair was getting into. She struggled to keep the look of impressed enthusiasm on her face. The reason for her being out in the lashing rain on a Friday evening was to watch the seven-a-side football matches which were being played out on the floodlit, all-weather pitches in front of her. The Midnight Soccer League was a new initiative. The facilities had been made available to the youngsters of Dumfries to come along and expend their youthful energy on the football pitch as opposed to smashing windows and daubing the walls of the town with graffiti. It had been running for some weeks and it seemed that there had been a measurable improvement in anti-social behaviour in various areas of the town. She had spent the first part of her visit touring these areas in a police car, noting how quiet and empty the streets were. The policeman had been enthusiastic about how it was all working. So had Dr Elaine Murray MSP, the local member of her party would had invited her for a Friday night in the rain. Elaine was now standing next to her on the touchline and looked every bit as wet and bedraggled as she felt.

"Well, Sally. I hope that you have seen enough?" The voice was hopeful. Between the lines the message was "Let's go somewhere dry".

"Yes. Yes, I have. I'm impressed Elaine. Truly."

"Would you like a quick coffee before heading back up the road?"

"Yes please."

Hands were duly shaken. A final photo was taken by a fed-up-looking stringer from the local press. As they drove back to the party offices she felt disappointed with herself. Of course she was impressed. It was what it was all supposed to be about. The technical term was "diversionary activities". Play football instead of breaking windows or drinking Buckfast. When she had entered politics she had promised never to ignore what was happening at the grass roots of the country. She despised those among her colleagues who spent all their days among the cosiness of Edinburgh. It was evenings like these which were supposed to have been the reason for her choosing her new career. A hundred kids splashing through the puddles dreaming of being the next Henrik Larsson. Sport at its best. She was angry at the black depression that had soaked through her coat with the rain. She wanted to feel more worthy. Instead she felt fed-up. She was middle-aged and single. She was a Junior Minister who had nothing better to do on a Friday night than to get soaked and watch seven-a-side football. She tried to tell herself it was all part of her new career path. It wasn't working.

Half an hour later she finished her coffee and made her farewells. The empty streets of yet another small Scottish town gave way to the blackness of the countryside. Her apartment in Edinburgh lay two hours away through the buffeting November wind. More coffee. Maybe some paperwork. Bed. And tomorrow? Tomorrow was hockey in Cumbernauld.

Was this as good as it was going to get?

By the time that Sally Hunter had hung up her damp coat and got the kettle on, darkness had descended in Washington DC. Like the song said, it seemed like it was raining all over the world. Larry Weinberg was a man in the mood for any number of sad rain songs. Another bad day had ground to a close. Another bad day to end another bad week. The boss had stomped off in an army helicopter to Camp David making noises about being sick to the back teeth of the "Middle Goddamn East" and going for a game of golf. He wasn't the only one to feel that way. Larry Weinberg was as sick of the Middle Goddamn East as anyone. But Larry Weinberg wasn't showing off to some big-haired bimbos in a wine bar like most of the Ivy League cretins who worked under him. Larry Weinberg wasn't sloping off to the golf course. Larry Weinberg was staring at yet another twisted, mangled lump of metal on his TV screen that only yesterday had been many millions of dollars-worth of Apache helicopter. Everything was going to hell in a handcart and there was nothing that he could do about it. Ratings were down. The media was wall-to-wall hostile. Just about every ex-member of the White House staff seemed to be publishing books and dishing the dirt.

The walls were closing in and his ulcer felt as if it were eating away at his insides, and all everyone seemed to want to do was to play golf and get into pairs of lacy Italian designer pants.

"Sons of bitches."

He spat out the words and hurled the TV remote across the room. It hit a mahogany drinks cabinet hard and smashed into pieces. Something had to change.

It just had to.

December was just days away. Autumn was fading into winter and the first real frost had taken hold of the empty hills. Steve Kenton had pondered on where to take himself and his rucksack. He had considered Nepal. He had considered the Andes. Instead he had chosen County Derry. For a week he had wandered the single-track country roads and stayed in small B&Bs. Now he sat by the side of the tiny road that had led him to the top of one of the grey hills. The view had opened up in the vivid clarity of the winter air. Far below him he could make out the town of Londonderry with the River Foyle wrapped around its old walls.

He had hoped that a few days in the grey hills might have helped to draw some of the poison that still tainted his blood. It was time to leave the memories behind, time to find a way of going to his bed with some confidence that he would sleep all the way through the night without waking covered in sweat. He had hoped that the ordinariness of the countryside in winter might dilute all the snapshots of his days here as a soldier. He had hoped.

Instead the landscape only drew the poison nearer to the surface. So much for that particular theory. He allowed his eyes to wander along the glittering north coast. Time for a new therapy. Golf. Why not? He hadn't played in years. A few miles to the east was the magnificence of Royal Portrush. He decided to find a hotel and spend a few days amidst the timeless sand dunes of the famous old course and get well and truly drunk in the evenings.

He got to his feet, made the rucksack comfortable, and started down the hillside to somewhere he would find a bus. He pictured Martin Sheen and the fan in his Saigon hotel room. "Saigon. Shit. Still only in Saigon." Waiting for a mission. Always waiting for a mission.

Chapter 4
February

Deek was hot. Next to him, on the plastic back seat of the taxi, Troll if anything looked even hotter. All the windows were fully down, but there was no chance for any kind of flow of air because they were inching through the traffic at an average of just under four miles per hour. For the umpteenth time since arriving in Bangkok five days earlier, Deek cursed Meg for being so stingy. His first event on the PGA European Tour was the Johnny Walker Classic at Bangkok's Alpine Golf and Social Club. The complex was a nest of five-star luxury built around the tropical splendour of the golf course. All competitors were offered the opportunity to stay at the resort at discounted rates. Meg had considered the rates to be not remotely discounted enough to allow Deek and Troll to move the overdraft up again. She had allowed economy class seats on a red-eye flight and accommodation in a backpacker's hostel which was given a thumbs-up by the Lonely Planet guide she had borrowed from the library.

Deek had considered putting up a fight, but not for long. Trying to win any kind of argument with Meg was something he had given up many years before. He rightly guessed that any efforts at persuading her that he needed the luxury of the hotel to maximise his chances would have been laughed out of court. Indeed, he had to admit that it was not something that was easy to argue from a man who had spent most of his adult life in a dilapidated caravan. Things had all looked easy when Meg had run through the itinerary in Dumfries. The Alpine Golf and Social Club lay twenty miles outside the city, no more than an easy ride in a taxi. Deek had discovered on his first day that twenty miles out of downtown Bangkok was an altogether different prospect to twenty miles in Dumfries and Galloway. They had left the hostel at ten in the morning and had sat for four sweltering hours as their taxi ground its way through the worst traffic on the planet. He had sweated through nine holes of practice before taking three hours to get back to base.

Not surprisingly, the day left both men with a considerable thirst which they quenched with a vengeance in a variety of down-market bars. The evening ended on an epic note as Deek treated a packed karaoke audience to a command performance of Rod Stewart's greatest hits. They had staggered out of the bar at 2.30 and managed two hours sleep before catching a dawn cab to make the 9.30 a.m. tee off time. By the time he stepped off the 18th green Deek was almost hallucinating with an acute mixture of hung-over dehydration, heat sickness and jet lag. He had virtually no idea how he had managed a level par 72. Having slept all the way back into town, they took showers and piled into the bright lights all over again. Thankfully, on day two his tee-off time was 2.30 in the afternoon which allowed for seven hours sleep. Troll filled the bag with plastic bottles of water to wash down the half-bottle of scotch that Deek had come to require on the golf course. He sweated his way round, taking great gulps of water to complement the crafty swigs of scotch and the chain-smoked cigarettes. The whole performance greatly amused his Australian playing partner who glided round in 68 to go with his opening 69 to sit a shot behind the second round leader. Deek was pleased enough with another 72. He was pleased enough to still be on his feet.

"Coming for a beer mate?" asked the big Aussie.

"I dunnae think I can. I'm not staying here, ken."

"No worries. I'm a guest."

After taking a much-needed shower, Deek joined his playing partner on the terrace. The ice-cold Bud was just about the best drink he had ever had. Two long gulps and the glass was drained and collected by a hyperattentive waiter.

"Bloody hell mate," chuckled Gerry Mills. "You're a thirsty wee bugger. Both of you. Good on you lads."

More bottles duly arrived and Deek steadied the pace. "You been on tour long Gerry?"

"Three years."

"Any good?"

"OK I suppose. Couple of top tens. Never really threatened a win. This your first go mate?"

"Aye. Bit different from what I'm used to."

The Australian shook his head in disbelief as Deek lit up a cigarette from the butt of the one he had all but finished. "Bloody hell mate, you're a throwback. Tell me, what do you have in that flask of yours?"

Deek pulled a face. "Ah. You noticed then. It's scotch."

"Need to stay wet do you mate?"

Deek wasn't entirely sure what staying wet meant, but he had a pretty good idea and nodded. "Aye. Something like that."

Mills smiled again. "So. If you're not staying here, where are you kipping down?"

"In the city. A hostel. We're on a budget."

"What's it like?"

"Basic. Nae bad though. The bars are great. We're having a big time of it at night."

"Girls?"

"Naa. Karaoke. I do a pretty mean Rod Stewart. It's playing huge with the locals. We did'nae have tae buy a drink all night last night."

"Bloody hell mate. Sounds a bit of all right. Better than this dump. Like a bloody morgue after eight o'clock. What's the name of the bar mate?"

"Benny Chow's."

"Bloody brilliant. I might just catch you later."

Mills was true to his word. He gave up the austere lifestyle of the professional modern sportsman in a big way and made a lasting impact with an energetic rendition of Men at Work's 'Down Under' before passing out on his way home in a taxi. The next day his pounding head took him to a 78. Deek on the other hand was becoming acclimatised and got round in a one under par 71. A study of the leader board told him that he was sitting respectably in 34th place, which warranted bed at eleven.

At ten the next morning he was feeling pretty good as he stepped onto the first tee. The temperature didn't seem anything like as bad now he was beginning to get acclimatised, and a solid nine hours of sleep had worked wonders. Anything on or around par would earn him somewhere between five and ten grand which would knock another big chunk off the overdraft. His playing partner was waiting for him. He was a tiny man from South Korea. The board had announced him as Hup Lee. As Deek and Troll wandered onto the tee the small man came over with a big smile. "Hello. Hi. I Hup Lee. You call me Jimmy."

"Jimmy?"

"Sure. Why not. Jimmy good name, no?"

Deek chuckled. "Aye. Why not. Lots of Jimmys where I come from. We having a punt then Jimmy?"

The Korean shook his head and shrugged. "Punt. What is punt? I not know any punt."

"Course you do. A punt. Wager. Bet. Gamble."

This lit up the Asian's face no end. "You want gamble? Sure. I like gamble."

Before Deek could suggest his customary £100 per shot on the card, Jimmy was in and pitching. "OK. Who hits longest drive, yes? $500 yes?"

"Bloody hell." Deek could hardly say no, having brought the subject up first. "OK. You're on."

The first hole was a narrow little par four lined with verdant tropical vegetation. Four three days he had taken a careful three iron for position and gone in with a six iron. From 250 yards the fairway narrowed in sharply. He turned to Troll and put the iron back in the bag and took out his driver. Troll gulped and muttered. "You sure, Deek?"

"Aye. $500. Give us a dram." He took a quick hit from the flask and took his shot. The ball went straight and true and settled down five yards from the rough to the right of the fairway. How far? Had to be 290 yards. He gave Hup Lee a grin and leaned happily on his driver. The Korean wasted no time and hit the ball with a resounding crack that belied his lack of inches. The ball took off like a jet fighter and bounded twenty yards past Deek's. This brought another trademark beaming grin. "So. We have double or quits, yes? Who is nearest pin. Is good?"

Deek nodded. "Aye. Is good."

His nine iron bit into the green hard eight feet past the flag. Hup Lee threw in a towering wedge to barely two feet. They both holed out and agreed terms for the next hole as they made their way along the path to the tee.

By the eighth Deek was $4,000 down and the stakes were going up by the hole. He clawed back $1,000 with a drive that rattled 310 yards down the par five ninth, and a peach of a three wood to the green got back another $1,000. However, the respite was short-lived. By the eighteenth he was back to $6,000 down. He drained his flask and looked across a shimmering lake to the green 200 yards away. Hup Lee was having the time of his life.

"So. Mr Deek. Nearest pin. Yes? $1,000, yes?"

"No. Double or quits. The whole lot."

It seemed as if Hup Lee would dance a jig of delight. "Is good. Is best. You good man Mr Deek. Good man who likes a gamble. I like you very much."

Troll looked as if he was about to be sick. "Christ Deek. That's nearly ten bloody grand. Meg's gonna kill us."

Deek gritted his teeth. "Only if we lose."

He decided on a club and settled himself. It was a mighty tough finishing hole and the flag was perched dangerously close to the water. He decided to play the percentages and hit a careful faded two iron which hit the middle of the green and gathered down the slope to fifteen feet from the pin.

Hup Lee seemed chuffed to bits. "Great shot Mr Deek. You good man. You make me work, yes?"

"Aye. That's the general idea Jimmy."

Deek lit up and felt his heart sink down through the tee as the Korea threw caution to the wind and hammered a four iron on a suicidal line over the water. The ball pitched inches over the lake and rolled to three feet from the flag.

"Jesus Christ, Jimmy. That is a shot. You're a wee bastard to be sure, but that is one hell of a shot." Despite feeling sick to his stomach he clapped his partner on the back as they crossed the elegant bridge over the lake. For the first time he noticed how many people were watching. More than watching, they were cheering. Hup Lee was all smiles as he waved his cap to all directions. Deek followed suit and gave a shy acknowledgement. He muttered to the sweating figure of Troll.

"Little do they know that I've blown $12,000." But Troll wasn't listening. Instead he was registering the leader board. They had both been so taken up with the chaotic betting that they hadn't paid the slightest attention to the score. Troll could barely believe his eyes. It took him a while to accept what he was seeing. 'HUP LEE. – 9.

BANKS – 7' There it was. Written bold and in red. BANKS -7. The fourth name on the board.

"Christ Deek. We forgot all about the score. Look. You're fourth. Jimmy's second. Bloody hell."

Deek followed his gaze. "Bugger me Troll. You're right. That's why they're all clapping so much. How much for fourth?"

"No idea. A damn sight more than $12,000 I reckon."

It was. Deek two-putted the eighteenth and nobody overtook his score. Fourth place earned him 49,272.83 euros. Even when he had paid out Jimmy he still had more than enough to send the account into the black for the first time in history. That night the three of them sang till 4.00 a.m. in Benny Chow's. Deek managed to claw back $2,000 on a show of hands for who could win the most votes from the audience. His rendition of *Sailing* beat Jimmy's murderous version of *Yesterday* by a landslide.

The next tournament was nineteen days away, the Carlsberg Malaysian Open at the Saujana Course in Kuala Lumpur. When they eventually surfaced the next afternoon they decided that the best preparation would be a few days on the beaches of Phuket.

Meg Cunningham was in the grip of wildly conflicting emotions. In front of her was the incontrovertible evidence that her number one problem account was no longer a problem. Numbers which had appeared for years with a minus sign in front of them all of a sudden were positive to the tune of over 14,000 pounds. Her ledger was all in order and her career was firmly back on track. The week before she had attended a manager's conference in Stirling where the high and mighty had dropped all the right hints over pre-dinner drinks. Barring tornadoes and hurricanes, there was nothing to stop her being appointed for the plum job in Edinburgh. It represented the sunny uplands. Edinburgh could take her in many directions. London. Maybe even abroad. Ten years of careful and diligent work were at last about to bear fruit. She knew that she should have been as happy as at any time in her life.

The problem was that she wasn't. She was beset by doubts. She had followed Deek's progress on the internet and had been relieved when each day showed that he was making solid progress in his first main PGA event. At the end of the third round he was positioned to earn a solid paycheque, which was all she had hoped for. She had been only too aware of the temptations of Bangkok and the ruinous effect they could have on Deek. The straightforward par figures that appeared on the BBC's website suggested that once again he was being true to his word.

She had been about to leave work for the health club when her dad had called and summoned her to his house. The pair of them had sat glued to the screen all evening as *Sky* gave generous coverage to Deek's hell-for-leather private duel with Jimmy Hup Lee. They had worked their way through two-and-a-half bottles of red wine and she had wound up sleeping in her old room. Frank Cunningham hadn't been able to sit still. He was constantly up from his seat and shouting instructions at the TV. Why the hell was Deek taking a driver? Was he mad? It had been Meg who had sussed out the situation.

"They're betting, daddy."

"What!"

"Oh come on. Just look at them. Look at that little Korean. He's having the time of his life. I would stake my mortgage on it. There. Look. Look at them talking. Look at Troll's face. He looks like he's eaten a raw kipper."

Frank Cunningham was almost beside himself as Deek almost wrestled a three wood off his miserable-looking caddie for a second shot over water to a sprawling par five.

"What the hell is he playing at? He's three under for goodness sake! He'll never make the carry. No way! Come on Troll. Talk some sense into him . . ."

The screen showed Troll trying to do exactly that. It was to no avail. Deek took one of his trademark swigs from his flask and a long pull on a cigarette before throwing every ounce of his slender frame into the shot. The camera framed the white of the ball in the rich blue of the sky as it flew towards the distant green. It landed five feet over the lake and settled down 40 feet from the pin.

" . . . *Archie Banks threw the kitchen sink at that one. Both these guys are having a real go today. Everyone else has laid up on ten all week and now both Hup Lee and Banks have made it in two. What do you know of this guy Tom? . . ."*

The camera tracked back to home in on Deek's face. Now he also looked as if he had swallowed a raw fish. Hup Lee was grinning from ear to ear as he playfully punched him on the shoulder. Deek tossed his cigarette to the floor and lit another.

"I told you daddy. Look at the pair of them. Betting."

Frank Cunningham couldn't disagree. "Aye. You're right Meg. That was a bet on who could get nearest to the pin. Hup Lee won it by six feet."

Meg felt queasy. How much was Deek losing? She knew him too well. It would get crazier and crazier. Double or quits all the way to the eighteenth. The crazy devil-may-care golf was bound to come unstuck. She guzzled her wine as he took on shot after shot. The holes went by and the anticipated disaster never came. Deek's name moved steadily up the leader board until, unbelievably, he walked onto the eighteenth green in fourth place. Her father couldn't help himself. When the ball hit the centre of the green he leapt to his feet and punched the air. Meg was quieter. She watched the image of him making his way over the bridge. She watched the look of surprise as the crowd cheered him home. She watched the old Deek smile as it spread over his face as he diffidently waved his cap to the stands. She noticed how well he looked with a tan. Later she was surprised to find a twist of jealousy as a big-haired, big-bosomed reporter interviewed him in front of some magnificent tropical plants. The bitch was flirting shamelessly and Deek was loving every minute of it as he wisecracked his way through the interview as if he had been doing it for years. Who did the jumped-up tart think she was?

Later, as she lay in her old bed and tried to settle her spinning head, she couldn't get the image of Deek and the overdone English tart out of her head. Was he with her? Were they carrying on with their repartee in some tropical restaurant in the thick warm air of the tropical night? Would they make their way back to her sumptuous room? She tossed and turned and sought sleep which wouldn't come. All kinds of images from some kind of twenty-first century *South Pacific* refused to leave her. The last thing in her mind was that of Deek and Jimmy carrying on their fun in the packed confines of Benny Chow's bar.

No matter how hard she tried she couldn't escape the simple, plain fact that she wished that she was out there with him. She engaged the hard, logical side of her brain that had always done her so well and convinced herself that it was just the wine talking.

The next morning she had a rattling hangover and to her horror the thoughts had not gone away in the night. When would she ever get over Archie bloody Banks?

Senator Joe Morton fixed his trademark Texan smile and worked the room. Although Joe was a lawyer by trade who enjoyed Scrabble and French films, his public persona was all cowboy. He favoured a white Stetson and flamboyant boots. The rest of the "anybody who was anybody" cocktail party was adorned in designer jackets and shirts from New York's Fifth Avenue. Joe sported one of his renowned collection of leather jackets with tasselled sleeves. He pumped hands as he mingled and was as big and brash as his media image demanded. Halfway round the room he spotted the cantankerous figure of Larry Weinberg deep in hunched conversation with the Senator from Iowa who was no doubt moaning on as usual about cheap pork imports. His old college pal was clearly in need of rescue.

"Hey Larry! How the hell are you? That son of a bitch treating you bad, huh?"

Larry's eyes twinkled. "And which sonofabitch might that be Joe? This sonofabitch of a hog farmer or the sonofabitch in the White House?"

"Hell, Larry. How the hell should I know? Everywhere you look in this town you find some kind of a sonofabitch ready to pounce."

The senator from Iowa wasn't at all sure what to make of this and beat a predictable retreat. "Idiot" muttered Weinberg under his breath. "All he ever talks about is hogs. Hogs, hogs and hogs. How are you Joe?"

"I'm good Larry. Real good. You?"

"What do you think?"

Joe's smile slipped a notch or two. "Yeah. Sure. Iraq."

"Iraq."

"You got a minute Larry? Got a favour to ask buddy."

"No hogs?"

"No hogs."

They moved to a corner. Larry lit up while Joe dropped the cowboy act and became all lawyer.

"Do you know Roland McMillan, Larry?"

"Sure. Rich guy. Really rich guy. Started in oil. Now it's everything. Never gave us a penny as far as I know. Never gave the opposition either. Tight-fisted Scot. Why?"

"He gives me, Larry. Gives me lots. Has done for years."

Weinberg raised an eyebrow in surprise. "Really? You kept that low."

"He doesn't like a song and dance. Have you heard about his pictures?"

Larry frowned. "Pictures? Oh yeah. Hell of an art collection or something."

"More than just a hell of an art collection. It is supposed to be the greatest private collection in the world."

"I remember. *Time* did a piece on it a year or two back. So?"

"So Roland is pushing 95. He's not a well guy. He's got to thinking a lot about dying. Got to thinking about his legacy."

"Like the pictures?"

Morton nodded. "Sure. Here's the thing. Roland came here from Scotland in the 1920s. He's torn. He wants to bequeath the collection, but he can't make his mind up who should get it. Scotland or the US of A."

"Ungrateful sonofabitch. What did Scotland ever do for him?"

"Exactly. Anyway. He's come up with a crackpot plan. He's going to arrange a golf match to settle it. America's number one against the Scottish number one. It's due to happen at Turnberry in Scotland at the end of May."

"Jesus. I haven't heard about this."

"Nobody has. It's all under wraps. That's why he asked me for some help. It will need some input from you guys. No cash. Just some oil for the wheels."

Weinberg was thoughtful. "Who's playing?"

"No idea. Whoever is number one for each side after the Masters. I guess it will be George Albright for the States. No idea who the Scot will be."

Weinberg lit up another and looked thoughtful. Maybe this was it. Maybe this was the thing he had been waiting for, for so many months. Maybe. A match. A big, crazy match and an art collection worth millions as the prize. An American way to settle an argument. Like gladiators.

Jesus. The media would love it. They would absolutely lap it up. And it was something that might just make the boss look good. REAL good.

"I like this, Joe. I mean I really like this. And I reckon the boss will like it too. You need to leave this with me a few days. OK?"

"Sure. No problem. You just call when you're ready."

Joe Morton was thoughtful as his old friend made his excuses and left. He had been hopeful of getting some kind of response. He hadn't for a minute thought he would get such a decisive reaction. Larry Weinberg hadn't merely shown an interest. He had grabbed at the idea like a drowning man pulling at the side of a lifeboat. How very strange. He made his way out into the corridor and called up Roland McMillan's number from the memory of his mobile.

"Roland. Hi. Joe Morton here. How's Texas today?"

"Texas is darned cold, but Texas is fine Joe. I bet you'd rather be here than Washington."

"Too right Roland. Too right. Look I've just grabbed a few moments with Larry Weinberg from the White House. I floated your golf idea like I promised."

"And?"

"And he's gone for it. I mean really gone for it big, Roland. I think he's away to pitch it to the President."

"You're sure?"

"Not sure. Just a hunch. A strong hunch. The President has always been nuts about golf remember. And the President needs something to take everyone's mind off Iraq. Who knows? Maybe he'll come along. Sure would make a pretty photo shoot. Turnberry's the one with that big island off the coast, yes?"

"That's right. Ailsa Craig. Do you really think he might come?"

"Hell, don't hold me to it. It's just a feeling right now. I'll stay in touch."

Roland placed the phone down thoughtfully. Abe had ghosted into the room with a silver pot of coffee and misread the expression on the old man's face.

"Are you feeling OK sir?"

Roland snapped out of his reverie with a smile. "Oh, Abe. It's you. Sorry. I was miles away. I'm fine thank you. More than fine in fact. That was Joe Morton. He's been talking with Larry Weinberg, you know, the White House Chief of Staff. Joe says he loves the idea of the match. He thinks that maybe the President will come along to watch. Now wouldn't that be something? I can't believe it, to be honest. It's too much."

Abe fussed over the coffee and thought about it. "Maybe not, sir. The President has never made a secret about how much he enjoys his golf. Remember how he followed big George around in the last round of the Ryder Cup. In fact, he has played with George a time or two in Pro Am's. I guess if George is playing for those pictures of yours, the President might want to be there."

"Do you really think so?"

"Yes sir. Yes sir, I do."

"Well Abe. I hope you are right. Anyway. I'm fine now. You knock off for the night. I'll see you at breakfast."

Abe nodded and took the empty tray back to the kitchen. He told the Indian chef and his assistant that they could head off for the night. He checked the time. A little after nine. He decided to make himself some coffee and do some work on the shopping list for the next day. Visitors were due at the weekend and it would do no harm to be ahead of the game. He stirred his mug and flicked on the wall-mounted TV with the remote control. The news was on. The pictures always seemed the same these days. Barren hills that hadn't seen water for some time. Soldiers.

Iraq.

Always Iraq. Or was it? He put his cup down and pulled his glasses from his breast pocket. There was something familiar about the scene. Something he knew here. Not Iraq. Not American soldiers. Israeli soldiers. Small houses built into the rocky hillside. Good lord. It couldn't be. It couldn't be, but it was. It had been over 50 years and he had only been seven years old, but he could still recognise the place. His village. His family's village. The same hills. The same tiny mosque. The same blighted fields with their thin goats. He upped the volume.

" . . . *every day Ariel Sharon's wall gets a little longer. Soon this wall will lock in the whole of the West Bank. In villages like this one, the wall can split communities in half. This man has lost over half of his land. Here is his house. His fields lie over there . . . beyond the wall. People are angry here in Al Jaleel. People see this twenty-first-century wall as a last straw. People here see the wall as a clear message. Ariel Sharon may talk security, but the residents of Al Jaleel see only repression and they are in the mood to fight. It is hard to see how the much-talked-about American road map for peace stands a chance. The wall may just prove to be cul-de-sac. This is John Tanner for CNN News in Al Jaleel . . ."*

Al Jaleel. How long since he had heard those two words? Al Jaleel where his family had farmed their land for so many years until 1948. Al Jaleel where so many of his family had died fighting the Jewish soldiers who had come for their houses and land. Al Jaleel where he might have lived himself with a wife and family if things had been different. The pictures had changed now. This time it was Gaza. Children throwing stones at tanks. Helicopters raining death from the skies. Normally he turned his eyes from the screen. Normally the guilt would make him change the channel. Guilt that it was the children who fought for what his people had lost. Guilt that nine-and ten-year-olds with scarves about their faces still went out every day to face death in the name of all that that they had lost. Guilt at the fact that he had run away to America to live out his life in the security and comfort on the McMillan estate. Guilt because there were times when he knew that he had sold his people short. Guilt at the thought of what his father and grandfather would think if they could see him now making up his shopping list in the magnificent chrome kitchen.

And for the first time in his life, something stirred in Abe. He wasn't Abe Haston, manservant. He was Ibrahim Hassim of Al Jaleel. For sure he was 63 years old. But did that mean he was finished? No. Did that mean that he had forgotten his people for ever?

No.

No it didn't. Why should it? On impulse he took his mobile phone from his jacket pocket and dialled. He called his oldest friend, Ali. Ali ran a carpet shop in Dallas and sold the magnificent rugs of Persia to the fabulously rich of Texas. Abe had known him for 40 years. Whenever he was in Dallas, they would drink mint tea and talk of life in Arabic.

"Ali. It's Abe. How are you?"

"I am well, my friend. This week Allah is generous. He sends me the wife of a man with many thousand head of cattle. She was a woman who had no consideration of the idea of 'Too expensive'. She was a woman who realised her home needed the kind of rugs that only Ali can provide. A good week my friend. A very good week. What about you, my friend. Are you also well?"

"I am. I am very well. Tomorrow I will be in the city. Will it be convenient for me to call my friend?"

"But of course. Why do you ring? I am always here. You know this."

"Then I will come. I will come in the morning before you are too busy with more women whose husbands run many cattle."

The next morning Abe arrived at his friend's Emporium a little after nine. The incense and the smell of the carpets always took his mind far back into the past. The two friends settled down in the back room and chatted with the ease of old men who had shared a lot of life. But Abe felt a tension which he was unaccustomed to. At last he could bear it no more. It was the moment. The time to stop hiding from his past.

"My friend, there is something that I must tell you. Maybe you will be able to use the information. Maybe you will not. My master Mr McMillan has come to a time when he has started to plan for his death. He is planning on what to do about his collection of art. I have spoken of this to you before. It is a magnificent collection worth hundreds of millions of dollars. He has decided that a game of golf will decide whether the collection should be left to America or his to homeland of Scotland. The game will be played by the champions of the two countries. The match will take place at a golf course called Turnberry on the 30th and 31st of May this year. It will be a big event for the media."

He took a sip of his tea and prepared for the moment when he would at last be at one with the children who threw their stones at the tanks. "I learned last night that the President may well be there to watch. He is a big fan of the game of golf. If he comes, it will be a secret until near to the time. There are people who would like to know of the place where the President will be before it is announced to the world. There are people who could use that information, my friend. I know of no such people. I came today because I think that maybe you might know of someone. I do not expect you to speak of this. I am happy that I have done my duty and made this knowledge available to you."

Ali slowly placed his glass of tea down on its saucer as the colour drained from his face. Slowly, very slowly, he nodded.

Larry Weinberg got his chance to pitch at the President two days later. The Oval Office was quiet, the President was dolefully working his way through a bowl of the cardboard-tasting bran flakes that his doctor had insisted on. The doctor had also suggested camomile tea, but that had been deemed a bridge too far, and a mug of full caffeine coffee steamed on the desk.

"Morning Larry. Don't talk to me about Iraq. Don't talk to me about poll ratings. And don't talk to me about my approval rating. Cheer me up Larry. Let's talk about football or something."

"I'll do better than that Chief. I'm going to talk to you about golf."

This brought a glimmer of a smile to the increasingly haggard face of the most powerful man in the world who was sentenced to cholesterol-reducing breakfasts. "Good man Larry. Shoot."

Larry shot, and as he shot, he saw his boss's face come alight just like he knew it would. "Hell Larry. Ain't that just something? I forgive him right here and now for never writing us a cheque. That is going to be a thing worth watching. You bet. Keep the diary clear for a few hours in front of the TV with a beer or two."

"Well that is the thing sir. The diary is already full for that weekend."

The enthusiasm fell from the face. "What with?"

"NATO conference. Friday 29th May. Paris."

"Damn and Hell."

"Saturday is a banquet at Versailles."

"Uggh."

"Sunday is pretty clear though."

"So?"

"So maybe you could take Airforce One up to Glasgow. Maybe you could hitch a ride down to Turnberry. Hell, maybe you could spend a day walking round supporting the USA."

The President thumped his hand down on his desk with a delighted thwack. "Damn it Larry, that's just about the best bit of news I've had in for ever. Me and George have a 100 percent record on these things. Remember the Ryder Cup? Remember George rolling over that Swede? What was it, six up with five to play? Oh yes, I'll be there to see George bring the bacon back Stateside."

"That is, of course, assuming that it will be George representing America."

"Course it'll be George. Who the hell else will be number one? George has been number one for years."

Larry fiddled with his tie. "It might not be quite that simple sir."

"What are you telling me Larry?"

"Well. McMillan says it is whoever is the number one or the calendar year. Whoever is top dog from January 1st to the finish of the Masters."

"So what the hell. That will still be George."

"Probably not, I'm afraid."

"Why?"

"You must have forgotten sir. George is on Sabbatical. Remember? He's out in Iraq doing his Bob Hope routine for the boys."

Once again the President pulled his "I'm thinking about Osama Bin Laden" face. "Hell Larry, I forgot. He hasn't played a single tournament. When's he due back?"

"We don't know. It doesn't seem as if he's in any great hurry."

"Well get him on the phone. Now. Call the Pentagon. Call anyone. I want to speak to George this morning."

"Of course, sir. I can take it that you are inclined to support McMillan's idea?"

"Obviously I do. Don't be so stupid."

"Joe Morton was wondering if you could make a call to the British. Get them on board."

"It's done. Hell, if I can get them on board to the tune of 10,000 men in Iraq, then a golf game just is not going to be a problem. I'll call this morning. Boy, this is really going to be something. Really something."

George Albright the Third was coming up to his grand finale. It was his fifteenth show on a quickly put-together tour that had taken him up and down the length and breadth of occupied Iraq. The first time he had been more nervous than ever before in his life. Twenty thousand spectators lining the eighteenth hole at the business end of a major championship was as nothing to playing to an audience of a thousand battle-hardened Marines. It had only taken five minutes for the nerves to evaporate. The young men were desperate for any break in the miserable cycle of their lives. The boredom, discomfort and homesickness were constant. The nagging fear was the same.

FEBRUARY

Moments of sheer terror were only now and then. The official propaganda painted pictures of a highly-motivated army with every hi-tech toy that American science could come up with at their disposal. The reality was very different. The reality was over 100,000 lonely kids from small towns nobody had ever heard about.

It seemed strange that he had to travel halfway around the world to find the real America. He had been born into a fifth-generation American dream. His had been a life of indoor swimming pool pampering and luxury. Even before he had become one of the most famous sportsmen in the world, he had been cosseted from the grim daily realities of the land of the free. Only now had he at last found the true America over cans of warm Budweiser in stifling-hot tents on the edges of miserable dusty towns. He found the true America in burgers which crunched with the sand that was blown into every nook and cranny by the wind of the desert. Wherever he went, there were young faces growing old too fast. Accents from all corners of America. Everyone wanted to shake him by the hand, not just because he was famous, but also because he had come. He had taken the time to remember them when so many at home were in the process of trying to pretend that they weren't there.

He had spent a week practising his trick shots before flying out. He had managed to master a repertoire that Ballesteros would have been proud of. He hit shots with extra long clubs and clubs designed for toddlers. He hit them one-handed and behind his legs and through his legs. He hit them right-handed and left-handed. He used a crazy rubber wobbly club. He teed off with a baseball bat and a hockey stick. In his college days he had found it almost impossible to persuade a volunteer from the crowd to lie on their back and hold a tee in their mouth for him to hit a drive off. There was no such problem here in Iraq. The percentage of volunteers in any Marine or Airborne crowd was close on 100 percent. The prospect of having a few teeth knocked out by a metal driver seemed pretty tame compared to a rocket-propelled grenade.

He wore a head mike which allowed him to keep up a running commentary as he performed trick after trick. Much to his surprise, he found that his jokes went down a treat. Soon his show ran for over an hour. On three occasions the sound of distant explosions had interrupted his flow. The first time it happened, his agent had wanted to hustle him into a waiting helicopter. For a moment he had been about to leave. Then he took a look around the young faces, every one of which was a mask of disappointment. There were no helicopters to take these guys to the safe zone. He just couldn't do it. His agent had got all worked up and in the end George had fired him and carried on. A legend was born that day because he had forgotten to switch off the head mike when he had called his agent a "lily-livered money-grubbing sonofabitch" and sent him packing. He was presented with a full Marine uniform after that show and now he wore it with pride.

The blues that had almost swallowed him up in Arizona were now far behind him. He was having the time of his life. No agents. No advertising men. No personal trainers and image consultants. Just soldiers. Lots and lots of plain American soldiers. Life was simple at last. Life made some sense.

He had developed a finale that was guaranteed to please. He had brought out two twenty-foot-tall plastic images of Saddam Hussein and Osama Bin Laden. He would call on volunteers to pace their way 275 yards out and set up the two targets. More volunteers would have a go at hitting them before he slammed the targets with his famed driver. Every time a ball crashed into one of the figures, the cheers would ring out, and for a few short moments those who watched were able to forget just how down and miserable they were.

He made sure that there were always crates of beer enough to go round. The army bean counters had initially balked at this. After a few hours of getting more and more wound up, he had solved the problem by getting his new agent to have him put through to a main board member from the Budweiser Corporation. They hadn't dithered for a second. The deal was done in record time, and within weeks George's desert shows became the centrepiece of a new Bud advertising campaign. In return, his audiences had access to an unlimited supply of Buds for the night.

He always made a point of never leaving until he had signed an autograph for every man who wanted one. Sometimes this could take two or three hours, and by the time he signed the last one he would be pretty well pissed out of his head. He didn't care. Nobody cared. It was a war zone. That kind of thing was OK.

He was halfway through his signing session when a colonel came running over to him to tell him that he had a phone call.

"Tell them to go to hell, whoever they are."

The colonel grinned. "Well I'm afraid I can't do that, sir. It's my commander in chief."

"What? The President?"

"Sure is, sir."

"Christ. Sorry guys, you'll have to give me a minute. Looks like I'm being summoned. Dig into those Buds, I won't be long."

He shook his head as he trotted after the officer. How many cans had he had? Too many. How pissed was he? Too pissed to talk to the President, that was for sure. He couldn't help but laugh. How the hell had he arrived at this place? Here he was, dressed up in full Marine combat fatigues, more than half-drunk having given a tricks show to 2,000 troops on the outskirts of Najaf. Crazy world. Crazy, crazy world. The colonel led him into a small private room which had once been some kind of storage facility.

"All yours sir. Just pick up and talk."

"How drunk am I, colonel?"

"As far as I can see, not in the slightest, sir."

"And there was I thinking that you Marines swore to tell the truth."

"Absolutely, sir. Don't worry. You'll be fine."

George took a deep breath and picked up.

"Mr President."

"George! Good to hear you. My people say you've taken some tracking down. Just where the hell are you?"

"Outside of Najaf, sir."

"Jeez. Ain't it kind of hot round there?"

"It's OK, sir. At least it is for me. I get to take the chopper out every night."

There was a silence on the line. Maybe he shouldn't have said that. Maybe it was the six cans of Bud that had done it. Damn. When the President's voice came back on the line the tone was still friendly enough. "It's a damn fine thing you're doing out there George. Truly. But I need you home now."

"No can do, sir. I've still got events booked. I can't let the people out here down." Christ, he had even started speaking like a Marine.

"Now listen up, George. I'm serious here. Give me a minute." The President spelt out the bones of Roland McMillan's plan. "So George, surely you can see that we need you. This is a big deal for

America. You need to get home now. You need to play in as many tournaments as you can if you are going to be number one. Surely you see that? Hell, George, I'm not playing the game by even telling you all this. McMillan would have a fit if he knew. I just know that it should be you out there at Turnberry."

George tried to clear the beery fog of his brain. He couldn't quite believe the words that came out of his mouth next. "Tell you what sir, from where I'm standing, a few pictures seem a hell of a site less important than the boys in field. I'm not cancelling anything. I'll be back in time for the tournament before the Masters and the Masters itself. That's the best I can do sir. If I win them both I might just make it."

This time the silence on the line was a good deal less friendly. "Are you saying no to me, George?"

"Yes sir, I am."

"You sure about this?"

"Yes sir, I am."

More silence. "What if you don't win those two tournaments?"

"Then I won't be number one sir."

"No. I don't suppose you will. OK George. Thank you for making yourself so clear. We'll speak again."

The line went dead. George knew that he should have been mortified, but instead he was elated. The colonel poked his head around the door at sound of George's laughter.

"Everything OK, sir?"

"Fine."

"And the President? How was he?"

"None to good colonel. He wants me back Stateside ASAP. He wants me to cancel the rest of my tour."

"That's a real shame, sir. The men will be pretty ripped up."

"No they won't, colonel. I told him to shove it up his ass. You see, that is where you and me are different. He ain't my Commander in Chief because I'm a civilian from the land of the free and the home of the brave."

"You told him that?"

"Not quite in those words, but something along those lines. I didn't exactly tell him to shove it up his ass. I just implied it. You ready for a beer, because as sure as hell I am."

The colonel was lost for words. Things could be weird and things could be really weird, but never, ever before had they been this weird. "Sir, I think we should do exactly that, and I'm buying."

The President's mood didn't improve much when it took his people 30 minutes to track down the British Prime Minister to his offices in the House of Commons. Among the expletives there was a deal of venomous comment about half an hour would be no pissing use to anyone if the Ruskies had fired off a nuke or two. His instincts told him that his number one ally was hiding, and in fact his sharply-honed political instincts were right on the mark. The Prime Minister was trying to prepare himself for what had become a routine mauling at Question Time, and the last thing he needed was yet another bout of bellyaching from his principal ally in Washington.

It came as a pleasant surprise when the President revealed the reason for his call. His own political antennae quickly started to twitch. He had no great love of the game of golf and he couldn't care less about the fate of a few over-priced paintings, but he liked the set-up. More to the point, he knew a feel good story when he saw one and he knew that the media would take an enthusiastic big bite out of this one. The ingredients were all there and the thing offered him a better than even chance of looking good for once. He happily gave the President full assurance that he would personally ensure that all was in apple-pie order on his side of the Atlantic. Yes, he quite understood that everything was to remain confidential until an announcement at the end of the Masters in April. Yes, he would limit knowledge of the event to a small, personally selected team. Yes, he would put in place a security plan for a one-day presidential visit for the day of 31st May.

The better than usual transatlantic call put him in good spirits and he marched into the chamber with a seldom-seen confidence and was able to land three meaty blows on a rather bemused Leader of the Opposition. Once he was back in his office, he tossed his jacket over the back of a chair and asked to be connected to the Scottish First Minister in Edinburgh.

Their conversation was as it should have been to start off. After all, even though Roger Temple was in theory the leader of a semi-independent country of five million souls, he was still no more than a bit-part player in the Labour Party. Temple duly congratulated his

London-based leader on his performance at Question Time and the London-based leader graciously took on board the flattery. It wasn't turning out to be such a bad day after all.

"Now Roger. I need to discuss something with you. It is all rather secret at the moment, but we will have to make some preparations." He proceeded to fill Temple in on his conversation earlier, making great play on the fact that the art collection would be heading north of the border should the Scots champion be successful. "So Roger, I will be arriving some time on the Saturday afternoon to meet and greet the press. We might as well use Saturday night as an opportunity for a statement of unity and all that. I guess that Airforce One will land at Prestwick, so you will have to ensure security down to Turnberry and back. You know how the Americans are about security. If not, you'd better prepare yourself. You will be invaded by hundreds of them wanting to dot their 'i's and cross their 't's. Work with the security men. They know the drill. I would expect that we will both depart early Sunday evening."

There was a pause on the line and then came words that ruined not only that day but also many days to come.

"I don't think that it will work that way, Prime Minister."

"Excuse me?"

"I am not convinced that it is appropriate that you meet the President on this one. It isn't really foreign policy. The way I see it, this is very much a domestic event, a sporting occasion to determine a bequest of artwork to the nation."

"Yes of course." The Prime Minister's voice was tetchy. He wasn't enjoying the man's cocky "know it all tone" at all. "Your point?"

"My point is that this is a purely Scottish issue. I feel that it would be inappropriate for you to come up north for this one. We will take care of everything from this end. I will do the honours for our American guests as the First Minister."

"This is outrageous."

"Not in the slightest."

The Prime Minister was losing his cool fast.

"You can't do this!"

"Possibly with all the distraction of your adventures in the Middle East it may have slipped your memory that we enjoy a degree of independence up here. All matters relating to sport and the arts are run from Edinburgh. So I am more than confident that I can do this sir."

"Just you wait, I have no intention of allowing this to happen . . ."

"I hope that you are not proposing to invade us again sir. I rather hoped that our two countries were well past all that."

The phone in London was crashed down. "The lousy arrogant jumped-up little prick! Forgets that he's just an overblown union man from a bloody shipyard that closed down years ago."

The problem was that the overblown union man had the Prime Minister by the short-and-curlies and he knew it. It seemed as if half the world had him by the short-and-curlies these days. He wondered for the umpteenth time what on earth had possessed him to give up the comfort of the law for this lousy job.

Roger Temple roared with laughter at the crash of the phone. He was a man cut from the rough industrial cloth of Old Labour and duly despised the Prime Minister as a public schoolboy dressed up in pretend working-class clothes. He had waited many years for the moment that he had just enjoyed. Roger was first and foremost a Scotsman, and like generations of his predecessors there was nothing he enjoyed more in life than putting one over an arrogant lord and master in London. There would be endless moaning and groaning, but he knew that he would win this one. It wasn't a full consolation for Culloden, but it helped. He made an internal call.

"Sally. Could you pop over for a minute? Great."

Half an hour later Sally Hunter left her boss's office feeling as if she needed to pinch herself. All morning she had been dealing with the thrilling issue of some threatened playing fields in Falkirk. Now she had been put in charge of the first full presidential visit to Scotland and the greatest game of match play in the history of golf.

By chance, Ali El Kali had a business trip scheduled to Chicago two days after his meeting with Abe. He fitted in coffee with an old friend who had worked for many years acting as a consultant to those doing business with the Saudi oil industry. The friend in turn took the news of the golf match to an acquaintance who ran a perfume emporium on New York's Fifth Avenue. Fate again decreed that this man was due to attend a trade show in Paris the following week during which he was able to pay a visit to the man known as Abdullah in his penthouse suite at the Ritz Hotel. Three days later Abdullah moved on, this time heading thousands of miles east to the casinos of Macau. He had been there for three days when Anatoly Rykov came to call.

The Russian realised as soon as he stepped into the room that this time things were very different. In the surface Abdullah was his normal debonair self, it was his eyes that gave him away. They glittered with vivid excitement.

"My friend, our time has come. Everything that we have done together over the years has brought us to this moment. A historic moment. A moment that means that it has been placed in our hands to mould the future of many generations."

Anatoly said nothing. He had learned in Afghanistan that these were people who enjoyed flowery language. The Arab continued.

"We have received intelligence, my friend. Remarkable intelligence. Put simply, we have been made aware of the possible whereabouts of the American President on 31st May."

"I don't understand. The presidential diary is hardly a great secret."

"Of course, my friend. Of course. But this is rather different." He laid out Roland McMillan's itinerary of events. Anatoly concentrated hard on the facts and began to see. It was remarkable. Unbelievable. He kept his voice calm. Indifferent.

"You are sure that it is a secret?"

"As sure as we can be. The plan is to be announced at the end of April."

"But you cannot be sure that the President will attend."

"No. But we will be able to confirm it."

Rykov fell into thoughtful silence. When he spoke it was more to himself than to Abdullah. "So, maybe the President will be there, maybe not. Maybe he will stay in the hotel at this place Turnberry, maybe not. But if indeed he is there, he will be there to watch the golf. He has a passion for the game that is well enough known. He made a personal appearance at the Ryder Cup competition two years ago and followed the leading American round the course. Yes. Yes, I can see."

Abdullah nodded. "Yes, I think you do."

"If he is there, he will be on the course."

"Indeed he will."

"And a golf course is an open target. You are aware that this will cost, I presume."

"Of course. I thought that ten million dollars would be appropriate. Two million up front. Two million once we receive confirmation and six million on completion."

Rykov nodded. "Agreeable."

The money of course was hardly relevant. They both knew that. Should Rykov be successful, he would be the subject of the greatest manhunt in history. No amount of money would be able to hide him. The world was not large enough. In the end they would dig him out. It was merely a question of whether it was worth cutting short his time for the satisfaction of becoming the greatest of them all. It wasn't a thing that he needed to consider for very long.

"I'll do it."

"I knew you would, my friend."

"Of course you did."

Over the next hour he gave instructions about what he needed to be put in place. He told Abdullah that he would arrive in Scotland no later than Monday, 26th February. When there was no more to discuss he got to his feet.

"We will not meet again. This is the last time."

Abdullah crossed the room and embraced him. "May Allah be with you, my friend."

It was past three in the afternoon of the day after their night of celebrating when Deek's brain crawled its way back into consciousness. There was some reason why he was awake. He struggled to put it together until at last he realised that someone was hammering away at the flimsy door of his room. Beside him, Troll hadn't moved a muscle. He hauled himself up and his head felt like a carelessly eaten soft-boiled egg.

Outside one of the young boys from the front desk was waiting.

"Mr Rod. You have call. You come now."

His karaoke fame had reached the hostel the day before. Across several bustling Bangkok streets he had become known as Mr Rod.

"Aye. Shite. What's the time, pal?"

"Is three."

He blundered down the stairs and collected the telephone receiver. "Hello?"

An Australian voice hammered into his eardrum and made him wince. He mouthed beer to the boy who got the message at the third go and fished out a bottle from the fridge.

"G'day sport. It's Gerry. How are you, mate?"

"Shite. You sound as if you're in the pink."

"Big old night was it?"

"Colossal."

"Bloody good on you, mate. You guys still planning on a few days in country then?"

"Aye. We're heading out in the morning on the bus."

"The bloody bus! You won a stack yesterday, mate. Why the bus?"

Deek took a long pull from the ice-cold bottle and rolled his eyes into their top lids in pleasure. "We're not going all posh just because I've won a few quid. The boys from Sunnybank aren't five-star poofs pal."

"What the hell is Sunnybank?"

"A scheme. You won't know it."

"What about your clubs? You can't take them on a bloody bus."

"Jimmy's taking them for us."

The second half of the bottle vanished in three gulps and he waved for another. Gerry carried on. "Listen mate, I talked to my baby brother this morning. He hung out a lot in Thailand in his gap year before college. I said I had a couple of mates heading up to Phuket. Asked if he had any reco's."

"Cheers Gerry."

"No worries. OK. The town itself has become a touristy bloody nightmare. He says when you get there you need to grab a cab and ask for Scoobytown. Scoobytown is the place. It's 35 clicks north. Don't pay more than ten bucks."

"Scoobytown?"

"Proper Dingo of a name. Look, I've got to go, mate. See you in KL."

"What L?"

"KL. Kuala Lumpur. 29th May."

"Oh aye. See you there Gerry."

The heat and the excitement of their time in Thailand caught up and they hit the wall hard at nine and slept twelve hours straight. The next morning they negotiated the chaos and squeezed themselves onto a bus that slowly jarred and rattled its way to Phuket. Once upon a time the place must have been a real paradise, but not any more. The streets were lined with gaudy neon-lit bars and prowling kids from all corners of the western world. After a couple of beers they were both more than happy to flag down a cab and escape.

"Scoobytown. You want go Scoobytown? Scoobytown 25 dollar."

"Scoobytown ten dollar, pal. Take it or leave it."

Deek shook a B&H free from his pack and offered it. This won him a gap-toothed grin and secured the deal. They soon left the thumping music of Phuket behind and turned onto a dusty road which more or less followed the sparkling coastline as it snaked northwards.

"Beautiful isn't it, Deek."

"Aye Troll. That it is."

After 40 minutes they crested a low hill and a couple of kilometres ahead a nest of huts ran along the white sand of the beach. The driver turned in his seat and gave another trademark grin.

"Here. Scoobytown. Scoobytown very good. Scoobytown number one."

As they came closer, a limp Stars and Stripes came into view. There were ten huts in all, nestled around a large hut with bamboo tables and chairs arrayed out front at the top of the beach. There were a few bodies sprawled out on the sand and a few more lounging in the chairs.

Troll's face was filled with complete awe. "Just look at that Deek. Its like one of those Bounty adverts. I cannae believe it."

Neither could Deek. The cab pulled up by the main hut and they climbed out stiffly and heaved their bags from the boot. They sent their driver away with a five-dollar tip as a contribution towards a savings fund for future dental work. There didn't seem to be any obvious reception area and they looked a little lost. A young man looked up from his paperback and greeted them in a voice that was pure Essex.

"All right lads?"

"Aye," said Deek. "Who do we see about a room pal?"

"Bloody hell. Jocks are you?"

"Aye. I'm Deek. This is Troll."

This brought the man bounding to his feet with hand extended. "Big up for the names man. Huge up. I'm Deco. Deco from Basildon. Deek and Troll. Well cool. Well cool. Come on. I'll take you to find Scooby."

"Scooby as in Scoobytown?"

"Yeah. Pretty cool. Scooby's a dude."

Deek couldn't help but smile. It was all a long way from a rainy afternoon in Sunnybank. It seemed very dark inside the main hut. They took off their shades, and as their eyes adjusted, a ramshackle bar came into focus. The sound of a mournful Jim Morrison song drifted up into the bamboo rafters along with the scent of several incense sticks. At first they didn't notice the snoozing figure in the corner. Only when Deco went and tapped him on the shoulder did he move. He was a big man with a great spread of belly and long shaggy grey hair. "Oi. Scooby. Wake up, man. You've got guests."

The giant figure slowly came to its feet.

"Greetings, fellow travellers." The voice was all deep-south American. "Allow me to formally welcome you to Scoobytown. May you find some rest for your tired and weary souls. You want to see a room or do you want a beer?"

"We want a beer."

"Hey! Do I hear Scotland? I just know that I hear Scotland."

"Aye. You hear Scotland."

"Man. A big day. Another big day. 35 years and you guys are the first Scotsman in Scoobytown."

Scooby lumbered behind the bar and produced four bottles of local beer. "Cheers guys. Happy landings. Grab a pew. We'll share a beer or two and then I'll find you a hut. Happy?"

"Aye. Happy."

They settled down around what appeared to be the hut's master table. Deek felt that he was under intense scrutiny. Scooby's face was all wrinkled concentration. "Hell man, I know you. I just know that I know you. Where the hell do I know you from?"

Deek glanced over to the impressive wide-screen TV. "Does that work?"

"Sure as hell it does. It's how we run the calendar hereabouts. Scoobytown BS and Scoobytown AS. Right now we are sitting at 5 AS."

Deek smiled. He felt as if he had somehow blundered into a tropical version of *Alice in Wonderland*. "BS and AS."

"Right on. 'Before Satellite' and 'After Satellite'. The Dish was a big day for Scoobytown. May 1999, man. May 1999 and we got ourselves switched on."

"Do you watch the sport?"

"Yes sir I do. Cartoons and sports."

"Do you like golf?"

Scooby's face started to see the light. "Damn. I got you. You're the crazy guy from last week. Banks. Archie Banks. Sure man, I saw you. Crazy golf. Dinky dau. Hell for leather. That's how the goddamn game needs to be played. None of this iron off the tee for position shit."

"You play then?"

"Once. When I was just an itsy bitsy little boy back in the world."

"The world?"

"Sure man. Louisiana. Saturdays at the country club with my daddy. Another life, man. Another era. All I know of the world now comes through the dish, man. More beer. More beer."

He slammed more bottles down. "So guys. How long? How long in Scoobytown? How much R&R from that dinky dau world guys?"

Troll shook his head. "I dunno Scooby. What the hell is dinky dau?"

"Dinky dau, man. It's a 'Nam thing. Means crazy. Looney tunes. Over the rainbow land."

"I see." Said Troll when it was plainly obvious that he didn't. Deek was more on the ball. Once upon a time he had come within a hair's breadth of getting his History Standard Grade. Troll had become confused by the time he got to the Vikings. Deek worked out the maths. 2004 minus 35 = 1969. He'd watched enough videos to know the significance of the date.

"Is that how you wound up here? Vietnam?"

"Sure was. Drafted in '67. In country till March 68. Bummed around some when I'd done the time and then my granddaddy died and left me the money to buy Scoobytown. Been here ever since. Ever heard of the A Shau valley, son?"

"No."

"Heard of the 1st Air Cav?"

"Sorry."

"Hell, don't be. Nobody has any more. The A Shau is the most godforsaken piece of real estate on this whole planet of ours. Misty, rainy, shitty place. It was always Charlie's place until they sent us in there. We went in ready for bear. Hundreds of choppers. Jets. Napalm. Arc light. The whole thing. Hell, it even got to hand to hand. And there was me just eighteen years old and a month short."

"A month short?"

"Sure. One month left. One month left before being rotated back to the world. Well I did me something heavy thinking man. I couldn't see why the hell they had needed to send a Louisiana boy like me to the A Shau valley to do so much killing. What had Charlie ever done to me? I took against the whole thing. Didn't want the world any more. I came here instead. Made Scoobytown the world. Better world here man."

Deek looked out through the open door of the hut to the deep blue of the bay. He could see Scooby's point. It wasn't hard. He didn't have a A Shau Valley to run from. Just Sunnybank and the caravan. Lost years. A lost girl. A life propped up by half a bottle of scotch a day. He felt as if Scoobytown had been patiently waiting for him. "Aye. A better world. We'll be here a while. Don't need to be anywhere till the next tournament in Kuala Lumpur in three weeks. This looks like a place to hang out. What do you say, Troll?"

"Aye. Nae bother. How come you're Scooby?"

"What do you think?"

"Scooby Doo?"

"In one, buddy. You ever seen a cooler dog?"

Troll shook his head. He couldn't help but agree. There weren't too many dogs much cooler than Scooby Doo. "What about Shaggy then?" It was a lame effort at a joke and it fell flat on its face.

"Yeah. There was a Shaggy once. Right there. On the wall." Troll got up and studied an old photo of two young men in uniform. They were smiling in their shades. Their helmets bore the names "Scooby" and "Shaggy". Scooby looked ridiculously young and about a 150 pounds lighter. Shaggy was a tall, gangling boy with a big goofy grin. He reminded Troll of Banjo. There was a weariness to Scooby's voice. "Shaggy bought the farm in the A Shau, man. He was just ten days short. Fragged through the throat. Best friend I ever had. All I got now is that photo. Maybe someone remembers him back in the world. Maybe not."

They fell silent. A quiet wind rustled the makeshift curtains and somewhere outside some chickens were picking away at the ground. Further away was the gentle sound of the South China Sea lapping gently against the beach. Deek laid his head on the back of the chair and closed his eyes. All the clocks had stopped. Scoobytown was a place out of time. Out of the loop. Out away from everything. A contentment that he had never known before in his life was easing through him. He'd done his bit for Meg. The bank account was written in black and her road to Edinburgh lay clear. In his heart he knew that his efforts in Bangkok had probably lost her for good. At least he had found the right place to come to terms with it. He felt no need of the place that Scooby called the world.

Once they had been shown to their hut, Troll had dived onto the bed and been spark out within minutes. Deek decided against a siesta and instead took a long walk along the deserted beach. When he returned the sky was turning into an outrageous patchwork of spectacular colour as the light of daytime drained away into the South China Sea. Scooby was sitting on his own watching it all for the ten thousandth time.

"You OK man?" he asked Deek

"Aye. Great. Can I get a beer?"

"Sure. Lucy's inside."

Lucy turned out to be a spry 60-year-old without a tooth in her gums who grinned and nodded a lot. Deek joined Scooby outside for the last of the tropical light show. He felt no great need to talk and was quite happy to drink at a much slower pace than normal. His mind changing down gears to the speed of Scoobytown. Likewise Scooby was in no hurry to chat. They sat for half an hour before the big American broke the silence.

"Can I ask you something?"

"Aye. Why not."

"On the course you kept taking a hit from a flask. The commentators didn't make a deal of it, but I could see. Do you need that or do you just want it?"

Deek had asked himself the same question many times. In fact it had been one of the questions that he had rolled around his thoughts as he walked the beach.

"I think I need it."

"How is it if you don't drink?"

"My hands shake. I feel sick. Can't concentrate. I certainly couldn't play golf."

Scooby nodded. "Yup. Drinking to feel normal. I've been there myself. I hid from 'Nam in a bottle for years. You'll get through it. When you're ready, come back to Scoobytown. I'll get you through. OK?"

Deek smiled and nodded. It had been that kind of day. He had only known Scooby for a few hours but already it seemed like most of his life. Others started to drift out from their huts and join them. Introductions were made. Deco was with two friends, also very Essex, from Braintree. Two Australians were using Scoobytown as a prolonged pit stop on protracted backpack tour of Asia. A scholarly Canadian was in country for the butterflies, while a quiet Norwegian was hiding away from his creditors. Joints were rolled and passed around as the light dimmed to blackness and stars. A little after nine Troll blinked his way to the table looking as if he had hibernated for months, and his eyes almost popped out as he sucked in his first draw from a proffered spliff. They were both fairly accustomed to getting stoned. Dope had been a mainstream substance of Sunnybank for years. But this was different. This was St Andrews compared to a pitch-and-putt in a city-centre park. They found themselves taken to a different place in the cool sea air of the night as the sound of Jimmy Hendrix wafted over the white sand of the beach.

A little after midnight, Deco leaned across with pupils the size of soup dishes.

"You ever seen *Withnail and I* mate?"

"What's that?"

"A film. Top film. Richard E. Grant and Paul McGann. Set in Scooby's time. Two lads on the piss and every drug they can get hold of. There's geyser says he's going to roll a 'Camberwell Carrot'. Massive joint. Biggest joint ever. Someone says, how come you call it a 'Camberwell Carrot'? Easy, he says. Because the first time I ever rolled one I was in Camberwell and it looks like a carrot . . ."

Deco collapsed into giggles at the memory before reaching into his bag and pulling out a version of the Camberwell Carrot that he had prepared earlier. The waiting audience gave the fat, eight-inch spliff a reception similar the one Barbara Striesand got when she made her big entrance down the stairs in *Hello Dolly*. Deek, as a new guest, was given the honour of sparking it up, and the flashlight of Deco's camera froze the moment. Deek and Troll each had an arm around Scooby's massive shoulders and monumental grins on their faces. Deek had wedged the mighty carrot in the corner of his mouth like a movie gangster with a fat cigar. The picture was of men at the height of party. The next picture taken twenty minutes later was of the two of them sleeping like babies on the cool sand.

They left Scoobytown with great reluctance sixteen days later. Both were unrecognisable from the men who had arrived. They wore deep tans on the outside and an air of contentment on the inside. They bussed it to Bangkok and took a plane down to Kuala Lumpur. Deek called Meg at the bank from the airport.

"Hi Meg."

"Where on earth have you been?"

"Scoobytown."

"What?"

"I'll have to tell you later. I hav'nae got enough change. Did you find us a hotel?"

She had, and duly gave him details. When they arrived, it came as a pleasant surprise. Meg had clearly decided that his efforts in Bangkok had warranted a reward and the purse strings had been eased. An even pleasanter surprise awaited them when they had showered and changed and made their way down to the bar where they found Frank Cunningham looking very dapper and sipping at a gin and tonic.

"Bloody hell Frank. This is a turn-up."

"Indeed. What can I get you, lads?"

The lads, as ever, were in for the beer. They repaired to the pot plants and climbers of the terrace. Deek was bowled over.

"So come on, Frank. How come?"

"I took a look at the course on the internet. Wait till you see it. Unbelievable. Fantastic. I went and watched the practice today. It's like something out of a Disney film. Well, I just decided on the spur of the moment and sold a few shares and here I am. Meg thinks I'm crazy."

"Meg thinks we're all crazy."

"Well, in the case of you two she's always been right. By the way, your friend Banjo is coming out. He asked for the time off and they said no, so he told them where to go. He's landing tomorrow."

"You mean he's left the Job Centre?"

"He surely has."

"Bloody hell."

They shared another relaxed round and then strolled the streets before choosing to eat Chinese. Cunningham leaned back in his wicker chair contentedly and lit a cigar.

"I tell you what, Deek. This Scoobytown place seems to have worked wonders for you. I've not seen you so happy in years. Not since I knew you in the summer holidays way back when. I might just try it myself."

"You should. Everyone should. Meg certainly should. Scooby's right. We all need a bit of time out from the world."

The four days of the Malaysian Open were a time where everything was right for Deek. The swing felt as grooved as a German precision tool, the putts rolled in and the bounces were kind. He tapped in on the eighteenth to complete a final round of 68 to finish eleven under par. His second place earned him a stunning 105,435 euros. There were more interviews, some of them from sports reporters from the British press. He was becoming a minor celebrity at home where his chain-smoking and odd-looking caddie had been noticed. He fielded questions about what was in his flask awkwardly, and had a feeling that life was probably going to become less simple. He completed the interviews and retreated to the locker room and a long, steadying swig from the flask. Gerry Mills popped his head around the corner.

"Bloody good effort, mate. Where's next?"

"Madeira Island Open. Will you be there?"

"You bet. We'll catch a beer or two." Mills noticed his friend's demeanour and joined him on the bench.

"You OK, Deek?"

Deek smiled half-heartedly. "Aye. I'm fine. Just a bit melancholy, Gerry. Us Scots are good at that. Maybe I don't feel like going back to the world. Maybe I feel like just buggering off back to Scoobytown and staying there. See out my days on the beach with the man."

"No good, mate. You know that."

"Do I? Why do I know that?"

"The girl, mate. The Sheila. You told me all about her."

Deek was appalled. "I never."

"Didn't think you'd remember. It was when we were all pissed up in Bangkok. Meg, right?"

"Aye. Meg. I must have been pissed. There's no way that's about to happen, Gerry. I blew it with Meg years ago."

"Stuff that, mate. It's never over till it's over with a Sheila. Believe me. They're funny old buggers, but a bloke always has a sniff. You should stop moping about like a typical bloody Pom and get stuck in."

"I'm not a Pom. I'm Scottish."

"Just as bad. Christ, you lot needed an Aussie to play *Braveheart* remember."

Sally Hunter was still very much in pinching-herself mode. When the First Minister had buzzed her to his office she had felt a vague trepidation. In the first few months of her time as Sports Minister she had hardly set the heather on fire. How could she have? The heather of the Scottish sports world was soaked after years of rain and all she had been given to work with was a box of soggy matches. What did the bloody man expect? There was no money and no facilities and a generation of young people hell-bent on filling their leisure time with alco Pops and deep-fried Mars Bars.

The news of Roland McMillan's match had left her completely speechless. However, it was when her boss gave her a frank description of his discussions with his counterpart in Westminster that her jaw had really dropped. She had always thought the First Minister rather a dreary, spineless type of man. It had come as a complete shock to hear that he had told his London-based colleague exactly where to get off. This was going to be a Scottish show and said he didn't give a damn. They had done the Commonwealth Games. They had done Madonna's wedding. So why not this? No way they needed any public school gits from London to hold their hands.

He told her that he had given the matter a deal of thought and he had decided that she was the person to head the whole thing up. He said that he was very impressed with her organisational abilities and that the time was right for her to take on something big. He stumbled about when he tried to be politically correct in pointing out that she was a fine-looking woman. She would be a hell of a sight easier on the eye than the majority of his cabinet, who were almost to a man walking images of the Scottish heart disease crisis.

The problem was that there was almost nothing that she could do. The whole event would remain a big secret until after the Masters in the middle of April. As far as the hotel was concerned, the McMillan had simply block-booked their facilities to stage an extravagant bash to celebrate the 95th birthday of their founder. When the time to make the announcement came, the Corporation had made it very clear that it would be handling all its own PR. Sally's job would be to oversee things. To make things happen if it were needed. To say all the right things to the press and to make sure that Scotland was painted in bright exciting colours. Up until then, all she could do was to do some initial work on security.

To that end, she had flown down to London to keep an appointment with Sir Richard Rathbone, one of the head men at MI5, who would be in overall charge alongside the gargantuan presidential security team that would fly in en masse from Washington. By the time she made it to the waiting room outside his office she was feeling pretty fractious. The journey from the front door had taken almost an hour, and at every step she had been treated like a girl en route to a dressing-down from the headmaster. As she sat under the fierce gaze of Rathbone's secretary she wondered if this treatment was usual, or if news of the big Edinburgh snub had filtered out. The intercom chirped into life and the secretary got to her feet with extreme reluctance.

"He will see you now."

A door opened and Sally was confronted by a dapper 60-year-old with little hair. He was all striped shirt, cuff links and Etonian charm.

"Ms Hunter. Sorry to have kept you waiting. It is 'Ms' I gather?"

"Yes. It is 'Ms'." The bastard. He had pronounced the word 'Ms' with a studied derision.

"So difficult to keep a normal family life in the swirl of modern political life. Very unfortunate. The price we pay I dare say. Please. Take a seat. Would you like coffee? Tea?"

The swine must have checked up on her. Her skin crawled with indignation.

"Actually, my divorce was finalised before I entered politics. It was the swirl of life as a headmistress and a husband who was led by his dick. As for refreshment, I am fine thank you very much."

"Yes. Quite." She enjoyed an inward smile as she watched his momentary disquiet. He carefully ran his carefully manicured hand over what was left of his silver hair. "Now. The McMillan event. I gather that you are the person in charge."

"Yes I am."

"Super. I must say I am thoroughly looking forward to the whole thing. Bit of a golfer myself. I've always had a fondness for Turnberry. We are all in your debt for whisky and golf. Do you play yourself?"

"Yes." So you didn't check up on that part you lizardy spook. He smiled the smile of a golf club committee member who firmly believed that the ladies should only be allowed access to the course between the hours of 5 a.m. and 9 a.m. on Thursdays. "I play at Wentworth myself. How about you?"

"Muirfield. You may know it. It's an Open Championship course." The unsaid bit was "unlike Wentworth". His smile tightened a notch.

"How terrific. What is your handicap? I still manage to hold down seven, although it is a struggle. I'm afraid our war on terror rather eats into my leisure time."

She met his cold smile. "I fully sympathise, Sir Richard. My game has suffered since becoming a Minister. I finished the summer playing off one. It's the first time I have slipped off scratch since I was fifteen."

This really tested the cool smile that his parent's had sunk so many thousands into, during his grooming days at school. "Really? Very impressive I must say."

"Thank your, Sir Richard."

"Well. Let's see. I think you know that we will be handling all the events security from here. Our office in Edinburgh will keep us in touch of course. Once we get to the week of the event, we will operate from Turnberry itself. I presume that you are happy to leave us to it, Ms Hunter. We have a lot of experience in this kind of thing."

"Of course. A weekly report will be quite sufficient. I'm sure that you will be able to spare someone from the Edinburgh office to come and see me."

"Of course. Always assuming that you consider it strictly necessary."

"I do."

"Even as a Sports Minister . . ."

"As the Minister in charge of the event, Sir Richard. I am where the buck stops, as our American friends are so fond of saying."

"Yes. So they are. Fine. Now there is one issue where we would request some local input. The Scottish golfer."

"The Scottish golfer?"

"Yes. Whoever that may be. This will be a very high-profile event Ms Hunter. Let us not forget that it involves our country and the United States who are of course very close allies in the war on terror. A close association will make it a possibility that your man could be a target. I'm afraid that it is the world we all must live in."

She hadn't remotely considered this. He was right of course. There would be plenty of people who would dearly love to disrupt the event. Assassinating one of the players would certainly do that. It seemed so horrible.

"Yes, of course. I see. How can I help?"

"Nothing too arduous. Once we know who it will be, I'm sure you will want to meet him. When you do, you can take one of my chaps along with you. You can introduce him as a babysitter. OK with you?"

"Of course."

He fiddled around with the pens on his desk for a few seconds. "So who do you think it will be?"

"Excuse me?"

"Your player. Who is looking favourite?"

"It's really rather hard to predict. Most of our better-known players are in something of a slump. If the decision were to be made today we would be represented by a young player from Dumfries called Archie Banks. He is quite unknown. This is his first year on the tour. He has managed a couple of good finishes in Asia, but I expect he will be overtaken soon enough."

"I should expect that you are rather hoping so."

"Should I?"

"Well of course. The last thing you want is some unknown freezing like a rabbit in the headlights. Underdogs are all well and good, but it would be nice if you stood a fighting chance."

She couldn't resist it. "I seem to recall that the underdogs did rather well at Bannockburn."

He couldn't believe the woman. Just who did she think she was, coming into his office with her attitude? Bloody Celts. They should never have demolished the wall. As if it wasn't bad enough having a damn Scot controlling the purse strings in Number 11. Expense accounts were always so much more generous under the Tories. The Scottish Minister for Sport of all things. He decided that he had had enough of her.

"Quite. I seem to recall that Bannockburn was several hundred years ago, Ms Hunter. Now. If you would excuse me, I have rather a lot to get on with. If you ask my secretary she will arrange for you meet the man that I have in mind to provide close protection. It has been an absolute pleasure."

He rose and took the route march around his desk to shake her hand. He had one of those miserable limp shakes and she gave him a firm grip honed from many hundreds of hours smacking balls up the practice fairway.

"The pleasure has been all mine, Sir Richard."

His eyes glittered with anger as her grip sent a shot of pain up his arm as her handshake agitated the arthritis in his fingers.

The hard-faced secretary summoned a meaty security guard who silently led her down a succession of corridors to a small meeting room. Inside, a middle-aged man dressed casually in jeans and a woollen jumper rose to his feet. His hair was getting a little thin and his face had a mildly haggard look about it. He was everything Sir Richard Rathbone wasn't, a fact that was confirmed when he greeted her in a low Mancunian voice.

"Morning Ma'am. I'm Steve Kenton."

"Good lord. Not Ma'am, please. Try Sally."

He smiled. "Of course. So you've met Sir Richard?"

This knocked the smile off her face. "Yes I have."

He laughed. "I know. He's the sort who thinks that his own shit doesn't smell. Not bad at his job though."

She was momentarily shocked by his frankness, then she joined in with his laughing.

"He made me feel like some kind of colonial subject."

"Oh well. All done now. I dare say you won't have to see him again. I'm much more laid back."

"What exactly do you do?"

"I do security, Sally."

"Yes I suppose you do."

"Fancy a brew? We could go to the canteen."

"That would be nice. Thank you."

She took a seat while he collected coffee. When he sat, he pulled out a packet of cigarettes and offered them with a raised eyebrow. "No thank you. I don't."

"I suppose it wouldn't look all that good. Minister of Sport and all that. Everyone smokes here. Well, all of us in the field do. Goes with the territory. So, do you reckon it's going to be Deek?"

"Deek?"

"Aye Deek. Archie Banks. That's his nickname I gather."

"Why on earth does he call himself Deek?"

"Search me."

She thought about the question. "It is hard to say really. Logically he shouldn't have a chance. But the time scale is pretty short. There are only a few European events left. You never know. Maybe he will squeak it. The poor man has no idea what he might be in for."

"He'll be in the spotlight sure enough. I hear you play a bit yourself."

"Yes I do."

"Muirfield isn't it?"

So this one had been more thorough. "It is."

"Always fancied a knock round there. Happen you'll squeeze me in for a round when I get up there?"

The cheeky sod. "Happen I might."

Anatoly Rykov entered the UK on the Eurostar from Brussels. Had he been asked, he would have shown impeccable identification confirming him to be Helmut Schiller from the southern German city of Fribourg. He wasn't asked. As a respectably dressed EU national with expensive luggage, he wasn't given a second glance. He spent a night at a discreet hotel in the West End and the next day he hired a mid-range Mercedes and headed north. He stopped off at a large retail park on the outskirts of Manchester and purchased a thousand pounds' worth of golf equipment from a JJB megastore before checking into a hotel close to Preston. Over the next two days he played rounds of golf at Royal Birkdale in Southport and Royal Lytham on the Fylde coast. He had enjoyed golf in the lazy years after Afghanistan and the weather was placid and kind. The great seaside courses were a far cry from the pale imitations that he had played in Austria. Much to his own surprise he enjoyed himself as much as he had in years. The brisk winter air cleared his head and the deserted courses made him feel as if he was the last man alive.

On the fourth day, he left his hotel after breakfast and drove north for three hours to the Westin Turnberry Resort on the Ayrshire coast. He was no stranger to the fine hotels of the world, but the majestic white walls of the Turnberry Hotel were still something special. The great building sat atop a low hill, giving it a huge view over the Irish Sea. The volcanic island of Ailsa Craig seemed to be almost within touching distance in the crystal-clear February air.

Beyond, the coast of Ulster was etched clear along the horizon. He checked into his room and spent several minutes at the window drinking in the majestic scene. The course was laid out below him. The fairways snaked in and out of the towering sand dunes to greens surrounded by nests of bunkers. Seagulls swooped on the wind and the white walls of the famous lighthouse shimmered in the early afternoon sunshine.

It all seemed so strange. It was such a placid, peaceful scene. A postcard. A tiny haven for the rich and famous to steal a few short days from their merry-go-round lives. It amazed him how far he had travelled in his bizarre life. Turnberry was a different planet from the polluted hellhole where he had grown up in the Soviet Union. It was a different universe from the grim Afghan hill-villages smoking in the wake of Russian napalm strikes. And yet here was the place were his life would finally arrive at its culmination. For now, Turnberry was merely a one-hotel resort, built around one of the world's greatest golf courses. Soon the name would mean more. Much, much more. It would become a Lockerbie, a Dallas, a Munich, a scene of a great crime. A name synonymous with an event that would change the shape of history.

These thoughts teased a smile across his slightly bland, Slavic features. He had no particular feelings about the President of the United States of America. He was just a man. They were all just men. History would peel away his veneer once he was dead and buried. It wasn't the man that counted, it was the institution. America believed itself impregnable. The greatest army the world had ever known. Their bristling array of hi-tech weaponry could be brought to bear to within ten square feet of any target on the planet. They were so utterly convinced that their hegemony on the planet would last for ever. Anatoly knew better. He had read his history. He had read of so many who had once thought the same. Alexander the Great, the Romans, Genghis Khan, Napoleon, Hitler and his thousand-year Reich, all cocooned in their military arrogance. The brash confidence of the corporate American Empire that had been carved out on the back of their victories in the Second World War would never survive the execution of their President.

He had no idea what would follow the Americans. Maybe the Chinese. Maybe nobody. Maybe the human race would finally succumb to the temptation to render their planet a radioactive wasteland. He didn't care much. All that mattered was that he would become the axis of history. Just one man. One man, one event, one killing. A big killing. Maybe even the biggest killing of them all. All he needed to do was to work out how to do it.

He checked his watch and decided that there was just about time for a quick lunch followed by a few holes of golf. Once again as he sat in the Ailsa Bar he was struck by the quality all around him. So many of the great hotels he had stayed in were overbearing, as if the staff were trained to judge whether or not the guest was really good enough to merit their attention. This was different. The staff here managed a friendly style that was rare in the have a nice day world of the twenty-first century.

Over a sandwich he browsed through a glossy book of photos of the golf course in all weathers and seasons. Several of these pictures acted as seeds for his thoughts. These seeds germinated later that afternoon. He had decided to simply play until the early darkness of winter made it impractical. By the time he tapped a putt into the hole on the eighth green, the western sky was a deep red and visibility was closing in fast. He tossed his putter into his bag and decided that enough was enough for the day. He pulled out a windproof jacket and pulled it on.

A track off the back of the green led him round a rocky outcrop to the ninth tee. He had studied several pictures of the tee, and in real life it didn't disappoint. The small oblong of green had been created improbably on top of a rock pillar that climbed up from the grey waters of the Irish Sea. It aimed the golfer over a shallow beach that was bounded by similar outcrops to a narrow fairway over 200 yards ahead. There was no sign of the distant green, a player had to aim at a marker post and hope for the best. Any kind of hook would be sucked away into the black rocks and tussocky grass where a variety of sea birds made their homes. The tide was out, but he could imagine how spectacular the scene would be when the waves were pounding into the small bay.

It was one of the iconic views of the game of golf. Photos and paintings of the ninth tee at Turnberry adorned the walls of golfing fanatics from Tokyo to Tampa. When Turnberry played host to the Open Championship, the cameras drank in the view and beamed it out to the watching world. On a wild, windy day, the image of the golfers bent against the wind was an image of men fighting the might of the universe. On a still, fine day, it was an image of a perfect harmony between man and nature. Different angles created different views. A shot from the front of the tee framed the silhouettes of the players against the sea and the island of Ailsa Craig. The view from the back of the tee revealed the magnitude of the task confronted by the golfer as he prepared to calm his nerves and try to send his ball clear of the rocks and water and sand. Viewed from the rocky clump at the side, the image took in the white walls of the lighthouse.

It was quite magnificent. Of course there was no way that the legendary patch of grass was available for an amateur like him to use on a normal day in February. His tee was some 50 yards further forward and considerably less dramatic. The tee of the picture books was cosseted and only opened up for the greatest of occasions. He smiled as he pictured the scene at the end of May when the players from Scotland and America would fight it out for a collection of pictures. They would finish off on the eighth green. The crowd would be guided to the right of the fairway. No doubt they would run and scamper to find a spot where they could watch the distant figures hit their drives across the beach. Only a few would take the small path past the clump of rocks to the tee itself. There would be the players and their caddies. There would be some kind of gallery. Maybe there would be a cameraman. And there would be the VIP spectators. The area for everyone to stand was not big. Only a few feet. Over the back of the tee the beach would be crawling with security men and patrol boats and surveillance helicopters who would ensure that nothing could come close from the sea.

The President was a golf fan. He would want to stand right behind the players as they took their drives. He would want to stand with the caddies and the officials. He would want the photographers to be able to zoom in and frame him in front of the sea and the lump of Ailsa Craig. And because he was the President of the most powerful country on earth, he would get what he wanted. It was a predictable certainty, and predictable certainty was what Anatoly Rykov was all about.

Without making it too obvious, he paced out some distances. From the rock feature it was 35 metres to the back of the tee. The rocks were cracked and broken by thousands of years of erosion. When the rock had been split and fissured by ancient geological mayhem the wind had blown in sand. He poked with his putter and found the sand to be soft and easily moved. When he turned, he confirmed that the main rock wall faced the back of the tee.

He closed his eyes and pictured the scene. The players and entourage making their way to the tee. A shot of the island. Maybe a shot of a distant helicopter. Zoom in some sea birds. Cut to the golfer drawing a club from his bag, no doubt with a frown of focused concentration. Shot of the President's face. Relaxed. Smiling. Probably in a golf cap. A man loving every minute of his Sunday afternoon away from the cares of office. Pan out to take in the view of the drive facing the player as he went through a familiar routine. Golf fans all over the world wondering how on earth they would do if they had to make the shot . . .

BOOM!

Probably a blank screen for a moment as the shrapnel and broken rock sliced the cameraman and his equipment into a thousand pieces. Cut to the view from the tower-mounted camera a few hundred yards away. An image of unimaginable carnage on the small tee. Bodies reduced to pieces of meat. A horrible realisation in the studio that this is a picture that simply could not be shown. Cut. Cut to the studio. The ashen face of the anchorman or woman. Lost for words. Unprepared. Trying to come to terms with what had just happened. How could they? They were sports, not news. And all over the world viewers would slowly realise that they had just witnessed one of history's turning points. Cut to the newsroom. Another flustered anchor trying to hold things together. TVs and radios being switched on all over the world. Work stopping in factories. Conversations stopping in bars. Countless millions of eyes fixed to the screens of TVs trying to understand. The moment of the blast would be played over and over and over and everybody would know that everyone on the tee was dead. But they wouldn't actually say it. They would await some kind of official confirmation that the unthinkable had become a reality live on TV. Slowly everyone would realise that this was their Kennedy moment. This was the moment they would remember for ever. I was driving to Leicester . . . I was filling in my VAT return . . . I was out tending to the chickens . . . a genuine "Where were you when it happened" moment . . .

Anatoly took in the scene one more time, and then turned to collect his bag and walk back to the hotel through the thickening darkness of the winter evening. He decided to order a pot of coffee before taking a swim and a sauna before dinner. The bar was very quiet and he was more or less on his own. He placed his order, picked up a newspaper and settled himself on a comfortable sofa. He cleared his thoughts. All was in place. No need to worry about it for the night. The front page as usual was all Iraq. Another car bomb. The usual amateur job. Three dead civilians. Behind the bland mask of his face he sneered at the caveman efforts of bombers. He was about to turn the page when a surprising pain shot up from his hand. He leapt up to his feet and quickly understood what had happened. A young waitress had approached silently over the thick carpet. Her shoe must have caught on something and she had tripped. Somehow she had managed to just about keep her feet but the coffee pot had toppled over on her tray and splashed onto his hand. The girl looked wretched and was pouring out apologies and offering him a crisp white napkin. He took it and smiled. It was fine. Really. Don't worry. These things happen. She calmed down after a minute or two and scuttled off for another pot of coffee.

Once she had served him, she tried not to think about it for the rest of the evening. Her name was Heidi and she was halfway through her second week as a trainee. Getting the job had been her ticket out of the small town in Latvia where she had grown up. A few years before, such an opportunity would have been unthinkable, but the world was changing. The governments of Latvia and Scotland had agreed to get cosy and set up work opportunities in each other's countries. Superb English had been her ticket to ride and she had escaped the crumbling tower block estate that had been built as part of one of Stalin's five-year plans. As she waited for the next order to be put together she began to feel a little confused. "The man by the window. You say he is from Germany, yes?"

The man in charge of the bar area was Australian. Heidi liked him. He was nice and had patiently help her to learn the ropes.

"Sure. He's Schiller. Helmut Schiller. I was chatting to him earlier when he was in at lunchtime. He's from Fribourg. Why do you ask?"

She shook her head and smiled. "No reason. I was just interesting."

"Interested."

"Sorry. Yes. Interested."

She collected the next tray. There had been a reason but she had decided not to share it. She couldn't understand why a man from Germany had sworn in Russian when hot coffee had splashed his hand. The next day Anatoly checked out of the hotel and drove south through the forest of Galloway. Al Quaida contacts in the UK had rented a small cottage a few miles north of New Galloway and forwarded the key on to him in Brussels. He had found the place on a large-scale Ordnance Survey map that he had bought in London. Using the same map, he located a small car park and picnic area three miles from the house and pulled on a pair of walking boots. He covered the ground to the cottage in less than an hour and took up a position in some hawthorn bushes 600 yards away. Binoculars and a guide to Scottish bird life provided a cover story had one been needed, but all was quiet. For four hours he covered every bush and tree of the countryside that surrounded the tiny white house until he was convinced that he was indeed the only watcher. By the time he arrived back at his car it was nearly dark and a cold thin rain was falling on a freshening breeze. His was the only car on the small car park, just as it had been when he arrived.

The house was well enough furnished and it was warm through even though the central heating was set low. He busied himself in setting a fire and unloading the few provisions that he had picked up from a supermarket. Dinner was a steak and new potatoes washed down with red wine in front of the TV. A weather presenter gave him the news that he had hoped for and explained how the low pressure over the Atlantic would bring two days of high winds and driving rain to the whole of Scotland.

Perfect.

The next morning he followed the simple directions that he had been given and easily found the deserted shed in a nearby wood. Once upon a time it had been used for lambing sheep but it had fallen derelict many years before. Ten minutes of digging revealed blue sacks of thick blue plastic. He took two trips to carry them back to the house and spent the rest of the morning and most of the afternoon in his preparations. When all was in order, he packed a large rucksack with what he needed and left the house before eight o'clock. The drive back to the coast was difficult as the high wind lashed at the windscreen. By the time he drew the Mercedes into a small picnic area that he had found the day before, it was half-past ten. He pulled on his expensive dark blue waterproofs and a thick woollen hat. Next came the walking boots, then he lifted the rucksack onto his back and adjusted the straps until it was comfortable. Finally he put on a pair of night vision goggles and waited a moment or two until his eyes became used to the green view of the world.

A narrow path took him to the beach three miles south of the golf course. The wind had risen to a near gale and a cold rain lashed at his cheeks. The hike was hard going but he made it to the ninth tee a little after midnight. Even though he knew that it was almost inconceivable that anybody would be around, he still sat and watched for half an hour. Nothing. There was no sound or movement beyond the crash of the waves and the howl of the gale. He completed the last few yards to the rocky outcrop and took off his rucksack. Strapped to the outside was a collapsible military entrenching tool that he snapped into readiness. It took twenty minutes of sand scooping until he was happy that he was deep enough into the rock cleft. He then reached into the rucksack and started taking out kilo bags filled with Semtex explosive. One by one he carefully packed them deep into the crack in the rocks. Once all twenty were in place he carefully removed and set the detonating device. He then covered his work with a plastic sheet. Next, he went down to the beach to start collecting pebbles in a strong Hessian bag. Over the next twenty minutes he refilled the bag three times, each time unloading the multi-shaped rocks and pebbles into the space in front of the explosives. On detonation, the force of the blast would smash the rocks into a supersonic hail of jagged shards which would be forced out and away from the rock face to fill the air for hundreds of cubic metres around. His final task was to scoop back the sand and discard the excess.

Before departing, he took a final hard look at the area where he had worked. By morning the torrential rain would have erased all signs of activity. Not that anyone would have noticed anyway. It was just another outcrop on a coastline that held endless thousands of such features. The next time he would see the spot would be from miles away from a hide in the hills that climbed up from the coast.

Then he would watch through a telescope as the party made its way onto the ninth tee.

When the time was right, he would make the call from his mobile phone.

BOOM!

Chapter 5
April

George Albright stood as still as a statue on the eighteenth tee with his arms folded and took in the monster hole that stretched out ahead of him. At thirteen under par he was two shots behind the tournament leader who was putting out on the sixteenth green. He cocked his ears to the applause from the green two holes back. It was of the "polite" variety. A par. Still two shots behind then. The course which was staging the last USPGA event before the Masters was quite new. This was its first major competition and the word was that if it came up to the mark it may well be given a Major at a later date. For four days it had passed the test with flying colours. After the two leaders, the third placed player was eight shots back at five under. Being recently built meant that the designer had been able to take into account the power of modern golf equipment. Several holes clearly reflected this, none more so than the eighteenth.

Course designers had found that no matter how long they built their par fives, the sheer power of the players almost invariably reduced them to birdie holes. Building holes of 750 yards was not an option as they would be completely out of sight for the amateur golfers who would always be the bread and butter for any club. The designer whose work George now assessed had been particularly clever. 180 yards from the tee where he stood, a lake filled the whole width of the hole which extended for nearly a 120 yards. Beyond was a stretch of fairway which ran for 100 yards up to a second lake that stretched all the way to the edge of the green. The hole measured 587 yards. Any golfer attempting to reach the green in two faced two

153

monumental shots over the water. The alternative was to tee off with a six iron, carry the first lake with another six iron and then make the green with a testing four or five iron.

Only three players all week had taken the hole on, and all three had perished in the water. George had used irons in each of the first three rounds and had made three safe fives. Now he had to decide whether he should go for broke. The good news was that the third placed player was so far behind. He could afford a seven or an eight and still be guaranteed a huge cheque for second place. He nodded quietly to himself as he worked out the odds.

All along the fairway the crowds were packing themselves tightly as they converged from all corners of the course. Behind the tee was a large grandstand which housed a rather disappointed group of fans who had suffered a somewhat unexciting day of watching their heroes playing careful iron shots. They cheered at the sight of George pulling the cover of his trademark big-headed driver. The cheers were infectious and they soon spread down the fairways to the stands around the green. George was going for it. Taking it on.

A hush slowly fell over the waiting thousands as he took his customary two practice swings before carefully addressing the ball. A carry of almost 300 yards was always going to be a tough task. This was even tougher as a light wind was blowing into his face. He knew that nothing less than everything he had would do. He threw himself into the drive and made good connection. The cameras zoomed in on his tanned face as he squinted anxiously after his ball. It landed five yards clear of the lake and released an explosion of cheering all around. His face gave a small smile and he lightly touched his cap. The job was only half done. The next shot was almost as long.

He strode down the fairway to great encouragement. When he arrived at the ball, the second shot looked even worse than he had anticipated. His caddie marched up to a mark and returned to inform him that he still had 281 yards left to carry the second lake. From there it was just ten feet to the pin which was helpfully placed in a nightmare position on the front right of the green. This time there was no reason to give the matter much thought. He had made up his mind on the tee. No point in changing it now. Even so, more cheers greeted his selection of a three wood. He was halfway through his preparations when his eye was caught by a disturbance in the crowd. Five figures were running at him. For a moment he wondered whether he was actually awake. They were each wearing a Spiderman-style whole body suit. However, their suits were not the red and blue of the cartoon hero. Their suits were black and painted over with the white bones of skeletons. They were standard fare at $50 or so in stores specialising in Halloween attire; a rather unusual sight at the business of a major golf tournament.

For a moment the stewards were as stunned at the weird invasion as George. The incursion gained a head start of 30 yards or so before several stewards snapped out of their shock and took up the chase. It only took a few seconds for the ghoulish figures to reach George. For a second his hand tightened on the grip of his three wood. Were they about to attack him? No. Instead they had banners which they held high as they surrounded him.

> *"ALBRIGHT SUPPORTS THE KILLING!"*
> *"STOP THE ILLEGAL WAR"*
> *"AMERICA'S SHAME!"*

The fact that this was an anti-war demonstration dawned on him at about the same moment as the stewards completed their charge. Four of the demonstrators were taken into firm arm locks and moved away with two stewards to each of them. However, the fifth was treated somewhat less gently. A particularly burly steward in a yellow bib threw himself into the back of the much smaller protester like an NFL line backer. George heard an unmistakably female yelp of pain as they both hit the ground hard. With a satisfied grin, the steward turned and was about to land a kick when George pulled him back.

"Hey man, cool it. It's just a woman."

"Screw that . . ." He tried to release himself from George's grip but he had completely underestimated the strength of the tall golfer who dragged him back and pushed him hard in the chest.

"I said cool it."

The realisation that he had just been manhandled on live TV by one of the world's most iconic sportsmen suddenly dawned on the overenthusiastic steward.

"Hey, I was only . . ."

"Yeah. Yeah. Save it. You were about to kick a woman." George gently lifted the winded figure to her feet.

"Are you OK, Ma'am?"

George could tell that tears were close in the small voice. "Yes. Thank you. I'll be fine."

Two different stewards now took a gentle hold and started to lead her away. She turned her head back to where George stood.

"Thank you Mr Albright."

"That's OK Ma'am. All part of the service."

It took nearly ten minutes for the excitement to die down and the players up in front to hole out their putts. George prowled the fairway and tried to pull his concentration back into line. The adrenalin was surging. He knew that this needed to be harnessed. Used well, it would give him the power to clear the lake. Used badly, it would turn his approach shot into an ugly hook.

Silence settled over the Vermont countryside as George once again ran though his preparations. The silence was blown into a million pieces when his ball thumped into the green and settled twenty feet from the hole. Another crescendo of noise rolled back down the fairway as his putt rolled in for the first-ever eagle on the great par five. It was all too much for the tournament leader who quit out of his four iron approach a few minutes later to take a bogey six on the final hole and finish at fourteen under par. George won by a shot.

The Press Conference was unlike any he had given before. His career had ensured that he was an experienced hand with the press. He always kept it light. He cracked a joke or two which were duly laughed at. He was always polite about the course and his opponents and modest about his own efforts. He was easygoing George. Laid-back George. But today was different. The scrum of journalists were all baying different questions. Some from the golf magazines were keeping to the norm. ". . . does this result make you confident about The Masters next week, George?"

"Of course it does. Winning can be a habit, and when did I ever have any bad habits?"

". . . so you think you'll win?"

"You know. Golf is really a pretty simple game. If I play better than the other guys, then sure, I'll win. If they play better than me, then someone else will win. I guess having won the thing twice already at least means that I know that I have it in me."

". . . what did you say to the steward George?"

"I told him that if he didn't adjust his grip he would go way out to the right."

". . . surely he was right in dealing with the threat?"

"You think so? The way my daddy brought me up was that hitting women was a bad thing. Maybe you disagree."

"Surely this kind of dangerous situation needs firm handling?"

"It wasn't a dangerous situation. It was a protest. A peaceful protest."

"Are you saying that you approve, George? Surely you don't condone this kind of behaviour in America?"

To his own surprise he felt the temper rising up the back of his neck. He fixed the journalist with a hard stare. "'This kind of behaviour' you say. What exactly do you mean by that? Last time I looked, I thought this was a free country. In fact I know it's a free country. That is why I'm so proud of it. You all know that. Isn't this the kind of behaviour that Doctor King encouraged? Isn't this the kind of behaviour that stopped segregated schools and buses? If you want to look for un-American behaviour I suggest you look at the guy who was beating up a woman."

The collective eyes of the journalists almost popped out as they scribbled furiously.

"You are just back from Iraq, George? Are you supporting the anti-war movement? Are you against the war, George?"

The swine. He kicked himself for losing his cool. He knew that he had just opened Pandora's box. No point hiding now.

"Don't misunderstand me here. I have no position on the war. I leave that to the politicians. I went out to Iraq to see the soldiers. Maybe some of you guys should try it before you write your stories. We have over 100,000 of our young people out there. It wasn't their idea to go. In fact nobody asked them. They joined up mainly because they come from places where it is almost impossible to get a job. They chose the military over welfare. Now they find themselves in a pretty tough place. Every day they have to deal with the fear of bombs and rockets. And every day it seems like the people at home are turning against them. Let's not forget that we've seen it all before. Revisit your history, gentlemen, before you write your stories. Check out the old newsreels of the crowds spitting at the guys when they came home from Vietnam. I met a lot of decent young American people out there. All I want to point out is that this thing isn't their fault. They have been sent there and I just hope that the American people don't turn against them . . ."

"George . . ."

"No. That's it guys. See you all in Augusta." He made a fast exit and darted into the locker room where a couple of his fellow pros looked at him with quizzical expressions. One tossed over a can of beer. "Going for your shots today, George?"

He smiled. "Looks that way."

The beer felt pretty good. In fact he felt pretty good. He hadn't felt as good in years.

In Washington the President snapped off the TV angrily and threw himself down into an armchair.

"Hell, Larry, what is George trying to do to me?"

Weinberg braced himself for another protracted bout of paranoia. In truth he was beginning to get a little tired of it. What did the man expect? Being President of the United States was never going to be a bed of roses. Sure, the media were having a go. When did the media not have a go? His ulcer was on top form, and keeping a hold of his famed temper was proving to be far from easy.

"To be honest, chief, I don't think he's having a go at you at all."

"Aaw come on Larry. Just listen to him. He's sounding like some kind of a bleeding-heart liberal. All this talk about Martin Luther King and those poor small town boys and galls being sent into harm's way."

"Maybe it is worth remembering that we now have a national holiday in the name of Dr King. It is hardly sedition to remember the things he believed in."

The President fixed him with a look of petulant anger. "Don't you start Larry. Not you of all people."

"If I don't tell you how it is, Mr President, then nobody else is about to, certainly not those crackpot Neo-Cons who got us all into this unholy mess in the first place."

"Careful, Larry."

"Yeah, careful, Larry. How long we been on this road together? Twenty years? If twenty years don't get me a ticket to speak my mind then I don't know what does. Maybe you should consider listening to George rather than having a fit. If you want my opinion, he sounds pretty like the way I think an American should sound. Think about it. I got things to do."

He stomped out, leaving his boss with an unusually stupefied expression on his face. Back in his office, Larry took an angry swig at his medication bottle and fumed for a while. After a few minutes the medicine started to work and he calmed down a little. He replayed the Albright interview in his mind and couldn't help but smile. The things that George had said had needed saying for some months. Why did politicians have such a problem holding their hands up and admitting that things weren't so hunky-dory after all? When the hell would they get the message that the public actually quite liked that kind of thing? George had it spot on. Just because it was a mess they shouldn't forget the poor devils who were left with the job of trying to tidy it up. At least he had managed to toss a bucket of iced water in the faces of the Neo-Conservative intellectual pricks who were forever strutting their stuff in the corridors of the White House. Larry couldn't abide them and was in a permanently bad mood about the fact that he seemed unable to get the boss to listen to sense.

His instincts told him that George's impromptu speech would play pretty damn well in small-town America. Maybe the man could become an unlikely ally in Larry's personal crusade against the Neo-Cons. Why not? Stranger things had happened. The American people loved their sports heroes, especially when they had a look of a golfing John Wayne. Maybe George Albright might just help change the boss's mind. The question was, how could Larry Weinberg help? The McMillan thing was just a couple of months away. Should George Albright get the job of representing America, his profile would get even higher. Would he continue to use his profile to speak his mind? Probably. So what could Larry do?

He clicked onto the internet and trawled around until he found a list of the top current money earners on the US PGA Tour. George's spectacular win had lifted him up to tenth place. He scribbled a few sums and confirmed the fact that if George won the Masters he would more than probably move up to number one. Was there anything he could do to make that happen? Not a thing. It was in the lap of the gods. All he could do was to hope and assume that Albright would come through.

So what then? If George made it, who would he play? He hit a few more keys and found similar statistics for the European Tour. The first name with the letters SCO after his name was Archie Banks who was down at number fifteen. He surfed some more and discovered that Banks had just finished tenth in the Madeira Open and earned himself a few dollars. More surfing. Articles about Banks coming fourth in Bangkok. A colourful character, it appeared. A chain-smoker. A wisecracker. Photos of him with his weird scrumpled caddie called Troll. Troll! Who had ever heard of a caddie called Troll? The reports were light-hearted and made it clear that the reporters liked this guy. He was a character. A maverick. A breath of fresh air in the midst of the bland world of professional golf.

Weinberg drummed his fingers on his desk. Assuming George made it, this guy could be a problem. It didn't seem as if there would be a snowball's chance in hell of him winning. No way. He was just enjoying a lucky streak which would soon fizzle out and he would return to obscurity. The problem was that Larry knew the media. He knew the media both sides of the pond and they were going to lap this guy up. He was just such a perfect underdog, especially when put up against the might of George. Not good. Not good at all if Larry was to help give George the platform he wanted him to have.

So what to do about it? Where was the key? He carried on drumming his fingers and stared out of the window onto a clear spring day. It only took a few minutes for him to realise that the answer to the question was just the same as it always was. Golfer, politician, what difference? None. They were just guys whom the media wanted a bite out of. This guy would have his cupboard full of skeletons just the same as all of them. Probably more. It never took long for the media to turn a loveable maverick into an anti-social asshole. Sometimes they needed a little guidance, and that was where Larry Weinberg came in.

He was smiling as he flicked through his index and picked out a card. He dialled up the number.

"Yeah?"

"Hi Sam. Larry Weinberg here."

Samantha Latimer's voice dripped with the sultry air of her native Mississippi. "Why Larry, you darlin' man. I haven't heard from you in about a million years."

"I'm sure that cold heart of yours must have broken in two."

"Now, Larry. What kind of a thing is that to say to a lady friend? I always considered you a gentleman."

He chuckled. "Don't be silly. Are you in town?"

"I'm always in town, Larry. You know that. Always in town and waiting at the end of the phone like a lovesick teenager. How can I help you, baby?"

"Let's meet." He checked his watch. "Why not an hour from now? The usual place?"

"Why sure, Larry. I'm all of a tingle just thinking about it."

Samantha Latimer was 32 years old, but a fortune spent in a variety of beauty salons knocked at least six years off the truth. She was decked out in a trademark designer suit and daintily smoking when he entered the wine bar. She had come far since they had first met. It had been ten years earlier that she had marched into the Senatorial Campaign offices in New Orleans and volunteered her services. It had been pure chance that Larry had been there. There was something about her that struck him the instant that he laid eyes on her. That morning she had been fairly shoddily dressed in a sweatshirt and jeans, but for him she absolutely dripped class. More than that, he could sense the ambition in her.

He took her onto his personal team and started grooming. Over the next six years she became the consummate professional. She could sweet-talk a fat contribution from the hardest-nosed businessman. She could dissuade even the most idealistic journalist from printing a damaging story. She could tease information out of the tightest of lips. She flirted and charmed her way to the top and Larry had helped her every step of the way. When she had decided to make her talents available on a freelance basis, he hadn't objected. It was no more than he had expected. He had never been in any doubt that her ambition would carry her clear of his team. They still worked together. She would always drop everything when he needed something handling. It was perfect as far as he was concerned. There were often things that were better handled by someone outside of the White House tent.

He ordered more coffee and joined her in the corner booth that had always provided a haven from prying eyes. They had known each other for long enough to dispense with the small talk.

"So, honey. You got a job for me?"

Her smile was as warm as the Mississippi Delta but her eyes were pure Alaska.

"Of course." He bounced her through the McMillan story as they stirred their coffees. ". . . so the odds are that the Scots will be represented by this Archie Banks guy. I don't really want him to hold onto this loveable rogue image. It will detract from George. He needs taking down a peg or two. Some dirt needs dishing. Capishe?"

She nodded slowly. "Of course I do. No problem. You say this match will be announced after the Masters?"

"That's correct."

"So right now this dear little Scotsman has no idea that he is about to enter the big spotlight?"

"Nope. Right now he's just another loser on a streak."

"How quaint. Now sugar, it seems to me that your motivation here is to ensure that George Albright gets all the attention that you feel that he deserves. Am I right honey?"

"You're right."

"So if Georgy doesn't win the Masters, you'll not have any need for my services after all?"

"Correct."

"But you'll still pay?"

"Of course. I just won't need the dirt, that's all."

She smiled at the prospect of another fat cheque to add to her pile. "May I ask why you are so enthusiastic about this big hunk of a golfer?"

"Nope."

She lit up and blew a ring. "Maybe you rather liked that little speech he made this afternoon? Maybe you liked the way that he stuck a manly finger up at those nasty, nasty Neo-Conservatives that you just adore so much, baby?"

"And maybe you should just stick to the task in hand and leave the politics to me."

"Of course, sugar. Don't I always?"

Deek, Troll and Banjo returned to a Dumfries of grey skies and driving rain. After the bouncing colours of Asia and the sun-kissed shores of Madeira, the town looked terrible. The pavements were home only to the occasional pedestrian with their heads bowed into the downpour. The usual cluster of miscreants were smoking furiously outside the courtroom. The boarded-up shops seemed more boarded somehow. They got the cabdriver who had collected them from the airport to run them straight out to the caravan.

It did nothing to lift their spirits. Banjo had departed in haste and the evidence of his last takeaway meal had turned into silver packaged penicillin. The dampness of a wet early spring had crawled into every rusty corner.

"Christ. Welcome home boys." Deek's voice was flat. Suddenly the white sands of Scoobytown seemed to be from another lifetime. On the flight back from Madeira he had made any number of resolutions. At last he had the chance to start to turn things around. For the first time in years his financial situation wasn't a disaster area. He was on the tour. He had some resources and he felt fitter than at any time he could remember. Gerry's words of encouragement regarding the Meg situation had stayed with him. Maybe it wasn't too late after all. Maybe there still might be a flicker of a chance. As he surveyed the hellish mess all around him he determined that he would make a start on a new life the very next day. Just a few hours kip and he would knuckle down. It had been a long journey and they were all weary. Tomorrow would be soon enough. No need to break his neck. He idly picked up a bottle of whisky and took a long bracing pull. "Boys, we have an option. Tidy up or stick on the heater and bugger off to the pub."

It was never about to become a very serious debate. They buggered off to the pub where word of their return soon spread through the grey homes of Sunnybank estate. By seven o'clock the place was packed as the residents turned out in force to welcome home the returning heroes whose exploits had been beamed across the world into the satellite dishes of the estate. It was a night that went on deep into the next morning and the Sunnybank Three did not wake until the following afternoon. It took Deek a while to clear his head and get his bearings. He had woken to a feeling of utter darkness and claustrophobia and his panic had only receded when he had come to terms with the fact that he was in a sleeping bag on Troll's mum's living-room floor. The two others were still cocooned in their sleeping bags like caterpillar versions of Laurel and Hardy.

Deek heaved himself up into a sitting position and the crashing in his head felt as if it would fire his eyes right out of their sockets.

Another blazing hangover on another grey wet Scottish day. Every time it seemed a little bleaker. Every time it took another half slug from the bottle to get himself back up to the surface of life. An overwhelming sense of misery washed through him. He had to get a grip. Absolutely had to.

He unzipped the bag and pulled on his trousers. Mrs Troll was smoking her way through the *Daily Record* while a transistor radio blared out a stomach-churning melody from some anorexic starlet who sounded like a kitten having its teeth pulled. The tinny sound invaded his throbbing head and made him wince.

"Mind if I switch that down a tad Mrs Simpson?"

"Aye. It's all shite anyway. Want a cup of tea?"

"Please."

He slumped down at the formica table and picked up the paper. The kettle bubbled and the tea was produced.

"Bit of a head the day have you Deek?"

He nodded and sipped at the steaming mug. They sat for a while in an easy silence. The tea was helping, but not nearly enough.

"You would'nae have a wee dram would you Mrs Simpson?" He felt a terrible shame at asking the question.

She gave him a long, level look then lifted herself to her feet and rummaged in a cupboard. A bottle of whisky was produced and plonked down unceremoniously with a tumbler. He poured three fingers' worth and drained. He closed his eyes as the fiery liquid shot down and started to work.

"This is nae good Deek love. You ken that?"

"Aye. I ken. Christ knows I ken."

He poured another and it followed the first down.

"So what are you going to do about it? Carry on like this and you'll no see 40."

"Sometimes I feel like I don't want to, Mrs Simpson. There was this place where we stayed in Thailand. Scoobytown. The guy there said he could help me. Maybe I'll go back there. I'm going to try. Seriously . . ."

Talking was an effort. Everything was an effort. "Mind if I use the phone?"

"No, lLove. Help yourself."

He got lucky and was put through to Meg straight away. "Hi Meg, it's me. We're back."

"Oh hello Deek." A mild coldness to the voice.

"I thought I would come in. For an appointment like. I've got a cheque from the Madeira Open. We could discuss the account and . . . well, you ken . . .."

"I'm free at four o'clock. Will that do?"

"Aye. Nae bother."

He took a shower and picked up some new clothes which he put on in a pub toilet in the town. Four vodkas more or less put him back to normal, not that he had much clue about what normal was any more. He was ushered into Meg's office at the appointed hour and passed over the cheque for 21,000 euros. Meg busily tapped away at her calculator as she made the currency conversion and added the amount to the account total. When she was finished she sat back and smiled.

"Well. Quite a transformation. You are over 80,000 pounds in credit. I can hardly believe it. Are there any more expenses?"

"Aye. I need to pay Troll his twenty percent for the three tournaments. And I need to pay Banjo for Madeira."

"Banjo?"

Deek lowered his eyes. He knew this wasn't going to play well. "Aye. He lost his job when he came out to Malaysia. So we've decided that he will be my manager."

"Manager?"

"Aye. You ken. Travel arrangements and sponsorships and the like. There's a lot, Meg."

"I see. And are these commissions payable before or after expenses?"

"Before."

More tapping this time accompanied by a frown. "Well, that knocks a hole in things but you will still be over 50,000 pounds in the black. What are your plans?"

"I don't know really. More competitions I suppose."

"The caravan?"

"What about the caravan?"

"Well, I had rather presumed that you would be considering a house. You have the wherewithal for a good deposit. I was going to advise on our mortgage products."

Deek scratched at his head. "Oh. Right. I had'nae really thought about it. The caravan's OK . . ."

She carefully put her pen down and fixed him with a clear-eyed stare which he couldn't meet.

"You can't go on like this Deek. Can't you see that? How much have you had today?"

"What do you mean?"

"You know exactly what I mean."

He fiddled with his fingers and looked down. "I dunno. Four or five I suppose . . . or six or seven or eight.

Suddenly she was angry. Really angry. Her pale cheeks glowed scarlet and he knew he was in trouble. Big trouble. "Deek. Wake up. Smell the air. You're an alcoholic and every day it gets worse. You are a 32-year-old man living in a clapped-out caravan. Every penny that comes your way goes to the pub or the bookies . . ."

He held out his hands to try and stem the flow. "But Meg, Meg, Meg . . . what about the tour? The prize money? The account?"

It was no good. She was well past the point of no return. "And what change is that Deek? Drinking in different countries? Pissed in exotic locations? I can see exactly where this is all headed. A few months of hot streak and then back to your wretched caravan and scamming a few lousy quid off Asian tourists down at Southerness. Everything that you might win will just get thrown away as usual on booze and gambling and women."

"Women!!!!"

"Oh yes Deek, women. Do you think I'm blind? Do you think I don't watch the TV? Well?" She was on her feet now, hands gripping the side of her desk, leaning forward at him.

"I dunnae know what the hell you're talking about Meg . . ."

"Oh come on. Spare me. I saw that jumped-up, big-haired London tart."

"What big-haired tart?"

"Interview? *Sky TV*? Bangkok? Ring any bells in that drink-pickled head of yours?"

He was open-mouthed. "Meg. For Christ's sake. It was an interview. That was it."

"And you seriously expect me to believe that? Please Deek. Enough. I've completely had enough. I've had my interview and I got the job. Thanks for asking by the way."

"I was going to Meg, you just never gave me the chance . . ."

"Yes. Well. I have got it and that is all that matters. I start in June so I suggest you consider opening up an account somewhere else in town. You'll find no problems. Right now you're a man of substance. So. I think that is all. I have things to be doing. If there is nothing else?"

She sat down and stared defiantly with eyes that shone with tears. "But Meg . . ."

"No. Nothing else? Fine. Goodbye Deek."

She bent her head to her papers and started writing, hiding the tears that she didn't want him to see. He slowly got to his feet. He dredged about for something to say but came up blank. "Meg . . ."

"I said goodbye Deek."

He stood for a moment before shrugging and leaving the office. As soon as the door clicked closed, Meg reached for the box of tissues in her desk drawer.

Outside, another day of relentless rain had once again emptied the streets and swelled the river. He trudged along in a daze. What had happened? He had hoped that his successes might make things different. Instead they were worse. Everything was worse. Everything was suddenly as bad as it had ever been. He tried to tell himself that she was just having a bad day and that she would get over it. He tried but failed. She had been so angry. So full of contempt. And why not? A look in the mirror would tell him all he needed to know. 32 years old and he looked a decade older. A wreck of a caravan and a half a bottle of spirits a day problem that was rising fast. So she had been wrong about the women, but the rest had been close enough to the mark.

He met the others in a pub but said that he wasn't staying. He asked if they minded staying at Troll's mum's house for another night. He told them that he needed a bit of time to himself. His oldest friends saw the look of burning pain in his eyes and knew that things had gone badly with Meg. Instead of taking his usual cab, he decided to walk. With a half bottle for company he walked out into the countryside. The seven miles took him two-and-a-half hours and even though the rain at last stopped a little after seven, he was still soaked to the skin. Not that he cared.

When he at last turned the final corner on the overgrown track to the caravan, he was surprised to see a small Vauxhall parked up on the grass verge. Who the hell? Maybe some shooting pal of Roger

Swann's. It seemed unlikely. Not many of Roger's mates were accustomed to using a Vauxhall Corsa to take them to a shoot. It seemed even less likely when the driver's door opened and a young woman in her early twenties jumped out. She wore jeans and a sweatshirt and white shoes. She had dizzy blond hair and a smile full of gleaming white teeth as wide as the South China Sea.

"Hi there!" A buoyant all-American apple pie and cream voice. What the hell was this? *Alice in Wonderland* again.

"All right. You lost love?"

"I surely hope not. Are you Archie Banks?"

The husky deep-South voice seemed to reach into his drenched skull and gently massage his tormented brain. "Aye."

"Thank the Lord. I was just getting to thinking I was in the wrong place. Roger seemed so good with the directions but this is such a cute, dinky little track . . ."

Cute, dinky little track? Definitely back in *Alice in Wonderland*. Maybe he was about to wake up and find himself back in Scoobytown. "I've never thought about it that way. Just a track. Can I help you?"

"I hope so. Is this your caravan?"

"Well it's Roger's really, but I use it."

"I think you better get inside baby. You're wet to the bones. Why don't we go inside and you can change. Then I can tell you all about why I'm here."

"Well . . ."

"Honey. I don't bite. I promise."

She didn't look as if she would bite. "Aye, well I suppose so."

Only when he got to the door did he remember the appalling state of the caravan. He stopped and tried to think of a way out.

"Actually. . . maybe we could go and talk in a pub of something . . . you see . . . it's not too tidy in there ken . . ."

She knew only too well what the state of the interior of the caravan was. She had opened the unlocked door and photographed it all earlier. "Oh don't be so silly. You can't go anywhere in those clothes, honey. I'm a student. Untidiness is where I come from. Now you don't be so silly . . ."

She brushed by him and opened the door. A blast of heat swept out and he remembered how they had left the heating on full. The damp was well away but the smell was ferocious. Christ. The girl however seemed quite undeterred.

"You change honey and I'll straighten things up some. You got a bin bag?"

He used the back room to get out of the wet new clothes that had failed so miserably with Meg. The woman kept up a running commentary accompanied by the sound of bottles, cans and food cartons being swept into the bin liner. "I better tell you who I am. You'll be wondering. Of course you will. Who the hell is this weird American gal hanging out in your garden? Well sugar, my name is Tiffany McNeal and I'm from a small town in Mississippi called Rayton which you'll never have heard of. Don't worry about that, honey. Nobody has ever heard of Rayton. Just a bitsy one-horse kind of a place. Well, my great, great-grandaddy left Scotland in 1880 and took up in Rayton. I'm studying journalism at college and I have to do a project you see. A year. I decided to come and find my roots. I want to go into sports reporting. I just love sports and most of all I just love golf. You getting all this, sugar?"

"Aye. I think so." He emerged from the back room rubbing his hair with a rather grimy towel.

"That's good. Real good." She eyed the spirits bottles that cluttered up the shelf over the TV. "Hey Archie. Could a girl get a drink?"

"You best call me Deek. Everyone does. What's your poison?"

"Whatever you're having, sugar."

He cleaned out two glasses with a piece of newspaper and poured whisky. "Water in it? I have'nae got anything else."

"Now what would my great, great-grandaddy say if I drowned it?" She took the glass and raised it. "Cheers."

"Aye. Cheers." The treble measure slipped down the slender tanned neck in one practised gulp. "Mmmm. That's better."

"Another?"

Glinting eyes. "Well why not. 'When in Rome . . .' as my daddy always says."

He cleared space on the bunk seats and they sat. She told him all about it. She had to do a project that meant creating a magazine-style piece. Her idea was all about killing as many birds as she could with as few stones as possible. She decided on the state of professional golf in Scotland. After all, Scotland was the home of the game. She had pitched the idea to a monthly rag called *The Southern Golfer* based in Memphis. Her uncle was the editor and he said that he would run it. Well, only if it was good enough. So she had caught a plane and headed back to her roots. She had checked out the internet and here she was. He was her first interview.

"So why me?"

"Because you're the number one, sugar."

This made him nearly spit his drink out with laughter. "Bloody hell love, you must have found some nutty site on the internet. I'm not number one. I'm not number 51. You need to try and speak with Monty or Laurie or Andy Coltart. I'm nothing."

She met this with a sweet knowing smile. "I'm talking about this year, sugar. January onwards. It's you. Believe me. You are right this very minute the number one golfer in the home of golf. Ain't that just something?"

He smiled. "Not really. It's just statistics."

"Oh come on Deek. Don't go all British and modest on me. What you have done this season is brilliant. What about that last round in Thailand?"

He couldn't help but laugh at this. He carelessly refilled his glass and raised an eyebrow that was met by an eager nod. Jeez, this lass could put her scotch back. "Look Tiffany, you seem a nice enough lass. I only feel it's fair to make sure you're not wasting your time. That round in Thailand wasn't what it seemed."

Her eyes widened at this. "Why not, Deek?"

"This is just the two of us chatting, yeah? This is'nae for your paper, OK?"

"Of course not. I'm not that kind of reporter. I'm not any kind of reporter yet. I'll only write what you want me to write honey. That's a promise. Guides honour. You do believe that?"

How could he not believe the big white teeth of her small-town girl smile. "Aye. Course I do." He lit up a thoughtful cigarette. "I was paired with a Korean lad for the last round. Jimmy. Jimmy Hup Lee. Well, you ken how the Asians love a bet? I had a word on the first tee and it all got a bit silly. Longest drive. Nearest the pin. Christ, we'd have got to betting on how many parrots there were in the trees if we'd played much longer. We both completely forgot what we were supposed to be doing and went for everything like complete nutters. It was just sheer luck that it all came off and I finished fourth."

Her eyes were sparkling. "Wow Deek. I love that. You were betting all the way round? And is it true that you were having a dram as well?"

"Aye. I'm afraid so."

She giggled. "You shouldn't be. Most players today are just so boring." She pulled a comical face. "Uggh. Boring. Boring. Boring. I like my sportsmen to have a bit of an edge you know."

"Aye it seems that way. You like a drink yourself?"

"Sure. Why not? Nothing ever happens in Rayton, honey. It's all church and talking about how the corn crop is looking. Not much for a good-time gal like me. So I take a drink. I don't see a problem with that."

Her voice had risen at the end of the sentence and her eyes suddenly had an angry glitter to them. Ooops. He had blundered onto a very sore point. "Hey. No need to get angry love. You're among friends here. I understand. Believe me, I understand."

Her shoulders slumped and the anger drained away. The glitter turned to tears and she rummaged in her denim shoulder bag for a tissue.

"Sorry. This is pathetic. Damn. Damn . . ."

"Look. Seriously. It's OK. Dunnae worry about it. I know. OK?"

She was looking down now and her voice had lost about ten years. Just a girl now. A lost girl. "I wonder if you do. I don't know how it happened. It just did. I need a drink to get out of bed, Deek. I need a drink to get dressed. I can't face the world without a drink. All day, every day. Vodka usually. It doesn't smell none you see. I can't believe it. My Daddy caught me and he went crazy. I just screamed at him and ran away. I'm behind in my studies. I just don't know what to do next."

He wondered whether he should put an arm around her but decided against. Instead he talked. He tried to ease her pain by describing his own. He tried to help her by telling her that she wasn't alone. He tried to explain that drunks weren't bad people, just people with a problem. He explained how he could no longer even hold a golf club properly without tanking himself up. It was all OK when he was just thrashing around in challenge games, but now it was getting more serious. One or two of the papers had begun to suspect. They were watching him out on the course. He was having to be more careful, but if he didn't keep taking a nip every other hole or so, he just couldn't get round the course.

Tiffany calmed herself down and they talked their way through another full bottle and deep into the small hours of the night. In the end they were both just about comatose and more or less fell back onto their respective bunks. Tiffany McLean, AKA Samantha Latimer, stopped registering anything remotely sensible before midnight. She was smashed beyond all repair. Not that she cared a damn. In truth she had always liked a drink and she found Deek to be one of her more entertaining marks. Memory was irrelevant. She knew full well that the night would have dissolved into an almighty blur by the time the morning came around. It didn't matter a damn. It didn't matter because the tape recorder in her bag was as sober as a judge.

Meg had no exotic American student to unburden her troubles onto that evening. She had escaped the bank as soon as she was able and had punished herself in the gym. Once home, she had cooked a meal which she had barely picked at before finishing off the evening morosely clicking through the channels on the TV. There had been nothing on which had taken her mind off the afternoon. Off Deek. Off the dreadful way that she had behaved to him. What the hell had got into her? It had been over ten years since they had split up. During that time she had been in any number of proper relationships, some of which had lasted for several months. He had never once said a word about any of them, at least not verbally. She had never been left under any illusions as to how he felt by the burning misery in his eyes. She was painfully aware of the fact that he had never even begun to fall out of love with her. Maybe she had taken it for granted. Maybe his desperation had become important to her. Was that why she had behaved so appallingly? Was she threatened by the sight of him looking so smart and tanned? And yes, there was no denying it, handsome.

She couldn't believe that she had flown off the handle so completely on the evidence of a two-minute interview on *Sky TV*. It was beyond childish. It was pathetic. It was beneath all contempt. However, there was no hiding from the facts of the whole episode. The only reason for her behaviour was that she was still in love with the wretched man and there was no point in running away from the fact.

Sleep refused to come and save her until after three and even then it only lasted for three hours. She awoke to a feeling of utter depression and self-disgust. As the coffee percolator bubbled in the kitchen she made a decision to throw off all her careful instincts and to act rashly for once. She had behaved abhorrently and there was only one thing to do about it: apologise.

The roads were early morning quiet and the countryside was hushed and damp from a night of rain. As she bounced up the track to the caravan the branches of the hedges were weighed down by moisture and rubbed up against the side of the car. As she turned the corner her hackles started to rise a little at the sight of the Vauxhall Corsa. The suspicion grew as she made her way to the battered door of the caravan and gave it a firm rap. It was no surprise when it took several attempts to stir any movement inside. When it creaked open, Deek's face was still wrapped in sleep and he stank like a distillery. His eyes blinked at the light as they struggled to come to terms with too many unexpected events all happening at the same time. Being awake so early was unexpected. Seeing Meg at his door was utterly unexpected. Facing a complete and unexpected early morning crisis was very, very unexpected. The alarm bells were going off all over his fuzzy brain.

"Meg."

"Good morning Deek." Her voice was cool. Her voice was always cool.

"Aye. I suppose." He rubbed at his eyes which were a mile out of focus. "Kind of early isn't it?"

"Yes. I'm sorry. I couldn't sleep much. I had to come. The way I behaved yesterday . . . well . . . it was disgraceful and . . . I just felt . . . oh bloody hell. Are you going to invite me in for a coffee or just leave me standing out here?"

Now he was awake. Treble awake times ten. Complete, utter crisis was just seconds away.

"Actually Meg it's a right mess in there and I have'nae got coffee. No time to stock up since arriving back, you ken. Well, I've had time but . . . well, you know. We'll go to a café or something . . . the Little Chef opens at seven. Let's go there shall we . . ."

He stepped out and was clearly ready to drop everything and go straight away. Meg glanced down and shook her head.

"You've got no shoes and socks on, Deek."

He followed her glance and swallowed on a dry throat. "Aye. Don't need them. Stopped wearing them out in Thailand. Not all the time, ken. Just some of the time. It's good to get air at the feet. It's fine. The Little Chef won't mind. Let's go shall we?"

"Whose is the Vauxhall, Deek?"

A rabbit in the headlights look. "The Vauxhall? Oh the Vauxhall. Just one of the lads. Got a bit pissed so he did. Took a taxi." He started to make a move towards the car but only got two yards before standing on a king-size bramble which planted a thorn deep into his bare foot. "Christ! Bugger! Shite . . !"

As he hopped about in pain, her attention was taken by a voice from within. An American voice. A low sexy voice from a Southern Comfort advert.

"Deek honey? You OK out there?"

The red-haired side of Meg's nature took control of her and she stepped inside the caravan in time to see Tiffany AKA Sam standing up from the bunk. Her raging brain analytically took in the facts of the scene. News presenter good looks. White T-shirt. Nothing else. No way of telling if she had any knickers on. Endless long tanned legs. Hair all over the place but big hair all the same. A faint smile. Then the husky voice.

"Oh hi sugar. I'm Tiffany. Y'all wanting a cup of coffee or something. What's the matter with Deek? Is he OK out there?"

Meg felt an icy calm spread through her. "He stepped on a thorn. Apparently he gave up wearing shoes in Thailand."

"Really. How bizarre."

"Indeed, how bizarre. Anyway I will leave you to tend to him Tiffany. I'll be off now." She turned her back and stepped outside. Deek was perched miserably on one leg cursing fiercely as he picked at the thorn. She saw the opportunity and couldn't resist it. She slapped him hard across the face and sent him sprawling backwards into a hawthorn bush and headed towards her car without a backward glance. Behind her, he started to scramble to his feet.

"Meg! Hang on a second. It's not what you think . . . she's a reporter . . . well not a reporter . . . a student . . . she's from Rayton . . . and . . ."

The car door slammed on his protestations and the car started a fast reverse as he stood and watched. Meg took a brief glance at him then turned her head and focused on the task of backing into a gateway and turning the car. One more glance in the mirror once she had completed the manoeuvre showed him standing there with his arms spread in supplication.

As the car disappeared around the corner Deek couldn't believe what had just happened. Unbelievable. She had come to apologise and he had planned on being on his own in the caravan. They could have talked. They could have made it like the old days. After all these years this had been the big moment. Instead she had seen Tiffany and . . . well, what was she supposed to think? It didn't look very good. In fact it looked worse than bad. Worse than bloody bastard awful and then worse again. He hobbled his way back into the caravan.

Tiffany was sitting on the edge of the bunk looking somewhat apprehensive. Deek said nothing as he rummaged in one of the cupboards and rooted out a couple of cans of Tennants. He passed one over and sat on the bunk. With a sense of horror she realised that in order to maintain her cover as a tragic student alcoholic she was going to have to drink it and her stomach churned at the prospect. Deek flicked the ring-pull and drained half the can in a single gulp. She followed suit with a more ladylike sip that threatened the onset of long and protracted vomiting. Silently she vowed that Larry Weinberg was going to pay through the nose for this one.

"Best let me take a look at that foot, sugar. Those thorns can go septic on you."

Without speaking he dutifully lifted his foot. The thorn was a whopper and it took her some effort to get it out. She talked quietly as she worked.

"That didn't look too good, honey."

"No."

"She your girlfriend?"

"She was. Many years ago."

"She's very pretty."

"Aye."

She worked silently for a few moments until she was able to wrench out the thorn. Deek sat and stared into space. When she sat up and showed him the thorn she was shocked by his expression. She was a woman who had seen her share of despair, but the sheer abject misery on his tired features was something new. It was an unaccustomed feeling, but she felt her heart go out to him. He was such a strange, beaten sort of man. She reached out and gently took his hand.

"Looks like you never got round to stopping loving her, sugar."

He shook his head.

"Never."

She couldn't really think of much to say. There wasn't a great deal that would do much good, that much was clear. She sat for a while holding his hand as the hangover started to sweep through every inch of her body. Little did he know. If he thought things were crazy now! Give it a couple of weeks and the whole world was going to want a piece of him. Fame would be a whole new cross for him to bear and he would hide from it in the bottom of a bottle. All night she had wondered what it was that made him drink. Every drunk had a story. In her time she had heard plenty. Deek was no different in the end from so many of the men she had worked over the years. In the end it was usually a girl. A wife. A mistress. Someone. Pain, remorse, loneliness and memory all swept away every night in a million bars filled with lost souls.

At last she dropped his hand. "Honey, I'm going to make us some coffee. Things will look better with a cup of coffee."

"I doubt it."

"Listen to some wise words. A woman knows a woman. I can promise you that it is a very good sign that she slapped you. Really. She slapped you because she saw me and it made her mad. She was mad because she got the wrong idea and she was jealous. The only reason she was jealous was that she must still care for you. Think about it baby. It makes sense. All of this can get straightened out and things will be just fine."

Deek shook his head. "Things never get straightened out, Tiffany. Never."

Meg had not been alone in hitting the road early. Sally Hunter and Steve Kenton had made their way through the empty streets of Edinburgh and onto the A702 a little after six. He had flown up to the Scottish capital from London the previous morning. An hour on the European PGA's website had shown him something interesting. The only competition in Europe while the Masters was being played was a minor sort of affair with modest prize money. Even if one of the other Scottish contenders for the number one spot were to win, it was mathematically impossible for them to overtake Archie Banks. The only possibility of him being overtaken was if Colin Montgomerie were to finish in the top five at the Masters, and that seemed somewhat far-fetched given the form of the man from Troon. He told Sally on the phone that they could start assuming that Banks would be their man.

"I think it would be an idea for us to go and see him. As soon as this thing goes public the media will be all over him. It will do no harm for us to meet up for an unofficial chat first."

"Are we supposed to do that? I thought it was all supposed to stay a secret."

"A slight bend of the rules never does any harm."

"I gather that is your advice as the security expert?"

"It is."

She had considered for a moment. "OK. Fine. When are you headed north?"

"I'll be up for the evening."

"Tell you what. If you can make it for mid-afternoon I'll collect you from the airport and we'll have a few holes at Muirfield while we talk. Or have you gone off that idea?"

"No. Not at all. Thanks. That will be great."

He had done his homework on Sally Hunter and so it came as no surprise when he was handed out a golfing lesson by the Scottish Minister for Sport. He had brought her up to speed on the plans for the security for the event over sandwiches and a couple of drinks before she had dropped him at his hotel and arranged to collect him at six the next morning.

As they climbed up away from the coast and into the rolling hills of the Borders she asked him a question that had been in her mind since they had met. "Have you been doing this sort of thing for long?"

"Yes. Most of my life. It was the army first. Then intelligence."

"I suppose that means that you spent a lot of time in Ireland?"

He nodded.

"Is it something that you talk about?"

"Not really. Not if I can help it. It was a dirty little war and we fought just as dirty as the other guys. I've never felt very proud of it to be honest."

"Are you past it?"

He looked across, rather surprised. "No. Not really. I still get nightmares and flashbacks. It's part of the job. You're rather perceptive."

She shook her head slightly. "Not really. My uncle Bobby was a Scots Borderer. A corporal. He was always my favourite when I was a little girl. A big, funny bear of a man. He came back from Ireland in a bit of a state. He's on medication and sometimes he is like he used to be, but most of the time . . ."

"Battle stress." He spat the words out like a rancid piece of fat. "It isn't something the army has ever had much sympathy for. We're all still expected to show a stiff upper lip."

Sally nodded. "I looked into it. It was one of my great political ambitions you know. Instead they made me Minister of Sport."

He grinned. "Does that mean that you are in overall charge of the Scottish football team?"

"No, thank goodness."

They made the miles south to Dumfries quickly and arrived on the edge of town soon after eight. They took coffee in a Little Chef and he then plotted their way along the tiny little roads to the gates to Roger Swann's grounds using an Ordnance Survey map he had picked up in London.

"Nice map-reading," said Sally rather approvingly.

"I do have some uses. Banks lives somewhere in the grounds apparently." He looked about glumly. "Could be anywhere. We best drive up to the house and get some directions."

Roger Swann wasn't at all amused to have his door knocked at such an early hour and he let them know in a cantankerous flow of expletives. Somewhere in between he gave them directions to the track to Deek's caravan. Halfway up the track, Steve asked for her to stop and he got out and took several photos.

"What are they for?"

"Just general. We may need to post a few lads here on security. I bloody well hope not. This place is an ambush ready to happen. Funny sort of place in which to live."

"From what I can gather Archie Banks is a funny sort of bloke full stop."

Steve nodded. "That's true enough. Look, we'd better decide how we play this. I don't think that he needs to know that I'm a spook just yet. I'll be an assistant, OK?"

"Fine. And I'll do the talking?"

"It's what they pay you for."

"Watch it."

They parked up next to the Vauxhall and made their way to the door and knocked. The door was opened by a strikingly attractive blond woman with a beaming smile.

"Good morning." She rolled out the words like corn barges sliding their way down the Mississippi to Baton Rouge. Sally was rather taken aback.

"Oh. Good morning. We're looking for Archie Banks."

For a moment the tanned face was bewildered. Then the clouds cleared. "Oh, you mean Deek." She turned her head and shouted inside. "Deek honey. You got visitors."

"Aye." The voice from within was muffled.

She stepped back and allowed them in. "I'm Tiffany. Tiffany McLean. I'm a friend of Deek's. Well Archie. Y'all come in and find a seat while I make some coffee."

Deek looked up at them with little interest. Every syllable of his body language spoke of a man who had had enough. He waved them to the cluttered bunk and took a doleful sip at his whisky glass.

"It's a bit of a mess I'm afraid."

Sally felt that this was something of an understatement. It was more than a bit of a mess. The place was a pit of empty bottles and cans and piles of washing waiting for the launderette. Her brief political career had already taken her into many bizarre situations but none that could compete with this one. Her brain struggled to take on board all the extraordinary elements of the situation. First there was the utterly broken and beaten demeanour of Scotland's would-be golfing champion. Second was the poverty and squalor of his abode which seemed like an example of the kind of grinding rural poverty that had caused so many of her fellow Scots to emigrate to all four corners of the earth. Third was the undeniable fact that it was barely nine o'clock on a regulation Thursday morning and Archie Banks was on the whisky with the air of a man taking on board medicine. And fourth, but by no means least, just who on earth was the blond stunner who had stepped out of a Tennessee Williams story? Her developing political instincts kicked in and she put on her practised smile and held out a hand.

"Good morning Mr Banks. I'm Sally Hunter and this is my assistant Steve Kenton."

He shook the proffered hand without meeting her eyes. "If you're from the tax you'll have to see my accountant. I dunnae keep anything here."

She forced a laugh. "Good Lord, of course not. I'm an MSP. The taxpayer might well pay my wages but it is the job of others to collect it." She didn't think that her effort at early morning humour was that bad, but Deek met it with no more than a rather doleful, "Aye. I suppose so."

Sally pressed on. "No doubt you are wondering why I'm here. Well, I will try to explain . . ."

Deek looked up sharply. "What's he doing?"

Steve had pulled out his camera and was shooting off pictures. The last one caught a rather surprised-looking Tiffany McLean as she ferried in two mugs of coffee. Steve was unperturbed by the note of anger in Deek's voice. "Sorry mate. It's just for the record. The album. This is a bloody big thing you know. Massive. It's just for my scrapbook. Something for the grandchildren."

Deek shook his head to try and make some sense of what was going on. Another crazy morning. Another does of Alice and white rabbits. Maybe he was going nuts.

"Christ, man. Slow down will you. What's a bloody big thing. I have'nae a clue what you're both talking about."

Sally smiled thanks for the coffee to a suddenly rather grim-faced Tiffany. "Sorry Mr Banks. This must all be very confusing. Let me see if I can explain."

She was about to make a start when Tiffany interrupted. "Deek, sugar. I best be on my way. It sure looks as if these people have important business. I best be moseying along now. I'll try and call round again before I go home. Y'all take care now."

Deek was about to try and say something, but she was out of the caravan and halfway to her car before he could make his mouth work properly. Sally watched her through the window as she did a three-point turn and headed off down the track.

"She seemed very nice."

"Aye. She's a journalist. Well not quite. A trainee more like. Student. She's from Rayton."

"Oh I see." Not that Sally saw anything other than craziness. She was about to resume when Steve got up. "Excuse me Ma'am.

I need to make a couple of calls. I'll only be a few minutes. See you in a sec mate."

Deek nodded and took another sip while Sally started to tell him the strange story of the McMillan pictures. Steve pulled his bag out of the boot and took out a laptop computer. He slid the passenger seat all the way back to give himself room to work and switched on. He connected a lead from his camera and hit a few buttons until the image of Tiffany's surprised face filled the screen. He nodded to himself and saved the picture to the desktop. Next he opened up another index and requested a search for "Walter King" which instantly popped up a number which he dialled.

"This is the headquarters of the FBI in Washington. How can I help you today?"

"Walter King please."

It took a few moments. How long had it been? Christ. More than ten years. He had first met Walter on a training course in Quantico where they were taught how to use a newly developed communication system that was to become the norm for undercover operatives in Ireland. He and Walter had found their way into intelligence through similar routes. Walter had been a Marine and had seen his share of the rough side of soldiering. They had hit it off and had spent several drunken nights in each other's company. They had met up on two further occasions, once when Walter was on a family holiday in England and once when Steve was sent to Washington to do some liaison work. The connection was taking a while. It seemed as if his old friend must have been moving up the ladder. At last the familiar rough voice was on the line.

"Yo! Stevie. Long time, no hear, compadre."

"That's right enough. How are you mate? Corner office yet?"

"Not quite buddy, but I'm getting there. I got a desk all on my own-some and a view of an inner courtyard. Business is good Stateside with this war on terror of ours. How about you Steve? Those Irishmen are all quiet now, huh?"

"When is an Irishman ever quiet?"

This brought a laugh. "So buddy, we on business or pleasure here?"

"Biz. I'm on a bit of a minder job here. I could do with an ID off you. US national, or so she claims. Nice piece of work. Goes by the name of Tiffany McLean. The name's probably about as genuine as a Picasso at a car boot sale in Ramsbottom?"

"What the hell is Ramsbottom? Some kinda sheep's ass?"

Steve smiled. "A town in Lancashire. You'd prefer a sheep's ass. I've got a picture. If I email it, can you ID it?"

"Sure. Fire it over."

"How long do you think, Walter? By the close of play today?"

"Hell no. The Feds are in the Twenty-First pal. Not like you guys over there. We don't do the hanging around with tea and biscuits bit out here. Weez get the job done."

"Piss off. Your email address still the same?"

"Sure is. Zip it over. Have a smoke and if the lady has a past, I'll be back in five."

"Well, well Walter. Don't you have a high clearance these days."

"And the expense account to go with it. Next time you come over the pond we party in style, deal?"

"Deal. I'll send it now."

More buttons. An egg timer. A message saying things had gone to plan. He took the advice and lit up. It was all very quiet. The sunshine had the first warmth of spring and all around him the birds were celebrating. He wondered how Sally was getting on. There had been something about Archie Banks that had struck a chord inside him. Whatever was broken was badly broken. Banks didn't bother to hide it from the world. Unlike Steve, he laid his trauma out on the table for all to see. A wrecked face, a wrecked room, a wrecked life, all washed out of sight into the bottom of a whisky bottle. Steve had known enough drinkers to know one at first sight. He had seen friends hide from their demons in the drink. For a while they had continued, but in the end it caught up. A plane home. A quiet deal on the pension and back into the icy waters of civilian life. At times he had done it himself, times when the nightmares came on the very second he closed his eyes.

Poor bugger. As if he didn't already have his problems. Had he any idea what was coming? Of course not. How could he? Soon the cameras and the weasel reporters of the tabloids would be all over him. To make any kind of entry into public life a man had to be 100 percent certain that his cupboards were empty of skeletons. Something told Steve that Archie Bank's storage areas would resemble something out of a Hammer Horror movie. He snapped out of his daydream as his phone trilled.

"Yeah."

"Steve, it's Walter."

"Christ, that was quick. Anything?"

"Yup. Kinda weird actually. We have a Samantha Latimer. 32 years old. Born Mississippi. Full-time politico."

"What's that when it's at home?"

"Campaign work. Fund raising. Schmoozing. Handling reporters. You know the kind of thing. It's a boom industry here in DC."

Steve frowned. This wasn't at all what he had expected. "Who does she work for?"

"That's where it gets a tad sporty. She worked for the President's team for years. All the way from Senator to Vice President. Then she went freelance. Chased the big bucks. It says here that she still does work for Larry Weinberg."

"The White House Chief of Staff, yeah?"

"Ten points my man. Glad to see you are keeping up with things over here. Is this a problem?"

"I don't know. Maybe. If it is I'll let you know."

There was a brief silence. "I guess you better ring me at home on that Steve. Could be twitchy, comprendo?"

"Of course. I don't suppose it's any big deal. See you soon, yeah?"

"Sure thing buddy."

Steve lit another cigarette and took a moment to digest the information. What the hell was happening here? What was fairly certain was that it didn't represent any kind of physical threat to his new client. So what then? He mentally tried to lay out the pieces of the jigsaw and lifted them one by one. A golf game for an art collection. A head-to-head between Scotland and America. A huge media circus. A presidential visit. It was coming slowly. A presidential visit. A President on his backside with everything going to hell in Iraq. America suddenly looking anything but invincible. A President looking like an increasingly lame duck. So what? A favourite operator of Larry Weinberg. Larry Weinberg with an eye on the elections. Larry Weinberg looking for any PR he could get. Of course. His fingerprints were all over the whole thing. No doubt it must have been his idea for the great man to come to the game. Great pictures and a feel-good event to boost the flagging ratings.

There it was.

This was no time for a David and Goliath re-run. No way. There were already too many Davids out there in Fallujah and Najaf and Sadr City. The White House was no doubt sick and tired of pesky little Davids with their slings. No, this was not a time for David to come good. They wanted Goliath to come out on top. Of course they did. Once he had worked out the principle, the rest was easy. What does any politician do when he wants to get one over on an opponent? Digs the dirt. And Samantha Latimer was the in-house digger. A freelancer. A deniable.

He angrily threw down his cigarette and went back inside. Deek's face confirmed that the news had been imparted. He looked as if he had seen about a thousand ghosts. Steve joined Sally.

"You know then do you Archie?"

Deek nodded. "Aye. Call me Deek. Everyone calls me Deek. I cannae believe it."

Steve forced a smile. "Bit of a change for you. Anyway, look on the bright side. There'll be a quid or two in it. You should be able to trade up from this place."

"I like it here."

And Steve could understand why. It was a place to hide. A place to pretend that none of it was real. A haven that was about to be discovered and invaded. He saw little point in adding any sugar. It might as well come out clear and straight.

"Deek, we've got a problem." Sally looked round sharply.

"Have we?" Her voice was edgy. How the hell could there be a problem before the thing had even started?

"We have. I best come clean Deek. I'm a bit more than an assistant. I'm in security."

This was met by a look of bemused resignation. Little did Steve know of the complete and utter weirdness that had come into Deek's life.

"You know when I took those pictures?"

"Aye."

"Well I just emailed the one of Tiffany to a mate of mine in America. I asked him to check her out. It's not good."

"How not good?"

"Very not good. She's some kind of troubleshooter for the White House. Her real name is Samantha Latimer."

Sally looked a mile out of her depth. "Sorry Steve. You've lost me here. What on earth is someone from the White House doing here in Dumfries?"

"Think about it, Sally. You're the politician."

She shook her head and so he explained his theory. Deek shook his head and wasn't having any of it.

"That's a load of bollocks. She wouldn't do that. She was a good lass. I dunnae know what she was doing here, but it wasn't to have a go. We got on. She's like me. Likes a dram. Needs a dram . . ."

Steve's heart sank. "Let me get this straight. You're telling me that you two sat up and had a good old heart-to-heart over a few drinks?"

Deek nodded. "More than a few."

"And it all came out. Warts and all. Two lonely people sharing the pain. Something like that?"

"Aye. Just like that. So?" A shadow of concern was now on Deek's face.

"I suppose she had her handbag with her?"

"Aye. Right there. Just where you're sitting."

"Shit."

Sally couldn't put up with any more of the guessing games. "Sorry Steve. Can you stop speaking in riddles please?"

He nodded and shook out a cigarette for Deek before lighting one for himself. "It isn't good Sally. Worse than not good. It's bad. I'll give you five-to-one on that she had a tape recorder in the bag. Tell me Deek, you said you both talked about needing a drink, yeah?"

Deek's head was down now. He knew what was coming. "Aye."

Steve drove on. "You talked about all of it. How is it when you don't have a drink mate? Hands shaking? Sick to the stomach?"

"Aye."

". . . and no way you can play golf. No way at all. So you need a few drams to get you round the course, yeah?"

Nearly a whisper now. "Aye."

Steve sat back and looked over to Sally. "Are you there yet? As soon as the match is announced all this lot gets emailed to the tabloids. Good stuff. Pictures of this place. An edited recording. So much for the gallant underdog Scotsman I'm afraid."

Sally's reaction surprised him. He had expected her to panic and run for the hills to protect her career. Instead she reached across and took one of Deek's hands. "Look at me Deek. Come on. Look up. That's it. They told me that my job is to look after things. Well that includes you. Let them say what they have to say. It only matters if you let it get to you. It only matters if you bottle-out and get hammered. Got me?"

"I suppose so. So what do you want me to do?"

"Beat the American bastards. Beat them out of sight."

This brought a small smile. "You ken it will probably be George Albright, Sally?"

"I don't care if it's George bloody Washington."

As the spring sunshine bathed the luxuriant colours of the Augusta National Golf Course, George Albright felt in the form of his life. For the first three days of the Masters he had tried to play carefully. Georgia had enjoyed an unusually dry few weeks and the course was playing at its very toughest. He had never known the greens to be as fast and treacherous. Every hole for every player was a catastrophe waiting to happen. Already two seasoned players had suffered the ignominy of five-putting. George had followed a similar strategy to the majority of the field. He had carefully placed iron shots from the tees. He had eased his approaches onto the safe sides of the greens. He had carefully lagged his putts up next to the holes. His game had been the very epitome of safety and there had been a degree of media talk about a new, conservative George Albright. In fact he had hated every minute and only the prospect of representing his country at Turnberry had kept the harnesses in place. The completely galling thing had been that the new sensible strategy hadn't worked at all. On the home stretch of the third round he had missed three putts inside of six feet and had slipped back to one over par, trailing the leader by seven shots.

He decided that evening that maybe it had been for the best. A seven-shot deficit meant that tactics were easy. There was only one way to take on the task of the final round. The way he liked it. Head on, with all guns blazing.

He had met with a mixed reception when he had marched onto the first tee sporting the cap that had been presented to him by the Marines outside of Kerbala. There were probably slightly more boos than cheers. The Americans were getting rather tired of such gestures. They remembered the Ryder Cup team wearing similar headgear for the match at Kiawah Island in the early 1990s. Many found that their flag-waving patriotic instincts were beginning to wear a little thin. All too often the image of their flag was seen draped over the coffins that were being flown home from the Gulf. They didn't need reminding that things weren't working out as planned in that godforsaken country. They certainly didn't want reminding when they had stumped up a small fortune for a ticket for the last day of the Masters. George received several hearty cheers from die-hard fans who would have cheered just as loudly had he chosen to tee off wearing a pair of pink knickers on his handsome head. Some booed and took their opportunity to publicly vent their disapproval of their country's modern-day crusade. Others were simply mute, not happy, but not angry enough to actually make a noise about it.

George grinned at the reaction. His PR people had been in a near frenzy when he pulled on the cap. Well, that was just tough. What did he care if their ten percent was under threat. He had been presented the cap by the guys on the field and that was all that mattered. He knew for a fact that they would all be cheering him as they tuned into the satellite in the stifling heat of their dusty tents. He pulled out the driver from his bag and after about half his normal preparation time he crashed his ball 345 yards down the centre of the fairway.

Birdie.

For three-and-a-half hours he had gone after every shot and now needed just four up the eighteenth to complete a nine under par 63. The boos of the first tee had faded to a distant memory. Spectators had flocked from all corners of the course to join the stampeding crowd of cheering humanity that rolled around after the blazing George. Their cheers had echoed around the towering trees and put fear into the hearts of those who had led the tournament into the last round. All had fallen back as drives were quit on and putts were dollied up short. By the sixteenth George was out clear on his own. Now he stood at eight under par for the tournament, having collected seven birdies and an eagle.

"So Bob, what do you think? He's got a two shot cushion and there sure doesn't seem anyone out there who can stay with him. What kind of thing are we looking for on eighteen? Is this time for a quiet one iron and take par?"

"That would be the play for just about every golfer out on that course Gerry. I can't see it though. George just isn't in one of those quiet one-iron moods today . . ."

The commentary was interrupted by yet another roar from the crowd as the famous huge headed driver was pulled from the bag and wielded like some kind of medieval weapon.

". . . there you go Gerry. Out comes the driver. That little old golf ball better get itself ready for a big, big ride up eighteen . . ."

The little old golf ball got exactly that. George crashed his drive at the distant bunkers and allowed a late fade to ease the ball to the right where it landed and settled within a wedge of the flag. His second shot soared up high above the grandstands and thumped down three feet from the pin.

Birdie.

A record-breaking closing round of 62 and George Albright duly pulled on the green jacket of the Masters champion for the third time. There were no unusual mathematical permutations further down the field. The winner's cheque meant that George had earned over $45,000 more than any American golfer in the calendar year.

Later, as he was enjoying a drink at the bar after the post-tournament banquet, he was approached by a quiet young man.

"Excuse me sir, I wonder if I might have a moment of your time?"

"Well son, that depends. You a reporter?"

"No sir."

"Then you have a chance. What do they call you son?"

"I'm Jonathan McMillan, sir."

So. Here they were. He had been wondering how they would go about breaking the news. The fact that a member of the family had come in person rather impressed him. He made a note to be careful. Part of him was tempted to drop the President right in it by letting on that he already knew exactly what was happening. He quickly brushed the thought aside. There was little mileage in rubbing up the man in the White House the wrong way.

"OK Jonathan. Let's take a stroll outside and take in some air shall we?"

The night was cool and above them the sky was filled with a Walt Disney array of stars. Jonathan felt more nervous that at any time in his whole life. What if the man said "No". It would be a disaster. It would break Roland McMillan's heart. He took a deep breath and dived in and told the champion all about the pictures and the plan. George gave nothing away. He merely leaned against a railing and took in the scent of the flowers all around. When Jonathan had finished he gave a diffident shrug,

"Well sir. I suppose that is about all of it."

"Seems like enough to me, Jonathan."

"Will you play, sir?"

George beamed. "I try not to make a secret of the way I feel about my country. Hell, there are times where we screw up, but there will always be something special about being American. Well, that's how I feel anyway. Of course I'll play son. I'll be proud to."

Jonathan blew out his cheeks with relief. "That's wonderful news, sir. Really. I can mention now that the President is already fully informed about the event and I believe that he plans to come in person to watch the final round."

Now George was really impressed. "Are you telling me that you already knew all this and you didn't mention it until I had already agreed?"

"Yes sir."

"Why the hell not?"

Jonathan shrugged. "I don't think it would have been fair on you. It is best that you play because you want to, not just because the President will be there."

George laughed. "Quite right, son. Quite right. Mind you, I figure he would have been pretty pissed if I had told you to shove it up your ass!"

"No doubt he would, sir."

"Indeed. No doubt he would. So, who am I to play Jonathan? Who is the champion of the Scots?"

"Archie Banks."

"Archie who?"

"Banks. I doubt whether you will know him. He's a first-year rookie on the tour. Not a young one. He's 32. It is all something of a fluke really. Most of their top players have had a lean time of it and he just happens to have had a good run. I expect this is all going to come as a bit of a shock to be honest."

"When are you going to tell him?"

"Actually the company jet is taking me over there tonight, as soon as I leave here. I expect I will catch up with him tomorrow."

"Well, tell him that I say good luck and may the best man win. What's the schedule now then?"

"As soon as Mr Banks agrees to play, my grandfather will be staging a Press Conference in the middle of the week. That will coincide with an announcement from the White House and the Government over in Scotland. We would like to bring both yourself and Mr Banks down to Texas on the Wednesday before the event for a final Press Conference. We will then take you both across to Scotland to arrive at the hotel for Thursday evening. That will allow a day for practice before the match starts on the Saturday. I gather that you have played at Turnberry before, sir?"

"Sure have. Great, great course. Good choice. Well son, you can get on the phone and tell your great, grandaddy that it will be my pleasure to represent America and that I look forward to meeting him at the end of May."

Jonathan smiled with pure relief. One down and one to go. Against all odds his crazy idea was coming together fast.

The McMillan Corporation Press Office sent the release out across the ether two days later. The story had all the ingredients to make the media bite at it like hungry fish. There was no mention of the golf match. Instead the press release focused on the fact that Roland McMillan would be announcing the bequest of his famed art collection. The sheer Hollywood-worthy value of the paintings drew the press to Texas like flies to a jam sandwich. A procession of cars and vans started to arrive at the remote estate of the little-known billionaire soon after eight in the morning, even though the official conference was not due to start until two. TV crews and reporters vied for space in the allocated area to give a breathless account of the unfolding events. Roland McMillan was nowhere to be seen, but Jonathan was everywhere giving interviews and instructions. The rest of the clan started to arrive by car and helicopter from the late morning onwards.

At noon, the first main event of the day took place as the doors of the gallery were opened to the gaze of the public for the very first time. Not many of the journalists and cameramen who filed through had much of an appreciation of fine art. What they did appreciate however was money, and the estimated values of the pictures in the specially printed catalogues set their hearts pounding.

By one-thirty the area allocated for vehicles was overflowing. A large marquee had been specially erected on the eighteenth fairway of the golf course, and it slowly filled with the eager ranks of reporters who had all taken their fill at the lavish buffet that had been laid on in a separate tent. A clear consensus was emerging. The McMillans were a class act. A real class act. The reporters liked them. They liked their manners. They liked their hospitality. They liked the embossed folders that gave every detail that they desired. They liked the money that made everything possible.

By two, all were assembled and a respectful hush settled over the tent. Lights winked as the ranks of cameras started their feed. Jonathan, who was dressed in a smart three-piece suit, strolled out onto the podium and took up a place at a lectern.

"Ladies and gentlemen, may I first take the opportunity to thank every one of you for coming today on behalf of the McMillan Corporation and all of my family. Today is about a life. A truly remarkable life. When my great-grandfather got off the boat on Ellis Island in 1925, he literally had nothing. As you can see, things have changed somewhat over the last 79 years."

This caused an appreciative murmur of laughter.

"Roland McMillan's story has been a story of America. Where else on earth could a man have started with nothing and created all this . . ." He emphasised his point with a slow sweep of his arms. *"But let us not forget that it was not America that made Roland McMillan. It was Scotland. Like so many others throughout history, Roland McMillan was given his courage, stubbornness and sheer dogged drive by the hills and lochs of Scotland. Every one of us is proud of the tartan blood that flows through our veins. What is my point, you may ask. Well I suggest that Scotland made the man whilst America*

made it possible for the man to achieve things that most of us can only dream of."

Jonathan paused and was pleased to see that the hard nosed journalists were waiting on his every word.

"So. Possibly you can understand my great-grandfather's dilemma. I personally find it hard to believe that Roland will not be with us for many years yet, but let's face it folks, at 95 a man has to start to make a few plans. I know that most of you have taken the opportunity to view the art collection that Roland has assembled over the last half-century. Magnificent aren't they? Forget money. Priceless means more than money. Priceless means unique. Priceless means irreplaceable. Priceless means for ever. Roland has never been in any doubt about the ultimate fate of his collection. He has been determined to bequeath the collection to the nation so that the people can enjoy them for as long as man walks on top of this earth. The principle was easy. However, the hard question was always: 'Which nation?' America or Scotland? Scotland or America? The country that bore him or the country that made him? Well, ladies and gentlemen, my great-grandfather has at last made his decision after all these years which of course why we are all here today. So, with no more ado, allow me to present the man himself . . . may I introduce you all to Mr Roland McMillan . . ."

As Abe wheeled Roland onto the podium the assembled journalists surprised themselves by rising to their feet and applauding. They didn't really know why. It just seemed the thing to do. Roland seemed rather embarrassed by all the fuss and waved his shrunken hand limply to ask for some quiet. Even though his voice was small and frail, the microphone that was clipped to the lapel of his blazer beamed his words clearly around the tent.

"Ladies and gentlemen. I'm afraid you will find that I lack my great-grandson's flamboyance. I am sure that you will find me rather boring in comparison and so I promise to be as brief as possible. Johnny is quite right. The question of what to do with my collection has troubled me for some time now. Before I share my solution with you all, I would like to take this opportunity to make an apology for what I have done

over all the years I have spent gathering these wonderful paintings. I am ashamed to admit that I have hoarded them and kept them to myself. This has been unforgivable. All that I can do is to say sorry and try to make up for my selfishness before it is too late."

The speech had clearly tired Roland and he took a sip of water.

"So. America or Scotland? Which should it be? Such a terrible decision to have to make. America has given me and my family everything. Not just us, but millions and millions of others like us who came here with nothing but hope, faith and a belief that hard work would get them where they wanted to go. But Scotland is in the blood. Johnny is quite right about that. In fact, it was Johnny who came up with the solution that I will announce to you all in a moment. I thank him for that. I could have pondered for ten more years and never found an answer. Johnny came up with it in five minutes.

"In short, ladies and gentlemen, the destination of my pictures is to be settled in an very old-fashioned way. Once upon a time, to settle their differences, nations would send out their champions to fight it out on the field of battle. Now I have chosen a similar solution. My champions will not be fighting each other with armour and swords and lances. They will use golf clubs."

This caused a stir in the audience. What on earth was going on here?

"It has been agreed that America's number one golfer will play the Scottish number one over 54 holes of match play. The match will take place at Turnberry's Ailsa Course over the weekend of 30th and 31st of May. The champions who have agreed to represent their countries are the men who are number one in the world rankings for this current calendar year. Following his magnificent victory at the Masters, the United States of America will be represented by George Albright the Third. Scotland's champion is a less well-known young man, Archie Banks. So, ladies and gentlemen, now you have it. The fate of my collection will have been decided by the end of next month. Now, if you will excuse me, my stamina is not what it used to be and I must admit that I feel rather tired. I'm sure Johnny will be happy to answer any of your questions. Thank you."

As Abe gently wheeled the old man from the podium there was a second bout of prolonged applause. Jonathan patiently waited until it had finally died away before resuming the presentation.

"Before I take your questions, may I just point out one final fact. In one way this will be the greatest match of any kind in the history of sport. Never before has a single game been played for such a stake. And yet even though the prize, as you have seen with your own eyes, represents many hundreds of millions of dollars, the players themselves stand to gain nothing. The winner will receive no prize. There is no appearance money. Both men are simply representing their countries. The prize for the winner is a prize for their whole nation. You should know that."

Questions took well over an hour and when the formal part of the proceedings were completed there were many more interviews. It wasn't until nearly eight o'clock that the ranch was vacated by the visiting media. The story was duly fired out across the world. It was a story for the times, a good news story packed with human interest which provided blessed relief from the grinding misery of Iraq. George Albright watched the news at his home in Virginia. The President and Larry decided to let it run for 24 hours before staging their own press conference to announce the intentions of the world's most famous golf fan. Sally did the rounds of the TV studios assuring one and all that the Scottish Parliament would do everything that was required to ensure that the great match would run smoothly. Some of the more seasoned political commentators picked up on the huge relevance of the fact that it would be Scotland's First Minister who would meet and greet the President at Prestwick. Their instincts were soon borne out by a rather terse reaction from Number Ten Downing Street.

Deek was in his local pub in Sunnybank. His return from Asia had been a truly notable event in the life of the estate. However, the McMillan announcement was without doubt the greatest thing Sunnybank had ever known. The pub was packed beyond every conceivable safety standard. Some of the older drinkers said that they had seen nothing like it since VE Day six decades earlier. A big screen was tuned in to the news channels instead of the usual sport. It was a "pictures only" night, for there was far too much noise to make listening to the commentary possible. Every time a picture of Deek flashed up on the screen it was greeted with a great cheer. George's image was met with equally vigorous booing.

The euphoria helped to lift the colossal sense of gloom that had settled into Deek for the last few days. These were his people. They had always been his people. They had little enough to cheer about most of the time. Unemployment was an age-old problem on Sunnybank. Lives were eeked out on the weekly Giro. The local economy had been dominated for years by heroin which had wreaked havoc with all too many families. Hope was a rare commodity.

The drinks stacked up on the table of honour where Deek held court alongside Troll and Banjo. The Sunnybank Three had come good. Ever since they had been four-year-olds with mucky faces and cut knees, they had been the resident ragamuffins of the place. Deek had always been a favourite topic of the gossip that was at the beating heart of the community. There had always been plenty of serious head-shaking when the subject of his life was up for discussion.

"The booze will kill him if he does'nae ease up . . ." "All the boy has to do is to knuckle down and he could make a fortune . . ." ". . . it all went wrong when he split up with that Meg Cunningham. Remember her? Bit posh, but a nice lass. Deek never got over her. That's when he really started to hit the bottle . . ."

Troll and Banjo received their own fair share of talk. The Sunnybank Three were all kinds of things. Idiots. Prats. Wasters. Nerds. Not bad lads at heart. Salt of the earth. Top men. Everyone had a view. And now, against all sensible odds, they had become heroes. It was unbelievable. Something that called for a big, big night – and that was exactly what it got.

Steve Kenton had spent two days at the Turnberry Hotel. The service had sent a team of five to start the process of building up the security ready for the visit of the number one target for every terrorist on the planet. Every guest would be checked as soon as they either booked or checked in. The staff were to be talked to and asked to keep an eye out for any suspicious behaviour. The course itself was carefully studied with a view to the deployment of a water-tight security cordon once the match was under way. The Navy were given the task of patrolling the sea whilst the RAF would ensure that at least two interceptor jets roamed the skies at all times. There were meetings and more meetings. Where would the inevitable protestors be intercepted and turned back? Would there be tickets on sale? Would those buying tickets be vetted? Was the roof of the great hotel suitable for snipers? It wasn't a loop that Steve played any particular part in. He was little more than an interested observer. He was the close protection man whose job was to look after his guy. It was for others to decide on how to hermetically seal off a chunk of Scotland for two days. He didn't envy them their task.

He joined a group of excited guests in front of a TV and eavesdropped on their conversation. Who was Archie Banks? Never heard of him. No chance against Albright. Not a prayer. Shame it wasn't Monty. At least Monty had plenty of Ryder Cup experience. It would have been miles better if it had been Monty . . . Poor old Deek. He hadn't asked for this and Steve knew only too well that the going was about to get pretty tough. How would he h ld up? Impossible to say.

Abdullah and his entourage had moved oack to the hotel in Monte Carlo ready for the Grand Prix. He watched the rolling news with a small smile that did little to betray the ferocious excitement that was glowing inside him. Their moment had arrived.

Anatoly Rykov was at his home in Austria. Every time the news used one of the archive pictures of Turnberry's ninth tee his heart beat a little faster. The clock was counting down. Maybe the security forces would find the bomb. If they did, there was nothing he could do about it. Would they guess that everything was already in place? Unlikely. They would feel safe in the fact that the news was new. All their preparations would flow from the announcement. Deep inside, his instincts told him that there was no chance that his work would be discovered. The clock was ticking and the clock was going to count down all the way to the last second when only he would matter. He, Anatoly Rykov.

The Sunnybank Three had been ferried back to the caravan a little before dawn and had crashed out within seconds of hitting their bunks. Not one of them moved a muscle as Steve wrenched open the door and stood and looked down at them. He found the kettle and switched it on. Once he had made four cups of tea he started the difficult process of waking them up. He hadn't expected this to be easy and it wasn't. Troll was the first to come awake. Then Deek. Banjo was out for the count.

"Morning lads."

Deek tried to sit up but it took three attempts. When he spoke he felt as if his mouth was filled with wire wool. It certainly sounded that way.

"Bloody hell Steve. What time is it?"

"Just after seven."

"Christ man, we did'nae get to bed till five-thirty. Can't you leave us be?"

"Nope. Here you go. Cup of tea."

Deek took it and tried a tentative sip. "I dunnae understand, Steve. Why so early?"

"Because you're about to be invaded. I thought you best have some time to brace yourself."

"Invaded? What do you mean, invaded?"

Steve passed over a copy of the *Daily Recorder* which he had picked up in Edinburgh having read the front page lead on the internet late the previous evening. Deek's eyes widened at the photos that dominated the front page. One was a fairly standard photo of him grinning to the crowd around the eighteenth green in Bangkok. It was the second photo which was beyond his comprehension. He looked up from the page and stared about the inside of his chaotic home with amazement. The two were one and the same. It was crazy. The front page of Scotland's best-selling tabloid was filled with a picture of the inside of his caravan in all its glory. Empty cans and bottles. Overflowing ashtrays. Piles of clothes. Food wrappers. Takeaway cartons. Screwed-up duvet covers that looked in dire need of a wash. It looked every inch the filthy pit that it was.

And it was right there, on the front page of the paper under the banner headline

'OUR ALKIE BRAVEHEART!'

Deek shook his head as he tried to come to terms with the words he was reading.

"We have always loved our underdogs in Scotland. It's lucky that we do because we produce enough of them. Yesterday the whole country started getting excited about our latest gallant sportsman to go out and fight the odds in the name of Robert the Bruce and William Wallace.

"At first glance Archie Banks seems to fill the role to perfection. He comes from a tough area on the wrong side of Dumfries. He likes a crack. He has a cheeky way about him. In fact he is a perfect candidate to become yet another of our wee loveable rogues.

"Sadly the investigations of the Daily Recorder paint a very different picture. On the surface of things Archie Banks, universally known as 'Deek', and his two henchmen 'Troll' and 'Banjo' seem to be colourful characters. We have found out different. Above, our readers can see the pig sty of a caravan where they all live. Their lives revolve around drink, fags and gambling. If it only stopped there, then maybe the people of Scotland would be able to accept their infantile behaviour.

"But it is worse. Much worse. Our new hero Archie Banks doesn't just like a drink. He needs a drink. He can't get out of his stinking pit in the morning WITHOUT a drink. This is what he had to say to one of our undercover reporters only a few days ago, 'I couldn't get down the first hole without a drink, my hands would shake so bad that I couldn't even grip the club.' Inside we have pictures from recent tour events that clearly show Banks taking on board his medicine whilst attempting to fulfil the role of a professional golfer.

"This is the half-a-bottle-a-day slob who will be representing our country next month. The view of the Daily Recorder is quite clear on this. We want him sacked, and sacked now. Archie Banks must not be allowed to bring humiliation and shame on this proud country!"

There were tears sliding down his pale cheeks when he allowed the paper to slip from his hands and slide to the floor. Before Scoobytown he couldn't have cared less. But now, just as he was ready to try and turn things around . . . Troll bent to pick it up and his face seemed to collapse as he read the bitter words. Steve collected a bottle from the side and poured a generous measure into Deek's tea.

"Sorry mate. It's a tough wake-up, I know. I just thought it best that you got due warning."

"Aye. Thanks Steve. I appreciate it." He took a gulp of tea and wrinkled his face as the hot whisky taste burned its way down. "This is Tiffany isn't it?"

"Looks like it. Tiffany, Samantha, whoever she was. Trouble in a bloody skirt, mate."

"I cannae believe it. I thought she was nice."

Steve couldn't think of anything much worth saying. He knew all about betrayal. Few pills tasted more bitter. Troll had finished the piece and was patiently shaking Banjo into life. It took him a while, but eventually a chaotic mess of red hair emerged from under a duvet. "You best read this, Banjo. We're all in the shite."

Banjo's boney fingers scratched around on the floor until he found his glasses which he pulled on. As soon as a bemused glance confirmed that the picture on the front page was indeed their caravan, he groaned. Deek lit a cigarette and succumbed to a prolonged bout of coughing. "Steve. You said you thought we needed warning. What about?"

Steve gave the paper a tap. "This is a can of worms, lads. A big can of worms. You've just become a piece of public property, Deek. It won't just stop with the *Daily Recorder* I'm afraid. They're all going to want a piece of this and it won't take long. Give them a few hours and they'll be all over you . . ."

Steve's prediction was proved wrong the instant it was out of his mouth. His sentence was interrupted by a loud hammering on the door. "Archie! You in there Archie! How's about a comment on today's story in the *Recorder* Archie!" The voice was aggressive and London.

"Piss off!!!" shouted Deek. "I'm no saying a thing."

Steve busied himself pulling the dusty curtains to cover all the windows. As he closed the last one he said, "Oh Christ. Two more cars. They don't hang around do they?"

Ten minutes later there were three voices shouting from different sides of the caravan. Another car pulled up, followed by an outside broadcast van from *Sky News*. The four men inside began to feel under siege.

"What are we supposed to do?" asked Deek.

Steve shrugged. "Christ, don't ask me. I'm a spook, not a PR man. I figure this is private property, yeah?"

Deek nodded. "Aye. This is Roger's land."

"Maybe you should give him a call. I haven't got a clue what the law is up here, but there might be something he can do to get shut of them. In the mean time I think the best thing to do is to give this place a bloody good blitz in case any of them fire off any photos. I'll make a start. You guys best get dressed. Try and look halfway smart."

They were just glad to have something to do to take their minds off the aggressive shouting that seemed to surround them. Twenty minutes later things looked a great deal more ship-shape. Steve had not been particularly scientific in his efforts. He had merely crammed everything into a selection of bin liners and stuffed them into an unused little room. Five minutes with a damp cloth made the place borderline acceptable.

Deek had managed to make himself reasonably presentable in black slacks, white polo neck and a red Pringle sweater. Troll, remarkably enough, came up with a cords, check shirt and a well-worn Harris Tweed jacket. Banjo's eclectic wardrobe offered no such opportunities for respectable conservatism. The best that he could do was his yellow shell-suit with a U2 T-shirt.

When he emerged with a hopeful lopsided grin, the other three buried their faces in their hands. "What?" he asked indignantly.

"Look at the state of you" said Deek. "Have you nothing else?"

"No. Just this. So what's wrong with it?"

For a moment Deek looked as if he was about to try and give a sensible answer to the rhetorical question, but the beginnings of laughter got the better of him. It only took seconds for the laughter to become infectious and Steve and Troll joined in. For a moment or two, Banjo assumed a rather hurt look, but their hysterics soon got the better of him and he joined in. When they at last managed to calm down, Deek still found it hard to talk without cracking up again. He wiped at his eyes as he spoke.

"Sorry Banjo. It's just that you look such a complete twat in that yellow shell-suit. Trouble is that . . ." He couldn't get the words out for another bout of laughing. He took a deep breath and tried to be serious. In the end he managed a few more words which set them all off again. ". . . you're the manager!"

Once the second bout of laughing fizzled out, the impact of Deek's words started to hit home with Banjo. "Look, Deek. I ken that I'm the manager and all, but what does that mean?"

"You ken full well what it means. The manager does PR. The manager deals with the press."

Banjo's face was panicky now. "You're kidding. You mean you want me to go and talk to that lot?"

"Aye. Dunnae bother yourself none. You'll be fine. That yellow suit of yours will look a bloody treat on tele."

"Oh shite."

Steve pulled a sheet of paper from his case and they put together a statement which Banjo picked up with shaking hands. He was muttering now.

"Nobody ever told me that it would be like this. I should'nae have ever jacked in the Job Centre. How can I talk to that lot. It's a bastard nightmare so it is . . ."

He maintained his diatribe as Steve gently nudged him to the door.

"OK pal. This is it. Shoulders back. Chest out. Deep breaths. You'll be fine. Just stick to the statement. I'm opening the door now. On three. One . . . two . . . three . . .."

The sight of the Day-Glo yellow shell-suit brought an instant hush to the crowd of nine journalists that had by now gathered outside. Before any of them had time to get over the surprising sight of the brightly clad beanpole figure, Banjo was already into his stride.

"Gentlemen. I have a prepared statement for you. I will not be taking any questions at this time . . ."

"Who the hell are you then?"

Banjo surprised himself by his crisp professional riposte.

"I'm Mr Banks's manager. Now. I'm only going to read this once. Mr Banks is both shocked and upset by the story in this morning's Daily Recorder. He is unwilling to make any public statements at this time and will be considering his position along with his advisers. Thank you. That is all for now."

He jumped back inside and slammed the door shut on the babble of questions.

Deek was delighted. "Christ, Banjo. You're a natural. Worth every penny, pal."

"You've never paid me a penny yet."

"Aye. Well. Just a detail. I'm going to try Roger again. Hopefully he'll have surfaced."

This time the call was answered.

"Who the hell is that?" Roger's phone manner had always left a lot to be desired and it had deteriorated badly over the years.

"It's Deek."

"Oh. Bloody hell man. Bit early isn't it?"

"Aye, sorry about that, Roger. Look. We're in a bit of shite down here at the caravan."

"Shite? What kind of shite?"

"Journalist shite. There are hundreds of them. Cars. Vans. TV. The lot. We're trapped mate. Maybe you get the police to come and kick them off. It's your land when all's said and done."

"Are they giving you a hard time Deek?"

"Christ, yes. The bloody *Daily Recorder* has me all over the front page this morning. It's a bloody nightmare."

"OK. Give me an hour or two."

"You going to call the police?"

This idea was met with derisory snort. "Don't be so bloody daft. That lot aren't worth a phone call. Bloody hopeless. No, I'll sort something out myself."

"What are you going to do?"

"You'll know when I get there. Just be ready to skip off. I'll only be able to get them out of the way for a while. You need to get to somewhere secret."

"Fair enough. Thanks for coming through Roger."

Deek reported back his conversation to the others.

"We could go to my mum's" offered Troll.

"Would she mind?"

Troll was about to say "Not at all" when Steve interrupted. "No. No good guys. Too close. That lot out there would suss it out in no time. Family won't work."

This led to a period of head-scratching before Troll had a eureka moment. "What about wee Donny?"

"Wee Donny?" Steve just managed to stop himself from rolling his eyes.

"Aye," said Deek enthusiastically. "Wee Donny's just the man. He's one of those lads who's half a sandwich short of a picnic, ken. A bit simple like, but a top man all the same. We've all kenned him for years. Since school."

"So where does he live?" asked Steve.

"Sunnybank. One of the blocks near the chippy. He's on the third floor."

Steve realised that all three faces were looking at him expectantly. This was ridiculous. "Listen guys, don't expect too much of me here. I'm supposed to be looking out for Al Quaida, not those clowns outside."

"But you'll help us?"

Nuts. Crazy. Stupid. But the problem was that Steve Kenton couldn't get away from the fact that he liked these guys. "Yeah. I'm in. This is how we'll have to play it."

By eleven-thirty three more cars had arrived. The early arrivals had lost much of their initial vigour. It had become clear that those inside the caravan had no intention of coming out easily. The members of the Fourth Estate settled themselves for a long siege. They had no fear about losing their prey. The caravan could only be reached by the rough track and otherwise it was guarded by a wood on one side and a field on the other. Nobody could get in or out without breaching their lines. The Sunnybank Three were bottled up as tightly as Paul Newman and Robert Redford at the end of *Butch Cassidy and the Sundance Kid*. The reporters caught up with each other amidst clouds of cigarette smoke while rotas were organised for volunteers to make the four0mile trip to McDonald's to bring trays of steaming coffee.

None of them therefore paid any particular interest to the sound of two approaching vehicles making their way up the track. This changed somewhat when two Land Rovers bounced over the rough ground at the side of the track and pulled up in front of the besieged caravan. Eight heavily-Tweeded figures emerged and lined up cowboy style in a threatening line with cocked shotguns cradled menacingly.

Deek peeked out from behind a curtain.

"Christ almighty. It's Roger. He's brought his shooting cronies."

Never could the collection of middle-aged lawyers, businessmen and landowners have looked more formidable. Roger Swann took on the role of the sheriff and stepped forward. His vigilante group had all stiffened themselves with a few drams as they had gathered up at the house and their faces were universally brick red.

"OK you lot. This is private property. My property. I'm giving you two minutes to get in your cars and piss off back to the road."

This caused a flurry of chatter. By and large the reporters were fairly young and were disinclined to be bullied by a bunch of middle-aged guys in wellies and Barbours. Roger stayed impressively still and watched the second hand of his watch complete first one circuit and then the second. When the two minutes were up and no move had been made by the reporters, he turned to his colleagues.

"OK lads."

The colour drained out of every journalistic face as the shooters cocked and raised their weapons. Their resolve cracked, and by the time the deafening roar of the volley shattered the peaceful spring morning they were nearly at the line of cars. Roger and his men fired high into the trees and a flutter of dead leaves and branches floated down as the convoy of cars did frantic three-point turns and headed back down the track. The sole casualty of the action was a three-year-old crow that had simply been in the wrong place at the wrong time.

Steve led his charges out as soon as the thunder of the guns roared. They emerged with a bag each and made straight for Steve's Japanese 4x4. Troll and Banjo tossed the bags into the back while Steve opened a gate into the field. Deek jogged over to where Roger Swann was watching the disorganised retreat of the trespassers with a satisfied smile.

"Cheers Roger. I owe you one."

"All of us actually" said Roger. "Tickets for Turnberry please. Five-star treatment. Full access. Fair enough?"

"Aye. You've got it. See you soon yeah?"

"Aye. You best bugger off now while they're still shitting themselves."

Deek joined the others and Steve bounced them across a couple of fields and out onto a small road. Fifteen minutes later they pulled unnoticed into the courtyard of Wee Donny's block of flats in the heart of Sunnybank.

The old school friend didn't disappoint and was more than happy to provide sanctuary. "Ah seen you on the tele Deek. You're dead famous now. Any chance of an autograph?"

Deek laughed, assuming that he was being ribbed about his new-found notoriety but Donny's face was completely earnest. "Aye Donny. Nae bother." He felt rather embarrassed as he signed his name for the lad he had known for twenty years. Troll produced coffee whilst Banjo slipped out to the local Spar to stock up on provisions. Steve wandered over to the window and looked out. All seemed normal and quiet. A couple of young mothers chatted as they aimed their pushchairs towards the town. A small gang of baseball-capped teenagers loafed about on a low wall whilst a dog-walking pensioner gave them a wide berth.

Steve took stock of the situation. It was over a month until they were due to fly out for the final meeting at the McMillan Ranch before returning to Turnberry for the match itself. Was the whole month going to be like this? As he stared out at the grey walls of Sunnybank he couldn't help but smile at the irony of the situation. He was more than familiar with this kind of bleak northern estate. There had been many such places in Ulster. Then the roles had been reversed. It had been the Bhoyos of the IRA who had been hiding up in the flats while he and 20,000 other British soldiers had been outside trying to track them down. What goes around comes around Stevie. He pulled out his phone and dialled up Sally who was in her Edinburgh office.

"Hi, it's Steve."

"Oh hello. How are you this morning? You've seen the *Daily Recorder* I suppose?"

"Yes. Things are hotting up here I'm afraid."

"Go on."

He ran her through the dramatic events of the morning and felt a despondent silence at the other end of the line. Sally didn't speak until he had finished.

"It's not very good is it? The First Minister was looking forward to a bit of Scottish feel-good factor. I don't suppose there's much chance of that now."

"Not a lot. The press don't tend to take it too well when they get volleys of buckshot fired over their heads. They'll be after blood sure enough. How are you going to respond to the *Recorder*, Sally?"

"In what way?"

"They want Deek off the programme. You read it same as me."

"It isn't my call. Only the McMillans have any say in that."

"Maybe you should give them a call."

"Yes. I suppose I'd better. I'll let you know if there are any developments."

"Fine. Me too. Things seem quiet enough at the moment. Let's just hope they lose the scent."

For a while it seemed as if they might. Then, a little after four, the cars started to pull up in the courtyard below. It was Troll who spotted them a few seconds before Deek's mobile rang with the same news. A few minutes later angry fists were banging at the door and questions were being yelled through the letterbox. Steve took in the scene outside and wasn't much surprised to find that the press numbers had swelled since the failed siege of the caravan. After half an hour, a new order of battle had established itself. A permanent advance party took up station in the corridor outside Donny's flat while the others stood guard over the cars and vans as the youngsters of Sunnybank gathered in an eager crowd.

The siege victims settled down rather miserably and were able to watch the scenes outside on the Border TV early evening news. Sally called a little after seven to report her dealings with the McMillans. Jonathan had discussed the matter with the old man and nothing had changed. As far as they were concerned Deek's status as number one wasn't altered at all. Roland sent a personal message to the beleaguered golfer apologising for all the problems he had caused. He suggested that Deek and his team might like to fly out a few days earlier than planned. They would be much more comfortable at the ranch where an iron ring of security would keep the press many miles away and the in-house golf course would offer an ideal place for undisturbed practice.

This news lifted the morale of the rather rattled Sunnybank Three and they took up the offer of hospitality gratefully. They were watching an early evening movie when a new commotion broke out in the corridor outside. Voices were raised and there was lots of angry swearing before a new and heavier hand beat at the door. This was followed by a loud, local voice.

"Donny! Open up will you. It's Gordo."

The name Gordo inspired little enthusiasm in the flat.

"Who's Gordo?" asked Steve.

Deek answered with contempt that was unusual for him. "Gordon Mitchell. Likes to call himself 'Grandslam Gordo'. One of our local hard men. He's a complete nutter. The whole family are. His dad is the big man round here. Fred Gordon. He's a hard-case as well, but he has a brain in his head. They make their money from dealing and money lending. I suppose we'd better let him in Donny."

Donny nodded with relief. He had no wish to get the on the wrong side of the dreaded Mitchell family. He eased open the door and a large shaven-headed man in a T-shirt three sizes too small burst into the room. Donny slammed and locked the door. Grandslam Gordo cut a striking figure. He was well over six feet tall and was carrying at least 50 pounds more than a doctor would have recommended. Most of the extra pounds were to be found on his belly which forced its way into the fresh air under the straining T-shirt. His arms were adorned with an array of tattoos that any merchant seaman would have been proud of and his muscles bore testimony to many hours in the gym. He was grinning from ear to ear and was obviously loving every minute of the unusual drama. His pupils were as big as a pair of soup plates in the centre of wild staring eyes that bore testimony to the two fat lines of speed he had snorted up a few minutes earlier.

"All right boys. Dunnae all cheer at once. Where's the beer?"

Donny dutifully trotted into the kitchen and returned with a can of Tennants. Gordo drained it in one mighty swig before crumpling the can and tossing it to the corner of the room for Donny to pick up.

"Right. Down tae business. My dad has sent me along. We're not happy about this lot." To clarify who he meant by "this lot" he gestured a contemptuous thumb towards the window. "As far as my dad is concerned they are bang out of order. We're not having any London twats thinking they can come lording it up on Sunnybank. No way."

"So what are you going to do about it?"

"I've got the lads sorted. Lots of them. We'll have them out of the court in a couple of hours." His manic grin spoke volumes about the tactics that the lads of Sunnybank were about to employ. "My dad says we've to get them out at least to the end of the road."

Deek shook his head. It was ridiculous, but there was little point in arguing. The word of the Mitchell family had been law on the streets of Sunnybank for as long as he could remember. Gordo dispatched Donny for another can of Tennants and lit up.

"We've found out how they got here. It was that wee junkie piece of shite Jamie Fletcher. He sold the information to some reporter in the pub. He must have seen you all arrive. The bastard sold you all out for a couple of tenner bags ae smack. Dunnae worry Deek. I'm going to sort him out later."

"Just leave the lad be Gordo. It's not his fault. You know how it is with those lads. You can't blame him." Over the years heroin had become a bitter fact of life for everyone on Sunnybank. It was behind every stolen bike or video. The community line was that the junkies were the scum of the earth, but few families were free of the chemical plague. Gordo's face hardened.

"What I may or may not do about Jamie Fletcher is none of your business Deek. We dunnae like junkies round here and we dunnae like grasses. You ken that well enough."

Deek's temper was frayed by the frantic events of the last two days. "Oh yeah Gordo. You go and break the lad's legs. How much does he weigh? Seven stone dripping wet? Real hard man aren't you?. And I wonder where he bought his tenner bag of smack? Wouldn't be the Mitchell family by any chance . . ."

Gordo's face was hardening by the second. The speed was rattling round his body and he was on a hair trigger. "You best watch it Deek."

"Or what Gordo? You going to slash my face are you?"

"Deek . . ." Troll was about to try and shut his friend up but it was too late. Gordo picked Deek out of the chair and tossed him to the floor. The big man was getting very angry by now.

"You dunnae talk to me like that you wee bastard, I'm going to . . ."

"You're not going to do anything." Steve hadn't spoken loudly but his voice stopped Gordo in his tracks. He turned about slowly with his meaty fists bunched.

"Oh, am I not? And just what are you planning on doing about it Englishman?"

Steve smiled. It wasn't a warm sight. "I'll make you stop, actually."

This made something snap and Gordo leapt at the smaller, older man like a demented rhino. Everything seemed to happen very quickly. Steve stepped aside like a ballet dancer and caught Gordo's wrist as he charged by. Once he had the wrist in his hands, he straightened the big man's arm and bent his wrist back far enough to make Gordo yelp in pain. Steve then kept the wrist clamped with one hand and took a little finger in the other. He spoke in a soft, bored kind of voice.

"Now then Gordo. I'm going to give you a little lesson in anatomy. The bones in the little finger are some of the weakest in the body. Now. I have your little finger in my hand. When I bend it back it will hurt. Maybe you could just confirm that?"

Steve yanked the finger back and Gordo confirmed by way of a high-pitched howl. "OK. Good. Now Gordo, I suggest that you listen. I'm going to tell you how things are going to pan out and you are going to agree. If you don't agree I am going to snap this little finger of yours and it will really, really hurt. Got that?"

"Aye." Gordo's voice was little more than an agonised whisper.

"Good. Now, if I have things right here, smacking Deek wasn't part of your dad's plan at all. So I suggest we forget all about it. What you are going to do now is piss off out of here and do whatever your dad told you to shift these reporters. You're not going to go anywhere near Jamie Fletcher because if I hear that you have, I'm going to break every finger you have. Now. Is that clear enough Gordo?"

"Aye."

"Splendid. Now piss off."

He gave the arm a twist and sent Gordo crashing into the door. Within seconds the scourge of Sunnybank had let himself out and was bounding down the stairs two at a time. It was Wee Donny who reacted first.

"Bloody hell. That was like one of them action movies. Bloody brilliant that was." He dug in the pocket of his jeans and pulled out the folded piece of paper that carried the signature that Deek had written earlier. He held out the paper to Steve along with a much-chewed pen. "Can I have your autograph too, Steve?"

In the 1980s an unlikely song made it into the UK's top ten. The theme of Paul Hardcastle's hit was that the average age of the American soldiers in Vietnam had been nineteen. Compared to the young soldiers who fought the battle of Sunnybank, the Vietnam grunts were veterans. The plan that Fred Mitchell had given to his hot-headed son was commendably simple and it relied heavily on youth. The Human Rights legislation that had swept across Western Europe in the late twentieth century made it very hard for the police to do much about the dreadful behaviour of the very young. Bearing this in mind, Fred Mitchell marshalled a force of 30 of Sunnybank's finest whose ages ranged from seven to eleven. They were divided into two squads and fully instructed about the two-pronged attack on the invading media. The attack was staged as darkness was starting to fall. The first squad of ten youngsters burst into the courtyard in a flurry of baseball caps and war cries. They ran at full tilt past the parked vehicles of the press. As they passed, they ran coins along the sides of the cars and vans and smacked the windscreens with hammers. The wilful damage roused the small groups of journalists to an immediate fruitless chase. As the raging adults chased the laughing kids, the second squad took advantage and opened up a withering barrage of half-bricks and stones at the unattended vehicles. Three of the more gallant darted out and slashed at tyres. The sound of rock smashing into metal stopped the chasing pack in their tracks and brought them racing back to try to protect the vehicles. Once they were back, the second squad of mobile artillery withdrew down an alley.

While the angry panting reporters assessed the thousands of pounds of damage that had been done to their fleet of vehicles, Beth Flanders strolled out from the main door of the block. Beth was a spry 70-year-old who had lived on Sunnybank ever since it was built in the wake of the Second World War. With a trademark cigarette dangling from her ruby red lips, she marched over to the cursing journalists.

"You're better buggering off. The lot of you. There's a car park by the main road. You'll be OK there."

"You threatening us lady?"

Beth smiled at this. "How can an old lass like me threaten the likes of you. I'm just giving you a wee bit of advice boys. And that advice is to piss off over to the car park. We don't take kindly to the likes of you on Sunnybank. I suggest that you're gone in ten minutes."

With this she turned smartly and marched back into the block with a clatter of heels. There were some half-hearted talk of holding the line and the freedom of the press, but it was never very serious. Well before the ten-minute deadline had expired, the battered convoy had retreated from the courtyard to the car park. Access to the courtyard was only possible from a single avenue with a T-junction at either end. Within minutes of the retreat of the journalists, the residents of Sunnybank emerged onto the street with all manner of old furniture and rubbish. Barricades were erected at either end of the avenue and suddenly there was a carnival atmosphere.

Within a couple of hours barbeques were glowing and the smell of sausages filled the air. The Sunnybank Three emerged from their sanctuary and Deek's hand ached from being shaken. The valiant young warriors who had led the attack soon had their pockets filled with donations of sweets and pound coins. They beamed in the knowledge that they had become legends. All that crazy night Deek was given a very clear message. It didn't matter what the rest of the world may think. The people of Sunnybank looked after their own and he was one of theirs.

The repair bills were considered to be a modest price to pay by the newspaper and TV bosses. The battle of the courtyard made for tremendous copy. All that night, numbers on the car park swelled and the media circus became an alternative attraction to the swinging party on the other side of the barricades. For the first time since the Foot and Mouth crisis, the town of Dumfries was in the media spotlight. The extraordinary scenes brought out the Chief Constable to take a look for himself a little after ten. He made a few bland comments to the press before consulting with the officers at the scene. He faced a considerable dilemma. For years, relations between the force and the inhabitants of Sunnybank had been at best strained and at worst disastrous. The barricades were manned by young and old. At the forefront were a group of very determined-looking women who were well along the road to middle age. When he chatted to them they made it perfectly clear that the barricades would stay in place for as long as the press were bothering Deek. He knew full well that not a single person holding the line would have a hint of a criminal record.

Having given the matter some thought, he realised that any kind of forceful action against lines held by law-abiding women and children would lead to the mother of all public relations catastrophes. He therefore decided that pragmatism was the best course of action and instructed his uniformed officers to discreetly let it be known that as long as there was no violence, the barricades could stay in place. Secretly he was 100 percent behind the action of the good folk of Sunnybank. He was a member of the same golf club as Deek and had watched him since he was a gawky kid. Later, he got hold of Deek's mobile and told him, off the record, that the barricades would be allowed to stay in place. He also gratefully accepted the offer of a ticket for the big match.

The front pages of the next morning's tabloid papers were more or less unified in their near-hysterical condemnation of the people of Sunnybank. The behaviour of the pre-teen army in the battle of the courtyard was cited as evidence of the growing lawlessness of Britain's young. The fact that it was so obvious that they were actively encouraged by the adults of the estate was seen as a clear indication of the kind of chronic moral decay which was destroying a once great nation. No graphic detail was spared in the description of the sheer terror faced by journalists who were gallantly trying to pursue the public interest. All through every one of the bitter articles it was made clear that the root cause of the inexcusable mayhem was a drunken golfer called Archie Banks, AKA Deek.

In one way, the judgement of the newspapers was absolutely correct. The story did indeed hook deep into the public's imagination. Sales of papers were on average six percent up on a routine Wednesday in April. This caused great bouts of self-congratulation and expense accounts were hit hard as champagne was ordered to accompany designer lunches. The ad men had a big day as they filled their space on the promise that the Deek story was good to run for at least another week and probably more.

What the editors did not notice was that in another way their judgement was hopelessly wrong. They had made the age-old mistake of believing their own publicity and had become totally convinced that it was their absolute right to preach on about the moral health of the nation. They had grown to depend on their tried and trusted paper-selling formula of creating a celeb, digging the dirt, then knocking them to the floor. They just knew that the British public had an insatiable appetite for seeing known faces with their trousers around their ankles or blind drunk or bog-eyed with narcotics. What they had failed to notice was that the British people were getting rather sick of the holier-than-thou attitude that the tabloids and their editors loved to hold. They had never really forgiven the papers for the part that they played in the death of Princess Diana, and so when the people of Sunnybank took their dramatic action to kick the newshounds off their patch, there were people all over Britain who had raised a cheer.

The editors also got it badly wrong in regard to Deek. For them, he was just another easy mark. A bit of a lad who deserved to be taken down a peg or two. Once again they showed just how out of touch they were. The British had always loved their sporting heroes to be a little rough around the edges. Gazza and Hurricane Higgins and George Best and Ian Botham enjoyed enduring popularity where other clean-cut professional athletes seldom won the affection of the public. When they watched Deek's archived interviews from Thailand, people took a liking to him. He was funny without being cocky. He was like the sort of guy that everyone already knew. The guy down the pub. The guy at work. The guy who brightened up a rainy morning. Almost everyone thought he was the sort of guy they would get along with. He had no airs and graces. He wasn't just another jumped-up, overpaid celeb. He was just a regular bloke. And sure, he had a drink problem. Lots of people had that problem. It was something that could be understood, sympathised with, something that an uncle or sister had battled with. It wasn't a grand a night on cocaine. It was half a bottle of spirits a day. How many MPs and captains of industry and doctors and lawyers shared the same problem? They didn't get picked on. The only reason that the papers were having a go at Deek was because he was just a little guy who couldn't fight back. Well, at least his own people had looked after him.

The mood of middle Britain was surprisingly united. People talked about it at work and agreed that it was about time too. About time that the cocky journalists got a taste of their own medicine. About time that ordinary folk fought back for a change. And so the more the papers laid into Deek and his neighbours, the more the rank and file of the country raised their glasses to them.

The next morning Troll brought in the papers and it was more bad news. This time the *Recorder* focused on gambling. All of Deek's off-the-record conversation with Tiffany about his frantic round of betting with Jimmy Hup Lee was described in gloating detail. A representative of the European PGA had confirmed that it would not under any circumstances tolerate gambling and that the matter would be investigated. Deek tossed down the paper with resignation.

"Well that's it then."

"What is?" asked Steve.

"That." Deek pointed to the offending paper. "I'm stuffed. They'll ban me."

"No they won't. How can they? The only people that actually know are you and Jimmy. Sure, you told Tiffany, but she won't go public. How can she? All you need to do is talk to Jimmy. If you both stay quiet, you'll be fine. Have you got a number for him?"

"Aye. I have somewhere."

Deek dug it out and found Jimmy at home in Pusan. "Ah. Deek. How you?"

"Nae bad Jimmy. Have you heard any of the news?"

"Sure. Reporters on phone all morning. You big man in news Deek" Jimmy sounded more than a little amused.

"You did'nae tell them anything?"

"You crazy! I tell nothing. Who believe such crazy stories. Jimmy no make no bets. Never!"

"Good man. I'm going to do the same. I'm real sorry about it. Some bloody American woman played me for a complete sucker, but there is no way she can ever go public. So long as we stick together we'll be OK."

"So. You play big George. You make win, yes?"

Deek chuckled. "I wouldn't count on it Jimmy. He's a bit out of my league don't you think."

"Hey, Deek. You win big. You should see odds here in Korea. Yesterday I get 40-to-one."

"What? For me to beat George?"

"Sure. Big, big price, yes?"

"Big price but I figure the bookies have it about right."

"No. They wrong. I bet $10,000."

"What! On me?"

"Sure Deek. You going to make win. I have big, big faith."

They reminisced about their Bangkok karaoke nights for a while and ended the call with the promise to do it again. Steve had gone dangerously quiet when he read the new dose of vitriol in the

Recorder. Once again the paper loudly called for Deek to be banned from representing the country. It was beginning to make Steve's blood boil.

"That's it."

"What?"

"I'm putting a stop to it. That's what."

He thumped a number into his phone and tapped his foot impatiently as he waited for an answer. "Hello."

"Walter, it's Steve again."

"Jeez, ain't I honoured. Not a peep for years and now I hear from you twice in a week. Was my Intel on Miss Latimer useful buddy?"

"It was. The problem was that it was too late. Have you seen any of the news about this big golf match. George Albright and the McMillan art collection?"

"Sure have. It's playing real big over here. I hear the President is going get his face in front of the cameras." The American's big voice dripped with sarcasm.

"Has there been much coverage about our guy?"

"Deek! Sure. He's all over the papers and TV. Sounds like he's getting a tough time of it."

"He's the guy I'm baby-sitting."

"Ah. So the pennies fall into place. You with him in this Sunnybank place?"

"I'm speaking from the very place."

"Looks pretty well like Dodge City from where I'm sitting."

Steve grinned. "Dodge City and then some."

"So. Let me see if I can put a few pieces together. Do I gather that Miss Latimer masqueraded as an American student and got your man to tell her more than he should have?"

"You're on the money Walter."

"And surprise, surprise, all that cosy pillow talk has mysteriously turned up in the hands of the media."

"Right again."

"OK. I'm with you so far. What do you want from me then Steve?"

"I want a direct phone number to Larry Weinberg."

"Jesus Christ Steve, that is one hell of a big ask."

"It is, but you know that nobody would ever find out how I got it."

There was a silence for a while on the American end of the line.

Eventually Walter spoke again. "OK Steve. I trust you. You know it would be my career, yeah?"

"I know that."

"OK. I'll text you. Give it five minutes."

The text duly beeped its arrival a few minutes later. By now all eyes in the room were glued to Steve. "Are you sure you want to do this Steve?" asked Deek.

"I am. 150 percent."

He took a breath and tapped in the number. It was answered on the second ring by an ill-tempered sounding voice.

"Weinberg."

"Good morning Mr Weinberg. You don't know me."

"Too right. And I don't speak to people I don't know."

"I am reasonably certain that you'll want to speak to me."

"Oh yeah? So who the hell are you?"

"I'm Steve Kenton from MI5. That's British Intelligence in case you don't know."

The American voice was rising now. "Of course I know who the goddamn hell MI5 is. What do you think I am? Some kinda schmuck? Who the hell gave you this number!"

"Never mind the number Mr Weinberg. I got it. It is the kind of thing that officers of the security services are good at. I am ringing to mark your card and I suggest that you listen."

"I'm all ears. You might as well know that your career just became toast."

"We'll see about that. Miss Samantha Latimer. Something of a protégé of yours I gather. She did rather a nice little song and dance act over here recently. The 'butter wouldn't melt in your mouth' college girl with a drink problem. It seems like the details of what was a private, 'off the record' conversation are finding their way into the hands of the media."

"So. What the hell do I care about Samantha Latimer? I don't know nothing about her any more. She's freelance."

"Oh I think that you might care Mr Weinberg. You should know that two can play your little media game. You should know that I have a photo that places Miss Latimer in the very same caravan that has appeared on the front page of the *Daily Recorder*. Maybe I could send that along to someone with a press release describing

Miss Latimer's past employment history. I think the media would be more than a little interested to hear how a girl who helped put the President into the White House came to be in a caravan in Scotland. How about you Larry? What do you think? Do you think the press would like that?"

"So what do you want?" The voice was quieter now. Less aggressive. Larry Weinberg knew only too well when someone had him by the balls.

"I want a deal. I figure that you do deals Larry?"

"Sure. I do deals."

"Then it stops. All of it. As from now. If America are going to win this thing, then George Albright is going to have to manage it all on his own. Agreed?"

"Agreed. It's done. This thing goes away now?"

"It does." Steve was about to say his goodbyes but the line was already dead. He looked up at the three expectant faces. "Sorted. No more problems from Miss Latimer."

"Great" grinned Deek. "So that just leaves the rest of the planet outside of Sunnybank."

The next morning Troll's face was, if anything, even more grave than the morning before. It was becoming a ritual. He handed over the paper and slumped down in a chair. The headline would have been visible from across a busy street.

'FIRST THE DRINK . . . NOW THE DRUGS!!'

Beneath was the photo from Scoobytown. The glassy eyes of Deek and Troll stared into the camera as they sat with their arms around Scooby's huge shoulders. Slack grins. Glazed expressions. An unmistakably tropical backdrop. And, in pride of place in Deek's hand was a glowing Camberwell Carrot.

"Oh shite." Deek wondered just how bad things had to get before they got better. Maybe they would never get better. This was unbelievable.

"What's my Mam going to say?" Troll's question was more or less rhetorical. His voice was pure misery.

There wasn't much anyone could say. It was Steve who spoke up first, his voice dangerously angry. "That lying bastard. I thought I could trust him. That's it now. All bets are off . . ."

He was reaching for his phone but Deek stopped him. "Don't Steve. This has'nae got anything to do with America. This is a little bastard toe rag from Essex called Deco. He took the picture. The wee shite must have sold it to the paper."

They all tried to put on a brave face on but it wasn't easy. The constant stream of bad news from the papers was taking a heavy toll.

"Christ," said Deek. "I just wish this whole pictures thing had never happened. Life was'nae great before, but this is a bloody nightmare."

Nobody could think of much to say to disagree. They were all very down and quiet when Deek's phone rang. He picked it up rather gingerly, clearly nervous that it could only bring yet more bad news. "Hello?"

"Is that Archie Banks speaking?" The voice was soft. A stranger.

"Aye."

"Hello Archie. This is Roland McMillan speaking."

Deek sat up in surprise.

"Oh. Hello Mr McMillan. You best call me Deek. Everyone calls me Deek"

"So I've noticed. Deek, I've seen the papers and I just felt that I should call."

So this was it then. The *Daily Recorder* was about to get its way. Well, he could hardly complain. None of it had been lies.

"Not pretty reading I'm afraid Mr McMillan."

"No it isn't. I just feel that I should apologise, Deek. Without this golf match of mine, none of this would ever have happened. Is there anything at all that I can do to help?"

Deek felt a surge of relief. Suddenly he knew that he really did want to take up his place at Turnberry and represent his country. "No Mr McMillan. I don't think that there's anything. All I can do is try and keep my head down and ride it out. I'm just glad that you're not ringing up to dump me. I'd understand if you did, you ken?"

"Now why on earth would I want to do that?"

"Pretty obvious isn't it. Drink, drugs and gambling. Does nae look very good does it?"

"You're no speakin tae some toff here Deek. Ken a'm a lad frae Korkonnel. Thenk a'hd hav'ae problem wi a few wee things like?"

The sudden switch into broad Scottish took Deek completely by surprise. When Roland resumed, he reverted to his normal quiet tone. "Seriously Deek. I'm delighted that it's you. You and me come from the same kind of place. Life was pretty tough when I grew up in Kirkonnel when it was a coal town. Since then I have spent years of my life with Texas oil men. I would rather it was someone like you than someone from a nice big house up in Edinburgh. You haven't committed any great crimes here, Deek. The press with muck rake to sell a few papers, but I believe that the people will like you well enough. I'm 95 years old and the biggest lesson of my life is that the only ones who matter are the people."

Deek was taken aback. This wasn't close to any preconceived ideas he had about how billionaires spoke. "Thank you for saying so, Mr McMillan."

"It is no more than the truth. I gather from Johnny that you will be joining us early to spend some time practising."

"Yes. Thanks for the offer."

"Is there a park or anything on Sunnybank estate?"

What the hell was this all about? "Sort of. Just a big field really. Why?"

"I will make arrangements for a helicopter to pick you up and take you to the airport. It will keep you clear of the journalists. It is the least that I can do."

Unbelievable. A helicopter ride out of Sunnybank. *Alice in Wonderland* again.

"That's great. Fantastic. What can I say?"

"No need to say anything. Just try to keep your spirits up as best as you can."

The call from Texas had a positive impact on the morale of the room and they decided to go outside for bacon rolls from one of the barbeques that had evolved into a permanent outdoor café. Deek was relieved to find there was no difference in the way that the people of Sunnybank were responding to him. Maybe Roland McMillan had been right. It made sense that a man who had come from nothing to be worth more than many small developing countries would tend to be right more than he was wrong. The only ones that matter are the people. An interesting thought. A thought that was so often forgotten. The people around him had come through. Even with yet another miserable slating on the front pages, they were all still foursquare behind him. What a difference it would make if only the people of Sunnybank could be like this all the time. For some strange reason he was a catalyst.

The scenes all around him gladdened his heart. It was a sunny Saturday morning and everyone seemed to be out on the streets. They had called the collapse of communism in Czechoslovakia the Velvet Revolution. This was the Barbeque Revolution. The pavements and the street had become the communal area. Everybody was talking to each other and for once it seemed as if everyone was smiling.

He had just taken a big bite out of a bacon roll when he spotted the postman staggering towards him with a mailbag hefted over his shoulder. As the sweating rotund figure drew nearer, Deek realised that it was an old pal from school.

"Bloody hell Dave. Got a load on have you?"

"Aye. And those miserable old cows on the barricade wouldn't let me through in the van. I think they were just having a laugh. There's another sack as big as this one still in the back."

"Christ, Dave. Is all that lot just for the one street?"

"Is it buggery. It's all for the one address. Deek. Sunnybank Estate. Dumfries. The lads at the sorting office cannae believe it. You're a Beatle pal. Can I dump these here?"

Deek was struck completely dumb for a while. In the end he nodded, and the bag was dropped at his feet. He opened it tentatively, and inside were hundreds and hundreds of letters of all shapes and sizes. The senders were young and old, male and female. There were typed letters and handwritten letters and cards. 95 percent were completely supportive. Children begged autographs, old men told their war stories, females from girlhood to middle age offered marriage and an open book of passion. Golfers offered earnest support. Widows wrote as to a long-lost grandson. And in one in three of the envelopes there was money. Some held a pound coin, some five pounds, some ten pounds. There were cheques and postal orders. He was staggered by the simple gestures of support contained in just about every letter he opened. Roland's words came back to him. Only the people mattered. And here the people were talking to him in a very British way. They had sent their letters to say "Keep the faith, don't let the bastards grind you down, chin up." It was utterly mind-boggling.

Tables were brought out, and soon an assembly line was set up to open and sort the mail. Money was tossed into a plastic dustbin after being counted. All morning the sum rose until, when the last letter of the second sack was opened, the sum had risen to over seven thousand pounds.

"Being a bad boy isn't a bad little earner, hey Deek." Troll's face had lost every trace of the misery of the morning.

"Naa. I cannae keep this Troll. It would'nae be right."

"Well, you're going to have to do something with it."

"Aye. That's for sure."

They were in the process of scratching their heads when a small voice from the permanently formed group of wide-eyed youngsters piped up.

"I've got an idea, Deek."

It was Charlie Phillips who had won his spurs two days earlier by putting an impressive dent on the bonnet of the *Sky News* van with his uncle's lump hammer.

Deek smiled. "Come on then Charlie. Let's hear it then."

Many nine-year-olds would have been hindered by an onset of shyness at being such a centre of attention, however Charlie was an Artful Dodger in the makings and held no such fears. "Well." He was very serious. "If us lads hadn't helped oot, they reporters wid still ae been here, ken?"

"Aye. Fair enough. I'll give you that."

"Well I reckon we deserve a wee reward for getting rid ae them."

"Do you now. And what kind of a wee reward have you in mind Charlie?"

"A skate park. Half pipe. The lot. We've been asking for one frae years Deek. You ken that."

Deek was thoughtful. Of course he kenned it. Everybody kenned it. There was often public money invested in things to keep the young people of the town occupied and out of trouble. The problem was that it always seemed to be spent everywhere but Sunnybank. It had been a running local sore for as long as he could remember. Maybe Charlie had something.

"You know, wee Charlie, I just reckon you're a genius. You've got it. Nae bother." He gave the dustbin a gentle kick. "This is now the Sunnybank Skate Park Fund."

In the end the only thing that matters is the people. Too right Roland. Too right. The announcement called for beers and they were duly brought down from the new American walk-in style fridge that they had bought as a gesture of thanks for wee Donny's hospitality. Deek noticed a new shifty expression on Banjo's face. It was a look that he had been familiar with for over 25 years. Banjo had always been the brains of the outfit. The schemer. The man for the scam. "Aye aye. Look at you Banjo. Spit it out."

"Well . . . as the manager I need to take care of the details. Seems to me that this skate park thing is short of something."

"Aye. And what's that?"

"We cannae just keep all this cash in a dustbin can we? Beside, there's cheques. An appeal needs a bank account."

"I suppose so." Deek was somewhat disappointed that Banjo's scheme was so dull.

Banjo saw this and grinned mischievously. "And a bank account needs a manager." His smile stayed in place as he paused. "Or even a manageress."

And then the penny dropped. Of course. Meg.

"She wouldn't do it. She hates my guts."

"She has 'tae do it! It's charity. She cannae say no."

Deek shook his head. He couldn't handle another rejection, not when things at last seemed as if they were looking up. "No Banjo. I cannae face it. She'd just put the phone down on me. I can't."

"You dunnae have to. That's why you have a manager my man. Leave the detail to me."

Deek wasn't at all sure, but in the end he knew he was bound to agree. If there was any kind of straw to clutch at when it came to Meg, he knew full well that he would reach for it like a drowning man. "Go on then."

He looked on miserably as Banjo took himself off to one side and chatted in animated fashion on his mobile phone. He could barely contain himself when the call was complete.

"So?"

"Nae bother. She's coming."

"What, now!"

"Aye. Now."

"Oh shite."

Word was passed down to the guardians of the barricades and Meg's Ford Focus was allowed free passage. As they watched it turn the corner, Banjo dug in his pocket and pulled out a handful of papers.

"Christ. Nearly forgot. Remember all those notes I got from reporters wanting an exclusive?"

"Aye. We told them all to piss off."

"Exactly."

Deek didn't get it. "What do you mean 'exactly'?"

"Here." Banjo pressed a business card into Deek's hand. He studied it.

Lynn Headley. Sky Sports.

Something familiar about the name. Of course. The woman from the interview in Bangkok. He smiled as he followed Banjo's devious train of thought. In response he received a knowing wink. He was watching the car make its way up the road when he realised that Steve was at his side.

"You all right Steve?"

"Grand as owt mate. Give me a minute with her, will you?"

Deek frowned. What was going on now? He was about to object but he had got into the habit of trusting the hard man from Manchester. "Aye. If you need one."

Steve stepped forward and opened the driver's door. "Excuse me ma'am. I wonder if I might have a quick word." He surreptitiously flashed his ID card. "I'll just jump in the passenger side shall I? It will only take a couple of secs."

Before Meg had a chance to reply, Steve marched round the front of the car and jumped in. She was far from pleased.

"I suggest that you show me that card again. I didn't have a chance of reading it before."

"Of course." He passed it over and she studied it with a frown.

"I don't understand. What does this mean?"

"MI5 miss. The Security Service."

"As in 'spy'?"

"Not really. All that stuff is for the tele I'm afraid. I drink pints of lager, not vodka Martini shaken, stirred or anything else."

Her mood was showing no sign of improving. "Look. I am a small-town manager. I have come to find out about some hair-brained scheme to open up an account to build a skateboard park. I cannot for the life of me see what any of this can be of the remotest interest to the security services. Aren't you lot supposed to be chasing Arab terrorists or something?"

"Absolutely miss."

"So what in God's name are you doing here on Sunnybank Estate."

"Believe it or not, it's my job to protect Deek from Arab terrorists, or any other nutter who gets out of bed on the wrong side for that matter."

"And do I look like an Arab terrorist or a random nutter?"

He grinned. "Nope. But you look pretty pissed off."

She tried hard to maintain her fierce demeanour but it wasn't easy. There was something unavoidably appealing about his bluff northern manner. He had a lived-in sort of face and eyes that spoke of a hard life. A face a bit like Deek's. She allowed some of the tension to ease out of her shoulders. Most of the tension had built up as she had driven across town wondering if Deek would be waiting for her. He was. He was waiting on the pavement looking like an abused puppy.

"So, Mr . . ."

"Steve. I'm Steve."

"So, Steve. What can I do for you? Am I to assume that you consider me to be a threat to your charge? Have I a long-lost uncle called Mohammed?"

He laughed. "Oh you're a threat all right. Probably twenty times more of a threat than anything that Al Quaida could muster."

"What on earth are you talking about?"

"Oh come on Meg, you know. One look from you does him more damage than a fragmentation grenade."

She looked down at this. There wasn't much to say. It was true enough.

"Look love. Sorry. That was out of order. It's just this. My job is to keep Deek safe. Simple as that. Close protection we call it, not that there is any real threat as far as I can see. The thing is . . . well, he's become a mate. He's a good guy. I like him. Know what I mean."

"I know what you mean." She replied in a small voice, still looking down.

"There's something you should know. That woman. Tiffany. The one you met when you called round the other morning."

This brought her head up with colour flowing into her pale cheeks. "What about her?"

"She was a fake. She played the part of a journalist with a drink problem. She completely suckered Deek. Got him into an all-night heart-to-heart over a couple of bottles of scotch. Most of the time he talked about you. The rest of the time he told her about how he couldn't pick up a club without a drink. She had a hidden tape recorder. That's how all that stuff found its way into the papers."

Now Meg's blood was really up. "The stinking bitch. Who was she working for?"

He looked a little uneasy. "It's sensitive. Can I trust you?"

"Of course you can. I'm a bank manager."

He thought about it a little longer. Why not? She didn't seem the leaky type and who would believe it anyway? Even if they did, the Yanks probably had it coming. He felt no particular loyalty to the "Special Relationship."

"The White House."

"What!!"

"I know. Unbelievable isn't it? They obviously don't want the gallant underdog stealing their PR thunder."

"Bastards."

"Quite."

She sat and fumed for a while. "So you're telling me that nothing happened?"

"Exactly that, though it is easy to see how it looked."

"I thumped him."

"So I heard. No harm done though."

She looked straight at him now. "You think so?"

He smiled. "I know so."

Meg nodded. "Thanks for telling me, Steve. It would seem that Deek has made a good friend."

Steve gestured to the crowds of Sunnybankers who filled the street in the spring sunshine. "Deek has lots of friends."

This brought a smile to her face. "Yes. Yes he has. Anything more?"

"No. That's all. I just wanted to help put the record straight."

They climbed out and Deek's face twisted another few notches as Meg approached.

"Hi Meg."

"Hello Deek. You look well."

"Aye. And you. Here. I've got this to show you." He passed her the *Sky Sports* business card which she examined with a look of incomprehension. "What is it?"

"It's from that bird. The reporter. Her with the big hair from Bangkok. She wanted an exclusive interview. Sent this over from the car park. Offered 10,000 quid."

"And?"

"I told her to piss off."

The tension drained from her and she had to laugh. "You really are the daftest bugger I have ever met, Deek."

"So we're friends then?"

"Aye. We're friends. Are you going to buy me a drink then?"

He grinned. "I thought it was the bank manager who bought the drinks for the client?"

"Don't push it."

He held up his hands in surrender. "OK. You win. Let's walk shall we?"

As it happened there wasn't a chance of either of them buying a drink. Deek's money was no good on Sunnybank. They spent a pleasant couple of hours wandering from group to group, chatting and sharing a drink and a drumstick from the barbeques. The sudden outbreak of raging community spirit astounded Meg. Only a week ago, all these people had been hiding from each other behind double-locked doors. None of this would have happened without Deek. Suddenly she was very, very proud of him. She took his arm and they strolled to the middle of the acres of empty grass which were earmarked for the skate park.

"What are you going to do about all those letters, Deek?"

"Christ knows. I cannae reply to all of them in person. There's thousands of them. Banjo is coming up with a general thankyou letter. I'll make sure I sign them all."

"You really should try and say thank you in person."

"What do you mean?"

"The tele. I think you should do an interview. Say thanks and tell everyone what the money is being used for."

His face darkened. "I'm giving no interviews to any of those bastards out there." He waved his are angrily in the direction of the car park where the slowly thinning band of media men had made camp.

"No. Of course not. But what about someone local? There's the evening papers and West Sound. What about the BBC? Didn't you once do a couple of interviews with them. Remember? When you made it to the semi-finals of the Scottish Amateur Championships."

He nodded. "Aye. That was Willie. Willie Johnstone. Willie's OK. He's on the tele these days as well. The news and all that."

"Well, there you are then. Why don't you get Banjo to give him a call. An interview with the BBC would go right out across the country."

Again Roland's words came into his head. The only ones that matter are the people. He nodded slowly. "Aye. You're right. Happen I might talk folk into a few more donations."

She smiled. "Happen you might."

"Might even get enough for a youth club. Sunnybank has been needing a youth club for years."

"You're becoming quite the social campaigner, aren't you Deek?"

He shook his head. "No it's not that Meg, well it's just, well . . ."

"There's no need to make excuses. I like it."

This stopped him in his tracks and he fiddled about with a piece of wood he had picked up as they walked. "Really?"

"Really. In fact there is quite a lot that I like about the Deek who came back from Asia. Something changed, didn't it?"

"Aye."

"So why don't we sit. Maybe you could tell me about it?"

They found a patch of grass that was reasonably clear from the dog dirt and discarded cans and bottles. He told her all about Scoobytown, about how Scooby himself had managed to find a way of getting his wrecked brain clear of the horrors he had seen in the A Shau valley. He told her how every day he would walk on his own for miles along the tiny dirt roads through the forests. He told her how he had made up his mind that enough was enough and somehow he had to try and turn things around. There had only ever been one thing on his mind during all those quiet days of tropical contemplation. Meg. Only her.

"Then I get back here and . . . well you ken how it has been. It was bad enough when I had to buy my own drinks, but now I cannae walk down the street for five yards without someone offering me a dram."

"I know. But you say that this man Scooby says he will help you, yes?"

"Aye."

"Well, there isn't much point in worrying about it until you get the chance to go back there and see him, is there?"

He bowed his head again. "You know that I need a drink, don't you Meg? I cannae manage without one anymore. My body needs it."

"Yes. I know that. I've probably known that for longer than you've known it yourself."

She was surprised to see that tears were trickling down his cheeks. This was not like him. Always before, life had always just bounced off. Scoobytown had changed him, of that there was no doubt.

"The thing is, Meg, I'll have tae drink at this Turnberry match. I just can't get round the course without one. Everyone will know. All the cameras will watch me every time I take a swig from my flask. I won't be able to hide it . . . I'm scared, Meg."

She reached over and took him to her. She could feel the tears of shame as she cradled his head and gently ran her fingers through his hair. "No need, Deek. If they see you, then so what. Who cares? Do the people here on Sunnybank care? No. Do all those thousands of people who sent the letters care? No. Does Roland McMillan care? I don't think so. You are what you are, Deek. And people like you for it."

His voice was muffled as he spoke in a rather choked voice. "In the end the only ones who matter are the people."

She smiled down at the unexpectedly profound sentiment. "And if it is of any help, I will be with you every step of the way. You're not the only one who has woken up, Deek. For twelve years I have behaved like a nasty stuck-up cow thinking of my crappy career. You weren't the only one who needed a wake-up call. If you will forgive me, then I'm back. And I won't be going anywhere again."

He pulled away from her and stared into her face with a look of incomprehension. "You'll come with me to Texas and the Match?"

She put on just about the worst cheesy Hollywood accent that had ever been heard in Sunnybank. "Where you go, I go sugar."

He grinned. "Including Scoobytown?"

"Absolutely including Scoobytown."

"What about work?"

"Stuff work. I'm through with being sensible. I'll take the gamble that Scotland's number one golfer will win enough to keep me in the style that I've become accustomed to. And if he doesn't, then I'll live in the caravan."

Deek shook his head. It seemed like every day of his new life was filled with moments when he couldn't tell if he was actually awake or not. "I cannae believe it."

"Well you'd better, because it's true. You've got the girl and the movie still has half an hour to run. Are you going to stare at me all day with that daft look on your face or are you going to kiss me?"

And Deek realised that *Alice in Wonderland* was a fairytale all along and kissed her.

There was a sense of seething resentment among the encamped journalists when word filtered through that a BBC van had been allowed through the barricades. They dropped everything and took up station opposite the grinning women and mocking kids. How had they swung it? The Beeb never had a budget for cheque-book journalism. Every one of the tabloid papers had been following instructions from their head offices. Day after day they had been passing higher and higher financial offers across the lines to Banjo for an exclusive. The word about the massive volumes of support mail going into Sunnybank was well and truly out. This had been borne out by a much higher than usual level of abusive letters to the increasingly beleaguered editors. Over the course of a few days the tabloids had completely lost control of the agenda. They had opened up their familiar Pandora's box and had unwittingly created a cult figure.

All of a sudden Deek was the man. He had become A-list. He was the man of the people. The trouble was that no matter what carrots they waved in front of his nose he just kept on telling them to piss off. All the reporters had been looking over each other's shoulders amidst an atmosphere of increasing paranoia. Who would manage to snare the exclusive? How much would they pay for it? Nobody wanted to lose out. Which made it all the more galling when it was the BBC who got the nod.

Willie Johnstone couldn't quite believe it. London hadn't been on the phone since he had received his surprising call from Banjo. The Corporation was gearing itself to feature the interview across its worldwide digital network. The extent that the story had gone global had come as a shock to everyone. The story had obvious appeal in Britain and the States, but the whole David and Goliath theme played well in countries far and wide. This of course was helped by the fact that the David in the tale was such a colourful and flawed figure. It also did no harm that the Goliath represented the world's ultimate superpower that had managed to piss off most of the planet with its arrogance. The Asian world was hooked by the unsubstantiated rumours about Deek and Jimmy Hup Lee's betting spree. The Third World loved the underdog bit. Most of the former Soviet Bloc found a collective sympathetic chord in the alcoholism. It was the story for everyone, and against all odds the telling of it fell on Willie Johnstone.

He shook Deek's hand and looked about at the extraordinary scene. He had done many stories on Sunnybank estate and couldn't remember a single one of them that would fall into the "feel-good" category. Big drugs raids. Overdoses. Joy-riding. Steepling unemployment. A couple of particularly nasty domestic killings. Nothing like this. This was from another planet.

They decided to the interview walking around the various barbeques and little stalls that had been set up. His idea was that it should all be as informal as possible. The world that evening was to watch the pair of them strolling about Sunday-morning style, chatting as they went.

"We'll start with what has happened here on Sunnybank, shall we Deek? We've both lived here for all of our lives. There has never been anything like this has there?"

Deek smiled. "No. That's right enough. I dunnae suppose anyone can quite believe it. I think the people here just got kind of sick of being called bad, you ken? It's not just here. It's the same in every wee town in Scotland. There's always that area where the bad people live. Well, I guess we all just decided that we'd had enough of it. At least people can see the truth now. We're just the same as anyone. There's good and bad everywhere. At least we've managed to stick together."

"Is this that the motivation behind your appeal?"

"Well, it's not really an appeal. People just sent me money. I could'nae believe it, to be honest. After what the papers had been saying, I felt as if the whole world must hate me. Then the postman turned up with two big sacks of letters. You should have seen it. We had to set up an assembly line to open them all."

"And that is when you came up with the idea for the skate park?"

Deek laughed and shook his head. "Hell no. It was'nae my idea. It was wee Charlie Phillips. You'll have tae have a word with him before you go. But I'm chuffed to go with it. You see, the kids here never seem to get anything. It's always in the town. That is why they get into bother most of the time. I was just lucky. I found I could play golf and it kept me out of bother."

Willie smiled. "Really?"

Deek read his thought. "Well, I mean real bother. Crime and drugs and the likes. Most of it's just boredom. Nothing to do. But look. That's why I wanted to do this interview. I just want tae say thanks to all the people who've sent in donations. And I want tae let them ken that the money will be put to good use."

Willie steered the talk on. "There has been a lot in the papers about you having a drink problem, Deek. What are your thoughts on this issue?"

Deek shrugged. "What can they be? I wish they had'nae printed all that, but there's no point denying it. Sure. I need a drink. I can't get by without one. I'm not pretending any different."

"What about the game at Turnberry?"

"I was worried about that. I ken where you're coming from. Will I be drinking out there on the course? The answer is yes. I've no choice. If I dunnae take a drink, I cannae play. Simple as that. Nobody's going to be shocked any more. Not after all this."

"Are you concerned about how the McMillan Corporation will feel about it?"

"I was. Of course I was. Who would'nae be? But Roland McMillan gave me a ring and we talked. He's a good guy. Unbelievable really. Ken he's a Kirkonnel lad?"

"Yes. He left a long time ago though. 1925 I believe." Deek couldn't resist it. "Aye, but you ken what they say. You can take the man oot ae Kirkonnel . . ."

Willie duly took his cue and finished the sentence. ". . . but you cannae take Kirkonnel out of the man. You like him then?"

"Aye. We've only talked on the phone, but he's dead down tae earth."

By now they had made their way out onto the great expanse of empty grass. The cameraman who was walking backwards stood in a hefty pile of dog droppings and cursed loudly. Willie chuckled. "I think we'd better edit that bit out."

They talked some more about the site of the proposed skate park and Deek floated the idea of a youth centre if the funds kept rolling in.

As they made their way back towards the flats, Willie steered the chat onto the subject of the match.

"So Deek. George Albright. What are your thoughts?"

"Bloody terrified basically. The man is a legend. Have you seen the way he hits it off the tee? Christ, his swing is something off another planet. Bloody brilliant to be honest."

"So you're not exactly confident then?"

"Confident?" Deek spat the word out. "You have tae be kidding. How could anyone be confident going up against Big George over 54 holes."

"So you can't see a way of winning then?"

Deek took some time and lit up a cigarette. "I did'nae say that. Nobody ever gives us Scots a chance. Too be honest, we never seem to have much of a chance. We always seem to get our arses kicked, usually by the bloody English. But every now and then it is different. About every 300 years. We only get one Bannockburn for every twenty Culloden Moors. But you never know. Maybe I might just get my own Bannockburn. On paper I dunnae stand a snowball's chance in hell. On the golf course, who knows. Funny things can happen."

George Albright watched the interview at his home later that evening. Like most of the golfing world, he had been keeping up with Deek's daily tribulations with a keen interest. Initially he had felt sorry for his fellow beleaguered pro. But after a few days, much to his own surprise, he began to feel envious. On the surface of things he was everything that Deek wasn't. His image was sufficiently clean-cut and perfect for some of the largest corporations in the world to be willing to pay him endless millions to put his name to their products. He had been at the very top of the golf tree for many years and there seemed no likelihood that this position would be seriously challenged in the foreseeable future. He was rich, famous and owned majestic properties in four countries. He flew his own helicopter and he had a Lear jet at his disposal 24 hours a day.

But if things ever went really bad for him, he knew that he wouldn't have the likes of the Sunnybank estate there to stand behind him. Instead there would be lawyers and smooth-talking PR men. His family would probably come through. However, if it had been his face on the front page with a big fat joint, he didn't think that their support would have been particularly enthusiastic. Maybe things had improved a little. He took some heart from the thought that he would have a few thousand Marines and Airborne troops rooting for him should he ever hit the bricks. It was more than there had been a few months earlier.

Everything he heard about his Turnberry opponent made him like the guy. There was no side to him. He liked the way that he chain-smoked his way around the course and didn't appear to have any sponsor for his clubs or clothes. He had got hold of what videos he could of Deek's recent efforts on the European Tour and they had fascinated him. The Scotsman's style was all his own. George wondered if he had ever had a lesson in his life. What was most impressive was the array of shots that he could play. There was something of the Trevino about him. Most impressive of all was the fact that he seemed able to find the most outlandish shots and pull them off when the chips were down.

He found that he was smiling all through the Sunnybank interview. One thing was for sure. Archie Banks had class. Real class. About fifteen tonnes of it. He raised a can of Bud to the screen as the interview closed. "See you on the first, Deek."

On impulse he picked up his phone and dialled up his main PR man and asked for the a contact number for Jonathan McMillan. He then asked for and got a mobile number for Deek and dialled.

"Hello."

"Hey. That you Deek?"

"Aye. Who's that?"

"George Albright."

"Aye, and I'm centre forward for Celtic. That's you isn't it Banjo, you wee twat."

This was unexpected. George chuckled. "Christ Deek. How the hell can I persuade you? Tell you what. I'll put the phone down and ring again. Check out the incoming call number. You'll see it's American."

At the other end Deek stared at his phone in horror. "Oh shite. It is you isn't it? Bollocks. Sorry about that, mate."

"Not a problem. Listen. I've just watched your interview. You did good. Real good."

"Thanks George. It's good of you to say so."

"I hear we'll be meeting up at the McMillan place before the game. I look forward to it."

"Me too." Deek couldn't believe just how easy-going his opponent was. Like most golfers in the world, he had been in awe of the big man for years.

"OK. Now this Sunnybank place of yours. Those people sure came through for you, huh?"

"Aye. They're a good crowd sure enough."

"You're a lucky guy Deek. Real lucky. This youth centre sounds pretty cool. Tell you what. I'm going to send over $500,000. That should get you well on the way. But listen up, Deek. This stays between me and you. OK? I don't want the press getting wrong ideas about me brown-nosing my way onto the bandwagon or anything. Anonymous American benefactor. Cool?"

Deek could hardly speak. "Aye. Of course. Christ, it's bloody good of you George. You sure you don't want people to know?"

"Sure as hell. It's better this way. It's nice to have the chance to do something useful for a change."

"I hear you've done more than your share in Iraq."

"I hope so. More to life than thrashing a little white ball around some cut grass huh?"

"Aye. You're right enough there."

When he had finished the call, George made his way into the study and dialled up the internet. His first keyword was "Bannockburn". As he read, a small smile played on his lips. "Crazy Scottish sons of bitches."

Unbelievable. It had been nearly 700 years ago and they still hung onto the memory of slaying the might of the English heavy cavalry as they got bogged down in the mud. "Culloden" told a different story. The same manic courage, but a different result. Carnage.

Massacre. A defeat that was never avenged. His country was so young in comparison. And they had never really tasted the bitterness of defeat. Vietnam had been a humiliating failure, but they had never been invaded and enslaved.

He sat back in his leather chair and gazed out across the green acres of his estate. One thing for certain. At Turnberry nothing would be certain. In his heart he knew he had a real match on his hands.

Chapter 6
May

Steve Kenton thought it a sight for sore eyes. The town of Dumfries seemed to have declared an unofficial public holiday to mark Deek's departure for America. By the time the helicopter from the McMillan Corporation thumped down from the sky, there must have been in excess of 2,000 locals present to cheer him off. For a few minutes Steve felt a familiar knot of tension as the Sunnybank Three and Meg clambered on board and turned to the crowd for a last wave. If something was about to happen, then it might well be now. The only security was provided by four uniformed policemen and they were clearly enjoying the spectacle just as much as everyone else. Otherwise there had been no screening whatsoever.

He wondered just what his lords and masters in London had in mind. Close protection. Oh yeah. Just him and an unmonitored crowd of about 2,000. Dream on, guys. He was still scanning the faces when he realised that Deek was yelling at him from the hatchway.

"Steve!!"

Steve turned and only half-caught the words over the din of the rotors.

"We'll see you in Texas!!"

"Right-o. Now go on. Bugger off."

Soon the chopper was a mere dot on the horizon and the crowd started to melt away. Steve stood and watched the scene for a while. Sunnybank would now return to normality after nearly a month of excitement. The barricades would come down and the journalists' car park would empty out. His grandmother had often told him tales about how it had once been in Salford during the days of the Blitz. She had

237

always been nostalgic for the time that he had found strange. How the hell could anyone be nostalgic for night after night in a bomb shelter whilst Goering's boys did their utmost to turn the whole place into an inferno? He felt that he could understand now. His sabbatical with the rucksack had done little to drive away the demons that haunted the hours of the night. But a month in the craziness of Sunnybank seemed to have gone a long way to keeping them at bay. For seven consecutive nights he had slept undisturbed in his sleeping bag on Wee Donny's floor. Not once had he woken in a film of sweat and terror. Maybe he was at last beginning to return to the human race.

He hefted his rucksack onto his shoulder and made his way to where his 4x4 was still parked in the courtyard of Donny's block. Deek had been disappointed when Steve had told him that he would not be joining them on the Lear Jet to Texas. There was no need. It was pretty well inconceivable that there would be any threat while the Sunnybank Three were wrapped in the tight cocoon of the McMillan security team. Instead, he had decided to take a last look over the security preparations up at Turnberry before flying down to London for a final briefing with his boss. He would take a flight out to Dallas on the Wednesday morning.

The McMillan ranch was a five-star version of Scoobytown. After the chaotic events of the last few weeks in Sunnybank, it seemed almost unreal in its total quiet and seclusion. Deek had never been anywhere so flat. The monotonous fields seemed as if they stretched out far beyond the ends of the earth. Somewhere out there the rest of the world was going about its business as usual, but it all seemed very far away. Their rooms lacked nothing in luxury and they certainly made a welcome change from the joys of Wee Donny's.

As the days rolled quietly by, all of them fell into a relaxed routine. In the mornings Deek and Troll would accompany Jonathan for a round of golf. The course was quite deserted and they felt like the last men on earth as they wandered the perfect fairways which were closely hemmed in by the imitation dunes that had been bulldozed from the surrounding fields. The two players were a complete contrast. Jonathan stood a good five inches taller and swung the club with a textbook grace. Deek's swing wouldn't have got close to any teaching manual. The American was a good 40 yards longer from the tee and he generally emerged the victor in their good-humoured games.

"I cannae understand why you don't turn pro," said Deek as they wandered off the eighteenth tee on the third day of his stay.

Jonathan smiled. "It was Turnberry that did it you know. Up until then I was going to. Then I realised that there is more to golf than hitting a six iron the same distance every time. I just don't have it in my hands to make it at the top level. The magic. The touch. Understand?"

Deek nodded. "Aye. I suppose so."

"You should, because you have it. I bet you've never had a lesson in your life."

"Not really. Roger used to help me a bit, but I suppose I kind of made it up as I went along."

"It's called being a natural. The likes of me are fine on a course like this in a light wind. Put us out on Turnberry or Muirfield or Pebble Beach when it's wet and blowing and we don't have the tools for the job. You do. All the tools you need."

Deek lit a cigarette and sat down at a table overlooking the endless empty space of Texas. "Maybe. I doubt if I have the tools to handle George Albright though."

Jonathan laughed. "You and the rest of the planet, Deek. I wouldn't worry about that."

"Course I worry. Who wouldn't? I've got tae play him next weekend with half the bloody world watching. I dunnae expect tae win. I just don't want tae get hammered."

They both opened up cans of beer that Jonathan had retrieved from a fridge. He knew that the Scotsman was becoming increasing terrified at the prospect of the match.

"Do you want a bit of advice?"

"Aye. I'll take anything that I can get."

"Then don't try to keep up with him. George hits the thing about 70 miles off the tee. That's just a fact of life. You just need to get your head around it. Expect it. You need to mentally adjust to the idea of playing from a long way back of him. Just focus on getting on the greens in regulation and leave it to the putting. Golf always comes down to putting. Sure, George is as good as anyone out there at putting, but at least it is fairly even on the greens.

Deek nodded slowly. "Aye, there's sense in that. Sometimes the putts drop and sometimes they dunnae. If they drop, I stand a chance of getting close. I'll go with that."

On their first morning at the ranch they had met Roland McMillan and he had shown them the gallery. Troll and Banjo had been polite enough but had been quite unable to get their heads around the fact that the air-conditioned room contained so many millions of dollars. Meg tried hard to understand what was so particularly special about the old works of art but couldn't really manage it. She liked the pictures well enough, but that was all. Deek however found that they touched him somewhere deep inside his chest. He had asked the old man if he minded if he stayed a while. A while turned into three hours and for the next few days he had taken to spending time in the gallery in the afternoons.

Roland had joined him on the second day. Deek had been disturbed by the soft sound of the old man's electric wheelchair approaching over the thick carpet. Roland had a bottle of Glenfiddich in his lap and a crystal glass.

"I thought you might like a drink."

Deek was rather embarrassed. It was as if Roland had read his mind. His mind really didn't want to drink at all. His mind wanted to be clear. It told him that these days were days of magic. The morning golf, the long walks with Meg, their nights together talking for hour after hour . . . and the pictures. However, his body had long since given up listening to instructions from the brain. His body was beginning to scream out for a drink. His face was sweaty and his hands wouldn't stay still. He was mortified when the glass shook so badly that he spilt some of the whisky on the floor. He swallowed half the glass and felt his body start to normalise. He sat down heavily on one of the viewing chairs and took his head in his hands.

"Sorry about the spill, Mr McMillan."

A thin hand gently rested on his shoulder. "No need. And for God's sake call me Roland will you?"

Deek still kept his head down. "Aye. Course I will."

For a while all was silent barring the distant hum of the air conditioner. Deek sipped at his glass until it was empty and filled another. There was something about the old man that made silence easy. Or was it the pictures? Or the velvet feel of the malt kissing the inside of his throat? Or was it all three? In the midst of all the craziness of his tortured life he had at last found some quiet places. The beach at Scoobytown. The strange deserted golf course. The non-judging expressions on the faces of models painted many hundreds of years before. The soft, caressing hands of Meg through the empty hours of the night.

For years he had thought of nothing other than the next bar. He had been hiding without knowing it. And now he was slowly beginning to wake up, and it wasn't half as bad as he had thought it would be. He became aware of the small old voice at his side.

"Would you mind if I talk a little about the old days. It is a rather common pastime for many at my age. Alas, not me. I have never really talked about my time in Scotland. Not to my wife. Not to my sons. Only Johnny. And Johnny didn't really understand."

Deek looked up and nodded. "Please do. I'd like to hear."

And so Roland talked of the things he had kept bottled away from the sunlight for 79 years. He talked of his mum and his dad and his miserable life in the valley. In the end it took him three days to scrub his memory clean.

"You've never been back then?"

"No. Never. I don't suppose I ever will return."

Deek nodded. "Maybe that would be for the best. Kirkonnel's not great now. I've a couple of mates who live up that way. All those wee towns are the same. Sanquhar, Kirkonnel, New Cumnock. Nothing ever replaced the mines once they closed. There's not been any work in the valley for years. It's all a bit grim to be honest. Too much booze. Too many on anti-depressants. Smack all over every scheme."

"Johnny told me that. I couldn't quite believe it. Kirkonnel doesn't seem the kind of place for heroin. Maybe I am just out of touch. For me it is something for the big cities."

"Not any more. It used to be that way in Scotland too. twenty-five years ago it was just Glasgow and Edinburgh and Dundee and Aberdeen. Not any more. Heroin is everywhere now. Every wee town."

"But why?"

Deek smiled. "Come on Roland. Think about it. You ken well enough what wee Jocks are like. We're gloomy buggers. Why not? Grey cold place where it rains eleven months a year. We've always drowned our sorrows for hundreds of years. It's the national pastime.

Smack just drowns the sorrows about three miles deeper, or so they tell me. Thank Christ I never got sucked into it all. None of us did. You could say that Scotsmen and heroin were made for each other."

Roland nodded slowly. "Very philosophical, Deek. You are a constant surprise. Maybe that is what my dad needed when he came home from the war. Something to drown his sorrows three miles deep. He never spoke of what happened, you know. Not a word. Not to anyone. I watched it eat him alive. He could never sleep. Night after night after night he would just sit there at the table staring into space, too afraid to risk sleep. I've read up on it over the years. I can't get my head around how it must have been in those tunnels they dug under the trenches. No wonder it broke him. It would have broken anyone. I have never forgiven myself for leaving him, you know. Never."

"We all have things that we can't forgive ourselves for. At least you don't need this." Deek waved the glass vaguely.

"I suppose so."

They fell back into their now familiar silence. After a while Deek decided that it was time to speak the thought that had come to him the moment he had first walked into the gallery with magic all along its walls.

"Can I ask you something Roland?"

"Of course."

Deek made a sweeping gesture. "It's about the pictures."

Roland was all attention. "Yes?"

"Let's say for a minute that I win. Not that there's much of a chance, but let's just say that I do."

"Go on."

"I would like you to send the pictures to Kirkonnel. Think about it. It would need a new gallery to be built of course. Something special with a big car park and a restaurant and some landscaping. It would bring in people from all over the world. Hundreds of them. Thousands even. Just imagine what that would do for the town."

Roland was suddenly bolt upright in his wheelchair. "Good lord."

"You like it then?"

"Why on earth did I not think about it before? Of course. It's perfect. This collection could start a regeneration. So obvious. How could I have ever missed it?"

"Maybe there could be one more thing."

The old man was animated now. "What?"

Deek looked deep into the watery eyes. "Maybe it could be called the Hamilton McMillan Centre?"

Suddenly the eyes were filled with tears which soon spilt out onto over-tired wrinkled cheeks. Roland's voice was barely a whisper. "Yes. Yes it could."

And a new shadow of regret briefly passed over his face. He fought it away and wiped at his tears angrily. "There is but one problem young man."

"Aye I know. I have tae win first."

"Yes. You do."

Anatoly Rykov chose a different route for his return to Britain. The chances of him attracting any suspicion were remote to the point of being negligible, but he was a man who was forever careful. This time he was Friedrich Weiner from Nurnberg. He took a flight from Paris to Dublin and stayed for two days in the Irish capital before taking the ferry to Holyhead in Wales and then a train to Birmingham New Street station. After an overnight stay in England's second city, he hired another Mercedes and took the M6 north.

After following identical precautions to those he had taken on his first visit, he made his way up the track to the small cottage. All the tiny pieces of his hair were still in their places. Nobody had been inside the cottage. All was on track. He lit the fire and prepared himself a meal. It was the evening of Tuesday, 26th May. Five days left. Five days before he would enter the history book of infamy.

After two days Steve was more than happy to leave the Turnberry Hotel. What had once been a place of genteel tranquillity had been transformed. The Americans had arrived on Monday afternoon and they had arrived in force. There seemed to be hundreds of them. They were fiercely fit looking young men and women with power suits and earpieces. Not one of them looked as if they had laughed at a joke in their lives, let alone told one. He wondered if there was an ultra-secret school of earnestness which created these clean-living security clones. They went through every nook and cranny of the venerable old building. They treble-checked every member of staff through their high-powered laptops. They ran similar checks on every guest who had stayed at the hotel since the White House made the announcement the month before. They seemed to spend hour after hour involved in grim-faced conversations on their mobile phones. In their brief leisure time they hammered their magnificent tanned bodies in the hotel gym and took sparkling mineral water with their salad.

Two days of them was enough. Steve felt completely out of it and spent most of his time in the bar with a couple of cronies from Ireland. He was amused at the complete uproar his expenses account would cause when it was presented to the bean-counters in London. He found time for a round of golf early each morning and watched the US army erecting their operational command and control tent on the beach. Out in the bay the Royal Navy were standing apart from the whole thing with an aloof air.

As he sat in the sauna on the evening before his departure he tried to put himself in the mind of a potential terrorist. It was something that he had done many times before during the dark years in Ulster. He found it harder now. He had been able to understand the mindset of the Republicans from the tough estates of Belfast and Londonderry. They weren't so different to him. Take away the politics and the history, and Andersonstown and the Creggan weren't so very different from where he had grown up in Salford. He knew the kind of men who were his enemy. Hard, resourceful, scheming. Their Manchester equivalents sold drugs and protection. Few of them were crazies. The IRA never even came close to the idea of suicide bombing.

Things were different now. If Al Quaida could find a way of getting someone close enough to the President to blow him and themselves into kingdom come, they would do it without a second thought. Bin Laden and his fellow leaders would be able to choose from a list of volunteers that would number many thousands. But could they get close? It was hard to see how. Only a single small road approached the hotel complex from north and south. It would be bottled up impossibly tight. Similarly, any attempt at an approach from the sea would be doomed. The Americans were world experts in the art of overkill, especially when it came to looking after their main man. The world had moved on a long way since Kennedy had been knocked down in Dallas. When was the last time a major Western leader had been topped? Not for years. It had indeed been Kennedy. When was the last time anyone had come close? Of course. The IRA in Brighton in 1984. That had been close. Really, really close.

The thought made him sit up and wipe the sweat from his face with a towel. Was there a similarity? Of course there was. At the time Thatcher and her Conservative government were about as unpopular as it was possible to get. She had thrown the gauntlet down at the feet of the IRA in typical fashion. A war on terror. She had fought hers harder than most, and the Bhoyos had waited for their chance to knock her down. How and where? A hotel. So. Similarities there then. A hotel that had been booked for months. That was the "how" part. They had placed their bomb months and months in advance. Could the same be done here? It was hard to see how. The President wouldn't be staying overnight and ever since the announcement had been made, the whole place had been bottled up tight.

He sat back and winced as the heat of the wood burned into his back. It was inconceivable. But he still couldn't settle. The worm of unease wouldn't stop wriggling around in his brain.

The next day he took a plane down to London and spent as little time as possible with his boss before catching an early evening flight out to Texas. As the plane roared through the night he found sleep elusive. There was something that he knew was just around the corner, something he could only see fleetingly from the very corner of his eye, something that he just couldn't manage to get hold of. Maybe he was just getting old and paranoid. The young Americans had made him feel like a dinosaur. Maybe he was. Part of him had had an inward chuckle at the thought of any of that lot growing their hair and donning a pair of old jeans and an anorak and going undercover in the Bogside or the Falls Road. Their laptops and earpieces wouldn't have done them any good back then. But those days were all gone away. The 30-year dirty war had fizzled out and both sides had cobbled up a Peace when they had at last given up trying to beat each other. All that was left were a few hundred broken up middle-aged men like himself who found sleep hard to find as they tried to come to terms with the things that they had done. Maybe he was just another yesterday's man. Maybe the answers to today's threats were to be found in the exertions of the bright young things with their high-tech toys.

He finally found a couple of hours sleep over the Southern States and awoke feeling stiff and tetchy as a bland female voice informed him that they were about to commence their approach to land. Getting into America was more time-consuming than he remembered and it was more than an hour-and-a-half before he collected a hire car and started the five-hour run out to the McMillan ranch. Soon the country was bleak and empty and his mood sunk a notch or two.

No matter how he tried, he couldn't rid himself of a sense of unease. He flicked the radio from station to station before settling for silence as his big car rolled along the long, straight roads across the plains.

When he arrived at the ranch the security people were ready for him and he was ushered through with polite smiles. It was a further ten miles through field after field of grazing cattle before the ranch came into sight. As he parked up, a young man walked up to the car and waited for him to get out.

"Hi Steve. I'm Jonathan McMillan. I've sure heard a lot about you. Glad you're here."

Steve gave a rueful grin. "Don't be believing all that those nutters tell you lad."

Jonathan insisting on carrying Steve's bag and they made their way inside. As soon as he was shown into the main reception room Deek leapt to his feet and crossed the room with a great grin on his face.

"The big man arrives! How you getting on pal? Let me do the introductions . . ."

He led Steve over to where Roland McMillan was sitting close to the fire.

"Here he is, Roland. This is our in-house spook. MI5's man in Sunnybank."

The sound of a falling cup distracted Steve. When he turned, he saw that an elderly man in the uniform of some kind of a manservant had disturbed a teacup as he poured. The cup was on its side and tea had spilt onto the tray which he must have carried in from a kitchen somewhere. Just for the very briefest of seconds their eyes met and locked on. For that instant Steve saw something that he had seen before.

Fear.

Sheer, naked fear.

The man looked down almost immediately and busied himself with mopping up the spilt tea.

"I'm very sorry sir. Getting clumsy in my old age."

"Don't worry about it Abe," said Roland who was holding out his hand to Steve.

For the next few minutes Deek talked ten-to-the-dozen about the time they had all spent at the ranch. Steve only half-listened. Instead he kept up a surreptitious watch on Abe as he made his way around the room serving them all drinks. On two further occasions the man's dark eyes flicked onto him, only to instantly look away again. There was something not right with him. He had certainly sounded American, but he didn't really look that way. He had the olive skin of the southern Mediterranean. Nothing unusual about that. Americans came in all shapes, sizes and colours. For a moment Steve was too distracted to notice that Roland was addressing him.

"Sorry. I missed that. Bit dozy today. Probably the jet lag."

Roland smiled. "I was just saying that I must introduce you to Abe. Abe tries to pretend he's just a servant, but he's one of the family here. We've been together for over 40 years now."

Abe put down his tray and wiped his hands with a cloth before shaking with Steve.

"Good to meet you sir. I hope you enjoy your time with us."

Was the fear still there in the eyes? No. Nothing he could see. Just an easy friendliness to go with the Texan accent. Had it been there in the first place? Yes. He knew it had. Roland was chatting on happily.

"I call Abe my sounding-board. He stops me being stupid. If I ever have to make any big decisions, I always run them by Abe. He keeps me straight."

Interesting. "So what do you make of this big match then, Abe?"

Abe shrugged. "No offence to Deek here, but I've always been a big fan of big George. I just hope he goes easy on our boy here."

"So you gave the thing the thumbs-up when Mr McMillan came up with the idea?"

Abe grinned. "Sure did. I've always loved my sports. I can't think of a better way to settle an argument."

Steve didn't want to make his interest too obvious and so he turned back to Deek. "So how's the practice going? You all ready?"

"Aye. As ready as I'm likely to be. To be honest, Johnny has been stuffing me most of the time."

Steve concentrated as hard as he could on being normal. The

manservant was collecting up glasses and cups and seemed to have completely settled down. When Abe had left the room Steve turned to Roland and asked.

"Tell you what I've been wondering, Mr McMillan, ever since I got this job. Just how on earth did you come up with this idea?"

"It wasn't really my idea at all. It was much more Johnny's work. We were talking away and it just came. In my experience it is the way that the best things usually happen."

"And when on earth did it all happen?" Steve hoped that he wasn't making his questions too obvious. He had already noticed that Deek was watching him with a mildly quizzical expression. There was no choice. It was now Wednesday afternoon and the following day they were all due to fly over to Scotland. Forty-eight hours later the President would be landing at Prestwick Airport and every instinct in his body was screaming at him that something was badly wrong.

Roland considered the question for a moment. "It was November. I had only been out of hospital for a few days. That was what had got me back onto thinking about what on earth to do with my collection. Mind you, it was a while before the whole thing came together. It wasn't until February that Senator Morton got the White House on board. By then Johnny had the hotel all booked up of course."

Steve forced a complacent smile onto his face.

"It's a truly amazing tale. And all of this was just you and Johnny and Abe the sounding-board?"

"Yes. That was more or less it. I have always been a believer in small teams. Possibly the same applies in your line of work, Mr Kenton." The old man spoke with a mischievous twinkle in his eye. Steve was too wrapped up in his accelerating thoughts to notice. He needed time to think on his own. Time to put it together.

"Listen guys. That plane has left me as sweaty as hell. I think I'll just go and take a quick shower and get a change of clothes. Whereabouts am I bedding down?"

Jonathan showed him his room. He stood for a quarter of an hour under the strong pressure of the shower and allowed the pieces to slot together in his head. He would have much preferred to have left it until the next day. The long flight had drained him and he was knackered, but the clock was ticking and there was no time.

A manservant called Abe. An olive complexion, but an all-

American accent and 40 years of service with the McMillans. Inconceivable on the surface of things, but there had been that look of fear in his eyes. Pure fear. Pure, naked fear. And Abe had been in on the thing all the way. Abe had known that the President was going to be at Turnberry two months before the rest of the planet. A look of fear that went way beyond a spilt teacup.

Was there anything else? No. Not a thing. Just a glance. A mere second's view into the eyes of a fellow human being. Had there really been anything there at all? Was it merely the gnawing gut feeling of trouble that had been bothering him for days? Was it the paranoia of a man who was too tired and too old?

A look of fear. Nothing else. Nothing at all. Nothing worth having.

Steve stepped out of the shower and wrapped the towel around him. He lit a cigarette and sat on the edge of the bed and considered his decision. More facts to weigh. What was to lose? Not a lot. He might look like a paranoid old git, nothing more. Well, he could deal with that. So what should he do? There was no point reporting any of this to London. They would call a few meetings and get their collective knickers in a twist as they stuck rigidly to their procedure and protocol. By the time a decision would be made, the cards would have already fallen one way or another.

No. London would be a waste of space. He had weighed the options out of habit. He already knew that there was only one realistic course of action and it was time to take it. He picked up his phone and dialled.

"Hello?" Walter King's big voice was as upbeat as ever.

"It's Steve again, Walter."

"Jeez Steve, you're chasing me like I'm some kind of high-grade hooker undercharging by 100 bucks a night."

"Your turn of phrase is as eloquent as ever Walter."

"Sure thing. You sound tired buddy."

"I am. How open is your mind today?"

"Hell, open enough I suppose. Fire away."

Steve ran him through the meagre facts that were the unimpressive core of his suspicions that something monumental was about to happen. It only took him a few minutes. "So Walter. That's it. All of it. Next door to bugger all. But believe me, I can feel trouble in my bones. Are you willing to go with that?"

For a while the line was silent. At last Walter spoke and now the tone was that of the high-flyer fast tracking his way to a corner office. "You've been at this game for years, Steve. Same as me. I don't give a shit for all the techno stuff in the world, you can't beat the gut-feeling of an old timer. Course I go with it. Shit. We're talking the President here man. Let me think."

Another pause. "Look. Give me five. I'll run this guy Abe Haston. Let's see if anything pops up."

"Good enough for me."

The phone rang when Steve was just finishing getting dressed. His old friend's voice was much harder now. "Looks like those guts of yours have a point, buddy. Listen up. Abe Haston got off the boat in the early 1950s. Back then he was Ibrahim Hassim. Came over from Palestine. Place of birth Al Jaleel. I checked it out. The Israelis cleared the place in the war of 1948 and booted all the Arabs out. That new wall of theirs runs right through it."

"Jesus."

"I've got a ways to go here, but a couple of minutes on the internet hit pay-dirt. You say that it was February when Senator Morton made the call to McMillan?"

"Yes."

"Jesus Christ. I have it front of me. When I typed 'Al Jaleel' into Google, the first hit it spat out was a CNN report from a reporter called John Tanner. 15th February. Story about Sharon's wall and how it is pissing off the Palestinians. The report was from Al Jaleel."

"Christ."

"You got it. OK. Here's what I'm doing next. I'll pull all phone records from Abe Haston's mobile and the house for the whole month. But the one to watch is the few days after 15th February. Then I'm on a plane. I'll get to Dallas late on this evening. Can you catch up with me in our Field Office? Say 11.30 p.m?"

"I'll be there."

"See ya pal."

Steve checked his watch. Just after four in the afternoon. What time was that in London? Christ, somewhere close on midnight. No wonder the tanks were feeling pretty drained. He spent a little time considering what to tell the household. It was still essential to keep his suspicions as far under wraps as possible. When he made it back to the reception room, the old man had retired for a nap and Troll and

Banjo were off out somewhere. Jonathan was sitting forward in a chair chatting to Deek and Meg who shared a sofa. They all looked up when he walked in.

"That better?" asked Deek referring to the shower and change.

"Yeah. Great, thanks. I'm afraid I'm going to have to love you all and leave you though. Something's come up. I need to drive back to Dallas."

This produced the looks of alarm that he had anticipated.

"Is everything OK?" asked Jonathan.

"Well, not really. But there's nothing for you guys to worry about." Steve made play of careful consideration before speaking again. "Look. I shouldn't really tell you this but I know it won't go any further. It's an Ireland thing. The word is that some toe-rag is about to try and do something stupid. I knew him once. Well, I followed him around the place. They want my input and that means the communications centre at FBI Field Office in Dallas. It's a bitch, but there you go. It goes with being a spook along with the society girls and the fast cars."

This brought a laugh and a sense of relief. The troubles of Ireland seemed many thousands of miles from the ranch on the flatlands of Texas. Steve said that he was sure he would be there to meet them at the airport the next day and then he hit the road. The five-hour return drive to Dallas was a lingering nightmare of fighting sleep as the long straight roads offered no relief to the tedium. By the time he was checked through the FBI security he felt completely strung out.

Walter in comparison looked as fresh as a daisy. The ex-Marine jumped to his feet and crunched Steve's hand hard enough to make him wake up fast.

"Good to see you buddy. Take a pew. Want a coffee? Looks like you need some, brother. Long old day huh?"

"Pretty long. Coffee would be great. How are you doing?"

"I'm doing fine. It looks like we're headed for the deep dark woods here. Sit down Steve. You ready?"

"Yes." Every line on Walter's face spoke of trouble. Big trouble.

"OK. Here's what we've got. 10.03 p.m. 15th February. Haston calls a Dallas number. Residence of a Mr Ali El Kali. He runs an upmarket Persian rug shop. Fancy carpets for the wives of oilmen. The call was timed twelve minutes after Tanner's piece on CNN from

Al Jaleel. Next day we got a transaction on Haston's VISA card putting him in a garage filling up with ten gallons of gas at 7.50 a.m. The garage is half a mile down the road from the carpet shop. I figure the odds are that he paid this Mr El Kali a visit. So. Ali Al Kali. Came Stateside form Jordan in 1959. No criminal record in the USA. No hits on any terror stuff. Looks as if Haston simply knew him as a friend and figured he might know someone."

"Christ." Steve spoke softly.

"OK. More phone records. That afternoon Al Kali makes a call to Chicago. He talks to a Zaheer Khan. This guy is some kind of a consultant to companies doing oil business in the Gulf. Came to America from Kuwait in 1975. Once again, no record of any kind. Credit card records show that Al Kali made a business trip to Chicago a few days later. He made a call to Khan from his room one evening at six. I figure that we can assume that he set up a meet."

Steve was absolutely hooked. The speed with which the Americans were finding all this out was staggering. Walter King carried on.

"OK. Khan. We checked his calls for the next couple of days and nothing jumped off the page. It was one of the girls up at HQ who spotted something strange. He made a call to a high-class perfume shop on Fifth Avenue, New York City. What was kinda weird was that the call only lasted fifteen seconds. What kind of conversation about perfume can a guy have in fifteen seconds? Not much of one, she thought. Maybe it was just a wrong number but his credit card told us that he flew over to New York a couple of days later. So we checked out the shop. We thought that someone had told him pretty damn firmly to get off the line and go use a pay phone. It turns out that the store-owner is a Mustapha Haj. For the first time we got a guy who turned up on one of our lists. He's a Syrian and has been over here for fifteen years now. The immigration papers suggested that he turned up Stateside without much in his pockets. It makes it tough to understand how he turns up a few years later buying such a classy piece of real estate. Need more coffee?"

Steve did and Walter poured out a couple of mugs from the percolator. "We must have picked this stuff up a while ago, part of all the post 9/11 investigations. Seems like we haven't got any further so far. So. Next. NYPD have a camera outside of this perfume shop and we're checking out the pictures for the two days that Khan stayed in

New York. It should come through sometime in the morning. Anyway, for now we just assume that the two of them met up. Three days later Haj got on a plane and flew to Paris and it seems that he must have had a cash-only visit. No credit card spend in hotels, restaurants, nothing. Now who the hell goes to Paris and lives offa cash?"

Steve nodded. It was suspicious, but nothing more than circumstantial. "What next?"

Walter shook his head. "A big fat zip, that's what. We got nothing to show us what Haj did in Paris or who he saw. That's where I am buddy. Don't know where to go next. Any ideas?"

Steve wandered over to the window and opened it as far as it would go so that he could sneak a smoke without setting off the alarms. Outside, the air was warm and the quiet hum of the late-night traffic reached up from the street eighteen storeys below.

"All your computers work on a database principle, yeah?"

"Sure."

"And am I right in thinking that after 9/11 everyone got linked-up? FBI, CIA?"

"That's right. Just so long as you have the right clearance."

"Have you?"

"Yup."

Steve closed his eyes and forced his weary brain to work it out. Slowly the idea filled out. "OK. Let me run this by you. Why not ask the computer for a list of targets who were in Paris around that time. Once we have the list, we can see if we can back-track someone to Haj. Cameras, surveillance, whatever . . ."

Larry clicked his fingers and launched himself at the keyboard. "OK. I'm there. All the way there . . ."

An hour later they had their list. It meant nothing to either of them, but one of the names turned out to be under surveillance at the Ritz Hotel. A camera had been installed in the corridor that led to the suite where Abdullah Faisel was due to stay as soon as an electronic reservation had been detected a few weeks earlier. It took several conversations and a lot of Marine language, but a little after three in the morning the pictures from the camera were emailed out to Dallas. Steve was fast asleep in a chair in the corner of the office by this stage, and Walter decided not to disturb him. He poured himself the umpteenth coffee of the night and started the laborious task of scanning through the video feed from the corridor. He started three hours after Haj had landed at Charles De Gaulle Airport. At quarter-past four he found it just as the window of the office was showing the first light of the dawn.

"Holy Christ." There he was. Unmistakable. Mustapha Haj making his way along the corridor in the company of a couple of big-chested goons at 11.04 a.m. the morning after he arrived in Paris. "Nailed you, careful son of a bitch."

He froze the image and went to shake Steve awake.

"You just won yourself a prize, my man. We got him. Here. Come take a look."

Steve rubbed his eyes and studied the evidence. "It's him all right. What happened next?"

"Dunno. Let's take a look."

Haj stayed in the room for twenty minutes and then left. A phone call informed them that Abdullah had departed Paris for Macau a few days later. It also confirmed that there had been a surveillance operation in place when he arrived.

"OK. We're getting there. Time to take a little look see at Mr Abdullah Faisel I think."

Walter tapped his keyboard until a screen told him that he could go no further.

"Shit."

"What?"

"Classified. Big-time classified. Too high for me." He got to his feet and stretched out his tall body before kicking a wastepaper bin across the room. He paced a while and Steve decided to leave him to it. After five minutes he seemed to come to a decision and picked up his phone.

"Well my friend, this might be a mighty fine career about to go down the toilet."

He waited for a few rings until he got an answer.

"Hey Hal. Walter King here. How you doing?"

An amused frown, then. "For Christ's sake stop being such a wimp. Sure it's early. Who gives a shit. Get your lazy butt out of that bed and call me back . . . Dallas. FBI Field office. OK?"

Steve raised an enquiring eyebrow as Walter ended the call. "That was Hal Benton. We go back some. He's CIA. Way up there these days. I met him out in Nicaragua in the 1980s. Remember those days? Reagan's all-out war on the Commies. He was junior Agency and I was on Special Ops. We hung out some in Managua. You know the kind of thing. A few nights trying to drink away all the bad things we were doing. Bad times, man. Real bad times. I ain't much proud of it now."

"I know that feeling."

Walter looked over and nodded. "Yeah. I guess you do."

"Will he help?"

The American shrugged. "Hell, who knows. All I can do is ask."

The phone rang and Walker sketched out the situation as it stood. The response was disappointing. "No way, Walter. You're crazy even calling. This stuff ain't for you. It's way over your head. If you give me more details I'll see what I can do."

"Bullshit Hal. Don't give me this." Walter's voice was suddenly very hard.

"It's all you're getting Walter. Live with it."

"Now you best listen up pal. I am talking about a clear and present danger to POTUS and I'm taking a time frame of less than 72 hours, so you best drop this need-to-know shit in about ten seconds flat. Capishe?"

"POTUS you say?"

"Yeah."

"And you're serious?"

"Deadly."

A pause. A decision. "OK. I'm on my way to Langley. I'll call you with the stuff you need, OK? Find a safe place to talk. If this leaks out my ass is in a sling. You best not be selling me a line here Walter."

"I might just make you a hero, pal. How long?"

"An hour, max."

Walter slumped back in his chair and stared up at the ceiling. "Sometimes we're our own worst enemies. Everyone protects their empires, their sources and secrets and their goddam dirty laundry."

"What the hell is POTUS?" Steve had been trying to follow the one-sided conversation as best as he could. It hadn't been easy.

"President Of The United States. Nothing gets folks jumping around like the idea of POTUS buying the farm on their watch. I best get some secure comms sorted out."

An hour later they were sitting in a bug-proof room with a telephone line that was scrambled by the maximum amount of modern technology that the FBI had at their disposal. They waited just over ten minutes before the phone rang. Walter hit a button and Hal Benton's voice oozed agitation as it came through on the speakerphone.

"OK. Is it just you I'm talking to here Walter?"

Walter put a finger to his lips and shook his head at Steve.

"Sure is, Hal. All on my own here. What you got for me?"

"More than you want probably. This whole thing is hot, Walter. You touch it, you're probably going to get burnt. OK?"

"You know me, Hal. Just another dumb-ass Marine."

"OK. I'm going to put a colleague of mine on the line. You don't need to know who he is. No questions. Just listen. OK?"

"Sure. Fire away."

A cracked, quiet voice that spoke of many cigarettes over many years came on the line. "Hi Walter. OK. Back in 1981 I was working for the Agency out in Afghanistan as a special adviser to the Muhajadeen forces fighting the Sovs. You remember how it was in those days? Hal tells me you were in the whole Reagan Cold War thing, yeah?"

"Yeah. Up to my neck man."

"So you know how it was. I worked the same sector as Bin Laden. He was one of ours then of course. We all thought he was the bees-knees back then. Big guy. Intelligent. Great leader of men. No fear. He brought over lots of young Saudis, all of them itching to send their souls to Paradise. Abdullah Faisel was one of them. He was a nice young guy. Kind of quiet, but tough enough. He was in one of my teams. I trained them. Watched them all kick plenty of Soviet ass. He came from some kind of fancy family back home and they didn't know he was out there. Someone must have talked to him and he went back. I always figured it must have been Bin Laden. I don't think anyone else could have persuaded him to leave. He sure wasn't the quitting out type. Anyways, once I finished my tour and did my debrief, we kept him on file. Didn't seem like anything to worry about for years. His family are richer than hell and he just became a kind of playboy. You know how it is with these rich Arabs: casinos, yachts, fast cars and fast women. Our Abdullah sure lived high. We started getting interested once Al Quaida got going in the 1990s. After 9/11 we watched him wherever he went. Never really got nothing, but he smells pretty bad to me. You ask me Walter, that Bin Laden connection is still there. This whole playboy shit is just some kind of a ritzy cover."

"Jesus guys, this ain't no way good."

Hal was back on the line. "It gets worse. Tell him."

The cracked voice once again picked up the narrative. "We ran into problems in 1982. Several of the local leaders got whacked. It seemed to be the work of one guy. Always the same MO Bombs. Carefully placed bombs detonated by someone watching the camp from up in the hills. Morale was getting hit pretty hard and then one day the hitter took out one of our guys. An American. Agency. I got onto Langley and they told me to make the problem go away, no questions asked as to how. By this time I had some pretty good Intel. The hitter was a kid called Anatoly Rykov. Spetsnatz. We had a way to him via a couple of labourers at the Sov base. I offered him cash to come over to our side. Big bucks. I mean huge bucks. It was a long shot, but he went for it. The deal was that he made five hits for us and then he was home free. He completed the contract and away he went. I tell you, he was one hell of a piece of work. Used to stay on his own at the edge of the camp. Never spoke much to anyone and always worked alone. In fact if I remember right, the only one of the other fighters he ever talked with was Faisel. It was because they both had a bit of English. I tell you, he was one seriously scary individual. I've met plenty of killers in my time Walter. Hell, the Muhajadeen were all killers. But this guy was something else. He was clinical. No emotion. No nothing. He just took off into those hills on his own and came back a few days later like nothing had happened. He never missed. Five hits in a few months."

Walter looked over to Steve and shrugged. Neither could work out where any of this was headed. Hal Benton came back on the line.

"We paid Rykov enough for him to disappear. What did we care anyhow? You'll remember how it was in the 1980s. Oliver North and everybody calling the Agency a bunch of cowboys. Guys like Rykov were embarrassing. We were happy enough for him to vanish. All the files got quietly destroyed. As soon as Gorbachov took over in Moscow, the Cold War got warmer and both sides wanted to forget all about the dirty things they'd done to each other.

"For years it seemed as if he was gone for good. Then we started hearing some pretty strange sort of whispers in the mid-1990s. We have six assassinations over the last ten years that seem to match Rykov's style of work. Three Serbs, two in Bosnia, one in Kosovo. Two Russian officers in Grozny. A Neo-Nazi crazy in Hamburg. All of them had been seriously pissing off the Muslim world. Each hit was the same. Bombs. Expertly placed. Detonated at exactly the right moment. Rykov written all over them. So we dug out the field officer who recruited him and he confirmed that in his time in the hills he had only ever seen Rykov get close to one of the other fighters: Abdullah Faisal."

"Holy shit." Now Walter and Steve could see where this was all going. Hal forged forward.

"There's one last thing. Last September we had surveillance on Abdullah in Monte Carlo. A discreet hotel away from the crowds. You need to be a big hitter to stay there. We got a picture of a guy going in there and we confirmed that he went up to see Abdullah. I'll email the pictures over. They ain't up to much. The guy is wearing sunglasses and a hat. We put him in his mid-40s. Caucasian. Looks pretty fit. My man here says it could be Rykov. No more than that. Just could be. So what happens two months later? A certain General Yuri Krishkin gets blown away as he enjoys his daily game of chess in a café in Moscow. Krishkin was a serious piece of work. He headed up the Russian interrogation unit in Grozny, Chechyna. A real asshole. No tears shed when he got blown away, certainly not in the world of Islam. Same old story. The hit had Anatoly Rykov written all over it. One last thing. In February Faisal was in Macau throwing big bucks at the roulette tables in the casinos. We had cameras on him. Looks like he got a visit from the same guy as in Monte Carlo. The pictures aren't worth a lot. Hat and glasses again. But there is enough. So Walter. There you have it. There has been no known assassination since February that bears the hallmarks of Rykov, which kind of points to the fact he hasn't done it yet. If you are telling me that there is a chance in hell that this guy might just have POTUS in his sights then we are all looking at one hell of a shit-storm. I don't need to point out the facts, but I will anyway. We recruited him. We paid him. And then we lost track of him. Now, Walter. I've shown you mine, I think that it's about time that you showed me yours."

By this time Walter was ashen-faced. It was every bit as bad as he had feared and then a whole lot worse on top. Not only was the threat that Steve had sensed absolutely real, it also came from a trained killer who had once done his stuff for the CIA. It was the kind of atomic secret that ended careers in a heartbeat. It was the kind of secret that got men killed. He shrugged at Steve, who looked every bit as lost as he suddenly felt. Steve simply mimed "Tell him".

So Walter told him. Every step of the journey that had taken him to the cul-de-sac of Abdullah Faisal. By the time he had finished, there was a chill in the air. When he spoke again it was clear that Hal Benton was choosing his words very carefully.

"Tell me, Walter. Have you got this Steve Kenton with you now?"

Steve shrugged and nodded. Walter gritted his teeth. "Yes Hal. I have."

"You bastard."

"Sorry Hal. I had no idea."

The silence seemed to stretch out for hours before Benton broke it.

"OK. No point in getting all busted-up about it. Good work Mr Kenton."

"Thanks." Steve felt up to his neck in ice-cold water and it was rising fast.

"If we can find a way to resolve this thing the United States of America are going to owe you big. OK. Let's see what we've got here. I see problems everywhere gentlemen. We all know that this is Grade-A condition black serious, but it's all circumstantial. POTUS is in trouble right now. Real trouble. He's behind in the polls and Iraq is going all to shit. He needs anything he can get to make himself look good again and he ain't going to give up this Turnberry gig in any kind of a hurry. If I take this to the guys in National Security, they're just going to scratch their backsides and cause as much shit as they can about the Agency's role in the whole Rykov/Faisal thing. I know these guys. They will be 100 percent sure that their security over there is watertight. No way will they recommend that POTUS cancels unless we have a whole lot more than this. Right now we have less than four days before POTUS arrives at Turnberry. The way I see it, we have two options. One, we build the evidence so we can absolutely prove that Rykov has been there. Or two, we find the bomb."

"You think it's already there?" asked Steve.

"I know it."

George Albright and his caddie arrived at the McMillan ranch by helicopter an hour after Steve's sudden departure on the Wednesday evening. It was a moment that the whole Scottish contingent had been rather dreading. George Albright the Third wasn't just famous, he was a legend, one of the top sporting faces in the world. They had been expecting him to arrive with a huge and intimidating entourage and so it came as a relief when it was just him and his good-humoured bag man.

George had become practised at breaking the ice on such occasions, and soon everyone was easy with each other. He was given the now customary tour of the art collection and he showed every bit of the enthusiasm that was expected of him. In private he really couldn't understand what all the fuss was about. Pictures had always been pictures as far as he could tell. That evening they all ate a barbeque out by the eighteenth green and washed down the fat Texan steaks with copious amounts of cold beer. The jet was due to leave a nearby airfield early the next morning, and so most of the party had drifted off to bed by eleven o'clock. George and Deek sat out longer than the rest under the massive sparkling sky above.

Deek talked of his madcap few months. George described his time with the soldiers in Iraq. They had both seen their lives turned upside down and had more or less arrived at the same place. They never talked of the match that was now just a couple of days away. There was no need. Getting along was fine. Unexpected. But they both knew how things would stand once they were out on the course. Both men were fiercely patriotic and knew full well that the other would be giving it 110 percent. As far as the bookmakers were concerned it was a foregone conclusion, but neither of the players saw it that way. They knew the game that gave them their livings far too well. Anything could happen out there – and it probably would.

The next morning they climbed aboard the McMillan Corporation Lear jet. As the sleek plane rose up and away from the flat fields below, Deek couldn't help but worry about what was going on with Steve. He had called at breakfast time to say that he wasn't going to be able to make it back on the same plane. He had sounded dog-tired and said that he wouldn't be able to get away from Dallas in time. They would all meet up again at Turnberry later on that night.

Something was wrong. Deek could feel it in his bones. He was used to things being wrong.

As Deek at last nodded off to sleep as they started out across the Atlantic, Hal Benton was stalking his office at the CIA Headquarters in Langley, Virginia, cursing everything and everyone. He had just put the phone down on a conversation with Larry Weinberg and there was black murder in his heart. All along he had known that there would be no point in talking to any of them, but Walter King had insisted that he should at least try. He had worked his way through a number of the senior men heading up the Presidential security team and he had got nowhere. They had all told him that their guys had got the whole of Turnberry shut down tighter than tight. The roads were sealed, the perimeter was closed, every member of staff had been exhaustively vetted and the whole place had been searched from top to bottom.

On four occasions, the thinness of what he had was pointed out. All he had were a few guys talking with each other. So what? People talk every day. If the President stopped what he was doing every time a few guys met up for a chat, then he would never go anywhere. His own boss had told him that he had to keep the whole Rykov thing under his hat. It was too explosive. If the goons in the National Security Agency got hold of it, the CIA would get crucified. His boss talked about bigger pictures. He talked about how the country needed a CIA that was strong and clean if it was going to fight the terrorists. What he didn't mention were the guys in the big offices whose fingerprints would never be quite erased from the evidence linking them to Anatoly Rykov and Abdullah Faisal.

Hal Benton had been round the block more times than most, but he was shocked all the same. They were willing to put the President at risk rather than expose the Agency to another round of attacks. His boss had been quite specific in his advice.

"You can try Hal, but you won't convince those guys to cancel with what you have. It's too thin. Dropping out would be a PR disaster right now and the White House isn't about to do that. Not on what we have so far. Even if we bared all and told them about Rykov, I doubt it would make any difference. These guys believe in their own publicity. They can't believe that anyone could ever be smarter than them. If you get nowhere with the security people, you can have a go with Weinberg, but you might as well save the breath. I agree with the assessment you came up with earlier. You need to find Rykov or find his bomb."

Speaking to Weinberg had indeed been a complete waste of breath. No way was the Chief of Staff going to start cancelling everything because of a few rumours. He had talked with the guys in charge over in Scotland and they had told him that there was no way that any bad guys were about to get close to POTUS. What did Hal think they all were? Goddamn pussies? The phone had been crashed down and that had been the end of it. He had done all he could. Now it was down to Walter King and Steve Kenton who were in the air en route to the west coast of Scotland.

Steve was asleep minutes after their plane was in the air and he didn't wake until they were an hour away from Turnberry. Beside him, Hal was wide-eyed and deep in thought.

"What time is it?"

"Five o'clock local. We land in an hour. There's a chopper waiting on us. We'll be there by about seven-thirty."

Steve rubbed the bristle on his chin and decided on a shave to brighten himself up. The prospect of the next few days made him feel even more tired. He had considered calling his boss but had decided against it. There would be hell to pay, but he knew that he would get the same response that Hal and Larry had got in Washington. Instead, he had called Sally Hunter and arranged for her to meet the plane when it landed.

She didn't hide her concern when she saw him. "Good lord Steve. You look awful. Are you OK?"

He gave a weary grin. "Never better, just too many air miles and too little sleep. Let's go sit somewhere quiet for a few minutes. I need to fill you in on a few things. This is Walter by the way, he's an old mate."

Their jet had landed in the private part of the airport and they found an empty office to talk in. Steve made it as brief as possible and watched the colour drain from the politician's face as she digested each terrifying fact. By the end of it she could barely sit still.

"Well, there is nothing else to be done. The President will have to cancel."

Steve shook his head. "Not that simple, I'm afraid. We're talking politics here Sally. You should know that. Huge politics. The President is on the slide and the people around him will do just about anything to turn it around. They think that they have the whole place wrapped up tight and that there is no way that anyone will be able to get close."

"Maybe they're right."

"Maybe, but I don't think so. We think that there is already a bomb in place."

"Jesus."

"Indeed."

Sally shook her head. "What on earth do you want me to do? This really isn't my field."

"No. I know it isn't and I'm sorry for dragging you into this. The thing here is that we only have a few hours. There's no time for people to piss about worrying about covering their arses. I need someone who will get on with things. I think you can do that Sally. Yeah?"

"I suppose so, but I really don't know what."

"OK. Here's what. I need you to go straight to Glasgow and see the Chief Constable there. I don't care if he's at dinner or in the bath or addressing a conference. Just get him. Tell him that I need the best six detectives that he has on his team down at Turnberry by nine o'clock tomorrow morning. No dithering. No arguments. Let him know that this is a complete must. And I need the best they have. Experienced men. No kids. OK?"

She shook her head. "But I'm only the Sports Minister, I can't . . ."

"Sally. You have to. Please."

"OK. I'll do what I can. You're going down there now?"

"Yes."

"I'll join you later."

"Thanks Sally."

Anatoly Rykov had cooked himself a steak and new potatoes. He washed it all down in front of the TV with half a bottle of red wine and then finished off with some of the German cheese that he had become fond of during his years in the West. The evening news showed familiar pictures of the President smiling and waving as he stepped off Airforce One onto European soil. The commentator said that the American could expect a hard time of it over the next couple of days from his many critics on the eastern side of the Atlantic. Anatoly gave the screen an icy smile. In just three days' time all thoughts of criticism from a few disgruntled demonstrators would be consigned for ever to the dustbin of history. He recalled newsreels that he had seen of Kennedy arriving in Dallas all smiles and waves. Little did he know what was about to happen outside the book depository. He watched the blank faces of the presidential minders with their dark glasses and suits. Their heads swivelled and turned in all directions, sniffing out any potential threat. The same men would do much the same thing up at Turnberry, but they stood no chance of seeing where their nemesis was waiting.

It seemed to Anatoly that there would be a kind of justice in the way that he would deal America one of its most shattering blows. As the highly trained guards looked to the immediate area for the threat, he would strike from many miles away. It was how they did their business, often from their mighty B52 bombers that rained their deadly loads down from the very edge of inner space. They used Tomahawk cruise missiles and computerised artillery that could pinpoint a target from twenty miles away. They were used to killing from safe places, far away from the carnage they visited upon their victims. Now it would be their turn.

He was still smiling as he flicked through the channels and settled on an old Bogart movie.

Early the next morning things started to hot up at the great Turnberry Hotel. The media invasion was in full swing soon after a rich spring dawn lit up the Irish Sea in vivid blue. TV vans set up. Newspaper journalists collected their information packs from the tented media centre that had been set up early in the week. For miles around, roadblocks manned by uniformed policemen carefully checked identification documents and tapped registration numbers into computers. A constant procession of helicopters ferried on and off the landing pad on the lawn outside the front door of the hotel.

The decision had been made that the match would be a private affair watched by a small gallery of a few hundred invited guests. The public at large would get to watch on the BBC which had won the contract from the McMillans even though their offer was a fraction of that of *Sky Sports*. Roland had been very clear that the whole event was nothing to do with making money and all he wanted was as many people as possible all over the world to get the chance to watch. All the guests had been allocated accommodation in the hotel and they started to arrive throughout the morning. Most of the McMillan guests were family friends and long-term employees of the Corporation with a smattering of key clients. Deek's crowd were rather different. True to his word, he had come up with the promised tickets to Roger Swann and his shooting cronies as well as the Chief Constable. Otherwise, his support was very much a Sunnybank affair and soon the venerable old hotel was filled with the unaccustomed sound of excited youngsters exploring its every corner. It was lucky that the McMillan Corporation had cash reserves running into the billions because the good folk of Sunnybank took every advantage of the free bars which were made available as part of their corporate hospitality.

On the plane across, George had asked Deek if he wanted to join him for a practice round. Deek had been sorely tempted. It had been a long held ambition of his to play with the great man and the idea of a casual practise stroll was appealing. However, he allowed common sense to prevail. He was already daunted enough without watching the huge power of his competitor on the eve of the game itself. They played their practice rounds an hour apart. George went out first, accompanied by a sedate group of mainly American spectators who watched with appreciation as he dismantled the old links with near casual ease. Deek's audience was rather more frenetic, being made up largely of youngsters from the estate. As he walked off the eighteenth tee he felt that he had enjoyed his round just about as much as any he could remember. However, he couldn't escape the fact that his score had been nearer to 80 than 70 and that he had spent most of his time larking about. Troll's face told him that his caddie was less than amused with the whole thing.

"Dunnae worry. I'll be fine tomorrow. You ken me, Troll. I never was a one for the practice."

He made the mistake of popping into the main bar before heading down to the leisure centre for a swim and a sauna. His idea had been just to have a quick one to wet the whistle, but it was always doomed to failure. The clientèle in the Ailsa Bar was a heady mixture. There were three distinct groups that had quickly intermingled as the drinking became serious. The first group were the reporters who were never shy about fully availing themselves of the opportunity of free drink. The second group was very much corporate American. Their habitual afternoon tipple would normally have been some kind of overpriced mineral water. Soon the air of excitement got the better of them and they collectively let their hair down and got stuck in. The third group was an amalgam of the Sunnybank crowd and Roger Swann's group. These were people for whom a free bar in such a majestic setting was a complete novelty and one they took to like ducks to water. Deek never stood a chance. By the time that Troll, Meg and Banjo came to collect him a little after six, he was at the very heart of the loudly singing throng.

Roland and Jonathan had spent a couple of hours with their increasingly rowdy guests before making a discreet exit a little after five o'clock. They collected a car from the back door and drove away without anyone but the security people noticing. Jonathan followed the same route over the empty hills that he had driven many months earlier. Beside him the old man was quiet as he took in the landscape that had once been so familiar. As they dropped down the steep hill into New Cumnock he sighed to himself.

"The last time I was here I was on the train heading for a new life. Sixteen years old. You know what Johnny, it almost seems like yesterday . . ."

He fell quiet again as they drove out of New Cumnock and along the valley to Kirkonnel. He asked his great-grandson to drive around the small town for a while before they parked up outside the pub.

"Everything is so different. You would never know there had even been a coalmine here. Gone without a trace. All gone."

Jonathan helped him out of the car and into the wheelchair and they manoeuvred themselves through the door of the pub. Inside, it was every bit as empty as it had been when he had walked through the door eight months earlier. It was as if time had stood still. The landlady was sitting at the same stool at the bar and the TV blared out the moronic sounds of yet another game show. She recognised him straight away and a broad smile lit up her face.

"Well, well. Young master McMillan. My word, there's been some talk about you since you were last in here."

"Evening ma'am. Allow me to introduce my great-grandaddy. This is Roland McMillan. Roland, this is Mrs Hough."

"Never mind any Mrs Hough. It's Sheila." She took Roland's hand gently. "Welcome back, Roland. I'd say it has been too long. Far too long. Now lads. What can I get for you?"

"Pint of lager for me please Sheila. Roland?"

The old eyes crinkled with amusement. "Maybe just a half. Heavy for me please."

"Still got the taste then?"

He smiled. "Actually no. Believe it or not, this will my first-ever alcoholic drink in Scotland. I was just a boy when I left."

Sheila busied herself getting the drinks while Jonathan wheeled the old man to the wall that was filled with old photographs.

"Would either of you mind if I made a couple of calls? There are a lot of people who would love to meet you both."

Jonathan looked concerned at the idea but Roland nodded and smiled. "Yes. Of course. We would be delighted."

"No later than eight-thirty." Jonathan felt like some kind of bossy parent. "I need to get you back in decent time, Roland. You don't want to be tired for tomorrow."

"Yes. I suppose so. Sheila, you have no idea how tiresome it is being as old as I am. There are still so many things to do but the body just keeps going on strike. Johnny's right of course. It is rather a big day tomorrow."

"Aye. I ken love. We'll all be rooting for Deek round these parts."

Two phone calls worked like jungle drums and within minutes the bar was packed beyond all normal levels. The clientèle could broadly have been separated into three distinct groups. There were the elder statesmen who gathered around a table in the corner where Roland held court. The talk was all about coalmining and how things had once been when Kirkonnel still had the beating heart of Fauldhead Pit. Then there was a mixed bag of general onlookers who took up station all around the bar. These were largely made up of young and middle-aged men who restricted themselves to respectful nods and the occasional handshake. The third group was young and female and had an age range of 16 to 22. Word had spread like wildfire about the handsome young American whose family had once come from the town and now were as rich as something out of a soap opera. Opinion had been united about Jonathan when they had all watched him at the press launch at the ranch a few weeks earlier. He was drop-dead gorgeous, and as soon as word was out that he was in the bar, the young ladies of the town flocked to see him in the flesh. Soon he was surrounded by a gaggle of young females in tiny tops revealing chalk-white bellies of various sizes. Tattoos were much in evidence and a variety of alco-pops were swilled down as they fired an avalanche of questions at him. Soon he was backed into a corner and wondering how on earth he would ever make his escape. He was also rather conscious of the rather less friendly looks he was getting from some of the younger men gathered around the bar.

A glance at his watch told him that it was already eight-fifteen. Where the hell had the time gone? An idea had been quietly fermenting in his brain for a couple of days now and on impulse he decided to act on it. Having fought his way out from the corner he managed to make to the bar and attract Sheila's attention.

"Would you mind awfully if I stood up on here! I think my shoes are clean enough."

"Course you can, love. Help yourself."

He climbed up and all faces turned his way with expressions of great interest, none more than Roland's. Sheila banged a pint pot on the bar to get some silence.

"Come on. Pipe down. The man here wants to say something."

Once she had achieved a hush he started his hastily prepared speech.

"We're going to have to go in a minute or two, but there are just a couple of things I would like to say before we do. I'm not going to go on and on. Here it is in a nutshell. The McMillan Corporation will soon be establishing a charitable Foundation. Roland here has decided that he's not about to leave any of his cash to the likes of myself. I think he's bothered that we would just become playboys and fritter all away."

This brought an amused chuckle. Everyone was wondering where on earth he was headed to.

"For better or for worse, Roland has given me the job of setting things up which, to be honest, is a pretty daunting task. It is early days yet, but there is one thing that I have made my mind up about. The Foundation will do its work on both sides of the pond. I have no idea where we will work from over there. Probably Texas, which is pretty well home to the family. However, as far as Scotland is concerned, my mind is already made up. It has been 79 years since my family have been in Kirkonnel. I figure that has been 79 years too long. So people, here's how it is. As long as everyone is in agreement, the European Headquarters of the McMillan Foundation will be set up right here."

At this he grinned and gave a shrug of his shoulders and jumped down from the counter. The watching audience didn't really know what to do for a moment of two. Then polite applause started up, soon to be accompanied by some cheering.

Sheila leaned over and shouted in Jonathan's ear over the growing racket.

"So we'll be seeing a lot more of you then?"

He looked around the enthusiastic faces that filled the bar.

"Aye. It looks that way."

By mid-afternoon, the hours without sleep were catching up with Steve. He was smoking far more than he was used to and the caffeine from constant cups of strong black coffee was giving him palpitations. He had been overseeing the work of the detectives from early that morning. They had been allocated the Hotel's elegant reading room as a base to work from and the management had worked out a rota whereby every member of staff would be interviewed before the end of the day.

By lunchtime he was beginning to give up any hope of a breakthrough. Literally thousands of guests had passed through Turnberry since Abe had made his call in the middle of February. There wasn't any reason why Rykov would have needed to book in at all. Even if he had stayed as a guest, why should anyone remember him? According to the inadequate surveillance photos, he was an extremely unremarkable-looking man. Early 40s. Average height. They had no clue as to what colour his hair was, assuming that he had any at all. In both photos his dress was expensive, casual and very much unremarkable. It was looking more and more like a wild goose chase, but what else was there to do? All they had at the moment was a collection of circumstantial evidence. Somehow he had to harden it up and time was draining away. He lit up yet another cigarette and paced the room impatiently, eavesdropping the interviews.

He didn't notice when Heidi came in and took a seat just before two o'clock. She had been talking with the detective for five minutes when he looked up and waved Steve over.

"We might just have something here Steve. Pull up a pew."

Steve sat down with them.

"OK love. Just go over that again can you? Just like you told me."

Heidi smiled and felt very nervous. Steve sensed this and spoke reassuringly. "It's all right. You're in no trouble. No need to worry. You just tell me."

She nodded and took a sip of water. "It was at the end of February. I can remember it because it was only my second week. I was working in the Ailsa Bar in the afternoon. A guest had ordered coffee and I took it out to him. I tripped up. I don't know how. I spilled some coffee on his hand and he jumped. It was a big shock for him because he was reading his paper and he didn't see me coming. I was really worried because I was still in my trial period. I was scared that he would complain and I would have to go back to Latvia, but he was very nice. He didn't make any complaint."

The policeman leaned forward. "Tell Steve what you heard, Heidi."

"It was very strange. When the coffee burned his hand he swore. I was surprised because he swore in Russian. I am from Latvia so I know Russian very well. Then when he told me that it was OK and that it wasn't my fault, he spoke in English. Very good English. I asked about it when I was back behind the counter. My supervisor said it was strange because he was a German. Schiller was his name. I am good to remember names always. Schiller. Helmut Schiller. I couldn't understand why a German would swear in Russian."

She looked at each of them and gave a small shrug. "It is all. Nothing more. I did not see him again."

Steve pulled one of the photos from his jacket pocket and passed it over the table.

"Could this be him Heidi? I know the photo isn't very good but . . ."

She frowned at the grainy image of a man in dark glasses and hat. She shrugged again. "I cannot say. Only maybe. This man is about his size. Maybe the same age. All I can say is maybe."

Steve gave an encouraging smile. "That's fine. Really. Thanks ever so much. You've been a great help."

He got up and gave the detective a pat on the shoulder. "Cheers pal."

The front desk was able to dig out the details of Helmut Schiller's two-day stay at the end of February including his credit card details. Steve and Walter headed to the American's room and started making calls. The combined resources of their two security forces soon started getting hits. Schiller had stayed a night in London. A Mercedes had been hired. The registration was noted down. The next hit was from a JJB store near Manchester. A generous spend on a full set of golf equipment. More transactions showed a stay in a hotel near Preston and rounds of golf in Southport and Lytham St Annes. Then there was a two-day stay at Turnberry. Each one of these transactions was written on A4 pieces of paper and sellotaped onto the wall of the hotel room. Then came a particularly interesting piece of the emerging jigsaw. £32.73's worth of unleaded petrol at a service station north of Gretna, 11.07 a.m. on 2nd March. This was followed by another overnight stay in London.

Steve stared hard at the collage on the wall and talked more or less to himself. "OK. What has happened here? He checks out of Turnberry on the morning of 28th February. Then nothing. So. Two nights and no cash on the card. Then he re-emerges on the morning of the second. So where were you? A bed and breakfast paying cash? Why? What would be the point? You like your nice hotels. You have a false ID. Good papers. So why go to a B & B and slum it? No. You wouldn't do that, would you Anatoly? Not your style. Not your style at all. So where were you?"

Walter handed him a coffee and left him to it.

"What would you be doing? You've stayed at the hotel. Played some golf. Had a look round. Recon, yeah? Got the feel of the place didn't you? Got an idea of the ground. Of course you did. It's the soldier in you. Know the ground. Always know the ground. So what did it tell you? What was decided? We know what, don't we Anatoly, because we know how you work. You decided where to put your bomb didn't you? Of course you did. Then you pissed off. Where to? Somewhere between here and Gretna. Somewhere in the south west of Scotland. You went there for two nights. Two nights unaccounted for. Then you got in your Merc and drove back to London and away. Come on Walter. Help me here."

"Hey buddy. You just keep on going. You're way out there in front."

Steve paced the room, smoking hard. "You make bombs Anatoly.

It's what you do. You're the best. You wouldn't let anyone else do it. You'd do it yourself. Of course you would. So what do you need? Somewhere secluded. Quiet. Out of the way. Somewhere booked in advance. Yes. That's it." He was grinning now. "Somewhere where the gear you needed was already waiting. No other people. Not you Anatoly. You work alone. You always have done. All you need is the raw materials. The explosives. The detonator. And somewhere peaceful to put the thing together . . . OK. Times. You leave on the morning of 28th February. You go to the safe house. You put the bomb together. Then what? You return at night. Of course you do. Not that same night. That would be too soon. No. The next night. The night of 1st March. You plant the thing and go back to the safe house. Then the next morning you pack up and leave and get a tank of petrol on the motorway . . ."

He turned to Walter. "We've got him, Walter. Has to be. You follow the Helmut Schiller line. I'll get every man I can looking for country holiday homes booked out second half of February. What's the time?"

"After five."

"Holy Christ. The clock's all against us my friend."

The American nodded grimly. "Sure is."

Jonathan's preparations for the pre-match banquet had anticipated a rather formal affair. His idea had been that the guests would make their way to the main dining room for a 10 p.m. start once the many Sunnybank youngsters were tucked up in their beds. This idea never really had much of a chance of coming to fruition as the young guests showed absolutely no inclination to go to their beds at such an early hour. In practice, the throng that had been hitting the free Ailsa Bar for several hours moved en masse into the dining room. The careful seating plan never stood a chance and cheerful chaos was soon the order of the day.

Deek had collapsed onto his bed, having been frogmarched from the Ailsa Bar by Meg three hours earlier. He awoke with the familiar thwacking head of the afternoon drinker. Two quickly guzzled beers from the minibar started to drag him back to something approaching normality. Meg watched him with arms folded.

"I don't suppose that it is worth me pointing out that you have the biggest game of your life to play tomorrow?"

He looked rather sheepish. "Aye. I should'nae have stopped off at the bar. It was a mistake. Sorry Meg."

She smiled. "I thought we agreed that we're all through with the sorry stuff. You are what you are, Archie Banks. There's no point either of us pretending otherwise. I presume that you will be on top form at the banquet?"

"Aye well, got to fly the flag and all that?"

"Of course. Shall we agree on 2 a.m ?"

"Three?"

"Two-thirty and that's my final offer."

He gave her a crooked grin. "Better get down there then."

"I don't suppose that George Albright has been stacking it away all afternoon. Gym, sauna and a swim I should think."

"Aye well. You ken what the Russians say."

"And what do the Russians say?"

"Don't drink. Don't smoke. Die healthy."

In fact Meg had it all wrong about George Albright the Third. A few months ago her prediction would have been unerringly accurate. But a new George Albright had returned from the heat and dust of the Gulf. It was the Marine version who had made his way to the Ailsa Bar half an hour after Deek had been dragged out. By nine o'clock he was well and truly into the swing of the evening and the famous tanned face was more than a little ruddy.

He was already seated at the top table when Deek and Meg made their way through the back-slapping crowd of well-wishers. He rose to his feet somewhat unsteadily and greeted them with the unmistakable grin of a man who had already had his share and was fully intending to have a whole load more.

"Deek. My man! Get yourself over here. These guys of yours from Sunnybank sure know how to have a party. Hell, I've not enjoyed myself so much since I can't remember."

Roland and Jonathan had just arrived and were both looking around the mayhem of the restaurant with vague trepidation. Meg gave them a smile. "Don't worry too much. It all looks worse than it really is. Welcome to Scotland."

Roland returned the smile. "It's good to be back. Truly."

George had draped an arm around Deek's shoulders; it looked as if it might swallow him up. "So buddy. We on for a big night here?"

Deek couldn't quite believe what he was seeing. This was a very different George Albright from the carefully manicured sports icon who advertised everything from beer to lob wedges. Unbelievable. "Aye. Looks that way."

"So what are we drinking? Should we just get a whole bunch of beers and a couple of bottles of scotch?"

"Aye. That'll do well enough."

George waved a young waiter over and Deek looked at him closely as he scribbled down the big American's instructions.

"Don't I know you pal?"

The waiter smiled and nodded. "Maybe. I'm from Dumfries. You've probably seen me about."

"And you've got a job up here? Good lad. What's it like? Lots ae famous people?"

"Aye. Just a few. You're pretty famous yourself Deek."

Deek nodded. How very strange. He was pretty famous. How the hell had it all happened? Nothing made sense any more. He was distracted by the extraordinary sight of George lifting his seventeen-stone frame up onto the table. The sight of the big man holding out his arms brought immediate cheers from the whole room. He waved for silence, which he eventually managed to achieve. Brandishing a bottle of beer, he surprised one and all by breaking into the American National Anthem. This brought every member of the US audience to their feet to join in. Deek looked over at Meg enquiringly and she nodded. Once George had belted out the last line, Deek joined him on the table to more cheering. Without hesitation he launched himself into "Flower of Scotland" which brought the Scottish contingent to their feet.

The singing set the tone for the evening. Any last vestige of formality was torn away. Children tore around the room, making the life of the serving staff a nightmare. Nobody stayed at their tables very long. The crowd became more and more intermingled as the drink flowed ever faster. It only seemed as if they had been there a matter of minutes when Meg gently shook Deek by the shoulder.

"I'm afraid it's after two-thirty, lover boy. Time to say your goodnights."

George's eyes nearly popped out. "You have to be kidding. Two-thirty! Hell, it's going to be some kind of crazy game of golf tomorrow. What the hell time are we playing again?"

"One in the afternoon. Thank God it's only the eighteen holes tomorrow." Deek had never in his life felt so relieved that he didn't have a morning tee-off time.

"So that's you off to bed, buddy?" Slurred George.

"Aye. The boss here gives the orders."

"Well." George made an effort to get to his feet, only for a huge head-spin to stop him in his tracks. It took Troll and Banjo to get him to his feet and hold him there. He grinned. "I hope you guys can get me to my room. Looks like I'm 'bout done here."

As soon as he completed the sentence he slowly fell forward like a great felled oak tree and crashed down onto the table. He never moved a muscle as a team of volunteers carried him to his bed.

The hotel was starting slowly to life at ten the next morning when Steve dragged himself out of a completely inadequate three-hour nap in a chair. Walter had emerged from his two-hour sleep an hour earlier and was talking hard into his phone. As Steve rubbed at his eyes the FBI man crashed the phone back to the cradle.

"Mornin'."

Steve's mouth felt coated in cat fur. "What time?"

"Just by ten."

"Anything?"

Walter shook his head. "Not really. Schiller spent another night in London. Same hotel. We've found another receipt from London when he first arrived. Bought some books and stuff. We're digging out the receipt. Should have it in a few minutes. Then nothing. He must have left the country that day. Helmut Schiller ceased to exist."

The fax started beeping and a sheet of paper slid out. "This is probably the bookshop stuff." He collected the paper and studied it.

"Well looky here. Ordnance Survey map. Castle Douglas and the Stewartry."

Steve reached out and took a look. "It's the most detailed version. Only one reason why he would have wanted this. The safe house. That narrows things down a bit."

He called the detective who was checking out that area. "We've tightened things up a bit. Chummy bought a large-scale OS map for Castle Douglas and the Stewartry. Get yourself back to the Tourist

Information Office and get details of as many holiday homes as you can. Fire the contact details up here, OK? Where are you now? OK. Should get something in a few minutes then."

Steve lit up and started contacting the other five detectives. Three were still in the hotel while two who had been covering Ayrshire and South Lanarkshire were called back in. The first list from Dumfries spat out of the fax after twenty minutes. The detectives immediately started working their phones and making contact.

Jack Sunderland was just about to open the front door when the phone started ringing in the small room that he used as his office. For a moment he wondered whether to just leave it to go onto the answering machine. He had only called back to the farmhouse to change out of his thick checked shirt into something cooler. The schedule that he had worked out for the morning was quite tight and already he had fallen behind. It was now approaching eleven and he still had to dash up to the top meadows to check on the lambs. If he was to achieve his goal of being back indoors in front of the TV ready for the tee-off at Turnberry then he didn't need to be getting distracted by any phone calls.

He started to ease the front door closed but the action lacked conviction. Times were just as hard for Jack Sunderland as all the other sheep farmers he knew. The phone call was very possibly a punter, and he couldn't really afford to ignore it. Ten years earlier they had invested heavily in refurbishing three old crofter's cottages and letting them out as holiday homes. The occupancy rates he had projected in his business plan had never materialised, and rather than creating a welcome boost to the income of the farm the project had merely added to its debts. It wasn't unusual for the phone to ring on a Saturday morning with a punter wanting to take him up on the cheap last-minute weekend offer. Generally it was just students who had trawled him out on the internet looking for a secluded place to spend a weekend smashed out of their skulls on whatever drink and drugs they could afford.

With a feeling of annoyed resignation he turned around and went into the office.

"Killen Farm."

"Is that Mr Sunderland speaking?" Official. Didn't sound like a punter. He cursed himself for not letting it go onto answering machine.

"Aye."

"This is Detective Sergeant Harris from Strathclyde Police. I wonder if you would mind helping me with a couple of things please."

His stomach took an express elevator from the fifteenth floor to the basement. Strathclyde Police! What did they want him for? He hadn't done anything. He was convinced that he hadn't done anything.

"Of course. What is it?"

"We believe that you have three holiday cottages on your property. Is that correct?"

"Yes it is."

"Are they occupied at present?"

"Two of them are. One is vacant."

"Could you give me some details of who is staying in them please."

"Aye. Of course." He put the receiver down on his desk and dug around in the clutter for his reservations book. Just the same as every day of his life, he vowed to free up some time to give the place a proper tidy up. The book was lurking under three old copies of the *Farmers Guardian*.

"Right. Just give me a sec while I find the page. OK. Cottage 1. Mr and Mrs Benson, 14 Stratton Road, Sandy, Bedfordshire. They have the place for a fortnight. Arrived last Saturday."

"And the second?"

"Hang on. Yeah. Here it is. Funny one this. The reservation was made by a firm of solicitors in London. Hendrick, Dean and Reynolds. They booked the place for four months back in February. Cash in advance. To be honest, I couldn't tell you if anyone has even been there yet."

"I don't understand. Surely they must come to you for the key?"

Jack shook his head. The call was looking like taking a while so he yanked his sheepdog off his chair and sat down. "No. They asked for the key to be sent on. Apparently their client was likely to be arriving late in the evening."

"His name?" The detective's voice was interested now.

"No idea. They said he was a writer. A reclusive type. They requested that he shouldn't be disturbed. It seems as if he is nearly done with the final draft of his latest book and the publishers are getting anxious. I gather that they are paying the bills. I don't know. I don't think the bloke has been there much at all. Maybe a couple of days in February."

"How would you not know?"

"Oh, the place is miles away. That's why they wanted it. It's seriously out of the way of everything. You have to go along a two-mile track through the forest to get there. I have a few fields up that way, but I don't use them much. I saw some smoke from the chimney a few weeks back when I was doing some repairs to the fences. Must have been back at the end of February. After that, I don't know. The place is paid for until the end of June, and that's all I'm bothered about."

"Mr Sunderland, are you in your office at the moment?"

"Aye."

"I don't suppose you have a map of your place on the wall by any chance?"

"Not on the wall, but I have one."

"I wonder if you could give me a map reference for the cottage."

Jack felt a chill run through him. What the hell was this? "Of course. Just give me a few minutes can you."

More rummaging found the map and he duly passed on the co-ordinates. The detective noted them down and continued in a tone that was firmer than ever.

"How far is the cottage from your farm?"

"It's a little over eight miles."

"OK. Now I have to request that you stay close to the phone for half an hour or so. I might need to reach you again. Will you do that?"

"Yes of course. What is all this about?"

"Just enquiries, Mr Sunderland. Nothing for you to worry about. However, I must ask that you do not tell anyone else about this at this point. That is very important."

"No. Of course I won't. I'll just wait then."

"Thank you Mr Sunderland."

Harris put down the phone and jogged down the corridor to the room that Steve and Walter had set up as the centre of operations. They both looked up hopefully as he entered.

"I might just have something." He quickly outlined the bones of his conversation with Jack Sunderland. The tiredness fell off them as they obviously agreed with his assessment that this smelt right.

"Hit me with the lawyer's name again will you?" asked Walter. He typed the details into his laptop and seconds later clapped his hands together. "We hit pay-dirt guys. OK. I've got a hit from the surveillance records. Abdullah Faisel has paid the offices of Hendrick, Dean and Reynolds two visits over the last eighteen months. Hang on. There's more here. Seems as if they have been his representatives in the UK for years. Looks like we found where our boy went missing Steve."

There wasn't even a hint of fatigue in Steve now. Adrenalin was surging. "Right. We have the bastard. Maybe there's still time."

"You think he's still there?"

Steve nodded. "Maybe. It would make sense. He'll want somewhere quiet to lay-up. I doubt if he'll move too early. We might just be in time. You get on to your people and see if this is enough for them to take this thing seriously. I need to make a call or two."

"You got it. What's the move? Are we going down there?"

Steve shook his head. "No. We're too long away for this stuff. This one's for the Regiment."

"SAS?"

Steve nodded as he dialled up a number in Hereford.

"Colonel Rogers please."

"Kenton. Steve Kenton. Yes. He knows me."

He lit up as he waited a few minutes to be connected. When it at last came on the line, the voice was pure public school and hundreds of acres.

"Steve. Bugger me. Long time. How are you, old mate?"

"I'm pretty good, Charles. No time for chit-chat though. I'd get crucified if they knew I was making this call. You good to listen?"

"Of course."

Steve managed to condense the whole story into five minutes of short sentences. Rogers made notes and digested them. When Steve was done, the soldier drummed his fingers on his desk. "You know I can't move without authorisation?"

"Of course. I just wanted to give you notice. Get a troop of guys ready and a chopper fuelled up. I'll make some calls. Hopefully they won't get their fingers stuck up their backsides. You have the details you need? We're talking rough wooded countryside. Probably a walk in from a couple of miles. Tell the lads to pretend they're off to South Armagh and they will take the right sort of gear."

"And chummy? Ex-Spetznatz you say?"

"Yes. Assume that he is one dangerous kind of bastard."

"Okey dokey. You make your calls Steve. We'll be ready to go at zero notice once we get the nod."

Steve's next call was to his boss in London. He told Steve that things would take a little while. It was deep-breath time.

"Look sir. Their man will need to be in position some time this evening. It's how he works."

"How do you know how he works?" The voice of his superior officer was suddenly very sharp. Steve cursed himself. Keeping up with both the investigation and the interminable transatlantic politics was becoming almost impossible.

"Look. Never mind how I bloody know. I just know. I'm a bastard spy, for Christ's sake. It's what I'm supposed to do. It's about an hour's drive from New Galloway to Turnberry. He's going to leave any time from mid-afternoon. It's . . ." He checked his watch. ". . . 12.20 now. A chopper from Hereford will take at least 90 minutes in the air and then the lads will have to . . ."

"Who said anything about Hereford?" The voice was cold as ice now. Steve took a frantic pull on his cigarette and took the plunge.

"For Jesus, sake! Listen will you? Our man is ex-Spetznatz. He's got umpteen conformed kills to his name. We can put him right next to senior guys in Al Quaida and the President of the United bastard States gets off Airforce One up at Prestwick tomorrow morning. Of course we're talking about bloody Hereford."

"You've been working with the Americans haven't you? Now you listen here Kenton. Your role here is quite specific. Your role is to provide close protection for Mr Archibald Banks, golfer. Your role is not to act like some bloody cowboy. It's the same with all of you Ireland types. Might I remind you that those days are long gone. No more Iron Lady. No more shoot to kill. We are a very different service now, we . . ."

"I'm not listening to any more of this crap. Get authorisation. Get a chopper in the air in an hour's time or I'm going over your head. Way over."

"You'll pay for this Kenton, when I'm finished with you . . ."

"When you're finished with me you can send me to the Tower of London if you like. But right now you'd better get your finger out of your public school backside and get something done. I repeat. One hour or I take this further. Got it?" Steve's voice was like iron. The man at the other end of the line got the picture.

"Got it. I'll call within the hour."

Steve didn't bother saying goodbye. Walter chuckled happily. "Well buddy, looks like we're both in the shitter. Ever fancy getting into the private security business pal?"

"Yeah. We'll be lucky to get work as a couple of bouncers by the time they're done with us after this bloody lot. Look Walter. Hold the fort can you? I best go and see Deek off. Poor bugger must be wondering what the hell is going on. If my man calls from London ,tell him to get me on the mobile."

Meg let Deek sleep until ten before shaking him awake and passing him a coffee. He dragged himself upright and screwed his eyes at the bright spring sunshine that was pouring in through the wide-open windows. For just about any member of the human race the sight of such a perfect May morning would have inspired them to poetry. Deek's response was summed up in one word.

"Shite."

Meg shrugged. "Come on, you miserable sod. Even you have to admit it's a bonnie day out there. What's the problem?"

"Only the usual." He coughed out the words along with his first fag of the day smoke. "The bright light is splitting my head open, and anyway, I was hoping for it to piss down. A bit of weather is about the only chance I have."

He eased himself out of the bed and gingerly made his way across to the minibar for a beer. He drank it whilst taking in the magnificent vista on view through the widow. The sea was a vivid blue that only made the emerald green of the fairways of the golf course look more dramatic. There was evidence of great activity wherever he looked. TV vans were clustered around the tented media centre. Guests from the hotel were strolling around the grounds and course. Helicopters hovered alongside the seabirds out over the bay. The decision not to sell tickets to the public meant that the scene was a good deal less frantic than when Turnberry staged the Open Championship, but still the air was thick with an unmistakable feeling of excitement. He found it difficult to believe that in less than three hours he would be at the very heart of it.

At last the *Alice in Wonderland* period of his life had reached its climax. This was it. No more anticipation. No more lying awake at night worrying. No more hiding away from reporters. It was now. The sheer cold shower reality of what was about to happen hit him so hard that he physically shuddered. He was about to go out and take on George Albright the Third over 54 holes of match-play golf and the world would be watching every shot on live TV. The prospect sent him darting back into the room for another beer which he swigged at as he sat on the edge of the bed. Meg sat by him.

"You know there's something that we haven't really talked about don't you Deek?"

"Aye. I suppose so. The drinking on the course."

"Mmm." She put an arm around him and squeezed encouragingly. They hadn't talked about it, but it had been on his mind for weeks. In fact it had more or less been on his mind since the chaotic morning that Sally and Steve had come to the caravan. It had been getting harder and harder for him to keep his on-course drinking a secret as the media took up a modest interest in him on the PGA tour. Now it would be impossible. The issue of his alcohol problem had been exhaustively aired by every newspaper in the land for weeks. Talk shows had examined it. Phone-in shows had discussed it. The watching audience would be spending as much of their time watching to see if he sneaked a dram as they would watching him play the game.

He had tried a round in Texas with Jonathan without a drink to see if it was possible. The experiment had been an unmitigated disaster. By the seventh hole his hands were beginning to shake, and by the back nine he could barely hold a club. There was no possibility that he could play George Albright without his flask, and there was no possibility of hiding it. He had thought and thought, but there were no answers.

"I've no choice Meg. I didn't tell you, but I had a go at getting round out in America with Johnny."

"And?"

"A bloody disaster. Complete nightmare. I cannae play dry any more. I just cannae. Sorry."

His head dropped and he felt terribly ashamed. She cupped his chin and lifted his face to hers and kissed him. "No need. Really. Look at it this way. Your problem isn't any kind of secret. The papers saw to that. Everyone knows. The whole world. Of course they'll be watching. No way can you help that. And there will be someone who will turn their noses up and have a go at you. But think of all the others, Deek. All those thousands and thousands of others who sent you all the letters. They aren't judging you. They like you because you're you. There are no perfect people. The media invent their perfect icons and then they knock them down. At least you never had to do the perfect bit. You are famous because you are so bloody imperfect. It's the imperfection that everyone loves. There's no need to be ashamed, Deek. Just be you."

He looked hard into her eyes and saw nothing but complete truth. "To be honest, the only thing that really matters is what you think. I just wish I did'nae have to do it, but it's no good. After this . . . I promise Meg. After this I stop."

"Scoobytown?"

"Scoobytown. You're still coming?"

She smiled. "Try stopping me. OK. We'd better get the show on the road whether you like it or not. Breakfast. Non-negotiable. Here or the dining room?"

"Here. I need to start getting my head right."

"OK. I'll order something. Bacon butty?"

"Aye. Two."

She placed the call and started pulling out clothes. "I bought you these and there is no arguing."

She tossed over a pair of tartan trousers. He looked at them aghast. "Ah come on Meg. Tartan! You have to be kidding."

"No. You're representing Scotland and so you are wearing tartan. If you didn't have such pathetic skinny legs I would have had you in a kilt, so be thankful for small mercies."

"I hav'nae got pathetic skinny legs."

"Now if I were dressing George, I would have him in a kilt. That lad really does have a pair of legs on him. Like tree trunks."

He was about to protest but she put a finger to his lips and shushed him. "Only winding you up. No need to get all touchy. Go on. Try them on. If you hate them, then fair enough."

Deek obliged. To go with the trousers she had chosen a white polo neck, a black Pringle cashmere jumper and a cap of matching tartan. He was about to tell her, no way, never in a month of Sundays, but when he checked out the mirror he held back. He looked at himself front on and sideways and rather liked what he saw. He looked like a throwback. He looked like one of the guys in the black and white photos from the twenties and thirties. In fact he looked every inch the canny Scottish golfer who could knock a two iron under the wind and play a bump-and-run onto a dry green.

"Happy." Meg was standing behind him with her hands on her hips.

"Aye. Canny choice Meg. Canny choice."

The phone on the bedside table rang and Meg picked it up.

"For you. It's George."

Deek took the receiver and found the big American voice to be a little smaller than normal and somewhat croaky.

"Morning Deek. How are you?"

"Aye. Nae bad. Yourself?"

"I feel like the inside of a bear's ass, but I suppose I'll live."

"That's a pity."

"Hey, what about that famous British sportsmanship?"

"It's a myth."

George chuckled. "Seems that way. Look, they want some kind of interview before we hit off. You good for that?"

"Aye. I suppose so."

"I'll tell them to come down to the practice ground about twelve-thirty. Ten minutes. OK?"

"Aye. That's fine. I'll see you down there shall I?"

"Sure thing."

Deek put off going down to the practice area for as long as he could. The last thing he wanted was to spend too long watching George flexing his shoulders and smashing balls into the blue yonder. He waited until just before twelve and watched the first half-hour of the BBC's *Grandstand* special that was dedicated to the event. The anchor in the on-course studio made sure that the viewing millions were in no doubt as to the importance of what was about to take place.

"*. . . forget the Premiership and the Champion's league, forget Wimbledon, forget World Title Heavyweight boxing, forget the Superbowl and the NBA, forget even the Olympics. Forget every single event in the history of sport because over the next two days we are all about to watch the biggest money match ever. Two men. One prize. Two nations and only one winner. We're all ready here. The weather*

*is gorgeous, the course is perfect, the President arrives tomorrow
morning. We've all been waiting a long time for this, and now, ladies
and gentlemen, the time has come. It's time for the Match . . ."*

He let his words hang until a familiar montage of images took over
with U2's *Beautiful Day* blasting out in the background. There were
the trademark images of Turnberry: the lighthouse, Ailsa Craig, the
ninth tee, seabirds over the water. There were images of Deek and
George and Airforce One. There were images of Roland McMillan
and lots of shots of the priceless collection of paintings that were the
prize. Deek grimaced at the stark contrast between the pictures of
himself and George. All there was of him was a collection of shots
from him playing in recent PGA events. The most noticeable feature
was his rather crabby-looking swing and the sparse handfuls of spectators watching. George on the other hand was framed by huge teem-
ing masses as he strode down fairways and held trophies aloft. The
music faded out on a view of the sun setting beside the dramatic cliffs
of Ailsa Craig.

*"So. There you have it. It's just about the most uneven match up since
David trotted out to take on Goliath. On one side we have one of the
world's true sporting greats, a golfing colossus who has won every
prize the game has to offer and who has been untouched as the world
Number One for a record four years. On the other side we have a
little-known Scotsman who before all this blew up wouldn't have been
a household name in his own living room. Since then of course Archie
Banks, better known to all of us as Deek, has gained more than his
fair share of notoriety. Let's just say that he probably lives in the most
famous caravan on the planet."*

He introduced his experts and they started the process of analysing
the match. After a few minutes Deek switched off the TV. They didn't
give him a chance in a hundred. Not that he blamed them. Over
eighteen holes, well maybe. Weird things did happen every now and
then. But 54 holes. No way.

By this time Troll and Banjo had arrived and Meg had them
decked out in the same outfit as his own. It was the first time that he
could remember seeing Banjo in a pair of trousers that were actually
the right length. He had to admit that the three of them looked
halfway decent.

At noon he realised that he could put it off no longer. It was time. Time for the practice ground. Time for the cameras. Time to play. There were plenty of well-wishers in the corridors of the hotel, and as he got to the main door he could hear that the Ailsa Bar was already in full swing. He felt a bitter envy for those inside who would spend a happy afternoon with a free bar and pictures of the match on the TV. The hotel had a buggy waiting outside and the three of them clambered aboard. Their drive down the hill to the course was filmed by a TV crew on a similar buggy, and all the way people gave him cheers and thumbs-up signs.

The scene at the practice ground came as something of a surprise. A decent-sized crowd had gathered and there seemed to be a good deal of laughing. It soon became clear that George was running through his Iraqi trick shot routine and many of the Sunnybank youngsters were lapping it up. The smile on the face of the cameraman showed that the BBC was treating the exhibition as an unplanned bonus. As Deek's buggy pulled up George marched over and shook his hand warmly.

"How's the head?"

"Aye. Getting there. Yours?"

"Better. You can't beat a bit of sea air."

Deek nodded at the watching crowd. "You've been doing the tricks I see."

"Sure. I just thought, what the hell, you know? Us guys do enough practising."

If only, thought Deek. A familiar young Sunnybank voice chipped in.

"Can you do any tricks Deek? Go on. Let's see."

Deek grinned and shook his head ruefully. "Sorry lads. I'll have tae leave that department to George here."

Troll emptied a bag of practice balls out onto the turf and Deek started with a six iron. The balls started to land in a rather discouraging widespread cluster. He moved down to a four iron and did little better. Things didn't improve much with successive clubs and his morale took another notch downwards. He was in the process of pulling his wedge out of the bag when a hand on his shoulder made him turn. Frank Cunningham and Roger Swan had come up without him noticing.

"Remember that morning on the practice ground Deek? Long time, hey."

"Aye Frank. Bloody long time." He aimed a good-humoured punch at Roger who swayed away "And you were a right bugger, Roger. Betting wee yins for their chip money. You should be ashamed of yourself."

Roger shrugged. "You won though."

"Aye. I suppose I did."

"How are you feeling?" asked Frank.

"Scared shitless, to be honest."

Roger smiled. "Don't blame you. Rather you than me, that's all I can say."

"Cheers Roger. Good of you to say so."

"Any time. Put that wedge away Deek. You were always crap on the practice ground. You'll do no good going through the motions. Save it for the course."

Deek weighed the club in his hand for a moment and then tossed it back in the bag. A few yards away, George lazily threw a drive 280 yards into the distance with what appeared to be no more than a flick of his thick wrists. He looked over to Deek.

"You ready?"

"Aye. Ready as I'll ever be. Let's go shall we?"

He was about to climb aboard the buggy when Steve came running over to him. When he arrived he was breathing hard and a cough was refusing to stay inside. It took a good few seconds of hacking before he could speak properly.

"Christ Steve, you OK pal?"

Steve wiped the tears from his eyes. "Yeah, fine. Too many bloody fags, that's all."

"You look like shite. What's been happening?"

"A few problems. Nothing too much to worry about. I'm afraid I won't be able to be out there with you this afternoon. I'm sorry. Really sorry. You know how it is."

Deek frowned. "Not really. Anything I can do?"

Steve patted him lightly on the back. "No. Not a thing. Just give it your best shot. I'll see you later. All the best, yeah."

Deek nodded. "Aye. Thanks. Hope things go OK, whatever they are."

He stood for a moment and watched Steve head back towards the towering white walls of the hotel. Something was wrong. Very, very wrong. Both players ran through their pre-match interviews before spending five minutes of the putting green and making their way to the first tee. Roland McMillan was waiting alongside several members of the family. Hands were shaken and luck was wished. Apart from a hard core in the Ailsa Bar, almost all the guests were now out, ready for the game to start. The gallery was a little under 400, a fraction of what George was used to, but many more than was the norm for Deek. He had only been out of the hotel room for an hour, but already his body and brain were screaming out for a drink. Should he have one before the first shot? He couldn't. It would look terrible. He pulled his driver out and checked to see how firm his grip was. There was a slight tremor, but nothing much. He would get away with it for the first shot then he would take a big swig from the flask on his way down the fairway.

The nerves were climbing all over him now as an announcer gave their names to the crowd and the camera. Jonathan wheeled Roland forward and the old man tossed a coin. Deek called 'heads' and "heads" it was. He felt like going first and getting it over with, but it wouldn't look good.

"Go George. You have the first bash."

"Thanks Deek. Just a minute. I'm expecting someone . . ."

The young Dumfries waiter from the evening before emerged through the crowd at the back of the tee carrying a silver tray with a bottle of Jack Daniels and two crystal tumblers. ". . . ah. Here we go. Deek, I figured I best show some good American hospitality. This young man has agreed to follow us round. Would you join me in a wee dram before we get started?"

The team of commentators couldn't quite believe what they were hearing. They had discussed at some length the issue of Deek taking a drink during the round and reached a consensus that he wouldn't. It was one thing to take a few crafty hits in front of the two-men-and-a-dog crowds of the PGA tour. They couldn't believe that he would do so in front of the cameras and an armchair audience of millions. What nobody had ever dreamed of was that George Albright would join in. The American poured out two generous measures and passed a glass to his opponent.

"Have a great game, friend."

He held his glass and they clinked. Deek felt his eyes prickling with tears and was almost overcome by the generosity of the gesture.

"Cheers George. You too. And thanks."

They both put away their drinks in one and returned the glasses to the tray. George shook his head comically and made a big play of the burning liquor hitting the spot. He leaned in close to Deek so the camera wouldn't hear him.

"Every couple of holes, OK Deek?"

Deek nodded. "Aye. Perfect."

"I'll only be taking small ones. I haven't got your head for it."

He walked back to where his caddie was waiting and pulled out his driver. It seemed odd to Deek to watch George go through the routine that he had seen so many times on the TV. Complete silence fell as the world number one addressed his ball. He looked up once. Then again. Then a third time before launching into the shot with a huge swing. The ball took off as if it had been fired by an artillery piece. It flew up into the blue of the sky and drew gasps from the watching crowd. By the time it had finished rolling down the left of the close-shaved fairway it had travelled a few inches short of 325 yards.

"Holy Christ" Deek whispered to himself as the applause broke out for the immense tee shot. He had already decided to try for a safe one iron and fought off the temptation to try and keep up with a driver. Thankfully, the Jack Daniels was doing the business and he managed a solid enough swing. The ball started out up the right of the fairway and curled back in nicely. It settled down a good 70 yards back from George's position, but at least he was under way. The match was on.

Anatoly had packed everything that he needed into the boot. All there was to do now was to wait. He felt completely relaxed as he watched the build-up to the start of the match. Every time the TV showed an image of the ninth tee a small smile played on his lips. When the waiter appeared with the drinks tray he shook his head in wonder. Only an American could behave so ridiculously. The watching experts struggled to find the words to describe their reaction. The papers the next morning would be covered with images of the two players sharing their glasses of Jack Daniels. The morning after, the news would be rather more dramatic. He watched the two drives and then switched off the TV. He took a last look around and ran through a mental checklist. When he was sure that all was in order he nodded to himself and went out to the car. The next day when he returned to the lonely cottage he would be the most wanted man on the face of the planet.

"What time have you got Walter?"

"Jesus Steve, I wish you'd buy yourself a sonofabitching watch. I'm beginning to feel like some sort of a speaking clock here. It's two forty-five. Why the hell don't you wear a watch?"

"Too many surveillance shifts. You must have done your share yourself Walter. There's nothing worse than watching the clock. I just gave up wearing the time and never got back into the habit again."

He turned back to the TV where George was launching yet another howitzer drive up the eighth. Deek was playing OK, but OK wasn't nearly enough. He had got himself onto the first seven greens in the regulation figures and had been unlucky to see a couple of birdie puts spin out from the hole. George was carrying on from his last round at the Masters and was going for every shot as if it were his last. Already he was four under par and therefore four ahead.

The two players couldn't have made much more of a contrast. George was dressed in the vivid colours of America and looked like a cartoon-giant next to the more conservatively attired Scotsman who stood a good five inches shorter. However, the greatest contrast was in their demeanour. George to all intents and purposes looked like a man who was having the time of his life as he strolled from shot to shot with a beaming grin. Deek on the other hand was wrapped in concentration. Before every approach shot he and Troll consulted their yardage sheets carefully and he went about his work meticulously. Steve's heart went out to him. He could see that Deek was giving it just about everything that he had and was playing right up at the top of his game. The problem was that he was up against genius, and the genius was inspired.

The camera fastened onto Deek's ball as it flew through the air into the eighth green. The pin was set cruelly just a few feet over a cavernous bunker and Deek's ball landed well clear of it and settled at the back of the green 35 feet from the hole. George's drive had finished nearly 80 yards ahead of Deek's and he needed no more than a wedge to get home. He played the shot with a huge swing and a fat divot jumped out of the fairway. The commentator pointed out to the viewers that the swing, indicated that George was going for a really high shot to land just over the bunker and settle near the flag. As it turned out the shot was six inches short of perfection. It caught the very top of the lip of the bunker and trickled back inside into a miserably difficult spot.

The camera panned in on George's face which was wearing an easy-going "Aww shucks" expression. Maybe Deek had a chance to do something.

The consensus among the commentators was that George would do well to get the thing out at all, let alone get it close. Maybe a par would be good enough for Deek to nick a hole back. There was a sense of increasing alarm among the pundits. Winning the rights to show the match had been a major coup for the BBC and the last thing they wanted was a one-horse whitewash. At the rate things were going the damn thing was looking like being over before the last round even got a chance to start. George hammered murderously down into the soft white sand and against all odds the ball popped out and rolled quietly up to a spot six feet below the flag. The consensus in the studio was that he was a man at the peak of his powers. As Deek and Troll stalked about the green there was a great deal of talk of magnificent, awesome and phenomenal. Now the camera panned in close on Deek's hard-lined face as he at last settled over his put. Steve liked what he saw in the eyes. There wasn't the merest trace of defeat there. Deek was focused. In the zone.

He started his putt out a good five feet to the right of the hole, and for the last third of its journey it seemed as if it was bound to stop short. But it didn't. It kept going with ever-slowing revolutions until it clawed its way to the edge of the hole and dropped in after a heartbeat of hesitation. As the cheers of relief rang out, the commentators agreed that it was what Deek had desperately needed. At least he had now won a hole. Three down sounded much better than four down.

The players were making their way to the ninth tee when the phone rang.

"Is that you Kenton?" Steve's boss sounded colder than Greenland.

"Yes."

"I have a green light. An SAS troop will be airborne in five minutes. They have an ETA New Galloway in just over an hour. I'll leave it to you to arrange landing."

"Thank you sir" said Steve to a dead phone line. He wrenched a cigarette from a dying packet. "OK Walter. We're green. Let's go."

The American jumped to his feet and started packing away his laptop while Steve got on the line to Harris and instructed him to arrange for Sunderland to make a field available for the helicopter to land.

The journey south through the Galloway hills was like a long and protracted fairground ride as Walter threw the car at corner after corner like the wannabe rally driver that he had been for years. Steve decided that it would sound a bit pathetic if he asked his friend to slow down and so instead he gritted his teeth and concentrated on the radio commentary of the match. They covered the distance to the farm in an astounding 50 minutes, by which time Ge rge Albright had moved to five up after thirteen holes. The helicopte swooped down from the sky ten minutes after their arrival and the four-man team jumped out.

In civilian clothes, not one of them would have come close to public expectations of what a special forces soldier should look like. The tallest of them was barely six feet tall and the youngest was just over 30. Their first priority was to light up cigarettes as soon as they escaped the no smoking interior of the chopper. They dragged hard on the nicotine as they pulled on their bulletproof breastplates and then their flak jackets. Steve recognised the familiar bushy red hair of the sergeant as soon as he jumped down to the grass.

"Bloody hell Fish, they must be desperate to send you. Don't tell me you're in charge?" The redhead was a wiry little man called Derek Troutman from the wrong end of Swansea. His surname had inspired the nickname Fish while he was at school. He had served with Steve on three occasions in Ireland.

His face lit up as soon as Steve spoke. "Well bugger me. This your show then Stevie?"

"Fraid so."

"Bloody knackered then aren't we?" He spoke in the singsong voice of the valleys. Few would ever have believed that he had killed on four occasions. He was the friendly guy behind the counter at the local newsagents who let the kids off when they were ten pence short for a bag of sweets. He introduced Steve and Walter to the other members of the troop.

The smallest of the four at five foot nine was Goss. He was the son of a sheet metal worker from Scunthorpe who was sparing with his words to the point of barely speaking at all. This trait earned the nickname of Goss, a shortening of the word gossip. Terry Fenton was bred on a sprawling sheep farm in Australia's Northern Territories. He had transferred across from the Australian SAS to find more action and carried the uninspired handle of Oz. Purley was the mouth of the troop, and loved to play out the role of his cheeky cockney roots.

Steve had used their ten-minute start to secure the use of the farmer's two Land Rovers to carry them all over to a jumping-off point a mile from the cottage. Despite the apparent casual air of the troopers they were loaded up and rolling within five minutes of their arrival. The farmer drove the lead vehicle and was encouraged to drive normally and sensibly to the spot they had chosen to walk in from.

The soldiers didn't dally and set out straight away. All Walter and Steve could do was to wait. By this time the golfers up at Turnberry had completed the sixteenth hole and Deek had managed two more birdies to hang on in at five holes behind. The SAS squad took half an hour to make their approach and a further ten minutes to get up to the front and back doors. Their technology suggested that the place was empty but they went in with charges and stun grenades to be on the safe side. Steve got a radio message that all was clear just as Deek and George were halving the seventeenth.

By this stage a car had arrived carrying three of the detectives plus a forensic team who had been drafted in from nearby Dumfries. A careful search began ten minutes after the soldiers had reported the property to be clear and had taken up a comfortable position in the sunshine of the front lawn. They looked for all the world like a group of builders on a tea-break as they lazed around and awaited developments.

The search of the property began in earnest as the first round of the match finished with both players halving the eighteenth in par fours. Deek had managed one of the finest rounds of his life and had completed the great course in three under par. The problem was that

George Albright the Third had played like a man from another planet. He had gone for every shot and made almost all of them to finish his round eight under par. The consensus in the studio was that a five-hole lead was a huge mountain for Deek to climb and that his chances had slipped away from slim to none.

The first breakthrough in the search came at five-thirty. It was a credit card receipt from a car hire firm in Birmingham. This gave them details of the hired Mercedes that were immediately circulated. The second big find came ten minutes later when one of the forensic team announced that the glass by the armchair in the lounge carried a fresh set of prints.

Steve stepped out into the late afternoon sunlight to try and find a way of making this new jigsaw piece work in their favour. He took a walk for a few hundred yards through the pine trees that surrounded the cottage and the answer came as he was watching a red squirrel scuttle away into the safety of the high branches. He walked fast back to the house and called out to Walter.

"You need to get Hal Benton on the line, mate."

"Go on."

"The prints. Rykov used to be in the army didn't he. Somewhere in some dusty old basement in Russia there will be a copy of his service record. They won't have forgotten him. Forget Gorbachov and Glasnost. This lad took out five of their top guys. The Russians don't forget things like that in a hurry. The CIA and the FSB are supposed to be best of pals these days. So, it's simple. Benton gets hold of his oppo in Moscow and we email a copy of the prints out. If we can get a positive match on Anatoly Rykov, that looks pretty much like real proof to me."

Walter nodded. "With you all the way, man. I'm on it."

"Make the call and we'll get back to Dumfries with one of the forensic guys."

While Walter made the call to Langley, Steve went over to the flopped-out SAS men on the lawn. "Don't go pissing off back to Hereford, will you Fish? I've got a feeling we'll be needing you lot before the weekend is done. I'll sort it out. You'll need to get yourselves up to Turnberry."

Fish gave a small smile. "Oh, I see now. Turnberry as in this big game of golf the TV are getting so hyped-up about?"

"Yes."

"Turnberry as in the President of America turning up to watch tomorrow?"

"Yes."

"My oh my. How exciting."

Colonel Oleg Grishkin was getting himself ready to take his two daughters to the ballet when his phone rang. He tried to finish off the knot of his bow tie before answering, but the haste made his fingers clumsy. He angrily ripped the knot open and picked up the offending phone.

"Yes!"

The voice on the other end was all trepidation. Grishkin's temper was the subject of many a legend in the headquarters of the FSB. Things had changed in Russia, but not that much. The infamous Lubyanka Headquarters of the of KGB was now home to the much less feared FSB but they hadn't become all warm and cuddly overnight. Oleg Grishkin certainly hadn't. He was an officer of the old school and often spent his evenings in the company of the old guard pining for the days when a man could be taken down to the basement and sorted out with no questions asked.

"I am truly sorry for disturbing you sir . . ."

"Stop bleating and get on with it."

"There is a call sir. From America. He says he knows you. Says it's urgent."

"Who is it?"

"Benton."

Oleg rolled his eyes. Indeed, he knew Hal Benton well enough. They had been pushed together like the teenage children of matchmaking neighbours. They were expected to smooth out past difficulties. Past difficulties! Their two countries had been on the brink of nuking each other into oblivion for half a century and now they were expected to kiss and make up as if nothing had ever happened. Benton. How he despised the man. He was typical of the new breed of CIA man. He was all mineral water and Italian suits and half his government salary spent on his teeth. In the days when they had all been enemies it had been so much better. Then they would meet secretly to iron out their differences over vodka. He had always thought that vodka had kept the world safe. Now that the likes of Benton with their sparkling mineral water were in the chair, they would probably all wind up as ash.

"Thank you. I will call."

Cursing, he made his way to his office and picked up the secure phone. Benton was ready and waiting and took the call on the second ring.

"Benton."

"It's Grishkin. You wanted me."

"Indeed. Are you secure?"

"Yes."

"I need a favour, Oleg. A big one."

This brought a chilly smile to the face of the Russian. He could sense what those words must have cost his clean-cut adversary. Oleg! Benton never called him Oleg.

"Of course. Tell me."

"You're not going to like this much, so you might as well sit down."

Better and better. "That is what we Russians do before we go on a journey. We sit down. It is a superstition of ours. Am I about to go on a journey Hal?"

"I figure so. OK. Here's what it is. I guess you probably know the name Anatoly Rykov."

Grishkin stiffened and the good humour fell from his face. "I know the traitorous bastard. What of him?"

"I guess you have followed him over the years. Well, not in person, but followed his work."

"We have."

"I expect that you concur with our analysis that Rykov was responsible for the recent execution of General Yuri Krishkin in a Moscow café."

Oleg's knuckles tightened on the handset. "Yes."

Benton picked his words with the care of a gardener choosing orchids for a flower show. "We have reason to believe that Rykov is in contact with Al Quaida. We believe they commissioned the hit on Krishkin."

"Are you telling me that you were in possession of these facts before the murder of our officer?"

There was a pained silence for a moment. "I'm afraid I am."

Grishkin struggled to stay calm. "I was under the impression that our services are working on the understanding that we now share information. Anatoly Rykov remains one of the most wanted criminals in Russia. He is a murderer and a traitor, but of course you know that Hal because it was the CIA that paid him for his work."

"Now look Oleg, that was a long time ago, things have moved on . . ."

"When it comes to traitors things never move on. Not here in Russia. I suggest that you continue."

"We believe that Rykov is now in Scotland." Benton took a deep breath. He had no choice but to put the thing straight. "We have reason to believe that he is preparing to make another assassination attempt tomorrow."

"Who?"

"The President."

Grishkin felt as if the headset had fired an electric shock straight through his ear drum and into his skull. "Repeat that please."

"You heard right first time. The President." Benton went on to explain the President's plan to attend the second day of the golf match in Turnberry.

"You say you have evidence. How much evidence?"

"Enough to convince me. Not enough to convince the people over at the White House."

"Explain."

"They say that everything we have is circumstantial. They are convinced that they have the whole place wrapped in an iron ring of security. The President isn't doing so good at the moment. He's behind in the ratings and slipping back every day. He needs a few positive events like this for people to see him in a better light."

"But surely his people know how Rykov works. He is a bomber. If this is true, his bomb will already be in place. Do they know this, Hal?"

"Most of it." Most of it! What the hell was happening here? Grishkin closed his eyes and tried to do the jigsaw as fast as he could. His calculator of a brain did it in seconds. "Oh yes, I can see. How very embarrassing for the CIA if it came out that a paid assassin from Al Quaida turned out to have been recruited by Langley dollars. A difficult situation my friend. A truly difficult situation."

"OK Oleg. You have it. Come on, are things so very different over there? We do what we do. CIA, KGB, FSB. What the hell. We do what it takes and the politicians rip our balls off any chance they get."

Oleg's smile was back. He had never heard Benton so agitated. He wouldn't have thought it possible. "So my friend. How is it that I can help?"

"Rykov was a soldier in your forces. Somewhere you will have a copy of his fingerprints. We believe that we have a fresh set from the place where he has been holed up. Get me a match and I have real proof. Real proof and I keep the President away from Turnberry."

"But my friend. It is Saturday night. Such a thing will take time. Of course I would like to help but you must be aware that . . ."

"Cut the crap Oleg. If the President gets whacked then everything will come out in the wash. Sure, the Agency will look like hell, but what about you? This conversation is going on the record if I don't have those prints on my screen inside four hours. FSB collude in assassination of President. The assassin is a trained Spetznatz killer. Think hard, Oleg. I don't think your lords and masters would be too happy about that, especially when there are a few billion dollars' worth of credits headed Moscow's way at the moment."

Grishkin knew well enough that he had no choice but to co-operate. "It will be done. You want me to send to your usual email?"

"Yes please."

"One thing Hal. One thing I will ask. If you catch Rykov, he is ours. Understood?"

"If we catch him you are welcome to him, Oleg. But that isn't about to happen. If we get close enough he's going down. Down hard."

Oleg grunted. "I believe you people call it 'extreme prejudice'."

"As extreme as it ever gets."

Rykov arrived at the old quarry a little before five o'clock. He had found the place as he drove around the countryside after checking out of the hotel during his visit at the end of February. The place had clearly not been working for some years. A high fence topped with rusty barbed wired kept the public out and a formidable padlock secured the double iron gates. As far as he could tell, the nearest inhabited building was more than a mile away. A tiny amount of explosive popped the padlock off the gate and he dragged the gate open. The task was made difficult by the thick weeds that had grown up out of the cracked concrete and rooted the bottom of the gate to the ground.

He drove his car around the back of the factory buildings and parked it up in an old workshop area before returning to close the gate back up. The perfect blue sky of the morning was now becoming increasingly filled with cloud. The forecaster on the radio had predicted a major break in the weather and, sure enough, by six a thin rain was falling. He decided to wait until eight o'clock before heading out across the last line of hills before the coast.

By eight the rain was much heavier and a thick coating of mist had settled onto the hills. Visibility was down to less than 300 yards and the light of the day was fading fast. Anatoly opened the trunk and started to put on his gear. He carefully tied on his hiking boots and then thick waterproofs that were perfectly in keeping with the cover of a birdwatcher that he would use in the unlikely event of him meeting anyone. He ran a quick check on the inside of his rucksack and he contented himself that all was in place. He hefted the sack onto his back and locked the car. Earlier he had cut the fence at the back of the compound and now he eased himself through it and started up the rough uneven hillside.

According to his map reading he had three miles to cover. On a sunny afternoon he would have been able to make the distance in no more than an hour and a half. In the rain and the darkness it would take him more than double that time. He would need to concentrate hard on his footing. To come so far and fail at the very end because of a sprained ankle would be inexcusable. Even if the journey was twice as slow as he anticipated he would still be in position well before dawn.

As he trudged across the bleak hillside he felt the familiar thrill of the hunter setting out for his prey.

Deek had stopped off in the bar for a couple of drinks, having made his way up the hill from the course. He had done his best in the post-match interview. Everyone had been very nice: very complimentary. Three under par was a magnificent achievement for any golfer around the venerable old course, especially off the toughest tees. He had tried to smile and show dogged optimism about his chances the next day. However, he didn't feel as if he had managed to pull it off.

In truth he felt utterly shell-shocked. Never in his wildest dreams had he imagined playing alongside a player who was capable of such golf. George had been majestic. What had made it worse was how easy it had seemed. The big man never seemed to have a smile off his face as he strolled his way round, chatting to one and all. It seemed to Deek that he must have seemed pretty miserable in comparison. The only way that he had managed to make such a score was by wrapping himself in a cocoon of concentration. Never before had he been more focused on a golf course and it left him feeling utterly washed-out and drained.

George had already taken up station at the bar when Deek walked in. He had the look of a man who was settling himself in for a mighty session and gave Deek a big wave over.

"You did great out there today Deek. Real great. Here. Have a drink."

Deek took a sip at the scotch and nodded acknowledgement to the well-wishers all around him. "I dunnae quite know what to say about your round George. If I was playing golf I have'nae a clue what you were playing. Bloody unbelievable."

He raised his glass in salute with a small smile.

George became rather more serious. "Hey buddy, you need to look at this thing right. There's nothing new in all this for me remember. TV, crowds, media. Hell, I just notice a few less people watching. It's no big deal for me to play OK. It's different for you Deek. This is your first time out there in the fishbowl. Seriously, you need to be damned proud of yourself. First time I was out there in the big spotlight I was a damn sight nearer 80 and 70."

Deek nodded. The generosity of the man was astounding. "Have you always been like this George?"

Albright grinned. "Like what?"

"Oh you know. Drinks with the lads. Passing out. Singing on the table. The thing with the youth centre. You never looked that way to me on the tele."

"Christ no. Deek, for too many years I have been one dull sonofabitch with my head stuck up my ass. It was Iraq that changed things. So I won a few golf competitions. So what the hell. One day I woke up to the fact that my wife hates my guts and I ain't got a decent friend in the world. Time to wake up and smell the air George

I thought. So I went to the Gulf. Spent some time with regular folks. Sacked my asshole of an agent. Best thing I ever did, friend."

Deek shook his head. "Life can be a weird old bastard, hey George?"

"Sure as hell can. Would you want it any different?"

Deek smiled. "No. I don't suppose I would."

"You having another?"

"No. I'm shattered. I think I'll go up and get my head down for a while. Maybe have a bath. After all these years in Roger's caravan a bath is still a novelty."

He emerged from a long soak a little after eight and was getting ready for going down to eat when there was a tap on the door. Meg had left him to it and headed for the gym and he had enjoyed the space to get his thoughts together.

He opened the door to find Frank Cunningham and Roger Swann waiting outside in the corridor.

"Oh, hi guys. Come on in. You'll have a dram?"

They settled down and took their glasses of scotch.

"Tell you what, Deek" said Frank. "I've been watching you since you first got hold of that eight iron of mine. Well, so has Roger. I've never seen you play like today. Bloody fantastic. We were proud of you. Both of us. Everyone is. 68 round this track with all that pressure was unbelievable."

"Good of you to say so Frank, but it didn't exactly do me much good did it? Five behind might as well be 55. I never had a bloody chance did I? I'm not in the same league as George. The man is a bloody genius."

Roger got up and fixed himself another drink. "Aye. He's OK. But this thing isn't over yet. Not even close."

Deek shook his head. "Forget the mathematical options, Rog. I can't do any better than today and I dunnae see George going to pieces."

Frank sat forward with a serious expression on his face. "You've not had the TV on then?"

"No. I just grabbed some kip and a bath. Why?"

Now Frank smiled. "The weather forecast. That's why."

Now Deek was interested. "What are they saying?"

"There's a big fat area of low pressure coming in off the Atlantic. It has already hit the west coast of Ireland and it is due to reach here by the early hours of the morning. They're telling everyone to batten down the hatches. Two inches of rain and force nine gales, gusting up to 80 miles an hour in places. There are flood warnings out all over the west of Scotland. They are saying that it is going to be rough as hell until late afternoon tomorrow."

All three men were smiling now. The contest had just got a great deal more even.

Frank continued. "Maybe it would be an idea if you didn't get absolutely pie-eyed tonight."

Deek agreed. "Aye. Maybe that would be a plan. George might just have more than a sore head to deal with come ten tomorrow morning."

Steve found it impossible to sit down. They had been allocated an office in the Police HQ building in Dumfries and there was nothing they could do but wait. He paced. He smoked. He checked his watch every two minutes. Walter on the other hand had settled down to playing endless games of Solitaire on his laptop. It was just after nine when Walter's mobile phone rang.

"Yeah."

"It's Benton. I have just heard from Moscow. We have a match. It's Rykov. Confirmed."

"Are you going to talk with the President's people?"

"I'll try. You best get back up to Turnberry."

"OK. I'll call in when we get there."

Walter looked up. "Get that?"

"It's him isn't it?"

"Yeah. Confirmed. We need to get back up there."

Steve nodded. "Let me make a few calls first. I need to sort something out."

"Want to share it?"

"I best had. If this thing comes off you'll need to come with me."

Steve made two calls. The first was to Jonathan McMillan who couldn't for the life of him work out why Steve wanted him to go to the hotel shop and buy as many videos of past championships as he could. He also couldn't get his head round why Steve wanted the use of the company helicopter when he arrived back in Turnberry some time before ten.

The next call was to the headquarters of the Royal Ulster Constabulary's Special Branch in Castlereigh, Belfast.

Sally was feeling thoroughly strung out. All day she had been chasing around ensuring that all was running smoothly. She should have been enjoying a few relaxing drinks with the buoyant crowd in the bar. On the surface of things the day had gone to perfection. The TV pictures of the gorgeous golf course and hotel had attracted a sensational worldwide audience, and the image it had all portrayed of Scotland had been the stuff of dreams. Nobody in the Parliament could have wanted for a better image of Scotland in general and Scottish sport in particular. Maybe the match might provoke the biggest influx of tourists since Madonna's wedding.

However, the future prospects of the tourism industry were far from being the main topic of conversation when the First Minister made his regular calls. All he wanted was updates on the threat to the President. She couldn't blame him. No number of panoramic seascapes would ever make up for the image of a presidential assassination on Scottish soil. She couldn't understand how on earth she had become the person in charge of overseeing the efforts of the security services. It was ridiculous. She was the bloody Minister for Sport for goodness sake. Her boss had been very clear. She was the person on the ground. She was the person who was fully briefed about the situation. She had indicated that she wanted something bigger than sport. Well, now she had it. Get this one right and she would be put on an even faster track. He didn't actually say the bit about getting it wrong and she was finished. He hadn't needed to.

Steve had said that he would be at her room before ten. It had sounded rather optimistic unless he had Michael Schumacher as a chauffeur. When the door was knocked at nine forty-five she was mightily glad that she hadn't been any part of the car journey from Dumfries.

Steve looked awful. Days without sleep had aged him a decade and his eyes were ringed with grey fatigue. He was frighteningly wired and was quite unable to stay still.

"OK Sally. Here's where we are. None of it is good. We have firm confirmation that it is Rykov."

"How?"

"You absolutely don't want to know. Just take my word for it. It's him and he's here."

"Oh Jesus."

"It gets worse. I just got a call from the local uniform boys. They have found the car." He spread a map out on the bed. "Here. It's a disused quarry. There's no way of telling how long it's been there. OK. Look. If he follows his usual routine he will lay up in sight of the target. I guess that could be anywhere along the line of hills here."

He ran his finger along the tightly knit contours of the map. "Anywhere along here puts him within four miles with a clear sight of the course. My gut feeling tells me that is where the bomb is."

"What! On the course itself?"

He nodded grimly. "Think about it. He was here before anyone knew any of this was about to happen. He books in and plays a round of golf. Easy recon. He decides on a spot and checks out. Then he goes to the cottage by New Galloway. He probably comes back the next night. We checked the weather for the evening of 1st March. It was awful. Wind and rain. Perfect conditions to park up and hike it in. It would probably have been one or two o'clock in the morning. What chance was there of anyone being out there at that time on a wild winter night?"

"None." Sally was chalk-white and visibly shaking.

Steve lit up and continued to spit out the facts as he saw them.

"OK. So he plants the bomb and buggers off back to his safe house. He leaves the next day, fills up with fuel at Gretna, drives to London, stays overnight, checks in the car and disappears from view. Until now. Right now he is up there somewhere."

He waved a thumb at the bedroom window that was starting to slightly shake with the buffeting wind. "The weather is crap and forecast to get worse. We could deploy a regiment into those hills and we wouldn't find him. Look at the map. He has hundreds of acres to lay up in. This guy is trained. One of the best. In these conditions the only way to find him would be to tread on him."

"I wouldn't much like the idea of treading on the sonofabitch" muttered Walter.

Steve nodded agreement. "So. Number one, we have a needle in a haystack. Number two is the bomb. We have just over twelve hours and a whole golf course to search and lousy weather."

Sally sighed. "Not a chance then."

"Not much. Just one in fact. There's a guy I'm going to ask. It's a long shot but worth a go."

"Who?"

Steve gave her an icy smile. "You don't want to know. That I can promise you."

She nodded. God alone knew what kind of dark murky world these strange men lived in. It made her feel cold all over.

"OK Sally. Here is how things need to play out. There is about a tonne of politics around this thing. Rykov has a history that some pretty big people need to keep under wraps. I mean really big people. Dangerous players."

She couldn't quite believe what she was hearing. "You mean that the President's security team aren't getting the full story?"

Walter shook his head. "Not even half of it, honey."

She was angry now. "But this is outrageous. We are talking about a threat to the President of America. How can anyone keep secrets? It's ridiculous."

Walter gave her a tired smile. "That's Washington. Lotta secrets in that little old town. Lotta power and a lotta secrets. No point getting pissed about it, sugar. It's just the way things are."

Steve hammered on. "This is what you need to do. The McMillan jet is waiting up at Prestwick. Get yourself up there and get over to Paris. The President is staying at the Embassy. Somehow you're going to have to blag your way in to see him. I haven't the first clue how. Being a Minister has to count for something."

"Oh come on, you have to be kidding."

"You think so? Come on Sally. We're just about out of options here. Someone needs to get to him. Face to face. Who else is there?"

"But it's impossible. Surely you can see that. I'm just a junior minister."

Steve ignored her. "This whole thing is going to go one of two ways. If we don't find the bomb then everything is going to get called off tomorrow morning."

"But how? You have just told me that nobody is listening."

"They will listen when me and Walter go to the press at eight tomorrow morning."

She looked aghast. "But you will be finished. They would never forgive you. Either of you."

"No. I don't suppose they would. That is why we would both like you to get in to see the man himself and resolve things before it needs to come to our going public. There is another scenario."

"Go on."

"We find the bomb tonight and we disable it. Everything goes ahead as planned. Nothing is said. No announcements made. When Rykov tries to detonate it, we track the signal and find where he's laid up. No more Rykov."

"Would the President risk it even then?"

"I doubt it, but Walter here tells me that he usually travels with a double. Tomorrow morning is going to be pretty wild. A double wrapped up in waterproofs? I don't suppose anybody would tell the difference. If we get Rykov, the President can come out for the afternoon round."

Sally realised that she was expected to give some reaction. Did neither of them realise just how far out her depth she was? It was lunacy. Utter madness. And yet she could not get away from the fact that there probably was virtually no choice.

"Look Sally. It's quarter past ten now. Half an hour to Prestwick. A good hour to Paris. You can be there for soon after midnight. There's no room for dithering about. You need to just go."

"I suppose I do." She got to her feet and looked around the room for any excuse to put the thing off. Finding none, she gave a shrug of resignation. "I dare say I'll see you both tomorrow."

"That you will. Just give it your best shot. You'll be fine."

Sally left and the two men gathered up their coats and followed her out of the door. The McMillan helicopter pilot was waiting for them in the reception area. He didn't look a happy man at all.

"Listen guys, this weather is going all to hell. I really don't care what anyone says, there is no way that I'm about to take this bird out in all this . . ."

Walter casually strolled up to him with an easy-going smile. Any casual onlooker would merely have seen a big American in a raincoat with a wide good-natured face approach a fellow countryman and place an affectionate hand on his upper arm. What they probably wouldn't have noticed was the vice-like grip that sent a shot of pain to the bemused pilot's brain.

By the time he had the chance to cry out, "Jeeeezus Christ!!" he was already out the other side of the revolving door and being marched through the driving rain of the car park. Walter's voice was still as genial as ever. "Friend, me and Steve ain't too much interested in your pussying around about a few drops of rain. What is about to happen is that you ARE going to fly this chopper to Belfast or I am personally going to rip your nuts off. OK?"

The terrified pilot nodded frantically. Walter continued. "Piece of advice for you son. Never, ever, ever piss off a Marine. OK? Good. Then let's go."

Rykov ducked down out of the wind behind a broken-down dry stone wall. He switched on a small torch and held it between his teeth. First he checked the time. Ten-thirty. Next he checked his satellite navigation and cross-referenced the reading with the map. He was close now. Probably just another 200 yards to the edge of the hill. Visibility was zero and the wind was approaching gale force. The discomfort didn't trouble him unduly. He had learnt to deal with all kinds of extremes of weather as a young man and it had never left him. His waterproofs were new and expensive and the rain was being kept at bay. All in all he decided that the weather suited him. The forecast had predicted that the storm wouldn't blow itself out until the middle of the afternoon. It reduced the chances of any enthusiastic hill walkers accidentally treading on him down to near zero.

He bowed his head into the gale and trudged forward for five minutes until he felt the ground start to fall away. Once again he crouched down and this time he checked his compass. He was facing due west. Out there in the howling blackness of the night he knew that the golf course was laid out by the sea a mere three miles away. Perfect.

He turned 180 degrees and started to slowly pick his way along the brow of the hill. He had only travelled a matter of 30 or 40 yards when he almost stumbled into a hollow. He investigated it more closely and found the depression to be about three feet deep and it stretched about ten yards back from the edge of the hill. In the dark it was impossible to tell what had caused it. Probably rabbits.

He positioned himself at the hillside end of the shallow gully and laid out a groundsheet that he pegged down to stop it blowing away on the wind. Next, he pulled off his pack and laid it down. Finally he lay down himself and pulled out a large camouflage piece of sheeting that he pegged out as a cover. Next he used a trowel to throw a covering of soil and clumps of turf on top of the sheet. When he was fairly satisfied that it would hide him from all but the closest observers, he climbed under the sheeting and poured himself a coffee from his flask. Once he had warmed himself up, he pulled the hood as far as it would go over his head and tied it tight. Then he laid his head on his pack and was asleep within minutes. It was something he had learned in the rugged hills of Afghanistan. His mental alarm clock would awake him at six o'clock and he would be fully rested and ready.

Every step of his journey was now complete. All that remained was the final moment.

Steve's life had taken him into numerous hairy situations, but none of them even came close to the sheer unrelenting terror of the helicopter ride over the Irish Sea. The big machine felt like little more than a discarded crisp packet as the fierce gales threw it around. Never in his life had he felt so glad to feel his feet land down on a sodden piece of concrete. The pilot never said a word as he clambered out and raced through the rain to the light of the entrance door to the building. Steve and Walter were close behind.

Inside, a pallid-looking 50-year-old was waiting for them. As they jumped inside he tossed his cigarette to the floor and ground it out with his shoe.

"All right Steve. Long time." He extended a thin, heavily veined hand and Steve shook it and did the introductions.

"Walter, this is Harry Quinlan. RUC Special Branch. Harry, this is Walter King, FBI."

"Good to meet you Harry" said Walter, as genial as ever.

"If you say so." Harry's voice was pure monotone Belfast.

"Don't take any notice of him, Walter" grinned Steve. "Harry was born the most miserable bastard on the planet and you can bet your mortgage that he'll die that way."

"You know who I am then?" Quinlan spat the words out like lumps of rancid gristle.

"Sure. Steve filled me in some. You guys worked together a few years back."

"He probably told you that I don't take kindly to working with strangers."

Walter beamed. "He told me that you don't much like anyone at all. Don't bother me none. You just pretend I'm not even here."

"Have you found him then?" asked Steve.

"Aye. Wasn't hard. He's in O'Brien's Bar. Just like he is every night of his bastard Fenian life. I've put a couple of guys outside to make sure he doesn't bugger off anywhere. You want to go now?"

"Sure. No time like the present."

Quinlan marched them through the empty corridors of the police station and out to his car. Steve stared out through the rain-streaked passenger window as they made their way across the empty late-night streets of Belfast. It was all so familiar. Ordinary sights from any Northern town that set his stomach feeling queasy with gnawing fear. Things had obviously changed since he had left. The fortress-like police stations were dark and unoccupied and there were no checkpoints manned by bored soldiers. Belfast had become a place of peace, but the memories still crawled all over him. For a moment he was so lost in staring out of the window that he didn't notice that Walter was talking to him.

"Give me one last run through on this, Steve. I just want to make sure I'm properly up to speed."

Steve nodded and shook out a couple of cigarettes. He lit them both and passed one over to Quinlan, who hadn't spoken a word since they had got into the car. "There was a big bomb in London back in 1989. It took out the home of a junior Minister in the Northern Ireland office. Luckily nobody was home and the only casualty was an Alsatian dog. The forensic guys marked the bomb as being the work of a player known as Guido. You know, Guido as in Guido Fawkes. Guy Fawkes. Gunpowder plot and all that."

"Yeah, yeah. Remember, remember the fifth of November. We done it in junior high."

"Right. Well Harry's guys got word from a tout. Informer. They marked Guido as Michael Slattery. They'd been keeping the book on Slattery for years, but they could never pin anything to him. He ran a newsagent's shop on the Springfield Road and he never seemed to have a hair out of place. Things were changing by this time in the Province. We had stopped all the heavy-handed stuff with thousands of soldiers rampaging all over the place. Instead most of the work was being done by the Det. 14th Intelligence. We were a bunch of guys who were trained to go under cover and carry out long-term surveillance. Sometimes we would watch a player for months on end. That's how it was with Slattery. There were four of us.

"It seemed for a while as if we were barking up the wrong tree. During the time we were marking him there were three more bombs with the same kind of signature to them. We couldn't see how the hell he could have had anything to do with any of them. One of the lads was walking down his road in the evening when his neighbour's wife came out just as he was level with her door. She was a roughish piece of work with long bleach-blond hair. She was always one of the first to be out on the street banging her dustbin lid to celebrate a soldier getting blown away. Anyway, our lad just got a glimpse of something out of the corner of his eye. The bird needed a shave.

"So, that's when we put it together. Slattery had managed to come up with a way of getting next door without us knowing. It turned out later that there was a hatch in the attic. Then he dressed up as the neighbour's wife and walked out bold as brass. She generally wore this big fake fur coat, and a wig did the rest. From then on we kept watch on her every time she left the house. One night she walked down to the Falls Road and was picked up by a car outside the hospital. From there on in it was all pretty straightforward. We traced the car and got a tracking device onto it. Three weeks later it was bingo time. The car took our boy in his wig straight to a farmhouse outside Newry. The SAS did the rest. Slattery got fifteen years and the bombs stopped. In the end he only served ten and got out as part of the Amnesty in 1999.

"We reckoned that he had been active since the mid-1970s and probably had at least seven dead soldiers and RUC men on his ledger. He was one of the best they had. The thing with Slattery was that his bombs always tended to go off and usually at the right time. Whenever he did something, it was always planned properly and we had no record of any civilian casualties. Basically he was good. Just about the best they ever had."

Walter nodded. "And if anyone could guess where a bomb might be hidden then he is your man?"

"It's a long shot, but what the hell."

"And you think he'll play ball?"

Steve gave a grim smile. "I doubt it, but you never know until you ask. You sure that you're on for this?"

"Hey, in for a penny and all that."

They were making their way up the hill to the Falls Road now. The area all around would have looked desolate at the best of times, but in the miserable orange-lit night it looked at its very worst. Quinlan was tensing visibly as they waited at the traffic lights to cross over onto the Springfield Road. No matter how long the ceasefire held, there was no way he would ever feel right in this part of town.

He pulled up behind a police Landrover. "All right. You lads still sure about this?"

Steve nodded and pulled up the collar of his coat ready for the rain. "Walter?"

"I'm good. Let's go shall we?"

They climbed out into the lashing rain and walked 50 yards down the deserted pavement with their heads bowed. O Brien's was a bar typical of hundreds in the terraced streets of Belfast. It enjoyed a corner location, and on the side walls a mural of Bobby Sands, forever-young face smiled out into the darkness of the night. Steve paused for a second outside the chipped door, then he shrugged and walked in.

Inside, the bar was busy rather than packed. The clientèle was by and large 50-plus, the younger ones having already left for night clubs. All faces turned immediately to the two strangers who stood by the door. The adrenalin surged through Steve and any residual tiredness fell away. Christ, had he done this just ten years ago he would have been trussed up in the boot of a car within minutes. He focused on taking steady breaths as he allowed his eyes to flick around the room. It only took a couple of seconds for him to spot Slattery who was sitting at a table in the corner with three men of similar age. The years had not treated Michael Slattery well. He had always been lean, but now he was scrawny and his cheap clothes hung off him. His thin hair looked lank and greasy and his face had the greyish pallor of the long-term heavy smoker. His dark eyes were boring straight in to Steve and made him wonder whether it was such a good plan after all.

He shook the negative thoughts from his head and marched directly over to the table, aware that every set of eyes in the place were on him. Walter stayed a couple of paces behind and turned to smile happily at the bar in general when Steve reached the table.

"Evening Michael." Steve was relieved that his voice came out fairly steady and true.

"Am I supposed to know you?"

"I don't suppose so. But I know you Michael. I probably know you as well as you're own mother, believe it or not."

A fierce resentment burned in Slattery's eyes. "Then you'll know well enough that I'm not in the habit of talking to Brits, so I suggest you both piss off before things get unhealthy for you."

Walter half-turned and gave Slattery a beaming grin. "Hey buddy, don't go mistaking me for no tight-assed Brit now. I'm 100 percent pure bred US of A."

He turned back to the bar and Slattery shook his head irritably. "I don't give a flying shite where you're from. Either of you. It's finished, in case you hadn't noticed. Done with. All of it."

Steve smiled. "Why don't you lads take a walk. I need to have a little chat with Michael here in private."

Slattery's companions looked to him and eventually he gave them a nod and they got up and went to stand at the bar. Steve took a vacant seat and carefully lit a cigarette, having offered one to Slattery who had shaken his head and lit one of his own.

"So if you're not about to piss off, I suggest you start talking. There's back-up outside I suppose?"

"What? Do I look like I'm nuts? Course there is. And to be honest I don't see anyone in here who would cause Walter here much of a problem. So why not try and be civilised and hear me out."

Slattery leaned back in his chair and produced a mocking little smile that revealed truly awful teeth. "Go on then Brit. I'm all ears."

"Well. There's not a lot of point trying to put sugar in this. I was in the Det. Back in '89. I was there the day they took you down, Michael. Me and three others."

The colour drained form Slattery's face and the condescending expression was replaced by a look of sheer hatred. Steve ploughed on.

"That's why I'm here. You were always the best they had. You always had a brain in your head. You were a planner."

Slattery was so angry that he could hardly speak. "You bastard."

Steve shrugged. "Maybe. So what were you then, Michael? You did your job. I did mine. You were never a nutter and neither was I. We were on different sides. That's all. Come on, lighten up. You lads were forever claiming POW status. You said it was war, well fair enough. War means that you lose sometimes. I won. You lost. It was never personal."

Steve could see that his brutal honesty was starting to work. It was as he had hoped. "Why are you here Brit?"

"I need your services Michael."

This drew a short barking laugh. "What? You want me to blow someone away? In yer bloody dreams."

Steve smiled. "Not quite. I need to find a bomb before tomorrow morning and you are the best guy I can think of to help me do it."

Slattery shook his head but Steve had already noticed the flicker of interest in the dark eyes. He didn't give the Irishman the chance to speak.

"I've been reading your file Michael. I'm impressed, to be honest. You're a bigwig in the Ex-Prisoners Association now. Very commendable."

"Piss off."

"I'm serious. Just because I was in the Det doesn't mean I approved of Long Kesh. I suppose an organisation like that is always hungry for cash. In fact I heard that you want to buy up one of the H-Blocks and turn it into a museum. Quite right too. None of the guys like you and me who fought our nasty little war want to be forgotten. It's the bastard politicians who want to pretend none of us exist any more. My side, your side, all of them. They used us Michael. You. Me. All of us. You want to open a museum to remind people of what we did, then you get my vote."

Steve surprised himself with his little speech. He hadn't planned it. He hadn't even realised that it was the way he felt. It was the very fact of being back on the streets where he had lost his soul that had let out the poison. He could see a change in Slattery's eyes. There was recognition there. For a moment they saw each other as if looking in a mirror. The nightmares and the gnawing guilt were what they had in common. The old bomb-maker took a careful sip from his pint and folded his arms.

"Money you say. For the museum. OK. I'm listening."

Steve relaxed slightly. "Do you like golf, Michael?"

"Do I look like I like golf? You don't find many country clubs round here."

Steve smiled. "No. I don't suppose you do. You watch the tele though."

"Aye. I watch the tele."

Steve leaned close over the table to ensure that he wouldn't be overheard. "You watched the tele about the match over at Turnberry?"

Slattery followed his lead and leaned closer himself. "I have. Everybody has. Impossible to miss it."

"OK. I'll give it to you in a nutshell. Al Quaida have hired an assassin. He's a guy like you. A bomber. He started out with the Soviet Special Forces in Afghanistan in the early 1980s. Then he changed sides and worked for the CIA and the Muhajadeen. Since then he has been freelance, working for the Moslems. We know of at least seven hits. He watches his targets. Susses out their routine. Plants his bomb, and detonates it from far away. Same method every time."

Slattery's eyes were gleaming like 100-watt light bulbs now. "Jeez."

"Right now he is laid up somewhere in the hills above Turnberry. We have found his car. He stayed there at the end of February. That was his recon. We know that there was a leak that tipped off Al Quaida that the President would be watching the golf on the Sunday morning. Tomorrow morning. We reckon that he set the bomb back at the beginning of March. Now he's waiting to blow the thing."

"And just what the hell do you expect me to do?"

"We go back to your house and watch some golf videos. I have a few books as well. We think the bomb is somewhere on the course. You take a look. Figure out if it were you, where you would put the thing. You find the bomb for us and the Association gets a massive donation. It's a one-time deal and there will be no publicity."

"Who's going to pay the cheque?"

"The McMillan Corporation. If we don't find the bomb then the whole thing gets cancelled. This means a lot to the old man. He'll pay handsomely if you help him out."

Slattery took a long, hard draw on his cigarette as his brain went into overdrive. Where were the downsides? They weren't about to lift him. No way. Not having been so up front and public about their entrance into the bar. They wanted to go to his house, not a police station. And there was something about the Brit that he felt he could trust. The man hadn't tried to hide his past, and that must have taken some bottle. Like many other of the men who had spent many years rotting away in the notorious H-Blocks of the Maze Prison, Michael Slattery was determined to do all he could to ensure that the government in London didn't get its way and bulldoze the place. For anything in his miserable life to make sense, the things he did and the price he paid needed to be remembered. Like everyone else who watched a tele, he was more than aware of the money that the McMillan men were worth. Maybe it was worth a go.

He nodded and started to get to his feet. "Let's go then."

The speed with which the decision was made surprised Steve, and he was slow to get up himself. Michael made his way to the bar and informed his friends that there was no problem and then he made for the door. His house was close by, a mere five-minute walk. The rain if anything was even harder and a gusting wind howled down the terraces. He unlocked his front door and stood back to let his guests inside.

"There's nobody else in. The wife walked out soon after I was released. She would have done it when I was inside, but the boys would have sorted her out. Peace isn't all it's cracked up to be."

"Have you still got the shop? The newsagent's."

Slattery nodded. "Aye. I was luckier that most. At least I had a job to come out to. Most of them are still on the dole. Here. Have a seat. Take your coats off. I'll make a brew."

He disappeared into the kitchen and Walter looked about the neat and tidy living room with interest. It was just like a million other rooms in a million other towns. Steve read his thoughts. "You lot are a mile behind us in this war on terror of yours. This is how it is. Ordinary people from ordinary places. You can never spot them. Especially the ones who are best at it."

"Like Slattery here."

"Exactly like Slattery here."

Their host returned with mugs of coffee and threw a shovel of coal onto the embers of the fire. "All right. Picture books you say. Let's have a look then."

For the next two hours he barely spoke. First, he leafed carefully through the three books that they had brought from the gift shop at the hotel. Then he sat back and smoked cigarette after cigarette as he watched three videos of past championships. When the final video had finished he got to his feet.

"We going then?"

"Where?" asked Steve, surprised at the sudden burst of activity.

"Turnberry of course. How did you get here? Chopper?"

"Yes but . . ."

"So let's go then."

"Do you think you know where it is?"

Slattery grinned. "Oh aye. I know exactly where it is."

"Well tell us then."

"Not a bloody chance. Think I'm daft or something? No. This is how this is going to play. I will tell Roland McMillan once I have his agreement about the money. Not before. I suggest you make a call and get the bomb squad up there. As soon as the thing is found I get paid. Fair enough?"

This wasn't at all what Steve had expected. He was tongue-tied and it was Walter who spoke. "Sure buddy. Looks like a square deal to me. Let's roll guys. That clock's a ticking."

Steve glanced up at the wall and confirmed that the clock was indeed ticking. It was five past two.

To his own amazement, Deek had managed to behave sensibly. The first evening had set the tone for the whole event and once again the majority of the guests had arrived at the magnificent dining room revved up for a big night. George Albright was certainly no exception. Deek had never seen a man in such a hurry to make up for lost time.

Throughout the night Deek had gone steadily. He had taken on his fair share of drink, but not a great deal more than was required for him to stay level and even. Just after midnight he had claimed extreme knackeredness and returned to his room. In fact he had felt completely wide-awake and he took a trip outside to stand on the grass at the front of the hotel and feel the strength of the wind and the rain.

By now the weather was building up fast and in the distance he could hear the big waves smashing down onto the sand. After only a few minutes he was soaked to the skin, but it didn't bother him at all. Frank and Roger had got it absolutely right. This was his weather.

As the wind howled around the chimneys on the roof he knew that he had a chance. A real chance.

Sally's nerves had started the minute she got into her car and set off for Prestwick. Never in her life had she done anything quite so harebrained. It was complete madness. A big part of her willed on the strong wind that buffeted the car as she worked her way around the Ayr bypass. Maybe the airport would be closed down. Surely it would. How bad did things have to get for it to be impossible to get a plane in the air?

It took her a while to find the hangar where the McMillan jet was waiting. The pilot was ready and expecting her. How much did he know? If he did know the facts behind her extraordinary night flight he certainly wasn't letting on. She had been with Steve when he had gone to see Jonathan and had been amazed at the young man's cool. Steve had been sparing with the facts and had simply asked that Johnny should trust his judgement and that he hoped he would be able to give him a proper picture some time through the night.

The pilot was smart as paint in his uniform and greeted Sally with a warm smile.

"Good evening Miss Hunter. If you are all ready we'll get off."

"Surely we can't fly in this." She knew her concerns offered no more than a forlorn hope.

"Oh we'll be fine Miss. This old bird is good to go in far worse than this. It will be a bit bouncy for a minute or two, then you won't even know you're in the air."

As the jet roared up through the raging sky she decided that it was more than just a little bouncy, but it soon stopped, as the pilot had promised. An attendant brought her coffee and she tried to work out what on earth she was going to say once she reached the Embassy in Paris. It only seemed to have been a matter of minutes when the attendant collected her cup and asked her to buckle-up ready for their descent.

The pull of the McMillans was in evidence when they landed. An obliging immigration officer waved her through the formalities and a chauffeur was waiting for her outside the hangar. As the car sped through the emptying streets of the French capital her brain grappled with the task that was getting closer all the time. By the time they arrived at the front gate she hadn't come up with much of a plan at all.

A tall black Marine with a face like granite leant close in to the back window and asked her business.

"I am a Minister of State in the Scottish Parliament and I need to see the President on a matter of extreme urgency."

The soldier never batted an eyelid. It was as if she had asked directions to the nearest newsagent's.

"You have some ID, Ma'am?"

She passed him her parliamentary security pass and he disappeared inside the booth. Five minutes later he re-emerged and instructed her driver where to park, returned her card, and hoped she would have a nice evening. A young man in a dark suit was waiting for them as they parked up and he suggested that she follow him inside. He politely opened a door to a waiting room and said that someone would be with her shortly. Her watch told her it was just past midnight. Quite extraordinary. She picked up a copy of *Time* and attempted to focus on it, but soon gave up when she realised that her hands were shaking. Instead she got up and started to pace as she tried to decide on an approach that would stand any chance at all of success.

Ten minutes later the door opened and an older man came in.

"Good evening Miss Hunter. My name is Frederick Simpson and I'm a member of the White House staff. Maybe I could organise some coffee, perhaps a biscuit?"

He was silver-haired and as smooth as a new bathtub. "No thank you. I'm fine."

This brought on a practised smile. "OK. Good. Why don't we sit?"

He sat and carefully crossed his legs in such a way that the creases of his expensive trousers were all pointing in the right direction. She perched on the edge of one of the chairs and prepared to do battle.

He kept his well-practised diplomatic smile fixed firmly on his face. "OK Miss Hunter. Let's have a look at what we have here. I gather from our people at the front gate that you wish to see the President on a matter of some urgency. Correct?"

"Yes."

He met her answer with a slightly troubled frown. "I am sure that you are aware that there are certain protocols that . . ."

She cut him short. "Frederick. It's late. I'm tired. You're probably tired too. I think it would be a really good idea if we stopped pissing around, don't you?"

The smile never moved. She was impressed. All he said was "I see."

She had taken her jump into the cold water and all there was left to do now was to try and swim. "I know that you are being ever so polite and, believe me, I appreciate it. I really do. Maybe it is better if I say all the hard things. I am just a junior minister from the Scottish Parliament and that of course isn't really a proper Parliament at all. In fact, if we want to go into the protocols you were alluding to, we will find that the Scottish Parliament has no authority to follow its own foreign policy. All of which means that you probably think that I am some kind of a mad woman and your job is to get me out of this building with as little fuss as possible. Am I close to the mark?"

"Pretty close, Ma'am."

"And basically there isn't a snowball's chance in hell of my seeing the President."

He nodded, his smile still securely in place. "I very much doubt whether that outcome is an achievable goal, Ma'am."

Sally stood. She didn't really know why, but she felt worse sitting down. She couldn't decide what to do with her hands and so habit kicked in and she placed them on her hips and assumed the pose she had always used as a headmistress for lecturing the school in Assembly.

"Well, it is good that we are being honest with each other. Now Frederick. I'd better give you some facts to chew on. It had been my job as Minister for Sport to oversee the whole event at Turnberry tomorrow. Part of this role has been to oversee the work of the security people. We have been collecting evidence over the last few days which has now become more or less conclusive. There is no way of dressing this up in nice clothes. We are now over 95 percent certain that there has been a very large bomb planted on the golf course by a highly capable assassin working for Al Quaida. We are also more or less certain that the same assassin is already in place somewhere close to the course."

Now the smile fell to the floor. "Holy Christ."

"There is a great deal more, but I very much doubt that you are the person to talk to about it. Do you agree?"

"Yes Ma'am. I would tend to agree. You will give me five minutes?"

"I will."

He left the room with a great deal less poise than he had shown when he had come in. Five minutes later Sally was taken to an office on the first floor where she repeated her story to two senior officers from the presidential security team. These were hard-faced men who had little need for smooth diplomatic smiles. When she had finished, the older of the two made great play of tapping his pen on the notes he had made.

"We thank you for this information Ma'am. I can assure you that I will be working these things through with the team leaders in place over in Scotland as a matter of extreme urgency . . ."

"Actually. I'm afraid that isn't good enough. I have made it very clear that I wish to make this information available to the President himself."

The face got a few degrees harder. "I'm sure you realise that is not a viable option, Ma'am."

The dripping condescension in his voice switched on her temper. "I don't believe that you gentlemen quite understand the situation here. There is obviously some kind of history to this assassin which is embarrassing to some rather senior people in America. Well, quite frankly I couldn't care less. Unless I talk to the President in person I will be going to the press with every bit of information I have. And don't go thinking about keeping me here, because there are people over in Scotland who will do exactly the same if they don't hear from me very soon. I know and you know that as soon as the press gets hold of this there is no way that the President will be going within 100 miles of Turnberry and a whole lot of people are going to be very embarrassed indeed. Now. Is that clear enough for you both?"

The more senior man looked as if he would gladly pull out all of her fingernails one by one. It clearly cost him a great deal to retain his cool.

"Give me a few minutes, please."

He left the room and his younger colleague made no move to speak. Sally felt completely charged and it was all that she could do to sit still and hang onto a mask of calm. When the man returned, he stood in the doorway and said "This way please."

More corridors. She considered asking what was next but decided there was little point. She was ushered into a larger, more opulent office where a sour-faced man in his early 60s was sitting in his shirtsleeves behind an ornate desk. He didn't get to his feet when she entered. Instead he waved a hand towards a chair and said, "Take a seat."

As she sat he tossed his glasses down onto the pile of papers in front of him and rubbed at his watery eyes. "I'm Weinberg. Larry Weinberg. White House Chief of Staff. Just what the hell is going on here Miss Hunter?"

His attitude rekindled the flames of her temper. However, she managed to keep her voice reasonably steady. "I am quite sure that you have been properly briefed, Mr Weinberg. However I will repeat myself. I would like to see the President."

This provoked a dismissive laugh. "You ain't about to see the President, lady. You ain't about to get within a country mile of him."

"Oh really?"

"Yeah. Really. Lady, you've just dug yourself about neck deep in a pile of shit. You're not talking to a bunch of nobodies in some shitty Scottish town here. This is the United States of America. You might just have noticed that we don't respond well to threats, lady. Now if you think for a minute that you can come in here and . . ."

"I don't think, Mr Weinberg. I know. I either see the President or I will be leaving." She started to get to her feet.

"Sit the hell down! Have you any idea whatsoever what I am about to do to your pathetic little career? Have you any concept of who you are threatening here?"

Now the dam burst and she boiled right over. "Oh indeed I have, Mr Weinberg. More than you know. I know that you are the kind of nasty little reptile who sends someone who in my book is little better than a prostitute to go digging around for dirt. That's who."

She could tell that the words had hit home by the look of shock in his eyes. His instincts kicked in and he immediately went onto the attack and rose to his feet pointing a bony finger at her.

"I have no idea what the hell you are talking about lady!"

"Oh have you not? Well let me try a name out on you. Samantha Latimer. Maybe you know what I'm talking about now."

The eyes showed fear now. "Like hell I do." He was becoming strident.

She could see she was getting on top and lectured him in a voice that had once terrorised a generation of Dundee youngsters. "Oh yes you do Mr Weinberg. I know all about it because the man who called you told me all about it. I couldn't believe that a man in your position could ever stoop to such pathetic depths . . ."

"I think it's time for you to leave, Miss Hunter. I'm going to call security now . . ."

"I wouldn't do that Larry."

Neither of them had noticed the President as he had come in from the adjoining office. He had removed his bow tie and was standing in his shirt with his arms folded. Weinberg's face took a fast double-take as his brain tried to work out how much his boss had heard.

"Sorry about this, sir. We have a situation here. I'm dealing with it." He grabbed at the phone.

"No Larry. No call. You should introduce me."

"Sir. This lady is irrational. She has barged in here and she's making all kind of threats . . ."

"Fine. I'll introduce myself." He approached with a hand extended and the smile that was the most photographed on earth. "I gather you know me?"

"Yes sir. I do. I'm Sally Hunter. I'm the . . . well . . . I'm the Minister of Sport for Scotland."

"Nice to meet you Sally. Now. I'm familiar with the name Samantha Latimer even if Larry here claims he isn't. She used to work on my campaign team. Good girl. But I can't understand for the life of me what business she could have in Scotland. Maybe you could sit down and tell me."

"But sir . . ."

"Larry. Just shut up will you?"

Weinberg slumped back into his chair and rooted for his medication. The President leaned on the edge of the desk opposite Sally. She braced herself and spoke. "Miss Latimer masqueraded as a young trainee reporter called Tiffany MacLean. She duped Archie Banks and taped him when he told her all about his drinking problem. A colleague of mine in the security services took her picture and identified her. He discovered her real name and that she often did work for Mr Weinberg here. My colleague called Mr Weinberg and let him know that he would go public if there were any more similar stunts. Personally I found the whole thing despicable."

The President nodded slowly. "I would tend to agree, Sally. Now. I could hear from next door that you came here to see me. Well. Here I am."

She forced herself to meet his gaze. "Mr President, we have discovered that there is to be a major assassination attempt tomorrow. You are the target. Until today, all the evidence was deemed to be flimsy and circumstantial. Now we have proof that is more or less conclusive. We believe that there is a bomb already in place on the Turnberry golf course and that the assassin is laid up somewhere in the hills ready to detonate it. We were concerned that for political reasons there was a chance that this evidence might not be taken seriously. Sir, it is my job to oversee the event at Turnberry. I simply cannot allow tomorrow's event to go ahead under these circumstances. My final option is the press. However, I am aware that such a course of action would cause immense problems for our two countries. Therefore I found no alternative other than to come and see you in person."

The President stood up and took a seat next to her.

"Looks like I should be pretty glad that you did, Sally. I thank you and I apologise for the way you have been treated. Maybe you could fill me in."

Sally methodically ran through the details of Steve and Walter's enquiries. The President stared down at his hands which were folded in his lap, and concentrated. He nodded on occasion to make sure she knew that she still had his total attention. She took ten minutes and when she had finished there was a tight silence in the room. For what seemed to be an endless period of time he continued to stare down until finally coming to a decision.

"I can see a lot of heads are going to have to roll over this one Larry. It is only right and proper that yours be the first. I would like you to leave now. You can clear your desk in the morning and we will sort out the details then."

"But for Christ's sake sir . . ."

"No Larry. I don't want to hear it. Just get the hell out before we both say things we will regret."

Larry sat dumbfounded at the unbelievable speed of events. It simply wasn't possible. A career of nearly 40 years just couldn't end like this. He struggled for something to say. Anything. Anything that might turn everything around. But for almost the first time in his life he knew that there was nothing to say. He got to his feet and pulled his jacket from the back of the chair and left the room without a word.

The President watched his longest serving colleague close the door and shook his head sadly.

"I can only apologise, Miss Hunter. In this world of ours . . . well. Maybe you know it yourself. Sometimes people turn bad. Larry was a good guy once. A real good guy. And a good friend too. Now . . . he's got an ulcer and the polls are all shot to hell . . ."

His voice trailed off and for a moment she saw a frightening tiredness in his eyes. He made an effort and sat forward. "OK. I gather that you have something in mind."

"Yes sir. I have."

"Then the floor is yours, Miss Hunter."

"There seem to be two options. If we are unable to locate the bomb, there is no possibility that the event can go ahead."

"Of course. I am astounded how any of my people could ever have thought otherwise. We will look into all of this. I can give you my personal assurance of that."

She nodded. She had no doubt that the most powerful man on the planet was far from amused that his safety had been compromised to protect a few careers.

"However, there is a chance that we may be able to locate the bomb tonight."

He shrugged. "That sounds great, but just how on earth can you make that happen?"

Sally looked uneasy. This was the part that she had been dreading. "I'm afraid that I don't know. All Steve Kenton was willing to tell me was that it was a long shot and he would have an answer before dawn."

"Typical spook then." He smiled at her and she felt a huge sense of relief that he had taken it so well. "Miss Hunter, I can assure you that you are not the only politician in the world to have the wool pulled over their eyes by the cloak-and-dagger boys. It happens to me every single day. Has Mr Kenton got a mobile phone?"

"Yes."

"Good. Maybe you could get him on the line for me. Perhaps he might be willing to fill me in some."

"Yes. Yes of course."

She dialled the number from the phone on Weinberg's desk and Steve answered on the third ring.

"Kenton."

"Steve, it's Sally."

"Oh hi. How are things going?"

"Fine thank you. In fact I'm with the President right now. He would like a word. Is that OK?"

After a pause he said. "Is this for real, Sally?"

"Absolutely."

"Holy Christ."

"Indeed. Now, will you speak?"

"Yes. Of course. Just let me step outside will you."

She held out the receiver and the President took it.

"You there Steve?"

"Yes sir. I'm here."

"Helluva job you guys have done. Looks like I owe you pretty big-time. This isn't something I'm about to forget in a hurry. I gather you've got one of our FBI boys in tow."

"I have sir."

"Great. I'll speak to him in a minute. Now, Miss Hunter tells me you have some kind of a plan to find this bomb. She tells me that you're keeping your cards close to your chest. Would you be willing to let me in on it? After all, from where I'm sitting it would seem to be my ass that's on the line here."

"Urmm. Yes. Well I suppose it is. The thing is . . . well I'm afraid this is all a bit unorthodox you see . . . and . . ."

"Steve, the way I see it you've probably just saved my hide. So I really don't think I'm about to get too uptight about what and what isn't regulation procedure. There's just the two of us talking here. Tell me as it is. Will you do that?"

"Yes. Of course. Sorry. I used to work in Ireland. Northern Ireland. Undercover stuff. There was one guy we caught back in '89. He was an IRA bomber. Just about the best they ever had. Well he got out of prison as part of the peace process. I thought . . . well . . . I suppose I just thought he might just be the best person to ask where our man might have placed his bomb . . ."

"Set a thief to catch a thief, am I right?"

"Pretty well."

"And is the guy playing ball?"

"Yes. It would appear so."

The President was smiling now. He decided that he liked just about everything about this Kenton guy. He continued. "Is he helping out of a sense of patriotic duty then?"

"Not really."

"So what buttons did you push, Steve?"

Steve cleared his throat and went on rather reluctantly. "He is heavily involved in the Ex-prisoners Association. The ones who did time in the Maze. The H-Blocks. They want one of the blocks retained as a museum to remember the Troubles. I guaranteed him a healthy donation if he locates the bomb."

The President grinned. "Did you get the green light for this from your people Steve?"

"Actually, no. Not really. Not at all."

"I didn't think that would be London's style. So, is the money coming out of your own pocket then?"

Steve was clearly wishing for a hole to open up and swallow him up.

"No. Bit steep for me, sir. I am hoping that I will be able to persuade Roland McMillan to come up with something. I know how much this event means to him."

"So do I Steve. So do I. Don't go bothering the old man. Leave him in peace. Tell your man a million bucks. I'll guarantee that personally. Thankfully I do have some room for manoeuvre. That OK with you Steve?"

Steve was knocked over. "Yes. Of course. Absolutely."

"He finds the bomb and I pay. No bomb, no fee. I kinda like that. Seems pretty All American, don't you think?"

"Yes. Completely. I'm sure it will be quite an incentive. You won't want it known where the money is from I presume?"

"You presume correct. I'm going to leave you to it now Steve. I hope we get to meet up tomorrow. Now, could you put me onto my man please."

"Of course. Thank you sir."

Sally looked on and tried to appear calm and collected as the President gave his thanks to Walter. When he had finished he took up a place in Weinberg's chair.

"OK. I understand now. Here's how things will go, Miss Hunter. If your boys don't find the bomb, Airforce One will be redirected due to vital business. We will leave it to you as to how you handle cancelling the event. If they find the bomb, we proceed as planned."

"You have your double with you then?"

"No. He is still Stateside. His Pa is sick and he needed to be with him. No. If the bomb is disabled, then I will follow the match as planned."

"But how can we be sure that there is only the one bomb? Surely there is still some risk?"

"There is risk every time I wake up in the morning, Miss Hunter. There are a lot of people out there who would dearly like to see me dead, and that is something I have to accept. I'm certainly not about to send men into harm's way in this war on terror without showing a bit of courage myself. This guy has never used two bombs before and I very much doubt if he will now. I consider attending the match to be an acceptable risk and I will give you a witnessed statement confirming that to be the case before you leave here. Will you allow that, Miss Hunter?"

Sally felt her skin reddening into a blush. "Of course."

"Good. Now I think we have earned ourselves a drink. Can we accommodate you here or are you returning tonight?"

"I need to get back I think. A drink would be more than welcome."

They talked politics for a further half-hour over brandy before the President retired to bed and Sally rode back to the airport. She arrived back at Turnberry at 3.30 a.m., five minutes before the wind-blasted helicopter from Belfast splashed down onto the landing pad.

The helicopter pilot had called from Belfast to confirm with Jonathan that he did indeed wish the company's helicopter to make the return journey through the storm. Jonathan had done so reluctantly and decided that enough was enough. He liked Steve Kenton and the easygoing giant from the FBI, but things were going too far. The pilot had said about half-past three, and from quarter-past Jonathan waited by the old glass doors at the front of the hotel and peered into the night.

It was a with a feeling of considerable relief that he heard the booming of the rotors over the sound of the storm and then saw the landing lights loom out of the darkness. He pulled his waterproof coat tight around him and stepped out into the rain. Steve approached first closely followed by Walter and a weasely-like bald man that he didn't know.

"We need to talk, Steve. I mean right now."

Steve had been expecting this and nodded. Once inside, he spoke first to Walter. "Take Michael up to the room can you Walter. I'll be up in five."

"No problem."

Jonathan and Steve stepped into the deserted Ailsa Bar and Steve lit up hungrily. "Never, ever again. Christ, that was scary."

Jonathan wasn't playing ball. He was way past any idle chitchat. "I need to know what's happening. Taking the helicopter out on a night like this was ridiculous. I should never have given my consent."

Steve took another hard pull and grimaced as the smoke burnt his throat. "You best sit down Johnny. You're not going to like this, I'm afraid. Time is incredibly short, so this needs to be very quick. There's no need to question anything. Just listen and accept. OK?"

Jonathan had a really bad feeling now. He nodded and took a seat opposite Steve.

"OK. I'm afraid that your man Abe passed on the information that the President would be coming here last February. The information found its way to a senior Al Quaida commander and he commissioned an assassination attempt. The man they have sent is called Anatoly Rykov. He is ex-Soviet Special Forces and he has been killing hard targets for over twenty years. We are almost certain that Rykov came to Scotland at the end of February and stayed here at the hotel. We have clear evidence that he stayed in a rented cottage about an hour's drive from here. We know for absolute certain that he left that cottage this morning and drove a hire car to a disused quarry four miles from here, probably early in the evening. We believe that he planted a bomb during his first visit. We believe that the bomb is out there on the course somewhere and we are pretty certain that Rykov is holed up in the hills looking down on us right now."

Jonathan was reeling. "You say Abe. But how? Why? It isn't possible. I've known him all my life."

"Look Johnny. Like I said. We have no time here. I will tell you everything later. That I promise."

"But why the helicopter to Ireland? And the jet to Paris? I don't understand."

Steve forced himself to slow down for a minute. "OK. The jet. Basically there is some kind of connection between Rykov and the CIA. It goes back years, but it is very embarrassing. It could end careers. That meant that Walter and I were finding it tough to get people to take us seriously. Sally Hunter went over to tell the President face-to-face."

"Good God. Surely she'll never get in there."

Steve grinned. "She got in all right. I have talked to the President myself. He is fully up to speed. Now. The helicopter. You are aware that I worked in Ireland?"

"Yes."

"The guy off the chopper is ex-IRA. I was part of the operation that took him down in '89. He was a bomber. A bloody good one too. I asked him to come over and see if he can work out where Rykov would have chosen. It's a hell of a long shot, but unless we get the bomb, I'm afraid the whole thing gets cancelled. None of us want that."

"And does he think that he can do anything?"

"He seems almost certain."

"So where is it?"

Steve rubbed at the stubble on his chin. "Well this is the thing. He is involved with an ex-prisoners charity. I told him that if he found the bomb, the McMillan Corporation would reward him handsomely. I'm sorry if I was taking that bit for granted. I had to work fast."

"No. That's fine. Of course it is. How much do you need?"

Steve laughed. "As it turns out, nothing. The President has stumped up a million bucks. However, he doesn't want that to be public. I need you to come along and persuade Michael that the McMillans will pay over a million dollars if he finds the device. And I need you to do it yesterday."

Jonathan jumped up straight away. "Let's go then."

"One last thing. This is the bottom line. If we find the bomb, the President is coming and everything goes as planned. If we don't, then that's it I'm afraid."

"What about the assassin?"

Steve thought for a moment. This was something that really was not up for discussion, but nothing would have been possible without the use of the plane and the helicopter. Johnny had trusted him and it seemed only fair to reciprocate.

"I don't know for sure. I will recommend we play it this way. We disable the bomb and Rykov will not know. He usually uses a mobile phone to trigger the detonation. I dare say things will be no different this time. That is why he lays-up and watches the target right onto the device. We can track where the call comes from. The Russians did it first a few years back in Chechnya. One of the warlords made a call, they zeroed in on the co-ordinates and sent a missile straight down his throat before he had finished his conversation. We have a team from the SAS up here. They will be ready in a chopper in the morning. As soon as we get the position, they fly up there and take care of him."

"You mean arrest him?"

Steve shook his head. "Anatoly Rykov won't be appearing in any court, Johnny. This is one of those things that will be done out of the public gaze. Nobody will ever be allowed to know just how close he got."

The younger man's face became very pale. "So he'll be executed."

Steve just nodded.

They made their way through the empty corridors of the grand old hotel as the sound of the gale growled away outside. Michael Slattery was sitting on the edge of one of the beds watching *BBC News 24* as he sipped at a coffee, while Walter was standing at the window watching the rivulets of rain streaming down the glass.

Steve ushered Jonathan inside and wasted no time with elaborate introductions. "OK Michael. This is Jonathan McMillan. I have brought him up to speed with how things are. He has agreed to make you an offer. Johnny."

Jonathan found it hard to get his head around the fact that this rather anonymous little man could possibly ever have been one of the IRA's most feared operators. Ridiculously enough, as he had made his way to the room, he had an image of Brad Pitt in his mind from some movie in the 1990s when he had played the part of a Provo. About the only thing that Michael Slattery had in common with Brad Pitt was that they both had two arms and two legs. He snapped himself clear of it and shook the Irishman's hand.

"The deal is straightforward, Mr Slattery. Find the bomb and I'll see that your Fund receives a donation of one million dollars."

Slattery took a suspicious sip at his coffee. "Sounds good, Mr McMillan. How do I know this isn't just words?"

"One, I'll write you a cheque. Two, I will knock up an agreement letter. Who would you trust as a witness? I expect Miss Hunter would be able to do that. Would she be acceptable?"

"And who the hell is she when she's at home?"

Steve chipped in. "Minister of Sport for Scotland."

This amused Michael no end. "Minister for Sport. Jesus guys, this is a wild old show you've got going here."

Jonathan was feeling angry. "Look, Michael. You're suspicious of people. Fair enough. I can understand that. But when my family make an agreement we stick to it. That's the way we do business. If I say I'll give you a cheque for a million bucks if you find the bomb, then that is exactly what will happen."

Slattery gave him a long, hard stare. "OK. I'll risk that. Write the cheque out. No need to bugger about with the rest. This thing is never exactly going to see the inside of a courtroom."

Johnny wrote the cheque and passed it over. "I don't particularly want this making public. That's down to you. You trust us and we trust you. Either side can screw with each other, so let's show a bit of honour shall we?"

Slattery nodded. The young lad made sense. His company wouldn't look all that great bunging a big donation to a gang of reformed terrorists. "Fair enough."

Steve tossed over a cigarette and lit one himself. "Good. So where the hell is it Michael?"

Slattery grinned and pulled out a couple of the glossy books of photos. "If I'm right, and I think I am, you're all going to kick yourselves. You see, you need to think politicians. That's what I would do. Sure, it is the bomber who places the device. But the politician is the target. It is the way they act that helps the bomber to choose his spot. You with me?"

Steve nodded impatiently. "Yeah, yeah. Just get on with it."

Slattery smirked. He was going to take his time. "So I ask myself, why is the big man here? What is the President of America doing taking a walk on the Scottish coast? Does he love his golf that much? Course he doesn't. He wants to look good and win votes, just like every politician in the world. So what does looking good mean? Well, it means being seen in casual clothes and enjoying a sporting event. That makes him seem accessible and human. But how will the voters see him? Well, some will watch all four hours of the round. What about the rest? The rest watch a clip on the news and look at the pictures in the papers. That's what you need to think about, lads. The pictures. An image in a newspaper. A five-second clip on the tele. That's what his image-makers are paid for. They need to make sure he is always looking good in the right shots. Remember the overall plan. A down-to-earth guy enjoying his sport in the great outdoors. So where is the best picture going to be tomorrow morning? Where is the image for the papers on Monday morning? Once you look at it that way, it is really quite easy. Here. Look."

He opened one of the books and laid it out on the bed. The photo was spread over two large pages. It was the trademark image of Turnberry. The photographer had chosen the sunset to capture his image of the world-famous ninth tee. The tide was in and the green of the grass was darkened in the evening light. In the background the waters of the sea were tinted all shades of orange by a fat red sun that sat next to Ailsa Craig on the edge of the world. The small patch of beautifully mown grass was a symbol of man's tenuous grasp on a planet that was all wilderness. As soon as Steve looked down, his instincts told him that Michael was right. Pictures of the ninth tee were to be seen everywhere around the hotel. Sometimes it was bathed in a dawn light, sometimes at dusk. Sometimes it was lonely and deserted, sometimes it was occupied by legendary golfers. Sometimes the view was out to the sea and Ailsa Craig, otherwise it showed the daunting shot over the rocks and the sand. Straight away he knew that Michael was absolutely right. This was where the President would want to stand. Right at the back of the tee behind the players as they took on the daunting drive. The cameramen would zoom in on the face of the President framed by a backdrop of waves and sky.

Michael flicked through to another image. This time the photo was from behind and showed the eighth green to one side. "OK. Now the technical bit. Look at this outcrop of rocks. It looks like it's about twenty or thirty yards from the tee itself. Big heavy lump of rock. If it were me, I would dig into the sand here. Look. Pack the explosives in tight against the rock. Once the thing goes off, the rock forces the blast out this way. See. Straight out over the tee. Look at the shape of the rock. It is slightly concaved. It will throw the force of the blast. Imagine throwing a tennis ball hard at a wall. If the wall shapes inwards, it is almost to bounce the ball straight back at you. Understand?"

They did. It suddenly seemed so blindingly obvious. Steve saw no point in hanging about gazing at the pretty pictures. He had chosen the long shot and it seemed as if there was a decent chance that it might have come off. He checked his watch. Twenty-to-four. Still time. Not much, but enough.

"It looks good to me, Michael. This is how we'll play it. I have some people here. I'll get hold of them and we'll head out there and see if you're right. I'll organise you some waterproofs."

Slattery nodded. "Who's here?"

"I have a four-man SAS team and a bomb disposal guy."

"Sass men is it? You think your man is close then?"

Steve saw no point in pretending otherwise. "He's in the hills. Probably just a couple of miles from here."

"How does he usually detonate? Mobile phone?"

"Yes."

Slattery grimaced. "I get it now. You disable the bomb and track the signal. Then the Sass men go an do their stuff."

"Something like that. You got a problem with that Michael?"

For a moment the Irishman's eyes burned. Like all senior members of the IRA he had lost good friends to the guns of the SAS hit squads. "I don't hold with mercenaries, Mr Kenton. I have nothing in common with this man. I did what I did for freedom. He's just in it for the cash. So, no. If your Sass men want to slot him, that's OK with me."

Jonathan felt a long way out of his depth. As he looked from face to face he saw the eyes of men who were accustomed to violent death. He felt like he had opened a curtain a few inches and caught a glimpse of a dark place from a nightmare.

"No point pissing around then is there?" said Steve. "Let's get it done."

It took half an hour to gather up the team. They decided that it was best to walk out across the course, as any vehicle would have needed lights that could have been spotted by Rykov. By the time they reached the tee they were soaked through, despite being wrapped up tightly in their waterproofs. Michael examined the rock face with a torch which had been carefully masked with tape to allow only a narrow beam of light. Mostly he used his hands to feel the shape of the rock and to find where the sand had filled the crevices. The others crouched down and waited until he identified the most likely spots.

They started to dig. It was slow work as each time a spade was eased into the sand it had to be done so with extreme care. It took half an hour until they found the plastic sheeting, by which stage there was the first hint of grey in the sky. They stepped up the speed and scooped away the sand by hand. First the plastic was cut away. Then they removed the layer of pebbles one by one. Every man was aware of the speed with which the sky was beginning to lighten. Luckily, the face of the outcrop pointed away from the hills and gave them an element of cover. At last the device was cleared sufficiently for the disposal man to start his work. He told the others to get themselves down to the beach at least 200 yards away.

They braced themselves against the wind and waited for what seemed like an eternity until the bomb man joined them and handed Steve a small device in a plastic bag.

"All done. There's a serious amount of Semtex in there. If the thing had gone off . . ."

He didn't bother to finish the sentence. "We can use this to track the call?"

"Yes. The lads better get back up there and get the sand back into place before it gets too light."

It took them all another fifteen minutes to scoop all the sand back into the crevices of the rock. Then they moved off down the beach, a group of murky figures in the miserable grey of a soaking wet dawn.

Neither they nor Anatoly Rykov would ever know just how close it had been. Had it not been for Rykov's unusually high tolerance for physical discomfort, there would have been no way that he could have slept for six hours through the stormy night. When he awoke, he found that a vague light was easing into the sky. A check of his watch told him that his mental alarm clock had worked as well as ever. His limbs felt stiff and damp, and he spent five minutes stretching himself to normalise his circulation. He then poured himself a mug of coffee and took a few minutes familiarising himself with the view below.

On a clear day the vista in front of him would have been truly majestic. In the clear air of a sunny day in winter, his high position would have given him a clear view all the way over to Ireland. This was a morning when the cameramen for the postcard companies would stay tucked up in their beds. The world was wall-to-wall grey and the rain fell in a constant dismal curtain. Without the ferocious gale, he might have had a problem as some kind of a mist may have settled over the line of hills. The wind ensured that this was not about to happen.

He finished off his coffee and pulled a telescope from his rucksack and set it up at the edge of the gully. He spent a while checking out the various security points dotted around the complex. Every road in was blocked in several places and miserable groups of soldiers could be seen on the beach. Out in the bay, the grey of a Royal Navy cruiser blended in with the general gloom. He spent some time carefully focusing on the point where the ninth tee sat amidst the rolling waves. He made sure that the view through the lens included the path that would lead the players from the eighth green, past the outcrop, and onto the tee itself. Even if there was a large crowd of spectators, his high position guaranteed a view over their heads. The powerful lens pulled the view forward to what seemed little more than 50 yards. He would be able to see the expression on the President's face the very second before he disappeared into the history books.

The weather down at the West Freugh airfield a few miles outside of Stranraer was no better. Steve, Walter and the SAS troop had made the hour's drive from Turnberry as soon as they had returned to the hotel after disabling the bomb. Now they swigged at mugs of tea in one of the hangars. The soldiers had laid all their kit out on sheets on the ground and were selecting what they would need for later on before cleaning and checking. The helicopter that had brought them up from Hereford was waiting out on the apron outside the open doors. Since they had arrived, it had been joined by two others. The first had delivered the silver-haired Colonel in charge of the SAS team. He had briefly acknowledged Steve and Walter before crouching down with his guys and joining in with the tactical discussion of who and how. The second helicopter brought Steve's boss and two unknown characters in suits. They were simply introduced as being from the Home Office.

His boss was clearly not in the mood for lavish praise. Spending the early hours of a wet Sunday morning in a cold RAF hangar in Scotland was obviously not any part of his planned routine. He approached Steve with his two stony-faced companions.

"Morning Kenton. A word please. Alone."

Steve led them to a small dusty office where the wall still carried the breasts of a page three girl who had made her name in the mid-1980s. Nobody fancied the grubby-looking government issue chairs much, so they stood.

"Am I going to be introduced?" asked Steve.

"No. My colleagues are merely here to observe. Brief me please."

Steve ran him through the last stages of his investigation. He could see that his boss would have liked nothing more than to fire him on the spot as he digested the facts of their late-night visit to West Belfast. Every protocol in the book had been ripped up and thrown away, and both men knew it. They also both knew that it would all be ignored because Steve had come up with a result. A huge result. And not only had he come up with a huge result, but their American cousins and paymasters knew all about it, and that meant Steve Kenton was just about the most fire-proof man on the planet. His boss knew it, but was damned if he was about to show it.

Once Steve had completed filling him in on their successful discovery and destruction of the device, his boss allowed himself a small smile.

"Very good, Kenton. What do you have in mind now?"

"We have sent the receiver down to GCHQ in Cheltenham. As soon as Rykov makes his call, they will have his position within seconds. Then there are options. There is a Navy cruiser out in the bay which could stick a rocket down his throat, but we thought that might be a little too public."

The idea of this made the two angels of death from the Home Office look as if they had eaten a dodgy plate of seafood.

"We didn't think that anyone would have much enthusiasm for that idea. The lads outside have come up with something pretty simple. They get in the chopper when the golfers are about twenty minutes away from the ninth. By the time the match leaves the eighth green, the chopper will move into the area. Rykov tries his call. GCHQ tag him and fire the co-ordinates to the helicopter pilot, and he drops the boys in close. 50 yards probably. A low-speed run by, dropping each man off about 30 yards apart. Then it's up to you guys. They can try and arrest him if you like."

This idea prompted three firm shakes of the head. "Didn't think so" continued Steve. "They have silenced weapons. It will all be very quiet. No drama."

His boss nodded and seemed content.

"There's one more thing. I dare say you won't like it much."

"Kenton, to be quite honest, there hasn't been a great deal that I have liked about this whole cavalier operation. What is it?"

"The Americans want Walter to take a ride with the guys. They want one of theirs up close to see the thing through."

Now his boss also had the dodgy-prawn look about him. When he replied, his voice was dripping with sarcasm. "Well Kenton. We'd better not do anything to upset our American friends had we? You especially. I wonder whether you intend to emigrate to the bloody place after this. You seem to have made yourself unusually cosy with our beloved cousins in the last few days."

Steve gave him the most annoying smile he could come up with. "Of course sir. Now I need to get back up to the hotel."

"Don't be so ridiculous. You're staying here."

"Excuse me sir, but my mission is to provide close protection to Archie Banks. As far as I am aware, nobody has altered that. There's nothing I can do here anyway. It's all in the hands of the boys now. I'm off."

His boss thought better of an outburst and allowed Steve to leave the room. He crossed the hangar to where the SAS men sat cross-legged cleaning their weapons. Fish looked up with a cigarette dangling from his lips.

"That you away then Steve?"

"Yeah. Take good care of my man here won't you?" said Steve, nodding to Walter.

Fish followed his gaze and gave a puzzled frown. "Doesn't much look like a boy who needs a babysitter to me. As long as he remembers he's not in a western, he'll be fine."

Steve gave Walter a clap on the back. "No heroics, big man. It's not Iwo Jima. It's Scotland."

Walter shrugged. Steve could see that his friend had stopped being Walter the FBI man. Once again he was Walter of the United States Marine Corps. "I'll be fine buddy. See you later for a beer."

As he got into his car, Steve saw one of the men in suits watching him from the window. The blank pale face gave him a brief shiver.

Deek gave up on any efforts at sleep at seven and got up to take a shower. He stood at his window and checked the weather outside for a few minutes, although all night he had lain awake and tuned his ears into the moaning of the wind and the lash of the rain. He clicked on the TV and switched the sound right down so as not to wake up Meg in the bedroom next door. The picture on the screen showed the President and the First Lady climbing the steps of Airforce One in Paris. The time on the screen said 7.20 a.m. The flight would take just over an hour and they were due to touch down in Scotland at eight-thirty. The next item retold the story of the first round the day before and took the viewer through some of George's more impressive shots. Deek in comparison seemed a mere shadow as he holed out a couple of decent putts. A couple of pundits in the studio gave little for his chances. The anchorman wondered if the terrible weather might make a difference. This idea provoked doubtful head-shaking. Albright's power would enable him to deal with the wind better. No. It was open and shut. Archie Banks had played as well as he could and he was still five shots back. Albright had the thing in the bag.

Next came the weather, and the presenter pulled appropriate faces as she showed how a spectacular area of low pressure out in the Atlantic would ensure that the whole country would have a lousy Sunday. Rain and high winds would move from west to east. There was just a ghost of a chance that a bit of brighter weather might just turn up in western areas in the late afternoon, but she didn't recommend that anyone should hold their breath. With a breezy smile she suggested that her viewers get their feet up and enjoy a good afternoon movie and a cup of hot chocolate.

A low tap at the door took his attention away from the screen. It was Steve.

"Christ man, you look terrible."

Steve gave a weary smile. "You've got that right enough, Deek. Am I all right to come in?"

"Aye, course you are. Want some coffee?"

"Yeah. Magic."

Steve slumped down in an armchair in front of the TV and lit a cigarette while Deek made up the drinks and added a couple of generous shots of scotch.

"You need to close your eyes for an hour or two pal. You look all done in to me."

Steve took a sip at his cup and winced at the heat. "I'll be fine. Been there before, Deek. All part of the service. There'll be plenty of time to sleep tomorrow." He thought of Rykov huddled out there in the storm. He thought of the pale face at the smeared window in West Freugh. Anatoly Rykov would have plenty of time to sleep for the rest of eternity. He snapped himself out of it.

"Anyway. More to the point, how the hell are you? Going to take him?"

"Stranger things have happened."

"Not bloody many. What about this weather? Good or bad for you?"

"Bloody marvellous."

"Well, maybe I better stick fiver on then."

Deek grinned. "Maybe you had."

Sally Hunter hugged her thin jacket as tightly around her as she could and for the umpteenth time cursed herself for not choosing to wear a coat. Beside her the First Minister, Roger Temple, didn't look a great deal happier. It was just all so bloody typical. This was the biggest day in the young life of the semi-independent Scotland. They didn't come any bigger. The biggest sporting event on the planet and a presidential visit. It was summer and here was a chance for Scotland to look great in the eyes of the watching world. Everybody had hoped that just for once the weather might choose to play ball. Fat chance. The scene at Prestwick Airport would have been dismal enough had it been in the middle of November. For the end of May, it was positively soul destroying.

They had received word that Airforce One was just minutes away and had duly gone out onto the concrete to meet and greet their famous visitor. Alongside them, a marching band complete with kilts and bagpipes stood stony-faced. It would be just their luck if a sudden gust of the gale lifted the tartan and gave the morose tabloid photographers a bonus shot for the Monday papers.

Where the hell was the bloody plane? The damp and cold was eating through the thin fabric of Sally's nice designer jacket and she was finding it tough to keep her umbrella in place as the wind tugged at her grip. All in all, she felt completely strung-out. She had managed two hours sleep and as she emerged from a bracing shower the face in the mirror looked ten years older than it normally did. By the time she had applied far more make-up than she would have liked, she had an uneasy feeling that it made her look like a jumped-up tart. Her boss had done little to improve her tetchy mood. From the minute he had met her at the airport he had moaned and groaned about the weather as if she was personally responsible. Now he stood beside her looking like he was wondering if there were any vacancies for a First Minister in Barbados.

She could hear the roar of the engines now. At last the plane burst through the grey of the cloud and came into sight. It took her breath away. It was enormous. Bigger that she had ever imagined when she had seen it on the TV. Above it, the sinister shapes of two F16 fighter jets scoured the sky for threat whilst the great plane rumbled down to earth and made its way over to where they waited.

After a couple of moments, the door opened and the steps were wheeled into place. A group of suited men with big shoulders and dark glasses emerged and took up their stations as the bagpipes fired up. The TV crews and photographers were all attention now and every lens was zoomed in on the open door at the side of the plane. Finally, the famous couple stepped out and the President gave his trademark wave. Sally had wondered how his mood would be, but his smile seemed real enough. He strode over to where they waited and he appeared to be perfectly oblivious to the torrential rain.

He took Roger Temple's hand and shook it vigorously.

"Welcome to Scotland, Mr President."

"Why, thanks Roger. So what's going to happen then? You think your boy has a chance today?"

For a moment Temple hadn't a clue what on earth he was talking about. He quickly realised he was discussing the match, and found his feet clumsily.

"Well. Yes. I suppose. Hopefully." He was like a teenager on a first date, and it was all Sally could manage not to smirk. "Allow me to introduce Sally Hunter. She is our Minister for Sport. Sally has headed up the whole event. Sadly, her talents didn't run to organising the weather."

He gave a rather weak laugh at his attempted joke. The President's smile grew even wider. "Ah. The famous Miss Hunter. Tell you what

Roger, we've heard a hell of a lot about this lady in the White House. A hell of a lot."

Roger Temple looked as if someone had stuck an ice cube down the back of his underpants. "You have?"

"Sure we have. People tell me that Sally is the rising star. That she is on the fast track." He leaned into the First Minister conspiratorially and spoke in a dramatic stage whisper. "They even say that the first Prime Minister of an independent Scotland might just be a lady. Now what do you say to that?"

Sally was almost cross-eyed in her effort not to laugh, especially when the President turned his face from Temple and gave her a wink. The First Minister had never been quite so lost for words. This was all beyond bizarre. He attempted a smile.

"Yes. Absolutely. We're all very fond of Sally of course. I hadn't realised that her reputation had well . . . travelled quite so far. Anyway. We have some coffee inside. Shall we go in . . . out of all this . . ."

He gestured apologetically at the sheeting rain.

"Sure. In a moment. But I think I better say a hello to these guys first." The American leader gestured to the pipe-playing soldiers. "Kinda rude not to, wouldn't you say? Hell. I best get used to your Scottish rain sooner rather than later. Looks like I'm going to spend most of the day in it."

The First Minister nodded rather miserably and dutifully followed the President as he walked along the line of bagpipers. Once they were inside, coffee and warm shortbread were served and Temple introduced his famous guest to various dignitaries until it was time for the motorcade to head south to Turnberry.

"I hope you can spare Miss Hunter to ride with me, Roger. Show me the sights and all. That OK with you?"

Temple nodded with a rather dumbfounded expression. He was due to head back to Edinburgh and bade his farewells. As he was driven back east to the capital he couldn't even begin to work out how it was that The White House could be so impressed with Sally Hunter. Maybe he had missed something. He must have.

George Albright awoke just in time to watch the pictures of the President's arrival at the rainy airport. Outside he could see that things were no better at Turnberry. As he stood at the window he murmured to himself. "Jesus Christ."

His head felt as if a whole construction team with jackhammers were at work inside. The hangover the morning before had been bad, but this was outrageous. He took a long shower and pieced together his memories of the night before. Despite feeling beyond lousy, he couldn't help but smile. He was thoroughly enjoying his new persona. What would all his image consultants have said if they could have seen him? Here he was, two hours away from a match with the President watching, and he was so hung over he could barely focus in the mirror to shave.

After a handful of Paracetemol and three cups of coffee he felt strong enough to make it down to breakfast. Deek was already there looking alarmingly fresh. He was digging his way through a huge plate of fried food.

"Morning George. Bit wild out there."

George sat and poured a glass of orange juice. "Just a bit."

Deek waved an appreciative hand over his plate. "You want to get a bit of this down you. Keep you warm like."

The very thought of it sent George's stomach into somersaults. "Maybe not. I'm not sure I could take it."

"You were on pretty good form last night George. The Sinatra stuff was pretty good."

George rolled his eyes. He'd forgotten the Sinatra. "I think my daddy would say that you are pretty bad company buddy."

Troll chuckled. "He would'nae be the first." He shovelled half a sausage coated in ketchup into his mouth, which rather distorted the next bit. "You best be on your game this morning George. This is my man's weather you ken."

George looked up from stirring his coffee to find that the eyes of the Sunnybank Three were all fixed on him and there was more than a hint of a gleam.

"You boys certainly all seem kind of confident this morning."

Deek shrugged and speared a chunk of fried bread. "I was wondering if you might fancy a wee punt on the side."

"Oh really. And what kind of thing did you have in mind?"

"I dunno. How about a tenner a hole?"

"Pounds or dollars?"

"Pounds."

George reached across the table and shook on the deal. It looked as if it would be a good idea if he got himself sharpened up some.

Rykov watched the presidential motorcade as it pulled off the main road and made its way to the hotel. Motorcycle outriders were in front and behind and a helicopter hovered above the six-car convoy like an over-protective insect. He knew that the President's car would have been built with similar protection to an Abrams tank, but they were still taking no chances. The fleet of black vehicles swept up the road in front of the hotel and disappeared from his view for a few seconds until it re-emerged in the car park. He could clearly see the black-suited figures of the security team as they leapt out of their vehicles and formed a cordon ready to shepherd their man inside.

A film crew marked the moment as the President and his wife scuttled inside under the protection of an umbrella. His prey had arrived. A check of his watch told him that it was quarter to ten. Not long now. Tee off was due for ten-thirty. How long would eight holes take? About an hour and a half. Zero hour would arrive at about noon. A real-life High Noon. And then history would be made. He poured the last of his coffee and settled down for the last minutes to tick by.

Finally all the formalities were over. The President had changed into his golfing attire and had emerged resplendent in a Stars and Stripes set of waterproofs. Steve had rolled his eyes at the sight. He had just been in the process of thinking "only an American" when he realised that the colourful figure was headed his way.

"I gather that you are Steve Kenton?"

Sally was close behind with an amused look on her face.

"Yes sir. I am."

"I believe that I need to shake your hand, Steve. My friends will tell you that I am not a guy to forget when he owes a debt. I owe you a big one son. All you need to do is make the call. Understand me?"

"Yes sir. I do. And thank you."

The President gestured out of the window. "Are you coming round with us today son?"

"Yes."

"Great. I'll see you on the course."

The regulation photos were taken of the President with both players and the McMillans. The Sunnybank Three were once again adorned in Meg's tartan and she felt ready to burst into tears of pride as she took her own photos of the three of them alongside the practised grin of the American leader. When she had emptied her film her dad put an arm around her shoulder.

"Remember that morning on the practice ground Meg?"

"Of course I do." Her voice was choked with emotion.

"They've come a long way. All of us have. I'm so glad you're back together."

"So am I daddy. So am I." She rooted a tissue out of her bag and wiped away the tears that would not hold back. "Do you think he stands a chance?"

"Who?"

"Deek of course."

Frank smiled. "I thought you meant George for a minute. In this weather I wouldn't fancy anyone's chances against Deek. Just you wait and see. A lot of people are about to be pretty surprised."

Roger Swann joined them with a smile as wide as the Galloway Forest.

"Have you done it?" asked Frank.

"Done, dusted and wrapped. Thirty-five to one."

"Bloody marvellous."

Meg's face became suspicious. "You've not been betting, have you daddy?"

"Oh, just a little wager."

"How much?"

"Never you mind."

What on earth was it with the men in her life? Bookies and booze. Her suspicions were further aroused when she noticed that Deek was deep in a confidential-looking conversation with the President. What on earth was he up to now? As soon as he came over she asked.

"And what was that all about?"

"Just a wee punt."

"A bet! With the President. How much?"

"A tenner."

"Ten pounds. That's it?"

"Aye. But it's the principle that counts."

They headed out into the storm on a convoy of golf carts which took them down to the first tee where the cameras and the spectators were waiting. The gallery was noticeably smaller than the previous afternoon as sore heads and the weather had kept many in the warmth of the bar.

The Dumfries waiter was ready. He looked a strange sight swaddled in waterproofs with a silver tray holding a bottle and glasses. The players duly toasted each other and tossed a coin which Deek called correct. He gestured for George to take the first shot and the two shook hands and wished each other well. The shot of Jack Daniels flew up to George's head much harder than he had anticipated and he shook his head to clear his vision. He would have to watch it. The alcohol levels in his blood were obviously still sky-high from the night before. He bent down and placed his ball on the tee and strolled back to take in the shot ahead. The day before, the hole had looked like something from a postcard as the perfect green carpet of the fairway stretched out to the distant green. Now the wind was hammering straight into his face and the rain made him squint. The hole would play about 50 miles longer. He stepped back forward and pushed the tee further into the ground to help to keep the ball lower. He then ran through the routine that had stood him in good stead for all the years of his career before hammering into the drive. To start with it looked perfect as the ball took off into the gale with a vengeance, but as it started to rise higher the gale got a hold on it and dragged it to the left of the fairway. The ball landed and trickled into the very front of one of the pot bunkers.

"Unlucky George" said Deek with a wry grin as he tossed his ball straight down onto the tee. Without much fuss he lashed into a one iron which barely seemed to get into the air at all. It lanced up the right of the fairway before easing left and scuttling and scurrying along to finish 40 yards short of the bunker which had snaffled up George's ball.

"What kind of a shot was that?" George had never seen anything quite like it.

"A Scottish one."

"Looks like this could be fun."

"Aye. It could."

Deek more or less replicated his tee shot from the fairway and the ball clambered its way onto the front of the green like a busy crab. George had no option but to come out of the bunker sideways and his towering iron just made it to the edge of the green. He rolled his chip up to the side of the hole and Deek duly picked up his ball and tossed it back to him. Deek's putt was a dead length and George followed suit and conceded the nine-incher that was left. He reached into his pocket and passed Deek a ten-pound note.

"Nice four."

Deek pocketed the cash. "Thanks George. It's a good idea to keep them low on a day like this, ken."

"So I've noticed."

On the second tee George wiped at his face and eyes with a towel and looked at what was ahead with trepidation. The first hole had been a mere 350 yards and the day before he had put himself in position for his birdie with a drive and a chip. The wind had changed everything and even a drive and a mid-iron had only just made the front of the green. The second hole was longer again. 430 yards. From where he was standing it looked about 43 miles.

Deek nipped down a small whisky and tossed his ball onto the tee. Once again he played his extraordinary one-iron shot that never got much more than six feet off the turf and scratched its way down the fairway. Even so, it didn't get further than 200 yards. That left Deek with 230 more to go. No way. Five was probably about as good as he could do. George rubbed at his sodden chin and wondered whether he could make it. The sensible play would be to emulate his opponent and lay up short in two. That would give him a pretty well nailed on five and a chance of a putt for four. He was four up and the smart move was to protect. On the other hand, if he could make the green in two and win the hole in four he would achieve a double whammy. He would restore his five-shot advantage and immediately regain the high ground in the match.

Having worked out his options, he pulled out his driver and once again teed the ball down low before hitting it with everything he had. This time the spin of the ball was more controlled and it thumped into the wet grass of the fairway 30 yards beyond Deek. George gave himself a short nod. Two hundred yards left. Makeable.

Deek rattled his second shot to a good spot on the right of the fairway which gave him an open line into the green. George bashed a furious three wood that bounded to the back corner, about 50 feet from the pin. Deek gave him an impressed grin.

"Nice going, big man."

George stood to one side as Deek arrived at his ball. The shot that faced him was pretty awkward. It was no more than 70 yards, but the green was above him and the wind made it almost impossible to judge. As soon as the ball was in the air it would be quite impossible to predict the flight. Only a perfectly struck wedge would hold its line. He frowned when he saw Troll pull out a long straight-faced club. What the hell? Deek seemed to hit the shot with nothing more than a flick of the wrists, and the ball stayed under the level of the green until the very last moment when it rose up to meet the full force of the wind. This killed the momentum of the shot as effectively as a concrete wall, and the ball dropped straight down to land two feet from the flag. For a moment George was transfixed. He had never seen a shot quite like it. Well, that wasn't quite true. He had watched similar shots on his video of Seve Ballesteros defying the elements to take a four-shot lead on the first round of the Open at Lytham in the late 1980s. That day the Spaniard had carded a 67 that bordered on genius, and he had gone on to win the title. All of a sudden George knew that he had a serious game on his hands.

His putt was downhill and now the wind was behind him. There was a considerable swathe across the green and he knew he would have to start the putt at least ten feet right. How much effect would the wind have? Impossible to say. He found it hard to settle himself over the ball. The rain was spearing into his face and he couldn't seem to get himself right. At last he struck the putt and the second it was away he knew it was too hard. It shot twenty feet by the hole and he missed the one back. Deek tapped in for four.

George dug another ten-pound note from his pocket and handed it over. "What the hell was that third shot? A four iron?"

"Three iron."

"Where the hell did you find a shot like that?"

"Sunnybank playing fields. We used to take hits at this tailor's dummy we found in a skip. I would try and hit it on the head. Target practice ken. All the other kids would come out and watch and have bets on how many times I could hit the head out of ten goes. It's a canny wee shot for the wind, ken."

George shook his head. "Aye. I ken right enough."

Deek was delighted. "Hey big man. You're getting the lingo. Let's have a bloody dram shall we? Keep the cold out."

After the players had played off the third tee, the President joined Steve and Sally as they made their way down the fairway.

"Hey guys. Your man is incredible. Where the hell did he learn to play golf like this? I've never seen anything like it."

Sally smiled. "Don't ask me. I wondered the same thing myself."

Steve stopped and hid his head inside his waterproof jacket for a moment to get a cigarette lit. Then he emerged in a cloud of smoke that was instantly swept away on the wind. "There's a course down on the coast a few miles from Dumfries. Southerness. It is quite similar to this place, just not as famous. Lots of Asians go there and one of the hotel managers fixes Deek up with money matches. Ten holes start usually. The wetter and windier the better. It's how he's made a living for ten years."

"Looks like Big George has a game on his hands then."

"I would say so."

The President glanced about to make sure they could not be overheard.

"Is everything in place Steve?"

"It is. They'll call me when it's done. I'll let you know."

Sally put her head down. She had managed to get her mind free of what was about to happen for a few minutes, as she had become more and more engrossed in the golf. Now it was back and she found it hard to deal with. The President noticed.

"I'm sorry you've got wrapped up in this Sally. I'm afraid it is the kind of thing that crosses my desk from time to time. Never tastes any good, but it's how things are. We can never let people know when they get close. You understand that?"

She nodded. The logic was beyond argument. It was the cold reality that was hard.

"It's an ugly world I'm afraid, Sally."

"I know. I think they call it 'big boys rules' don't they?"

Steve winced at the phrase that was so familiar from his time in Ireland. Neither man could think of much to say and so walked on in silence as the rain swept over them.

At eleven-thirty the SAS team made a final check of their gear and climbed on board the helicopter that rose unsteadily up into the sky. In the doorway of the hangar the two men from London stood and watched their departure with cold, bored expressions.

In his hotel room in Monte Carlo, Abdullah carefully controlled his excitement as Deek and George walked off the seventh green having halved the long par five. The Scotsman had won the sixth and reduced the American's lead to two shots. All the commentators were getting excited now. Before the start of the round, they had all written the underdog off as not having a chance. Now it was beginning to appear as if they had all got it badly wrong. The local man had a better understanding of the conditions than the American. Abdullah had enjoyed watching him. He was clever. He used craft and guile where the American relied on brute force. In a way, what was happening in the match was highly appropriate. All around the President was a security screen that was unsurpassed anywhere on earth. The TV had shown pictures of the soldiers on the beach and the warship in the bay and the RAF jets in the sky. Even the fairways seemed to have as many agents as spectators. The thought made him smile. Their power and money made the Americans believe that they were indestructible. The cameras had shown many close-ups of the President looking happy and relaxed despite the awful weather. How dare he! All around the world his soldiers were doing his filthy work while he took a morning stroll around a golf course.

Abdullah allowed the familiar knot of cold hate to grow in his stomach. Let him enjoy his last few minutes. Let them all feel safe and secure in the heart of their dark empire. Soon all would change for ever. Soon his people would deliver a blow that would make the attack on New York pale into insignificance. It would be the start. After what was about to happen, events would begin to turn. Maybe it would take many years, but in the end Allah would deliver them their victory. It had all happened before. The Crusaders had once polluted the sacred soil of the Holy Land for many, many years. But in the end Saladin had thrown them into the sea at the Battle of Hattin. His people would prevail in the end, and what was about to happen would be one of their greatest victories.

TARGET ONE

He took a careful sip of his mint tea and was surprised to find that he felt a twinge of regret for the Scotsman. He rather liked the strange little man. He was clearly the worst of infidels with his constant drinking and smoking, but there was something about him that reminded Abdullah of the children on the dusty streets of Gaza who threw the stones at the Israeli tanks. In his own way he was exposing the weakness in the myth of American impregnability. A shame that he would not get to complete his task.

Just one more hole. Ten minutes. Then the whole world would know the power of Allah.

Rykov watched them as they marched out down the eighth fairway. Not long now. He packed his rucksack with the items that he needed. The waterproof sheets were already folded and hidden away under a pile of rocks. All he needed now was the telescope and his mobile phone which was safely tucked away in the pocket of his jacket. The battery was fully charged and the signal was fine. Just a few more moments. It would be the last time that he would watch his prey walk to their death. A part of him regretted that he would never again feel the fierce excitement that he had always known in the moments before making a kill. As ever, it seemed so strange that the figures so far in the distance were about to die at the hands of someone so far away. Someone they had never met. Death would come from nowhere. It would come without any warning. But it would come.

Abe sat in the huge reception room at the ranch in Dallas. He had risen early and hadn't missed a minute of the special programme from Turnberry. He was alone in the sprawling homestead. The family had departed en masse for Scotland and all the other staff had been given the time off. He had volunteered to keep an eye on things.

Soon after everyone had left, he had started to wish that there were more to do. The tension of not knowing was beginning to eat him alive. He had heard nothing from El Kali after the morning when he had visited him at the emporium in Dallas. His friend had said that it would probably be a good idea if they didn't see each other for a while. Abe had no way of knowing whether or not the nugget of information he had passed on had come to anything or not. Some days he had managed to get along with his work and not think about it at all. Other days it consumed him all his waking hours. Some days he felt a fierce pride at the fact that he still hadn't forgotten his people after so many years. Other days he felt like a Judas in the house of the man who over the years had become the best friend he had ever known.

Soon the waiting would be over. Just another day of golf and it would all be decided one way or another. Every time the cameras zoomed in on the relaxed face of the President, his stomach tightened. The half a century of the American in him actually rather liked the man. He had voted for him last time around. The terrible fact that he could be responsible for his assassination seemed too appalling to be true. But it was true. And if it was about to happen, it would happen in the next few hours.

For a few moments he sat with his head in his hands. When he looked up he saw George hit a wedge nearly into orbit. The camera watched it arc into the eighth green and thump down twelve feet from the pin. Deek had already played one of his trademark run-up shots to a few feet further. Probably a half. For a tiny fraction of a moment he forgot his worries and was engaged in the splendid game that was unfolding in the wind and the rain.

It didn't last. The demons soon returned and swarmed over him like hungry ants.

Deek crouched down next to Troll and weighed up the putt he had left himself. Playing down-wind was often even harder than against it. He had considered throwing his second shot up high, but had decided that the gusting wind would make it too unpredictable. Instead, he had driven his approach shot into the bank at the front of the green and allowed it to bump along toward the pin. He had made sure that it stayed short of the flag to leave him with an uphill putt. George had taken the aerial route and had hit his wedge so high that it had almost come down with snow on it. However, the wind had eased it past the flag and he was left with a fiddly downhill ten-footer.

"Three inches to the right. No need to belt it. The wind will roll it on."

Deek squinted along the line suggested by Troll and could find no argument with his reading of the putt.

"Aye. Looks good to me, mate."

Once the decision was made he didn't bother taking much time. It had always been his theory that the more time you spent agonising over a putt, the worse things got. He took a couple of glances at the hole and gave the ball a firm tap. It eased in from the right as predicted and dived down into the hole. A birdie three. It put him one under par for eight holes.

George nodded his appreciation and stalked his putt like a big agitated bear. He knew that he really needed this one. In just eight holes he had seen his lead whittled away to a mere two holes. As he had watched his second shot into the eighth he had been convinced it was going to finish just inches from the hole but the wind had gusted and taken it ten feet by. All of a sudden he needed a birdie simply to maintain his lead and the putt was a nasty downhiller. He knew it would come in from the left, but how far? The wind made it worse. The putt was downhill but the wind was against. What effect would it have? In the end he decided to give the putt a firm hit and try to negate the effects of the slope. For eight feet it never wavered from the centre of the hole. Then, in the last few inches, it swung to the right and caught the lip. Had he hit it softer it would have dropped in, but the speed of the putt sent it spinning out.

The lead was down to one hole. He gave a rueful smile and reached into his pocket for yet another ten-pound note.

The tinny voice was again in the earphones. Fish struggled to hear over the noise of the helicopter rotors.

"They've finished the eighth. On their way to the ninth tee. Stand by."

Below him he could see the streets and harbour of Girvan. The seagulls were gathered on the water like confetti. It wouldn't be long now. A couple of minutes at the most. That was if anything happened at all. He held up two fingers to his fellow troopers to give them a time check. In return he received four bored nods. It was the way of the Regiment.

Rykov sensed the adrenaline begin to reach its maximum. The eighth green was perfectly framed in his telescope. He saw the big American arch his back in frustration as his putt lipped out. The crowd all moved right to get a view of the famous drive up the ninth over the rocks and the raging waves. The players' party moved off the green along the path that took them to the tee.

He eased the telescope slightly to bring the tee itself into focus and watched them all arrive. There were iron railings at the back and the spectators lined up. The President was easily visible in his garish set of Stars and Stripes waterproofs. There were four obvious security men and ten others, two of them who appeared to be female. Albright stood to one side whilst the Scotsman bent to place his ball on a tee.

The President had laid his arms out along the railings and Rykov could sense that he was smiling. Of course he was. He knew that the sight of the angry waves behind him would make it an irresistible image for the cameras. A last smile for the dying man. He drew his phone from his pocket and gently depressed the "send" button.

It only took two seconds for him to know with a cold certainty that things had gone terribly wrong. His brain went into overdrive. Another jab at the green button had no effect. Only two conceivable reasons then. Either he had made a mistake when he had set the device or they had found it. He had never made a mistake. Not ever. Then he heard the sound of the helicopter.

Rykov's signal had flown south to where the receiver was waiting in an office in the GCHQ centre in Cheltenham. The computer took less than three seconds to establish the co-ordinates of the sending phone which were then instantly transferred to a sister computer in the helicopter. This system was designed for search-and-rescue operations that could pinpoint a man down in hostile territory to a few square feet. The pilot adjusted the direction of the helicopter and pointed it towards a line of dark hills.

"We have him lads. ETA twenty seconds."

The chopper swung up over the brow of the hill and moved in low over the tussocky grass. The team were now crouched and ready in the openings either side.

"Go one."

The speed of the reaction took Rykov completely off guard. Seconds after he was aware of the sound of the machine he saw it rise up over the brow of the hill. Part of him tried to tell himself that they couldn't know where he was. Just a routine flight. Stay dead still and they couldn't possibly see him.

Then, a figure dropped ten feet to the ground and rolled like a parachutist. Then another. Seconds later there were five of them, spread out in a line of 50 yards, ten yards apart and coming in fast. He knew instantly that these were trained men. Special Forces. SAS probably. There was no hesitation about them. They were moving in without any wariness or doubt. He didn't have a gun himself. What was the point? If he was discovered, a single weapon would be of no use whatsoever against the massive firepower that would be levelled against him. If he wasn't found out, he wouldn't need a gun.

But he had been found out. He had no idea of how or why. It didn't matter. It was always going to happen. Today was the day. He slowly rose to he feet and spread his arms high and wide into the driving rain.

Fish saw the figure rise from the grass and kept his rifle levelled as he moved forward. He stopped five yards short and stared down the sights to the placid middle-aged face. No panic there. Not even much resignation. The face of a man who had lost a bet on a horse race but could afford it well enough. He sensed that the others were alongside now. A semicircle of aimed weapons.

The man gave a small smile. More of a smirk. "No weapon. Unarmed." His voice was perfectly calm.

"Sorry Anatoly. We're not doing surrender and arrest today."

His finger flicked down the trigger twice. The SAS called it the double tap. One. Two. Two bullets that flew at hundreds of feet per second straight through the Russian's heart. Anatoly's brain just had time to register that they had known his name.

Then all was darkness.

Steve didn't watch the tee shots. Instead he scanned the line of hills that looked broodingly down on the course. He had watched the helicopter change course and disappear over the brow about three miles away. Then it was gone. Nothing. Just the roar of the wind and crash of the waves on the beach.

It was done then.

At West Freugh the word came in. "Target disabled. Team One returning to base. ETA 25. The two men from the Home Office got to their feet and climbed into their car and drove away while the Colonel looked on with a look of naked disgust.

Abdullah watched the American drop his driver back into his bag and start to walk away from the tee. Within seconds the camera panned away and showed the whole party leave the square of green in the midst of the grey waves.

Something had gone wrong. A great wave of disappointment washed through him. Now there would be the task of backtracking to try and understand where the weakness was to be found.

Outside there were muffled sounds. A sound of something falling. He was rising to his feet as a small explosive charge blew the door off its hinges. Two men came in. Big guns. Big silencers. The feet from one of the bodyguards outside were visible through the open door.

So this was it. Time for the Paradise that the Koran had promised him for all his years. One of the men stepped forward. Olive skin and ice-cold eyes.

Abdullah heard one last word before taking leave of his life.

"Shalom."

The neurons of his brain just had time to register a single thought: Israeli.

A website representing an obscure Shia group was later to claim responsibility for the execution of the super-rich Saudi whose face was so well known in the places where the world's super-rich had their fun. The pronouncement stated that he was executed because he had adopted the ways of the infidel.

Al Kali parked up his car in the one of the three spaces beside the bins at the back of his carpet shop. He had listened to the golf commentary as he had driven into work through the quiet Sunday morning streets of Dallas. So far nothing. He stepped out and was pulling on his jacket when two hooded figures jumped out from beside the dustbins. Black faces. A gun.

The Dallas Police Department later concluded that it was robbery and homicide. No doubt the assailants were crack addicts. Violent crime was on the up again. The story made a few lines on page four of the local paper and a ten-second mention on the evening news.

Zaheer Khan was watching the match in his hotel room in Riyadh. He had considered going down to the bar, but had instead chosen privacy. He was barely aware of his door flying open. A shot took him in the back of his skull before he could turn to see the eyes of the man who killed him.

The Saudi police concluded that his associations with American oil companies had made him a target.

The NYPD officers who took the 9-1-1 call from Mustapha Haj's neighbour concluded that he must have disturbed a burglar. His flat had been thoroughly ransacked and nothing of any value was left. Time of death was estimated at sometime during the morning of Sunday 31st May.

Steve hung back from the main group and made a call on his mobile.

"It's Kenton."

"The operation is conclusive."

He ended the call and caught up with the President as they made their way along the path to the fairway. He fell into step beside him.

"It's done sir."

"All?"

"Yes sir."

The President paused for a moment and gazed out over the white tops of the waves to the grey nothingness of the horizon.

"OK. Thanks Steve."

Jonathan noticed the exchange and stood to one side as Steve caught up the group.

"Well?"

"It's all over, Johnny. Nothing more to worry about."

Jonathan looked into Steve's haggard face. "Christ, I couldn't do your job Steve."

"I'm not sure I can. Not any more. Might be time to move on."

"*. . . and there's Jonathan McMillan. What a day for this young man. What a day for the whole family. It really is the kind of story* *that makes you feel pretty good about being American, wouldn't you say John . . ."*

Abe could hardly watch any more. Johnny was talking to the English security man who had frightened him so much when he had come to the house. What if something were to happen to Johnny? He wouldn't be able to live with that. He had known the boy all his life. He was a good boy. In some ways, Johnny had taken the place of the son he had never had. And now he had put him in danger. Terrible danger. How could he have . . ?

The doorbell took him by surprise. Who the hell? He opened up to find two men in suits waiting outside.

"We need you to come with us Mr Haston."

He knew it straight away. They had found out. Somehow they had discovered what he had done. Relief poured through him.

"So Johnny will be OK then?"

"If you could just come with us please Mr Haston."

He went with them. They drove for an hour through the empty plains. A dirt track took them to a deserted field with a neat hole. They gently walked him to the lip and put a bullet through his head.

When the McMillans returned home to the ranch, Abe simply wasn't there. There wasn't a single trace of him. Not a book, not an item of clothing, not a note. Nobody could understand it. For a while everyone expected that he would get in touch, but he never did. He just vanished. He had no family and barely any friends. It was almost as if he had never existed at all. Only Jonathan McMillan guessed at the truth. He had seen the truth in Steve's eyes on the path up to the ninth fairway at Turnberry.

It was a secret that he carried to his grave.

By the thirteenth hole of the afternoon round, viewing figure records all around the world were being shattered. The match was capturing the attention of golfer and non-golfer alike. The David and Goliath story was looking like it was about to pan out in line with the good book. The storm had raged without a break and Deek had punched and chopped his way around the great course to near miraculous effect. After 31 holes of golf in the most brutal conditions that the Scottish climate could come up with he was an incredible two under par. George Albright hadn't played badly. In fact, the consensus was that he had played out of his skin. But he was up against genius. Commentators talked Ballesteros and Trevino and Bobby Jones. They marvelled at the outrageous range of shots that Deek was able to produce like an impish conjurer. Every three holes he took a glass from the drenched waiter. Every few minutes he took a lit cigarette figure from a lanky man with wild red hair who was dressed in the same tartan uniform as the golfer and his caddie.

Camera close-ups showed a face set in lines of rigid concentration. Here was a man on a mission. Here was a man who had found his moment and was taking it with both hands. He was Cassius Clay standing over the prone figure of Sonny Liston. He was Bob Beaman leaping out of the long-jump pit at the Mexico Olympics. He was Maradona jinking his way through the flailing legs of the England defenders in the World Cup quarter final. The watching audience were told every few minutes that they were watching sporting history in the making and they tuned in by the million.

Deek had taken a careful two iron from the thirteenth tee and left himself with a five iron to the awkward raised green. Ahead of him, George's ball was less than 100 yards from the flag and slap in the middle of the fairway. The pin was cut cruelly close to the bunkers that guarded the front of the green, and the wind was sweeping in from the right.

Troll was staring suspiciously out to sea where the clouds were finally starting to break up and a dramatic beam of late afternoon sunshine was shining down on the waves.

"Weather's easing, Deek"

Deek followed his gaze. "Aye. The wind's easing too. What do think on this one Troll? Play it safe. Knock it up the right. Let it come in on the breeze. Steer clear of the sand."

Troll nodded. "Aye. Keep hold of what we have. He'll be like a wounded bloody rhino when the weather lifts."

Deek finished his cigarette and tossed it down to the wet grass. He decided on an easy five iron rather than a hard six, and hit it high over the right side of the green. The wind eased it in and it landed safely on the back right corner, 40 feet from the flag.

George stared at the green with arms folded. Time was ticking down. Three down and only five to play after this one. Deek had a

40-foot downhiller. Surely he wouldn't make that. Not that surely came into it. Not the way the Scotsman was playing. Taking on the flag was a risk. If he got it wrong and landed in the bunker, it could be four down with five to play. But he had to make a move. It was now or never time, and he knew it.

He thumped into his sand wedge approach and took a fat divot out of the carpet like turf. The ball landed inches to the right of the hole and spun back fiercely. Slowly and agonisingly the spin drew the ball back down the slope of the green until it dribbled over the edge into a bunker. George hung his head for a moment. It was beginning to look as if it was not to be his day.

This feeling grew stronger when he arrived at the bunker to find his ball hard up by the almost vertical wall. Even though he was on the green, Deek's ball was further from the flag and so he putted first to a foot away. All George could do was to hack the ball out and he was relieved to get the ball within 30 feet. His putt was downhill and had five feet of swing. As he squatted down behind it, he allowed himself a glance out to sea. The clouds were much lighter now and a hint of sunshine warmed his face. At last the weather was calming down. Somehow he just needed to stay in touch. As soon as the ball left the putter head he knew it was too hard. Way too hard. It was about to roll fifteen long, but at least it was on target. On target. Maybe. Just maybe. The ball hit the back of the hole and actually jumped an inch before diving inside.

He grinned at the crowd and mimed out the act of patting his beating heart. Three down and five to play. Still a ghost of a chance. Just a ghost.

Deek again played out a careful par four on the fourteenth. However, this time George's majestic approach shot fulfilled all its airborne promise and settled down two feet away. Birdie three. Two up and four to play.

As Deek took a glass of scotch on the back of the fifteenth tee, the sun wrenched itself out of confinement and lit up the course in an afternoon glow. He gave a worried grimace at Troll and waited for George to play. The par three hole suddenly looked stunning in the vivid light. It was just over 200 yards and guarded by a daunting array of rough and bunkers. Once again the flag was placed in a miserably tough position at the back left of the green. The smart shot was the safer right side, but George wasn't in that kind of mood. His towering six iron never wavered from its track and finished seven feet away.

"Best go for it. You agree Troll?"

Troll nodded and Deek fired a four iron straight at the pin. He underestimated the effect of the adrenalin that was pumping through him, and the ball pitched on the back of the green and flew into the long grass. He managed to hack it onto the cut surface but missed the twenty-foot par putt.

One up and three to play. The sixteenth was a par four which evened up the odds as a small stream wound around the front of the green. It meant that there was no advantage in George's longer hitting. Both men took irons from the tee and Deek's approach shot was only a couple of feet further from the hole than George's. For a dreadful moment he thought his putt was about to slide by, but at the last second it dived in. Deek felt almost faint with relief. Now the tables were turned. George was back in the hot seat. He had a ten-foot birdie putt to avoid going to two down with two to play.

The big man was smiling now as he eyed the putt. Every aspect of his body language spoke of utter confidence. This was his world. He had thrived on this kind of pressure for as long as he could remember. Not one cell in his brain considered missing the putt.

He didn't. Halves in three. One up and two to play.

The seventeenth was a long winding brute of a par five. Deek's spirits were sinking even as they made their way to the tee. No matter how hard he wound himself up, there was no way he could reach the green in two. He knew that George could do it in his sleep. The euphoria of his three-shot lead suddenly seemed like a distant memory, especially when George made the crowd gasp with a titanic 340-yard tee shot. Deek got within 40 yards of the green with his approach shot. George slammed in a three iron to leave a twenty-foot putt for an eagle.

" . . . you've got to feel for Archie Banks. Just a few minutes ago it looked like he had this thing in the bag, but ever since George banged in that big putt on thirteen, he's been in overdrive. Somehow Banks has to dig a birdie out here and hope that George misses his eagle putt. What a game. What a spectacle! This one is going all the way to the wire . . . ."

Deek took a cigarette from Banjo and stared at the shot that faced him. 40 yards. Maybe 45. The bunker in the way was what made it tough. He would have to go high. No other choice. He sucked in the smoke and took a sand iron from Troll. For a moment he caught a glimpse of the faces watching. All day he had been in his own zone. His own tiny little world that was restricted to Troll and Banjo and the occasional brief banter with George. He had blanked out everything else. The rain, the crowd, the consequences. He had fought his own private little duel with the might of the great old course.

Now for the first time he saw the faces. Steve and Walter were together at the edge of the group with Sally Hunter. Steve gave a thumbs-up, but his eyes were terrible. The President was in the midst of his minders who were all staring out at the crowd that lined the fairway.

"Best of luck son. Hang on in there."

Deek acknowledged with a nod. Meg was at the far edge of her group with her dad who was clutching her hand. Frank gave him a nervous smile. Meg's smile was different. It said to him that it didn't matter to her if he won or lost. It said that she would be proud of him no matter what. It said that she wasn't leaving any more. Not ever. He grinned back at her and turned to the shot.

He cut under the ball and threw it high. It bit hard into the green and grabbed. Seven feet away. Not bad. Better than not bad. Bloody marvellous under the circumstances.

"Great shot, Deek." shouted George as he walked onto the green and marked his ball. How many years had he been enthralled by this guy? Ten? Maybe more. And now after 53 holes in his company he knew that he had been right to feel that way. The man was the absolute epitome of a sportsman. No matter how hard things went, he had never wavered in his good-natured dignity. Deek nodded back and marked his own ball.

He couldn't imagine the American missing his putt. The man had hit absolute overdrive. Everything seemed possible. The ball never seemed anywhere but in until the last few inches when it eased to the right and finished on the lip of the hole. George pushed his visor back on his head and stared up into a patch of blue sky in frustration. A four. Just a four. Deek had a seven-footer to go down the eighteenth: one up and one to play.

He crouched down with Troll and looked it over. Nothing in it. Maybe just the right side. No more. One easy stroke. He locked his eyes on the ball and swung the putter with the shoulders. As soon as the blade connected with the ball, it kicked slightly off a slight imperfection in the billiard smoothness of the green and it slid by the hole.

" . . . *he's missed! You know, I would have put my house on him making that one. Let's see it again. Pretty good stroke . . . oh there, look . . . he got a kick . . . that's got to hurt. That's got to really hurt. What a time to get a break like that. Well, we all better get ready folks because we've got all square and one to play . . .*"

Deek stood for a moment with a look of complete incomprehension on his face. A kick. Unbelievable. What a moment to get a bloody kick. He stepped forward and dragged the ball back and took the putt again. This time it rolled straight and true into the centre. He bent down and collected the ball and started to brace himself for one more hole.

George was waiting to collect his ten-pound note on the back of the eighteenth tee.

"Tough break buddy."

Deek found a smile from somewhere. "Aye. It's the way it goes I suppose."

George patted him gently on the shoulder. "Are we having a last drink?"

"Aye. I reckon that sounds a decent idea."

Deek looked down the eighteenth as the waiter did the honours for the last time. 430-something yards. The wind was lighter now and blowing them home. The big clumps of gorse which had so famously snagged up Jack Niclaus at the end of his legendary duel with Tom Watson in 1977 waited down the right-hand side whilst a line of bunkers guarded the left. Distance wasn't a problem. Any kind of long iron would give him a straightforward approach. Then it would be all down to the putting.

He drained his glass and saw George taking the huge-headed driver from his caddie.

"Bloody hell George. You're never having a go at the green?"

George beamed at him. "Hell, surely you didn't think I was about to lag up?"

Deek shook his head. "No. I suppose not."

" . . . you're not going to believe this folks. George is going for the big one. He's got his driver out and he's about to go for the green. What can you say about this guy . . ? Unbelievable . . !"

George rolled his shoulders and stepped forward to the ball. As soon as he hit it, Deek knew that it was perfect. It was more than perfect. It was astonishing. The ball climbed high above the line of the great white hotel and landed 50 yards short of the green. The bounce was true and the ball ran up happily on to the front edge. As George returned the club to his caddie, the President stepped forward and shook his hand.

"Fantastic, son. Greatest shot I ever did see."

Deek looked up from placing his tee. "You're not on your own there."

He stepped back and tried to arrange his thoughts. His heart was pounding and somehow he needed to slow down. Troll pushed a one iron at him. "No heroics pal. No point. You cannae make it. Knock it down the fairway and get in close with your second. You can still get a half with a three."

Deek nodded. Troll was right. A three would do it. He needed to play the odds. He took a few long slow breaths and struck the one iron straight and true to 150 yards from the flag. As he strode down the fairway he concentrated on blocking everything out. He was vaguely aware of shouts of encouragement from all around him but he blanked them out. Instead he stared at the ball as he approached.

Troll dropped the bag down and marched forward to get the correct yardage.

"149. Decent wind behind. I reckon an eight to the front edge. Let it take a bounce and run up. Start it a touch right and let the green gather it in."

Deek nodded. It was seldom that he and Troll saw a shot differently. The sun was pouring down now and it lit up the brilliant-white walls of the hotel. What a sight. What a magnificent bloody sight. He sucked in the air and took the shot. It was as how they planned it and the ball wandered up the green to finish eighteen feet short of the flag. There was a chance. Just a chance.

As Troll dropped the club back into the bag, George came over and draped an arm around Deek's shoulder as they approached the green.

"Buddy, me and you need a chat."

"Do we?"

"Yes sir, we do."

Both men were smiling as they acknowledged the whistles and cheers of the crowd.

"I have an idea on how things should play out here. Interested?"

"Aye. Of course."

"Good. Now this is how I see it. I knock my putt up somewhere near the hole, then I pick up your marker and concede yours. You can then pick up my ball and concede mine. Simple. Half in three. Halved match. We tell old Roland that we ain't doing any sudden death play-off thing. He will just have to split his collection down the middle. Half of it comes to Scotland, half stays Stateside. He can swap over every couple of years or so. Sound good to you buddy?"

It sounded better than good. It sounded perfect. It was a game that would be better for no-one winning.

"I would have got that putt you ken."

George laughed. "Sure. But I'm not about to give you the chance of missing it."

"That's what Jack Niclaus said to Tony Jacklin when he gave that three-footer to halve the Ryder Cup."

"You bet. And I've been waiting all my life to say it. So come on pal. Do we have a deal?"

"Aye. We have a deal. Nae bother."

The cheering slowly settled as the players reached the green.

". . . so. Here we are. All square after 54 holes of some of the finest golf it has ever been my privilege to watch. This great course has thrown everything at these guys and both have stood tall. This is what this great game of ours is all about. But now it all comes down to just a couple more shots. Albright has this 45-foot putt for eagle. If this goes in, then there is nothing Archie Banks can do about it. If this goes in, the McMillan Collection will be staying in America. He's over it now. That old familiar routine. One practice stroke . . . and another

. . . and now over the ball . . . here it goes . . . looks pretty good . . . but wait . . . he's not hit it. No. It's short. Must be about six feet left. So if Banks can somehow make this . . . wait a minute! Good Lord. George Albright has picked up Archie Banks marker. Unbelievable. He's conceded . . . Banks is going over to George's ball . . . he's conceded too. That's it folks! What a gesture! What a finale . . . this was a game where nobody had deserved to lose and nobody has lost . . ."

Meg flew across the green and almost flattened Deek as she leapt into his arms. Everyone knew within seconds what had happened. There wasn't about to be any play-off. The two players had made their decision. The green was soon a mob of back-slapping figures. The President's security men didn't know whether or not to break a few heads, but their man was evidently enjoying every second. Suddenly he was just another guy in the middle of the crowd. Just another punter who had watched the greatest piece of sporting drama in his life.

Eventually the two players fought their way through the crowd and approached the frail figure of Roland McMillan who was waiting in his wheelchair with a thick blanket over his knees. He was smiling contentedly

"I don't suppose that either of you much fancy the idea of a play-off?"

"No sir" replied George. "I think we're about done for the day. We figure that the best thing is if you split the collection down the middle."

Deek picked up the thread. "Aye. Half for Scotland, half for America. Swap over every two years. What do you reckon?"

"Do I have a choice?"

"No sir. I don't believe you do" boomed George.

"Then that is how it shall be."

Much later that night, Deek and George were hanging over their drinks at the table in the restaurant. Airforce One had lumbered off the runway at Prestwick and climbed up into the setting sun to head back across the Atlantic. All the interviews had been wrapped up and the fate of the collection had been announced to the world. A similar celebration was in full swing in Kirkonnel where the news of the coming Hamilton McMillan Centre was toasted all through the night.

It was at last over. All around them the guests sang their songs and exchanged phone numbers and addresses. Their match had taken its place in the annals of sporting history where it would rest for as many years as people hit golf balls on Sunday mornings. George sank the last of his glass.

"So buddy. What next? Back to the tour?"

"Maybe. Not straight away. I'm off to Scoobytown first."

Epilogue
June

The sound of the approaching taxi woke Scooby from his doze in the chair. As he sat up, his great bulk made the hard-pressed bamboo creak in complaint. He squinted into the bright sunlight.

An old car threw up a cloud of dust as it bumped its way over the rutted track. Scooby wiped the sweat from his big face with a rather tired-looking neck-scarf and heaved himself to his feet. The taxi pulled up and the back door opened.

As the crumpled figure of Troll emerged from the back door he started to smile. Banjo came next and stretched his over-long limbs after the long confinement. Next came Meg who looked much cooler in a light cotton dress. His smile widened another inch as Deek clambered out from the other side and gave him a cheery wave.

The smile was replaced with an expression of complete disbelief as George Albright the Third emerged from the passenger seat and leant in to pay the driver.

"Well I'll be goddamned."

Later that night Deek and Meg wandered out to sit on the sand. The stars stretched away into the outer reaches of eternity and the waves quietly lapped at the beach. From inside the makeshift bar they could hear the sound of Jimmy Hendrix rolling out into the thick warmth of the night.

Deek held out a hand and Meg took it.

Other titles by Mark Frankland

One Man's Meat
£5.99

The Cull
£5.99

Terrible Beauty
£6.99

Red Zone
£6.99

The Drums of Anfield
£4.99

**To order copies please complete the
order form at the back of the book
or tel. 07770 443 483**

**All prices include P&P
to customers in the UK**

www.thecull.com

One Man's Meat by Mark Frankland

"Frankland turns crisis into drama"
Sunday Telegraph

November 1997 and British Farming
is being ripped apart by the BSE Crisis.
Vast areas of the countryside are facing devastation.
Finally one man decides that enough is enough.

Sir Alistair McIntyre, owner of the vast McIntyre
Holdings Corporation, makes the fateful decision to
save the Beef Industry. He hires a team of Mavericks
who claim to be able to solve any problem.
Their prize is massive. So is their task.

As their campaign gathers momentum
thousands of angry farmers at last start to fight back.
The story sweeps across the globe at breathtaking speed
from Argentina to Matabeleland,
from the windswept Scottish hills
to the shanty towns of Brazil,
from the Cabinet Room in Downing Street
to the Boardroom of a supermarket giant.

Every step of the way the team are sucked into ever
greater danger until their path inexorably leads them
to the lair of one of the most dangerous men on earth . . .

**To order a copy complete
the order form at the back of the book
or tel. 07770 443 483**

£5.99 (incl. P&P to customers in the UK)

www.thecull.com

The Cull by Mark Frankland

"Mark lifts the lid on Drug Town" **Sunday Post**

"Everyone who has lost a child to heroin will want to be Jack Sinclair. Tragic, thrilling, captivating." **Simon Houston, Daily Record**

Will Sinclair is dead. It seems as if he will be just another statistic. Another young man dead before he reaches twenty. Another Scottish junkie unlucky enough to shoot-up a bad bag of heroin. A few column-inches in the local paper. Ten seconds on the radio news. And then he will be added to the long, long list. Just another dead junkie.

But this time it is different. It is different because Jack Sinclair will not accept his son's loss with resigned grief. He refuses to forgive and forget. He was once Major Jack Sinclair of the Scots Guards. In three tours of Northern Ireland he learned all about fighting an unseen enemy. Then there were rules. Regulations. Restrictions. Red tape. His war against the drugs gangs who killed his son will be very different. This time the gloves are off. This time he has a free rein.

As Jack Sinclair lights his small fire, the story sweeps from the empty wilderness of the Galloway Forest to the war-torn streets of West Belfast, from the mean council estates of West Scotland to the Cabinet Room of 10 Downing Street. And the fire becomes an inferno.

"Like 'Trainspotting' before it, 'The Cull' takes the reader into the darkest corners of the Scottish drug world. Compelling. Harrowing. Always gripping. Nothing will stop you turning the pages."

**To order a copy complete
the order form at the back of the book
or tel. 07770 443 483**

£5.99 (incl. P&P to customers in the UK)

www.thecull.com

Terrible Beauty by Mark Frankland

*" Gripping and horribly realistic." **Glasgow Evening Times***

It is the story of the making of an outrage. An outrage which will be the greatest of them all. An outrage that will make Omagh and Enniskillen look like mere sideshows. An outrage that will blow the Good Friday Agreement into a million pieces.

It is the story of two men from West Belfast. It is the story of how their lives are swallowed up by the endless war of their peoples. Sean O'Neil travels the road of the IRA. For Davie Stanton it is the British Army and the UVF. Their journey carries them through thirty years of pain – Burntollet, the riots of 1969, the Battle of Ballymurphy, Internment, Bloody Sunday, Warrenpoint, The Hunger Strike, Loughgall.

Slowly their lives become intertwined. They become puppets in the dark game where their strings are pulled by the shadowy forces of the British Security Forces. And their destiny becomes one. In the end one man can no longer stand the Peace that he sees to be a lie. The Peace he sees a betrayal of his people. He plans an act so appalling that the fragile Peace will be shattered beyond repair. And there is only one man in the world who can stop him.

*"A compelling read. Terrible Beauty is lovingly written, imbued with compassion, humanity, and great attention to detail. It will keep the reader entranced from the moment they pick it up." **An Phoblacht – Republican News***

*"This book identifies the murky world of terrorism, it also shows how in more cases than not, an incident opens the path towards violence." **David Ervine – Leader of the Progressive Unionist Party***

*"Frankland shows insight and authority about the perennial problems of the Province. It is also a rivetingly good read!" **Rt Hon Sir Robert Atkins MEP, Minister of State, Northern Ireland Office, 1992 – 1994***

£6.99 (incl. P&P to customers in the UK)

www.thecull.com

Red Zone by Mark Frankland

"An unrelenting pile driver of a read"

An asylum seeker goes berserk on the late night
streets of Sighthill. Three local teenagers are hacked
to death. The worst riot Glasgow has seen
in a generation rages through the night.

The Israeli Defence Forces stage a dawn raid
on a house in Gaza city. Mahmoud Bishawa,
the most notorious of all Palestinian fighters,
is taken into custody to await trial and execution.

Two events. By pure accident they happen within hours
of each other. Two events that are in no way related.
Two events in two cities thousands of miles apart.

It is the plan of one man which draws the two events
together. Khalil Bishawa will go to any lengths
to secure the freedom of his brother.

He brings the savagery of fifty years of fighting
between the Israelis and the Palestinians
to the towering blocks of the Sighthill Estate.

He takes the people of Glasgow into the Red Zone.

*"You watch the news and see the pictures from Gaza
and the West Bank and think it will never affect you.
You won't feel the same after you turn the last page."*

**To order a copy complete
the order form at the back of the book
or tel. 07770 443 483**

£6.99 (incl. P&P to customers in the UK)

www.thecull.com

The Drums of Anfield by Mark Frankland

"A fantastic adventure book for all young
football lovers – even one as young as me!"
Sir Tom Finney

Once in every generation a great new star emerges
into the world of football. Out of the slums of Sao Paulo
came Pele. Out of the bullet-scarred streets of Belfast
came Georgie Best. Out of the shanty towns of Buenos Aires
came Maradona. When Liverpool's veteran captain,
Tony Hobbes, suffers a crippling injury and receives a long
ban for violent conduct, he decides to take his son to Africa.

He expects to find lions and elephants amidst the Dark
Continent's endless wild plains. Instead, far away in the East
of Uganda under the shadow of the Mountains of the Moon,
he finds a boy called Simon Matembo. He knows that the
boy's talent is so huge that he could become the greatest
of them all. He knows that this boy can take Liverpool back
to the great days. But first he has to find a way to take him
back, and to do this he must overcome many huge challenges
from the tribe, the club, and even the forces of nature.

"Anyone who loves football will love this book.
Football is about passion, unrelenting excitement
and, more than anything else, it is about dreams.
Exactly the same can be said about 'The Drums of Anfield'.
Gerry Marsden, from 'Gerry and the Pacemakers'

"Genuinely hard to put down", **FourFourTwo Magazine**

To order a copy complete the order form
at the back of the book or tel. 07770 443 483

£4.99 (incl. P&P to customers in the UK)
www.thecull.com

Order Form

Name ----------------------------------

Address ----------------------------------

Telephone ----------------------------------

Email ----------------------------------

Please send me ---------------- **Copies of**

Please send me ---------------- **Copies of**

I enclose a cheque for -------------------------

**Please make cheques payable to:
'Glenmill Publishing'**

Return this form to:

> **Glenmill Publishing
> Glenmill
> Dumfries
> DG2 8PX**

Or Telephone   07770 443 483